THE WILD CARD

PIPER RAYNE

ABOUT THE WILD CARD

Getting pregnant after a one-night stand with my brother's best friend was never part of the plan.

We're talking about Foster Davis here.

Chicago Colts closing pitcher.
The broody king of one-word answers.
And the man everyone knows keeps one foot out the door.

Surprisingly, when two pink lines turn my world upside down, Foster doesn't run. He steps in, he shows up, and he insists we do this together.

Pretending we're fine is easy. Pretending this is just about the baby? Not so much.

Because Foster is gentle when no one's watching.
Because he looks at me like I'm something worth protecting.
Because the walls he's built start to crack—and I'm the one he's letting inside.

Our arrangement was supposed to be simple. Boundaries were set. Co-parents and no catching feelings.

Okay, maybe a few sex lessons were added in too. Bad idea, I know.

Because the more time I spend with Foster Davis, the harder it is to remember why I ever thought he was the risky choice.

The Wild Card

CHAPTER
ONE

Callie

I f I was the heroine in a rom-com, seeing the father of my unborn baby in a Chicago Colts baseball uniform would ignite a warm, glowing sensation bursting through my belly.

Instead, my stomach mutters, *Congrats. You've officially outdone yourself.*

Was my pregnancy planned? Of course not.

Truth be told, I'm a lifelong safe-sex-always card-carrying member. We're talking VIP, platinum status here.

Condoms in my purse? You betcha.

Birth control pills? On them since college.

Regular testing for an STI? Mandatory.

But somehow, even with my type-A safe-sex checklist, I'm still growing a baby in my uterus. And a fucking Chicago Colts child at that. Yes, I realize for some women, that would be a dream. But I've sworn off baseball players my entire life, which leads me to the third problem in my dilemma—my baby daddy is... wait for it...my older brother's teammate and friend.

Don't worry though, neither of them has any idea I'm carrying said baby. Only one other person knows my secret so far, but time is ticking, and I need to tell the father and then my brother.

"So, give me a hint," Leighton whines. "It's, like, best-friend code. You can't tell me you're pregnant and then not give me the most important detail."

She's already asked me ten times today. "You're picking up bad habits from Monroe."

Please note, Leighton is my best friend, but she's also my brother's fiancée. She's in her happily-ever-after bubble with Hayes where everything is magical and sparkly, and life is perfect. Meanwhile, I'm choking on every thought that crosses my brain (and almost every piece of food that hits my tongue).

Can I navigate pregnancy and motherhood and maintain the success I've had with my podcast? Are women really telling the truth when they say I can have a family *and* a career? Or is that something society tells women so we inevitably feel as though we're failing when we can't juggle it all? I sure as shit hope I can handle both because I didn't put all my blood, sweat, and tears into this dream just for a few minutes of success.

Leighton's brows draw down. "You're comparing me to a six-year-old?"

We look down the row of seats behind home plate to see Monroe jumping in place and my dad getting up from his seat to go buy her ice cream.

I chuckle. "She's relentless, and you've been the same since I told you the news."

Thankfully, my mom can't hear us because she's busy pestering Lake to stay away from boys and telling Lincoln to sit down.

The fact that my BFF took guardianship of her deceased cousin's three kids last year makes her and my brother this cute-as-hell instant family. Just more sparkly magic shit for them. Sometimes it's nauseating to witness, but I'm still over the moon happy for them all.

"Okay, tell me one characteristic he has." Her eyes zero in on the field as the Colts take their positions. She taps her finger to her lips. "Is he quiet?"

I roll my eyes, knowing she's talking about Decker.

"Cocky?"

I glance over to where Easton stands in his shortstop position. "If I told you either one of those things, it would narrow the choices significantly."

Hayes jogs out to home plate, lifting his helmet and winking at Leighton before his gaze strays to the kids. Lake is too cool to give him any attention, but Lincoln jumps up and shouts at him. Hayes gives him a wave, and his gaze strays to Leighton one more time. She blows him a kiss.

"I think I'm going to be sick." I mimic a vomiting noise.

"Tell me about it," Lake says. "I came downstairs this morning to them making out on the counter."

Leighton scoffs and whips her head toward Lake. "We were not."

Lake only gives her a look, and Leighton waves her off.

My mom taps Lake's leg. "They're in love, let them be."

"Back to the question of the hour..." Leighton whispers, secluding us in our own little conversation once more.

"You'll find out after he does. You'll be the first to know, I promise."

I could tell her. She wouldn't spill the secret until after, but for some reason, I feel like telling the father first is the right thing to do. Allow him to digest the information before we tell anyone else. After all, we got ourselves into this mess together.

Leighton balks and straightens her back. "Your brother has such a great ass. Last night in bed—"

"Oh, so you're gonna play dirty?" I raise an eyebrow at her.

She shrugs. Leighton knows I don't want to hear the details of their sex life. Do I know they have sex? Of course, but I don't want to hear about it. Immature? Maybe, but believe me, once my brother finds out who I conceived his niece or nephew with, he's not going to want the details of my sex life either. Which, thinking about it, I wouldn't mind being a fly on the locker room wall when this secret comes out.

Hayes throws a runner out at second, and our entire row gets on their feet, screaming and cheering for him.

"Did the baby daddy just tag that runner out?" Leighton whispers in my ear.

I shake my head. "Like I said, relentless."

The game continues, and the best thing about her now being guardian to three kids is that her attention gets diverted a lot. The smart thing to do would have been to keep this news to myself until after I've told the father, but I was kind of freaking out. Me… pregnant? A mother? It's hard for me to visualize, and I'm sure it will be for others as well. I'm not exactly Mary Poppins.

By the time we get to the eighth inning, the Colts are winning, but only by one run.

Taz is losing his cool on the mound. Hayes calls time and walks out to talk to him.

Two girls who haven't been here the entire game stop beside the row in front of us, causing everyone to stand to allow them to pass.

Leighton and I glance at one another. We've seen women like them enough over the years. A player got them tickets. The question is who exactly? They definitely don't fit in with the rest of the crowd with miniskirts so short I'm about to put my hand over Lincoln's eyes. They've matched their skirts with tight crop tops that have their boobs spilling out.

Leighton leans in closer. "Aren't they cold?"

"I'm pretty sure they prefer to be nippin'."

"He told me as soon as the catcher guy talks to the pitcher, I should make sure I'm in my seat," one woman says to the other one.

Leighton and I glance at each other again, and she mouths, "Who?"

I have a suspicion, and my body plays war with itself on whether I care if I'm right or wrong.

Hayes jogs back to home plate. Taz, being the dipshit he is, walks along the back of the mound and sets up.

"Oh, so… no then?" the one woman says to the other.

I'm really curious where they've been seated up until this point.

"These seats are so uncomfortable." The other woman elbows the nice man to her right while trying to situate herself as if there's a cushion out of place. "If he's such a big deal, he couldn't get you a suite?"

"He said he wanted me up front and center." The blonde shrugs.

Taz walks the first runner, and it's over for him in this game. Ripley steps out of the dugout, meeting the infield on the mound, and Taz puts the ball in his palm.

The minute Taz is in the dugout, the lights cut out in the stadium. My stomach swoops as if it's in a stunt airplane.

The Jumbotron flashes ALL ABOARD! in bold, blinding letters as "Crazy Train" by Ozzy Osbourne plays and a train engine bursts from the shadows on the screen, wheels sparking as it barrels down tracks of pure lightning, racing straight toward the fans until it feels as if it might crash through the screen.

"Oh, is it…?" The blonde elbows her friend, whose attention is on her phone. "This is him, I think."

"Seriously?" Leighton grumbles.

"Ladies and gentlemen," the stadium announcer says, "it's closing time, and we all know what that means. Let's all rise for our… number fourteen… FOSSSTTEERR 'The Reaper' DAVVIISS!"

Foster jogs out of the bullpen and stops at the edge of the infield to let the umpire check his hands and glove. His tattoos sneak out past the edges of his jersey and up his neck and down both arms. You can't see much of his dark blond hair because of his ball cap, but his blue eyes shine on the Jumbotron screen.

"Okay, you're right, he's hot." The friend sits up in her seat. "Does he have any brothers?"

I feel like a mean girl in high school from the number of times Leighton and I have shared a judgmental look at these two women's expense.

"Decker Davis." Lincoln's voice has both mine and Leighton's heads swiveling to see him standing next to Leighton. At some point, he and Lake must have switched seats.

The lights are back on, and all the infield gives Foster slaps on the back and fist bumps.

The two girls turn around and look at Lincoln.

Lincoln points toward third base, and the friend's shoulders deflate.

"No tattoos?" Her disappointment is clear in her voice.

My eyebrows are at my hairline. Did Foster really get these women tickets? I look at the blonde. So, she's his type—blond, young as fuck, and doesn't know anything about baseball. Good to know he's as superficial as I thought.

I have no idea why it upsets me… well, that's not exactly true.

But it's not as if I had any delusion that Foster Davis and I would ever be romantically involved. He's only going to be the father of my child. I just need to get up the nerve to tell him.

CHAPTER
TWO

Foster

The only good thing about today's game was that we won.

I pitched like shit. My velocity sucked. My command was worse. Hayes's framing saved my ass, so walking out of the stadium and into the streets of Chicago, the cheering makes the oily feeling inside worse since I don't think I did anything to contribute to our win.

I zip up my jacket, ready to head to my condo to brood.

"Foster!" a woman shouts.

I don't even glance in the direction it came from, falling in line with Easton and Decker, but we're stopped when Hayes and Leighton's family find them ahead of us.

Lincoln runs up to me. "Did you see Miller fall to his knees on your last pitch?" He laughs.

What can I say? The kid loves me. He boosts my ego on a good day, but on days like today, I don't feel as though I've earned his enthusiasm. But I remember myself at his age, when I revered all my favorite players. That was so fucking long ago, and I don't think I was ever as innocent as him.

"I did." The one pitch of mine that did what I wanted it to today.

"I'm calling a sleepover at Grandpa and Grandma's tonight!" Hayes's dad shouts.

Lincoln disappears from my side, joining Monroe as they jump up and down, both asking their grandparents questions about stopping at McDonald's and what kind of ice cream they have in the freezer.

Growing up, I thought those kinds of families were only television sitcom shit. Turns out I was wrong.

"We can take them home." Leighton fights Hayes's parents about babysitting them, but from what I hear, she and Hayes get no alone time. Especially during the season. Our career isn't really meant for a family.

My gaze strays to Callie.

She looks good tonight. Her cheeks are a little flushed from the cool air, and her hair is tucked into a Chicago Colts winter hat. Why does she have to fucking be Hayes's little sister?

Our eyes lock for a moment, and although I should stay far away, I step forward to approach her, but something snags her gaze behind me. A sour expression crosses her face, and she rolls her eyes, turning to Lake to give her a hug goodbye.

"Foster!" a woman screeches right before she steps in front of me and catapults herself into my arms. She throws her arms around my neck, plastering her body to mine. She's so short, she's hanging off me like a monkey.

I see her friend standing next to me, checking out Easton and Decker.

"Thanks for the tickets," she coos in my ear. "Don't worry, I give great thank you blow jobs."

Oh fuck. I forgot I left tickets for this girl at will-call. What was her name?

This isn't my finest moment, and I'm pretty sure I just moved even farther down on Callie's list. It wasn't some master plan that I got Samantha... Sarah, maybe... tickets either—just me on autopilot.

"Introductions, Stephie," her friend says, her gaze rolling up and down my body.

Stephie. That's it.

Thanks for the save, friend.

Stephie removes her arms from around my neck and drops down to her feet.

My attention shoots to Callie, but all she gives me is a glance as she tells Leighton something.

"Foster, this is my bestest friend in the whole wide world. Like, ride or die. This is Millie."

Millie holds out her hand. "Family name before you ask."

I shake her hand, and when Easton catches on to the fact that two women are standing in front of me, he says his good-byes to the group and moseys on over.

"Easton Bailey." He introduces himself as if she doesn't already know, shoving his hands in his pockets. "Who do we have here?"

Stephie's eyes widen. "I'm Stephie, and this is my BFF—"

"Millie," she interrupts.

Easton eyes me as if asking which one is mine.

He can have both for all I care because apparently all I want to do is shove my tongue down the one woman's throat who is off-limits.

None of this is good. It's actually the worst thing that could happen to me right now. Callie and I have kept it quiet that we slept together once, which makes me an asshole of a best friend. I know the rules, and I broke them anyway.

Hayes has been a loyal friend who always has my back, so the fact I slept with his sister... I shouldn't be all that surprised she's still got a hold on me even after I already had her. It's just karma biting me in the ass for my bad deed.

But continuing anything behind his back would be even shittier.

Still doesn't stop me from wanting her though. At least so I can remember it clearly next time.

"We're going out," Easton says. "Care to join us?"

Stephie looks at me. I've been in this situation with girls like Stephie before. I could ask her if she wants to see my place. Send Millie with Easton. Both of us would probably get some kind of action, and it's only based on the fact that we're professional athletes and we're both good-looking. I have that bad boy edge and reputation, whereas Easton has the cocky athlete vibe that's approachable, and he flirts as though it's his second job. But I just don't have it in me tonight.

Getting Stephie tickets was a massive mistake. A real dick move. Not to make Callie jealous—I didn't even know Callie would be here tonight. But I thought that after being unable to get Callie out of my head, Stephie would help me forget her. Something easy and meaningless.

"We'd love to," Stephie says. "Right, Mill?"

"Sure." Millie smiles at Easton.

"Great. I'm just heading home, but you can wait for us down at Peeper's Alley." Easton makes the plan since he's more invested in the outcome.

Stephie's smile dims. "I heard about that mean owner though."

Easton laughs. "You just can't go to the backroom. We'll walk with you guys there first, so she doesn't give you trouble."

Easton saunters closer to Millie, and Stephie falls in line with me as we walk from Webber Field to our condo building.

I say goodbye to Hayes and Callie's parents as they venture the opposite way toward the parking lot.

"I'm gonna go. Good game, big bro. One day maybe I'll want to interview you," Callie says.

Hayes puts Callie in a headlock. She squirms, and the two

of them go at it as though they're eight years old. Her hat falls onto the concrete right at my feet as she wiggles out of his hold.

I bend down to pick it up right as Leighton does, but she stops and allows me to do the kind act. She looks at me with a puzzled expression, as if she's figured out a riddle.

Callie smooths down her hair, and I watch her search the area until she sees me holding her hat.

"Oh, thanks." She goes to take it, her gaze flashing to Stephie next to me. And there it is in her eyes. The label she's pinned and stitched on me—asshole, or maybe douchebag. I don't think the world's sharpest seam ripper could pry it off at this point.

"I want one of those," Stephie says. "Where did you get it?"

Callie's eyebrows rise. "At the store." She points at the corner souvenir store that houses all of Chicago's professional sports teams' merchandise.

"Can you get me one, Foster? Or wait… should I call you Reaper?" Stephie looks at me expectantly.

Hayes laughs, but when Stephie turns toward him, he pretends to cough. "All that dirt." He slaps his chest.

"Foster's good," I say.

"I'm Callie. We saw you were seated in front of us." She puts her hand out in front of Stephie.

Millie and Easton are already gone from view.

"You were?" Stephie's head tilts to the side.

I catch more than a hint of annoyance in Callie's expression. "Nice of Foster to get you tickets. That's a real sweet boyfriend move."

I narrow my eyes, and Callie's eyebrows rise slightly as if she's purposely doing this. Does she not remember that she was the one who left without a word? But now she's looking at me as if I'm exactly who she thinks I am. As though I've proven her theory right.

Stephie puts her arm around my waist and her cheek on my chest.

Callie's gaze flickers down to Stephie's hand tucked at my hip.

"I know, right? I feel like I won the debutante ball. The diamond girls say he rarely gives out tickets."

"You must be really special then." Callie looks at Hayes, who secures Leighton to him—as if she could get any closer.

"We have to get going," he says.

"No way, you're coming out with us," Decker says, sidling up next to Callie. "Looks like we're the odd ones out."

"Are you though?" Leighton asks, and Callie shoots her a look that would scare a gladiator.

"I meant because you and Hayes, Foster and…"

"Stephie," she fills in with a big smile.

"Foster and Stephie. Easton and Stephie's friend. Callie and I are the only ones unattached." Decker acts as if he's some master chess player and has to spell it all out for us. Get a fucking life.

My hand flexes in my pocket, so I wrap my other arm around Stephie. Fuck this. Decker and Callie? Just stab me in the gut and twist the fucking knife.

The only thing worse than being on a team with my estranged brother would be if he were dating the woman I want but can't have. As it is, Decker and I barely tolerate each other. I can't imagine things would get any better if he was dating Callie.

"I'm kind of tired." Callie slips her hat back on her head.

Good girl. She doesn't need to be doing anything with my brother.

"No way. I'm going out for the first time in a long time. And now that the season is starting, it will be a long time before I can again." Leighton moves away from Hayes toward her best friend. "I'm going. You're going."

"But…"

Leighton crosses her arms. "I'm calling in my BFF favor."

"We can just go home," Hayes says.

If I was him—which I'm far from—I'd want to be alone with my girl instead of out in a club. Then again, that has to get boring at times. No way they enjoy spending all that time alone together.

"Come on." Leighton turns to Hayes and puts her arms around his neck. "We could dance." She shimmies her hips, and when he doesn't play along, she takes his hands and places them on her hips. Then she leans in closer and whispers something to him.

"Please." Callie rolls her eyes. "I am not going to the club to see you maul my brother all night."

"You can maul me," Decker says.

My body vibrates with anger. He is *not* the Davis brother for Callie.

Not that I am either.

"You're going to let one of your friends talk about me like I'm an animal?" Callie asks Hayes.

"It's Decker, he's a rule follower." Hayes shrugs. "Now…" His gaze shoots my way. "Foster, on the other hand." He chuckles as if he's funny, and my heart lodges in my throat.

Fuck, that's not a look to say sure, take your shot with my little sister. And if the secret that I already had her ever comes out, I'm pretty sure I'd lose my best friend *and* fuck up the entire team dynamic as well.

"Well, she can't have him. He's all mine." Stephie squeezes her arms around my middle and giggles.

Callie sighs. "Fine. Let's go. But I'm leaving early." She looks directly at me when she says, "Decker, let's get a drink with Ruby first."

My jaw flexes as I watch her walk away from me—with my brother, no fucking less. I didn't bring Stephie here to play games. But that doesn't matter, does it? From the outside, it looks I did.

"Come on. Millie is probably ready to kill me." Stephie tugs at me.

Hayes and Leighton are clearly in a moment. She's still convincing him.

I wait a beat, but Hayes waves me off. "We'll catch up." Then he swings her around so her back is to the wall, and she squeals.

"They're really into each other. Did he get her tickets to the game too?" Stephie asks.

"She's got season tickets," I grumble.

"Oh, how do I get season tickets?"

You don't, I think. At least not from me.

CHAPTER
THREE

Callie

Without sounding too dramatic—stab a thousand needles in both my eyes.

I'm not jealous because I don't want Foster.

He isn't exactly boyfriend material. From everything I've ever heard about him, he doesn't do relationships. I'm actually a tad worried about his emotional state and whether he has any emotion besides grumpy. For our child's sake only, of course.

So, it's definitely *not* jealousy that's coursing through my body as I watch Stephie fawn all over him in the VIP booth Easton and I swindled us. We used our names and influence. Saffire is a pretty hot club in Chicago, so it's a miracle we landed a booth, but Easton is never against tossing money around to get what he wants.

Now I sit across from them. Easton and Millie are on the dance floor while Stephie looks longingly in its direction, trying to coax Foster out there with every new song that plays. Leighton and Hayes disappeared a half hour ago, and I question whether we'll see them again tonight.

"Come on, Reap," Stephie says, using his nickname—which grates on my nerves for reasons I'm not giving attention to right now.

"Yeah, *Reaper*, dance with the girl." I smirk at him.

His eyes narrow at me from across the booth. "I don't dance."

"Why not?" Stephie's head falls back. "You can just stand there, and I'll dance around you if you want."

Decker sits next to me, sipping his drink. "'Cause that's fun, and he's not fun."

I have no idea how Foster hears Decker's comment, but his gaze shoots over to him with a look that could kill a million blood-sucking vampires.

Why do I even feel like playing this stupid game of who can make who jealous?

It's childish.

It's immature.

But it's happening.

"Do you want to dance, Deck?" I place my water on the table. No one batted an eye when I didn't order a drink after I used the excuse of having a long day tomorrow.

"Sure." He places his beer on the table and stands, holding out his hand.

"Ugh… I guess I picked the wrong brother." Stephie wiggles her body along the seat like a toddler who was told she has to eat her vegetables before being excused.

"Fuck it. Fine." Foster slams his glass on the table, and the liquid sloshes over the rim.

The brotherly rivalry is thick between Foster and Decker, though I have no idea why.

Decker and I reach the dance floor, and when Easton and Millie see us, they dance over. Decker wraps an arm around my waist, his thigh between my legs, and links our free hands together, twirling me around the dance floor while his hips move to the beat.

"Holy shit, seriously?" My head falls to his shoulder in laughter. "You're, like, good at this."

"Single mom," he says, continuing to dance provocatively with me.

"Your mom taught you to dance this sexy?"

He chuckles. "God, no. She taught me the basics, and I had a couple girlfriends who loved to dance. I got comfortable with my body and how to move it, how to lead."

He turns us, and suddenly I'm facing the other direction as he steers us.

"Well, seems they were all good teachers. I've never danced like this."

"I figured you'd be surprised."

"Surprised is putting it mildly. I thought we were going to be dancing in place and snapping our fingers."

He shakes his head. "I'm used to being thought of as the boring one."

I rear back. "You're not boring."

He shrugs. "I like order, I like rules, and I like to be a stand-up guy. Unlike others..." His gaze veers to Foster.

Stephie is all over Foster, trying to get him to move his feet. She'd be better off persuading a drunk girl in the bathroom not to call her ex.

"And it's okay, you know? He's a lot of people's type." He says it as if he knows something.

I stiffen. Our eyes lock, and I divert mine, but it doesn't stop him from continuing.

"He's complicated. I should tell you to stay away from him, at least give you a warning, but..." He frowns. "He's my twin brother. My blood. And though we don't see eye to eye on almost anything, I'd still like for him to be happy."

I scoff. "You are way too much of a stand-up guy."

"I'm really not."

He twirls me again, and I catch sight of Foster over Decker's shoulder. He's finally wrapped his arm around Stephie's waist, and they're grinding. I watch him for a second, wishing I kind of did like Decker, but dancing with him is like dancing with my brother. Foster is the one who hits all my hot buttons.

Can't there be a vaccine for us woman who always want the bad boy?

Then I remember the baby growing in my stomach and how my days of cavorting with men like Foster need to end if I'm going to teach this little girl or boy to love…

I gasp, staring at Decker, not realizing until right now—he'll be my son or daughter's uncle.

"What is it?" He turns us so he's looking at Foster now. He doesn't make a comment about the fact that his brother isn't the dancer he is.

"Nothing. I just thought I saw an ex."

Decker seems appeased by my answer. I think I could tell Decker I'm pregnant, and he'd understand. Probably help me navigate how to tell Foster. How to judge his reaction. But that seems terribly unfair to Foster. They clearly have some kind of brotherly issues, and telling Decker before Foster would piss him off. Rightfully so.

So I keep my news to myself and finish the song with Decker.

A slow song comes on next, and he removes his thigh from between my legs, pulls me closer to him, and nuzzles his head closer to mine. It's intimate, but not one part of me zings with excitement. I might as well be dancing with Hayes.

My gaze goes to where Foster and Stephie were, but they're gone. Probably in a cab back to his place.

Well, that's good anyway because I need to put him in a box. A box labeled baby daddy, and that's all. And if he doesn't want to be a part of our lives, then I'll happily do this on my own. I do not need his help. I just need to tell him so I can move on and tell everyone else who *will* support us.

Now I just need to come up with a plan.

By the time Decker and I are done dancing, I've convinced myself that I'll be raising this baby on my own. In my head, Foster has already left us high and dry to fend for ourselves, and I've put a protective bubble that's more like a shield around myself and our baby. He won't hurt us. I'll never allow it.

Decker leads me through the crowd with my hand in his, and when we get to the VIP section, we find Foster drinking on one couch and Easton on the other, drilling him with questions.

"What the fuck? One more song, and I was going to ask her back to my place."

"Sorry. She wasn't for me." Foster finishes his drink and waves at the server for another.

"Wasn't for you? She was a hot blonde with an amazing ass." Easton looks at Decker. "I'm on your side now."

"I thought you always were." Decker motions for me to go in first, and we end up sitting between the two of them.

"Did Hayes and Leighton leave?" I ask, still not seeing either of them. She's going to hear it from me after getting me to come out and then bailing to go bang my brother.

"I think so," Decker says.

"Help me understand why I'm going home alone tonight after I had a woman ready and eager to sleep with me five minutes ago?" Easton isn't letting it go.

Foster waves toward the crowd. "Go get another one. They're all the same."

I can't help the way my stomach plummets. That's what Foster Davis thinks of women. Disposable, interchangeable, and only good if he's in the mood to bed one of them—otherwise they're of no use. That's exactly what I was to him. A warm, wet pussy to slip his dick into for a few minutes.

I hate how much it hurts.

Foster downs the drink the server brings him in one go.

Surprisingly, Hayes and Leighton rejoin us in the VIP section, looking disheveled and definitely freshly fucked.

I raise my hand. "Ready to go now?"

Leighton tilts her head, and I stand, turning back to Decker. "Thanks for the dance. If *Dancing with the Stars* ever asks you to be on the show, go for it. No one else stands a chance." I wave goodbye to Easton as I'm passing Foster. "Sorry about your lady. Maybe next time."

He doesn't hear me because he's rehashing the story to Hayes and Leighton.

As I'm stepping through Foster's open legs, he locks mine between his, causing me to stop. I turn toward him. Neither of us says anything as we stare at one another for an uncomfortable beat.

"Sorry it didn't work out with Stephie." I glance at his lap. "She not into whiskey dick?"

He doesn't spit out a sarcastic response. Instead, to my surprise, he says, "I'll get you home."

I lean down and pat his chest. "That's okay, big guy. Go find another girl on the dance floor to warm your bed tonight. They're all there for the taking, right?"

I straighten up, and he narrows his eyes at me. I step dramatically over his legs.

"Ready?" Leighton asks.

"Yeah. Let's go."

She swings her arm through mine, and we walk out of the VIP section.

Leighton leans close and says directly into my ear, "So it's totally the bad boy of baseball, right?"

I almost tell her. I'm sure that little stunt Foster and I just pulled gave us away. My brother is going to ask questions.

"Thank fuck, I think I'm too old for this place," Hayes says as soon as we're clear of the crowd.

Guess not.

"How would you know? You were in the alley fucking Leighton the majority of the night."

He doesn't say anything, and once we're outside, I take a big, cleansing breath. I just want to get home, but at least going to Saffire helped make my decision easier.

I'll do my duty and tell Foster, then the baby and I will move on with our lives.

CHAPTER
FOUR

Foster

I zip up my coat, jog down the outside stairs of the condo, and pass through the security gate. There's another sign with The Dugout written on it, along with a bunch of notes. Some are specific to one member of the team who lives here, and others are addressed to all of us with the hopes that at least one of us takes them up on their invitation.

The name The Dugout seems to have stuck for our three-condo building, but I don't really give a shit about it. Easton was pretty into the whole name thing. Not sure why he cares. It's not really about us, it's about them, and by them, I mean the diamond girls. They're the ones who put us up on some pedestal as if they get into the Hall of Fame if they sleep with us.

For years, I took advantage of women and what they hoped would come after a night with me. I do feel like a dick for my immature and childish behavior. Later on in my career, I learned to lay it all out before I slept with a woman. That stopped the online bashing and stalking afterward—for the most part.

I let the security gate shut behind me, leaving the sign on the gate. If it makes them think we'll get their notes, what's wrong with giving them a little hope?

For some reason, when I think of diamond girls, Callie comes to mind. Not that she is one. It's just that I think she feels like one since we slept together. I hate that, but I have no idea what to do about it. I certainly can't tell her I've been thinking about her nonstop.

As I turn right to head to the pancake restaurant to meet Jagger, my mind won't stop traveling back to Callie. I've racked my head to figure out what makes her different.

When Hayes talked about his sister when we played together in Seattle, I was always like *cool, you have a younger sister. She sounds badass, starting her own podcast and shit. That's awesome.* I thought it was great that he had a good relationship with her since I barely have any relationship at all with my one and only sibling.

Then I came face to face with her last year, and not under the best circumstances. My introduction to Callie was her coming at me with her finger wagging, dark hair flying in all different directions, face red. Even with my broken nose and mild concussion, my dick got hard.

I wanted to push her against the wall, sandwich my thigh between her legs, and tell her to go to town. Her anger toward me had turned me on, and out of all the sex I've had, that was a first. Usually if someone comes at me, I'll return the treatment ten times harder. My relationship with Decker is proof of that.

I wanted her so fucking badly, and even after having her, I want her again.

Lusting after your best friend's sister is complete and utter torture. I can't remember the last time I couldn't have something I wanted. Well, that's not exactly true. I should've grown used to that when I was a teenager. I mean it more in the sense of sex and women.

I cross the street and open the door of the pancake house, pushing away the thought of Callie because nothing can come of us anyway. It's an exercise in futility.

Jagger raises his hand when he spots me, and I weave through the tables, dodging the kids running back and forth from their table to the glass window where they can see the guy making pancakes. I slide the chair out across from him.

"Who dared put Jagger Kale in the corner?" I fold myself into the seat, turning over my coffee cup.

"Late as usual."

I lift my wrist, staring at an imaginary watch. "I'm not late."

Jagger lifts his wrist, where a very real, very expensive watch rests. "Five minutes."

I blow out a breath. "Sorry, Dad."

A server comes over and fills my coffee. "Do you need a few more minutes?"

"Yes," I answer.

"No," Jagger says over me. "Figure out what you want while I order."

"Okay, daddy dearest." I pick up the menu and scan it. I'm not really sure what this place is all about. There's a pancake guy who makes different shapes? This is some family shit right here.

"Egg white omelet, spinach, mushroom, and parmesan cheese. And I need a pancake in the shape of a…" He lifts his phone and scrolls with his thumb for a moment. "A rose?"

The server laughs. "I can't wait to see what she comes up with next."

"The family will be with me next month, so she can order herself." Jagger smiles.

"That's nice. You'll be here for the Falcons?" She leans a hip against the table.

I use the extra time I've been given to go over the menu again.

"Yeah. They're for sure gonna be in the playoffs again this year."

I roll my eyes. The Chicago Falcons are the "it" Chicago team. It's awesome for them, but I wouldn't hate it if they shared some of their success with the Colts. Being traded onto a struggling team wasn't my favorite part of moving here after being on a winning team for so long.

"Okay, genius, it's your turn." Jagger pulls me out of my thoughts, and when I look up, the server is staring at me.

"Three eggs, sunny side up, hash browns, bacon, and sausage, please." I hand her the menu after she writes it down.

"I guess you're not watching your diet." Jagger hands her his menu. "Thanks, Reese."

She walks away, and I settle in for the lecture I know is coming, sipping my coffee and acting as if I'm not interested in anything he has to say.

"I'm just going to cut to the chase. Your performance wasn't stellar."

I huff. "Tell me something I don't know."

He leans back in his seat and strums his fingers on the table, eyes laser-focused on me. I'll hold his gaze for as long as he wants me to without blinking. No one intimidates me, even the man who gets me my deals.

"You're roughly four years from retirement, at best."

I arch an eyebrow. "Putting me out to pasture already?"

His lips thin. He's never been one for my grumpy ass, but he came to me all those years ago. He wanted me, and over the years, he's reaped a lot of benefits from it.

"Put your pride on a shelf for a second. My job is to make you as much money as I can doing what you love. And when those days are nearing a close, I feel responsible to set you up for the future."

"Ah… that's sweet, Daddy."

He gives me his cut-the-shit expression I'm very familiar with, and I turn away from him, trying to remember that he only wants what's best and he's not judging me. He's not my dad lecturing me about my work ethic or the pitch I threw in the seventh that gave up the game.

"Sorry," I mumble.

He shakes his head with that disapproving father look except there's still affection in his eyes, something I'd never find in my own dad's. "You need an endorsement, Foster. A really good endorsement."

I open my mouth, but he continues.

"I'm not sure how you are with your money. You've had some great contracts. Sure, this last one wasn't what you were looking for, but it got you out of Seattle, which was our main goal. Chicago's management wanted you. You're the reason Vega was out as manager, because he wouldn't entertain you coming to the Colts. So, you're still wanted, and that's all that matters in this business, but there's going to come a time when you aren't. You'll have your own feelings about that at the time, and my job is to make sure you can survive while you're lost in your pity party. That you can support a wife and kids."

I scoff.

"Oh yeah, I forgot you're too cool for a family, right?"

"Some people aren't meant to be a husband, let alone a father."

He sighs and stares at me a long time, then shakes his head again. "I've told you this before, and I'm going to say it again—clean up your act."

My forehead wrinkles. "I have."

He glares at me.

"I've been good about my temper on the mound."

"Let's be honest, it's the Hayes effect."

I stare off because he's right to an extent. Having Hayes

behind the plate and working with him has calmed me, which doesn't bode well for the fact that I want to bend his sister over any available surface and shove my dick in her.

"Still. My trouble outside—"

"You and your brother got in a brawl outside Webber Field last year."

I sigh. "He hit me first in case it matters."

He holds up his hand. "You haven't had an endorsement since your first year in the league. Let's make this the year you get one. Be a good teammate, don't lose your temper, and keep all the shit off the field quiet. You hate Decker. I don't give a shit." He hums. "I do, but that's a conversation for another time."

I know Jagger has a point. I'm good with my money, I am, but there's a big dent in it now. I've always wanted endorsements. Some players earn a shit ton. And some endorsements go long past retirement. Let's be honest, I don't have a ton of job qualities past throwing a really great fastball and slider.

I let out a long breath. "Let me know what I need to do."

He smiles, and the server brings our food to the table. Jagger swings his tie so it rests over his shoulder. The man is everything I usually hate. What people must think seeing the two of us at the same table. With my neck and hand tattoos, they probably think I'm a felon and he's my lawyer, trying to negotiate me a plea deal. We couldn't be more opposite, and in all honesty, Jagger Kale is the first guy in a suit I learned to trust. When he first showed up at one of my games and said he wanted to represent me, I walked right past him.

I didn't want some guy in a three-piece suit, wearing a watch worth more than my dad made in a year. Figured I was just a paycheck to him. But Jagger showed up again and again. Eventually I listened, and even though my dad said we didn't need him, I've never regretted giving Jagger the opportunity to represent me. I've put him through enough shit to earn my respect.

"You baseball players always need me to dumb it down for you. Hayes was the same."

I chuckle, picking up my fork. No surprise there.

"First off, get your head right on the mound. No fights. No arguing. No swearing at the umps."

"That's my whole persona on the mound."

He lifts his gaze from his plate and stares at me with an expression that tells me my comment doesn't deserve a response.

"Fine," I grumble.

"And surprisingly, I don't have to lecture you about the women. Did you go celibate? There've been no new pictures for quite a while."

I bury my head in my plate. He can't know that the only woman I want in my bed would demolish everything I'm trying to accomplish this year. Hayes has made it clear that Callie can date whomever she wants, but Easton and I aren't the kind of guys he'd like to see his sister with. Truth is, I can't really blame him.

I shrug and stab one of the hash browns on my plate. "Not into it."

He laughs and places his fork on the plate. "That sounds like trouble."

"What is?" I bring my fork to my mouth.

"What hot-blooded pro athlete who can score multiple women a day isn't into sex? Are you sure you're not pining over someone?"

I stab another forkful of hash browns. "That life isn't for me."

Jagger doesn't bother trying to tell me I'm wrong like he probably did with Hayes.

He knows the truth—I'm not anyone's dream of a happily ever after.

CHAPTER
FIVE

Callie

"Why am I struggling with this?" I try to attach the mic once again, but it gets stuck on my bra.

"I think it has something to do with you being very off lately." Lex places the camera on the ground and walks over to me. "Take off the shirt."

"No dinner first?" I strip off my shirt, leaving me in my bra.

"Well, aren't you domesticated. No wonder you've been cranky. You're not getting laid in a flesh-colored bra that's squashing your tits like that." She snakes the wire and mic through my cleavage, and my back arches from the ice blocks she calls hands.

"Jesus, do you have any circulation?"

She stops what she's doing. "Do you want my help or not?"

"You threw the first dagger, making fun of my bra." I

haven't told Lex I'm pregnant, so I can't tell her that my boobs are so sore I need them to be squashed so my nipples don't drag across anything.

"It's just some friendly girl-to-girl advice. Doing my due diligence. I mean, you are with all those Chicago Colts guys all the time. I'd be showing off my assets if I were you." She gets the wire secure, and with my help putting my shirt back on, we get it into place.

"One of them is my brother, and the others are his good friends."

She scoffs. "You don't really abide by the brother's best-friend rule, do you? I think that goes out the window when your brother is a pro athlete."

I grew up around Hayes and his baseball buddies, so I'm used to being around athletes. Them being *professional* athletes makes no difference to me. If anything, it just brings more drama to the situation. I wouldn't mind a regular guy as long as he has an edge to him.

"Well then, I'll go buy more appropriate undergarments after we film just for you." I wink.

"And I'll expense some hand warmers."

"Thank you, I'd appreciate warm hands feeling me up next time."

We both laugh, and she goes back to pick up her camera. We leave my apartment, but as we're about to go down the stairs, Jerry's walking up.

"Well, hello, Slummy, how are you this morning?" Lex says.

I knock her with my hand.

"Funny." He narrows his eyes at Lex. "I was just going up to look at your garbage disposal."

I stop in the stairwell. Jerry is a good landlord. He always fixes things when I need him to, and he didn't raise my rent last year. But I'm not sure if it's his swollen belly that hangs over his pants or the fact he wears white T-shirts with matching velvet jogging suits, but Lex isn't completely off base when she calls him Slummy. Although I think it's mostly because he tried to hit on her once and had a hard time accepting the answer no.

"Oh, nothing is wrong with my garbage disposal."

He glances at Lex and back at me. "Huh, maybe I had the wrong apartment."

"Do better, Jerry. You only have six to remember." Lex walks down the steps. "Come on, I don't have all day."

"See you, Jerry." I leave him at the top of the stairs and follow Lex.

"Don't forget to talk to your brother about those tickets," Jerry says. "You know my property taxes are going up this year, and I'd hate to raise rent here."

I sigh, and Lex gives me a look as if to say, *what the hell, he's blackmailing you?*

I raise my hand, not turning around. "On it."

"Get on it faster." He laughs.

Lex's face transforms as if she's going to throw up.

We push through the vestibule and onto the sidewalk.

"He's so creepy." She does a full-body shudder.

"He's just lonely."

"There's something about him," she mumbles, setting up her camera as we walk toward the corner.

I need to find someone who looks interesting and might spare some time to talk with me. We walk down the street as I search for someone who looks as though they'll give us good content.

I spot a mom with a kid in a stroller, one strapped to her chest, and a fresh iced coffee drink in the cup holder.

"Let's try her." I walk toward the woman as Lex sighs behind me.

We usually shy away from the moms. They're generally

doing too much multitasking with too many distractions for us to have a good conversation.

"Excuse me, my name is Callie, and I have a podcast—"

Her eyes widen. "I know who you are." She stops and glances to my right. "Lex!" She acts as if they're long-lost best friends. "Oh my god. I can't believe this is happening to me. Just wait until everyone hears at pickup later."

Lex shoots me a look like *told you it was a bad idea.*

"So, is that a yes? May I join you wherever you're going so that we can have a conversation for the podcast?"

She lets go of the stroller, and it starts to roll away, but she grabs it quickly. "Oh that would've been bad." She sticks out her hand, and I take it. "My name is Amelia. Nice to meet you."

We move to the edge of the sidewalk, and she puts the baby in the second section of the stroller. It didn't look that hard. The baby is sleeping, and my stomach tugs at how adorable he is.

"Okay, hook me up." She holds out her arms.

Lex rolls her eyes. I really need to talk to her about hiding her judgmental expressions.

After Amelia is hooked up, we start walking.

"So, this is a lot." I wave toward the stroller.

"And I have one at school in first grade too. It's my life, but I couldn't love it more." Her perfectly slicked ponytail swings as she bounces in her running shoes that are paired with a matching jogging suit I'm wondering if she's ever sweated in.

"Did you always want to be a mother?" I ask.

Lex moves the camera to the side and looks at me. I usually try not to steer my guests in a specific direction with my own questions, at least at the beginning. It's more about allowing the person to say whatever, however they want. The conversation is always best when it flows organically.

"Who wouldn't? Children are our greatest gift." She picks up her drink and sips from her straw.

"I think there's a case to be made for women who don't want kids."

"They might change their minds if they knew what they were missing. Raising children, making them good adults, molding and shaping the next generation… there's nothing better."

Her answers are so polite and politically correct—there's nothing raw here. Lex moves in front of us as we cross the street. I rarely have to cut these conversations short because they're not working, but this is exactly what I hate now that my show has gained popularity—the fact that people know me and what the show is about. I don't want manufactured answers. That's not what my listeners want either.

"Yeah… right."

We turn a corner as she takes another sip of her drink.

I place my hand on her arm and turn off my mic. I don't want to waste my time or hers. "Hey."

She stops, and her smile still doesn't leave her face. I really can't tell if it's fake or not. "Did I do something bad?"

I shake my head. "No, of course not." I wave Lex over. "It's just… you seem to have a great life and love being a mother. You obviously know my show is called *If I'm Honest,* which is kind of a confessional about what you don't want other people to know. Something you might be keeping to yourself or advice to give others once you've gotten through a difficult situation. It's awesome that you don't have either of those. Admirable, but it just won't work for the show. I'm sorry."

She huffs and looks at the stroller. The baby fusses a little, and the toddler kicks his feet as if they sense their mother's mood shift. "Do you mind if we go to the park? I have to nurse, and he needs to get his energy out?"

"Amelia…"

She raises a hand. "I get it. I do. I actually do have something I want to share."

Lex raises her shoulders as though it's my call. I'm not someone who can just turn away when there might be something there, and my intuition said that she was someone I wanted to talk to.

"Sure. You lead the way."

We walk again, Lex filming in front of us. "I did always want to be a mother. I'm sure there are women out there who are appalled I didn't want more for my life. But I wanted a husband, kids… a family because I never really had one when I was younger." Her bubbly personality slowly fades. "God, I've told no one this… my husband obviously, but everyone else… well, I reinvented myself."

My head tilts to the side. "Why?"

"Because in the world I live in, a deadbeat dad and a mother who needed sex to feel loved isn't desirable."

We reach the park, and she undoes the straps on the double stroller for her toddler, allowing him to play on the small swing set while placing a blanket over herself and positioning the baby to feed.

"How did you reinvent yourself?"

"Full disclosure… I went to college to meet a husband, and that meant leaving my life behind and starting new."

She continues, telling me how she was smart and got into a good school on financial aid, but once she got to campus, she never talked to her mom again and has no idea where her dad is. She made friends, then borrowed clothes and makeup from them. When she met her husband her sophomore year, they fell in love.

"That's the funny part," she continues, her gaze never leaving her toddler.

I watch her body tense as the toddler approaches the stairs to the small slide.

He pushes off and falls on his butt at the bottom but jumps up and claps. "Mommy!"

"Way to go!" She smiles as the bubbly voice she used earlier returns for a second. "He's been trying to gain the courage to do that for weeks." She lifts the baby and places him on her shoulder. "My husband is everything I ever wanted, my end goal. Comes from a wealthy family, prestigious pedigree, great job, he's handsome... but underneath that country club exterior is the sweetest person I've ever met. He knows my story and doesn't judge me. He truly loves me for me and not the superficial girl he met at that frat party."

I lean back on the bench. This is why I do this podcast, because I never would have thought this was her story. I was looking for a mom who looked like her life had always been on a perfect path to lend me some wisdom on how I'm to navigate this new path I find myself on.

"So you really did get your happily ever after." I smile at her.

She laughs. "Believe me, I love my family and my life, but when I was younger and imagined it, there were no bad days. I imagined myself waking up refreshed and me being the patient mom who always explained things calmly to her kids. That's not what my life is. But even when it's crazy and the baby won't calm down and the other two kids are fighting, or when I'm salty at my husband for coming home late, I would never trade it for anything. I'm not sure if that's because I know what it's like on the other side or if this is just what I was meant to do. I'm sure some women think I'm a sellout. That we could hire a nanny, and I could want more for myself. I feel their judgment sometimes. But in the end, I'm happier than I've ever been and isn't that what life is about... being happy?"

I wipe a tear about to fall from my eyes. "Yes, absolutely. That's the point of life for sure."

"And I hope I'm making good humans too." She glances

at her toddler, who is still smiling, and I wonder if it's because he conquered one of his fears.

"Thank you so much for talking to me."

"Sorry about being so fake in the beginning. It's an old habit sometimes, but you really got me to spill my guts, and now when—or if—this airs, people will know my past."

"I won't air it if you don't want me to. Or I could keep you anonymous."

She shakes her head. "Nah. It's about time I tell my truth. For my sake and theirs. They need to learn that they're enough no matter what they endure. Learn to survive and that there's always something good coming after the bad."

Lex lowers the camera, and even she is no longer giving me those *this was a bad idea* eyes.

"Thanks again." I pull out my card and hand it to Amelia. "Here's my card, and if you want to give Lex your info, we'll be in touch when it airs. If you change your mind, just let me know."

She takes my card and slips it into the pocket of the stroller. "I won't. Man, when I woke up this morning, I thought I'd go get a coffee, head to the park, and have my usual day. I didn't think I'd be divulging all of this to a complete stranger. But it feels freeing." Amelia turns to me as she places the baby back in the stroller. "What a great job you have. Freeing people from the truth they keep chained down."

"It only works with courageous people like you."

We say goodbye to her, and on our way out of the park, neither of us says anything. I think we're both reflecting on the story we just heard.

But then my phone vibrates.

I pull it out of my pocket and look at the screen. "It's Jarrah."

We both stop as I answer and put it on speaker phone. I've been waiting for her call for a week.

"Hey, Jarrah."

"They're biting…"

My shoulders sink, and Lex's lips thin. "That's all?"

"Hey, they're the biggest streaming platform on the planet, give me a break. They're willing to commit. They just need one more thing from you…"

My forehead wrinkles. "What is it?"

Lex perks up, staring at the phone.

"They want you to interview five celebrities. They think this everyday people thing won't work—"

"But—"

"I know, Callie. I told them, but they have a point. After the tour last year, people are more familiar with you, and if you can't get an authentic story, then what's the point? They think you need to up the caliber of your guests. Intersperse public figures with the general public. So they want proof you can get five people with a public persona to talk to you, which shouldn't be a problem. You have an ace in your pocket."

"Hayes," Lex whispers.

I nod, already knowing who Jarrah is referring to. It's been a constant in my life as Hayes's younger sister—everyone sees a way I can use and abuse him to get what I want.

"Easy peasy. And once you have the five and they hear the conversations, I suspect you're in. They'll give you a contract."

I'm silent because I'm not sure where I can find the people they want. And unfortunately, I don't want to put my brother in a situation where his friends and people he knows feel as though they have to do it. Have to tell the truth to the world and be judged for it. My guests need to be willing, not strong-armed into it. That's the only way this works.

And honestly, it would be all athletes. That probably wouldn't work. But they're the only kind of connections my brother has.

"I have to go, but this is good news. Now go be that killer I know you are and make us both a lot of money." She hangs up.

Lex and I look at one another.

I don't know how, but I have to find a way to make this happen for us.

CHAPTER
SIX

Foster

"So, what exactly is up your ass lately?" Hayes asks as we sit down on the plane.

Decker and Easton sit across from us.

"He hasn't even been going out," Easton says.

"Maybe I don't want to hang out with you." I just want this conversation to end.

"You had Stephie willing and waiting." Easton hasn't let that one go, and I get it, he was disappointed, but he could go out and get any other woman, so why is he harping on this one?

"Why don't you get on Decker?"

My brother looks up from his book, and our gazes collide until I tear mine away.

I don't hate my brother like everyone thinks, but a lot of shit has gone down between us over the years. Coming to Chicago to his team wasn't ideal, but I needed to get out of Seattle. We never had an outright conversation about it, but it was an unspoken agreement that we'd live our lives on opposite sides of the country.

What are the chances that two brothers who didn't grow up together would end up in the pros? Unlikely, but we've been good at keeping our distance since I'm pretty sure we both resent one another for different reasons.

"Don't pull me into it." Decker goes back to his book.

"Decker will end up with some sweet girl he meets at the dog park or something." Easton elbows him and laughs.

"Speaking of, what's up with the dance moves with my sister the other night?" Hayes asks.

My jaw clenches, and I lift my gaze to see a smile on Decker's face that has a hint of competition in it.

Fuck him.

"I thought you and Leighton were having relations in the back alley?" Easton laughs.

"Relations? How old are you?" I shake my head at him.

Easton shrugs. "Well, it doesn't seem polite to say fucking now."

Even Decker looks at Easton with a *what the fuck* expression.

Easton holds up his hands. "I'm a gentleman."

"So do you ask the women you bring home really nicely to please get down on their knees and kiss your pee pee?" Hayes asks.

We all laugh and even Decker snickers.

"I'm just saying Leighton is in a different category now. She's in the wife category."

All of our eyebrows rise.

"You're kind of scaring me now." I give him a *what the fuck* look.

"And if he says that, then there's a real problem." Decker throws shade at me, but I let it go because I'm exhausted from the beef I already had with him today.

"I'm just saying, talking about you *fucking* Leighton seems wrong now that she's gonna be your wife." He shrugs one shoulder.

We all laugh again.

"Jesus, Kodiak, who would have thought?" Hayes says.

I lean forward. "I have a question then. So, are you thinking that once you get married, you'll change fucking to making love?"

Easton shakes his head. "I'm not giving you pointers on my dirty talk, Reap, but I'm just saying, I'm not going to ask you if you gave your wife a good fuck last night. It's impolite."

Hayes and I share a look. "Leighton wouldn't care. I won't give details, but rest assured, there was no making love the other night at the club. It was definitely fucking happening against that brick wall in the alley."

Easton raises his hands again. "That's fine if you want to say it, but I'm not going to."

"That's very admirable of you, and I don't mean to be a dick about it. There are a lot of nights Leighton and I have relations that aren't about fucking."

"Sap," I murmur.

"Just wait and see if you ever find her, you'll see how much more—"

Easton points at me. "That is my point. She's your person, the one. It sounds disrespectful."

"We get it. Let's move on." I don't wanna sit here and talk about any of their sex lives. I've never been one to really trade stories about the women I sleep with. Speaking of which, I pull my phone out of my pocket and see that Becca hasn't gotten back to me from my text this morning.

"All right," Easton says. "Let's talk about why you're not picking up women or going to clubs anymore."

Hayes turns in his seat to face me. Decker closes his book. All three pairs of eyes are on me now.

"Are you keeping a tally for me?" I lift my phone. "I apologized about the Stephie and Millie thing. And I might call her when we get back to Chicago."

"It's just weird. I mean, your reputation precedes you," Easton continues.

I think he thought that with Hayes now with Leighton and Decker never having been a guy who picks up women at clubs, I was going to be his wingman. But I don't need a wingman.

"I'm meeting with a woman tonight." Maybe that will shut them up.

"Becca?" Hayes asks. "She's still around, huh?"

"Whoa, whoa. whoa. You have a steady?" Easton's hands go up in the air.

Hayes chuckles. "Foster is more of a one-woman-in-every-city kind of guy." I cut him a look, and he shrugs. "They're our friends. They'll ask me later, so just tell them now."

"You started it. You can fill them in." I wave for him to go ahead.

"Just what I said. He has one woman in every city who he hooks up with when he's in town. So he won't be going out tonight, he'll be with Becca from San Diego."

Easton throws his head back and stares at me. "Really? That's kind of genius."

"And they know the score?" Decker asks. Of course he always assumes the worst of me.

I side-eye him and nod. "They get it. No strings."

Easton nods as though he's starting to see the benefit of it. "What if you don't want Becca from San Diego when you get there?"

"If I didn't, I never would've reached out. She knows the deal. We hook up while I'm in town, and when I leave, there's no texting or calls until I'm coming back to town."

Easton's eyes are wide. "Fuck, you really are a playboy."

I sit up straighter. Hayes is smiling and not because he thinks it's cool, more because he thinks it's funny that Easton's mind is churning right now. Hayes was never into that. He was my wingman for that one year, and I kind of pushed away my time with the women because he needed me. Now he's all happy and half married, so it's time to stop thinking about Callie and get back to my regularly scheduled programming.

"Why would you say I'm a playboy? I'm not lying to them. I make sure they're okay with it before we do anything, and if I think one of them is starting to get feelings, I end it before anyone gets hurt. The word playboy pisses me off. Every one of us here has hooked up with women we just met. Calling me a playboy means I'm giving the impression that there might be hope of something more."

"Eh…" Decker says, clearly not agreeing with me.

Of course he doesn't. He never does.

"I'm kind of with Deck, man. You're still a playboy," Hayes chimes in, and when I give him a cutting look, he raises his hands. "I'm not saying it's a bad thing, but I wouldn't want you dating my sister."

And there it is. What Hayes really thinks of me.

"And me?" Easton asks.

Hayes points from me to him. "You're one and the same. It's not about who you sleep with or how many women you sleep with, it's the fact that you don't want a relationship. I get that Callie doesn't take a lot of shit, and she's snarky as hell sometimes, but she's my sister. I want her to be with someone who sees her worth. Who will take the time to dig through those hard layers and let her trust him with the softness underneath."

"Fuck, I'm gonna cry." Easton blots at pretend tears.

I say nothing because fuck, if I didn't think I was the man for her before, now I know for sure I'm not. I've never been that for a woman, nor have I ever wanted to be. Hell, I've never even done it for myself.

"I guess Goldie is it then." Easton elbows Decker.

"I wouldn't date a teammate's sister," he mumbles, opening his book back up. "It's not like that with us anyway."

"Your thigh was on her pussy the other night," Easton says.

Again, my teeth grind as I remember how he spun her around and how happy she looked. It was what soured me on sleeping with Stephie that night. And when I told her I was tired and would be going home alone after the club, she got upset and grabbed Millie then left. But I'm not telling any of these guys that.

Hayes narrows his eyes at Easton. "Okay, if you're going to have respect for who Leighton is to me, the same goes for my sister."

Easton smirks, but nods. "Sorry, Decker's thigh was very close to her lady parts."

Hayes narrows his eyes. "Let's not talk about my sister. Decker said they're not like that, so let's just drop the Callie topic."

I inhale and rest my head on the back of the seat. I'm hoping my night with Becca will be successful in ridding Callie from my head. She's the complete opposite of Callie. Becca has blond hair, bright blue eyes, and she's very thin since she's trying to be a model.

Whereas Callie has dark-brown hair with a slight wave, and her eyes are dark and fierce. And fuck, her curves... her hips were made for my hands. I know from the way my fingers wound around them as I thrust into her. And her tits. Where Becca's are barely a handful, Callie's are plenty more than a handful.

So I decided I needed the exact opposite of Callie, so I don't think of her while I'm drilling into another woman tonight. Then my head will be back on what matters most. Baseball.

Easton puts his headphones in and gets out his phone. Decker goes back to his book, and Hayes turns toward the window, his eyes already shutting. I have no idea how he keeps up with the demands of his life.

I close my eyes too, trying to think about anything but *her*.

By the time we land, I've been unsuccessful, but at least I have a game to prepare for that will serve as a distraction. As we file off the plane and onto the bus, my phone vibrates in my pocket.

Becca. Finally.

I pull her message up and find a picture. Perfect. She's always good for a great tease of what I can expect tonight.

I open it, and it's not her in skimpy lingerie or even a titty pic. It's her left hand raised with a giant diamond on her ring finger.

"What the fuck?" I mumble.

Another message pops up right after.

> Becca from SD: I'm engaged! Getting married in August.
>
> I could see if any of my friends are down to party…

> No. Congratulations. He's a lucky guy. Have a great life.

She messaes me back, but I pocket my phone and get on the bus, not bothering to look at it. My mood going to shit really fast.

CHAPTER
SEVEN

Callie

"**I**n and out," I repeat to myself over and over again as I hurry up to The Dugout.

Thankfully, after Hayes moved in with Leighton, Foster took over his place, and if all goes well, he hasn't changed the security code to the condo.

Is my way of telling him the coward's way out? Maybe. Okay, it is, but I mean, Foster Davis isn't going to want this baby, and since I have no idea if or when I'll be pregnant again, I really do want the *we're having a baby* announcement I've always thought was cool.

The guys aren't due back for at least an hour since they're returning from Philly.

I punch in the security code, jog up to my floor with my backpack, and enter the code on Hayes's old apartment door.

Dumbass, he never changed the code. Probably hoping some girl Hayes had been with would surprise him by waking him up with a blow job.

You're the one who slept with him the devil on my shoulder says.

I walk into the condo, slip off my shoes at the door, and tiptoe into the primary bedroom. I'm shocked to find his bed neatly made and a few extra throw pillows there.

Obviously, a housekeeper must have been here. A man like Foster cannot make his bed every day.

I open my bag and pull out the onesie before laying it flat on the bottom half of the bed. I run my hand over it to make sure there are no wrinkles and I can clearly read what it says. Then I place a set of little booties with it just to make sure he gets the point. Although he'd be an idiot not to.

The pregnancy tests are next. Yep, not just one but all six of them in case he asks if I'm sure, which I would bet good money he will. Even I questioned the accuracy of one. There's one with two pink lines, another one with a plus symbol, and as if that's not enough, one that spells out the word pregnant.

Then I scatter little pink and blue sperm confetti all around the items.

I pull my phone out and hold it up above, snapping a picture. Then I head out into the main living area and send it to Leighton, teasing that she'll know soon enough who the father is. The picture is close up enough that she'd have to recognize the comforter to know whose bedroom this is.

That's how you're telling him? Are you waiting for him to come home?

No. I'm leaving it here for him to find.

You're playing games. Why?

I don't really have an answer, other than I'm curious if he can figure out who left it here—or more accurately, I'm terrified of watching his face when he finds out. Something to think about another day.

No judging.

I'm not judging, but if that's your plan, I'd get
out of there fast.

Relax. They don't land for another hour.

Um... Hayes has been home for an hour.
They got in earlier than expected.

I glance at the door that's still shut.

Shit.

Get out now.

As I read Leighton's text, I hear a beep from the condo
door and the lock slide over.

Fuck. Fuck. Fuck.

I panic and look around the room then rush toward the
bathroom, but I trip, catching myself on the breakfast bar
stool before I fall.

The door opens, and Foster stands on the threshold with
Stephie peering around him.

Well, this is awkward.

CHAPTER
EIGHT

Foster

I'm taking my own advice.

I have to do something because all these thoughts of Callie aren't going to get me anywhere. Hayes made his feelings clear—I'm not good enough for his baby sister.

And I'm not even upset about it. He's right. All it would do is fuck up our friendship and our team when I'm inevitably done with her or she wants more than I'm willing to give.

Just like Pen back in college. I swear women come out of their moms' wombs wanting to fix a man. Well, there's no fixing me.

So I did what every red-blooded male would—I called Stephie. I'm going to fuck Callie out of my system.

After Becca shared her news, I spent most of my time in San Diego with Hayes, exploring the city and doing tourist shit. It was cool to hang with him again like we used to when we played together in Seattle, which only convinced me even more that Callie is completely off-limits if I want my friendship with Hayes to remain intact.

While in San Diego, I texted Stephie and asked her to meet me for a drink after I landed.

We're off tomorrow, so it's the perfect time to go balls deep in a woman as many times as I can in one night.

She was more than eager, which I assumed she would be, and was already waiting at the bar when I arrived.

We had one drink, but she seems to be just as into the sex thing as me. Her exact words were, "I'm not looking for anything other than a few tickets and telling people I'm fucking you."

Works for me, so I paid for the drinks, and now as I'm putting in my code to the security gate, there's a sourness in my stomach that says this is a very bad idea. But I've ignored that feeling many times before in my life. What's the harm now?

The minute the security gate shuts behind us and only the concrete stairs are between us and my bed, I regret my decision even more.

"Oh, I'm behind the gate. Millie is going to be so jealous. She got mad at me for making her leave the club that night." She's on me like we're in a three-legged race, and my throat closes up.

"I'm sure Easton wouldn't mind her phone number."

"Really?" Her excitement is palpable.

I inhale deeply, wishing this didn't feel like pulling out my teeth. I step onto the first step, and somehow it feels like I'm heading down death row. "All the way up."

"Tell me who lives where." Stephie's arm is linked through mine because apparently, she can't move more than two inches away from me.

"Decker." I point at the first door we pass. "Easton," I say when we get to his floor. "And I'm on top."

"Just the way you probably like it." She giggles at her sexual innuendo that's more like middle school humor.

Fuck, I need to stop judging her. I asked her to be here. I just wish my plan was working.

I press the code on the keypad outside my condo door and the lock slides open. Turning the knob, I push open the door, and I'm about to tell Stephie to go first when a streak of dark hair breezes by, then falls toward my breakfast stool.

"Callie?"

There goes my whole idea of getting her out of my system. She's wearing tight yoga pants that show off her amazing ass, and her tits are straining against the T-shirt under her unzipped hoodie.

"Hey, girl." Stephie sneaks by me.

Shit, I forgot about her for a second. In about two minutes, I'm gonna be the biggest asshole because I don't lead girls on, and my ridiculous plan just went into the shitter. If I fuck Stephie, I'll be imagining Callie the entire time.

"Oh, hey." Callie stands and brushes her hair out of her face. "I completely forgot that Hayes doesn't live here anymore."

I narrow my eyes at her. *Bullshit.*

Then it dawns on me. She's here because she can't get me out of her system either. I can have a second round with her.

"Did you clean out the closet? I left this sweatshirt..." She's tiptoeing toward my bedroom door. "Mind if I just check really quick?" She thumbs in that direction, and when she's close to the door she turns around.

"I'll help you look!" Stephie follows. "What color was it?"

Callie grabs the handle of my bedroom door and slams it shut. "Oh wait, it was in the second bedroom, I think." She points toward the door on the other side of the kitchen.

Stephie swivels around and heads that way.

No way, did Callie do something kinky like leave sex toys

and lube on the nightstand? I really hope it's nothing romantic like candles or some shit. Does she know me at all?

Stephie disappears into the spare bedroom. "There's nothing in here. It's all empty," she shouts from the other room.

"What's going on?" I murmur to Callie with the hope Stephie can't hear.

"I'll check the bathroom!" Stephie calls.

Callie cringes. "So… I had this whole plan…"

My curiosity gets the better of me, and I go to open the door, but she gets in front of me, her hand covering mine.

"Please don't," she whispers.

We're chest to chest, our eyes locked, and I'm trying to figure out what's going on with her.

"I hoped you'd be back," I say in my seductive voice that usually gets women to undress. "Let me get rid of her." I press my body to hers, weaving our legs together. "We just can't tell Hayes, okay?" I thrust my thigh up against her core, and she swallows audibly, her face flushing.

Yeah, this is what I needed.

I feel like an asshole for going behind Hayes's back again, but it's already happened once. One more time, and I'll get her out of my system and can move on with my life.

"Yeah, that's not—"

"Nothing there." Stephie's voice is close enough that she's definitely out of the bedroom. "What are you guys doing?"

Callie peers around me. "Foster is being protective of his bedroom. Must be sloppy and doesn't make his bed or something."

"Well, I planned on unmaking the bed anyway." Stephie's voice is so certain she's still going to have me tonight. I am the asshole everyone thinks I am.

"You know what? You should take Stephie up to the rooftop." Callie pats my chest then looks around at Stephie again. "You'll love it."

We're still not moving, and I'm not sure how Stephie hasn't called us out on the fact that Callie's tits are pressed to my chest, and my thigh is wedged between her legs.

"Oh, I would love that. Let's go! Callie can find her sweatshirt and leave. And then the real fun will start." Stephie's tone is full of excitement. I'm going to hurt her, and I fucking hate it when I hurt people.

"Great idea. Now let go of the doorknob," Callie whispers to me, but she's crazy if she thinks I'm going to give her a chance to get rid of whatever is in that bedroom.

"Do me a favor, Stephie, go ask Easton for the code. I forget what it is." I don't move my gaze from Callie.

"One floor down, right?" She heads toward the door.

I'm thankful I'll have a few minutes alone with Callie. And even better, the door will shut behind Stephie and lock automatically in ten seconds.

"Yup." I pop the 'p' on the word.

"Wait... Stephie..." Callie calls, but I press my thigh against her core again, and she squeezes my shoulder. Yeah, there's definitely something in that bedroom.

"BRB!" The door opens and shuts.

"Foster," Callie says my name with a bite in her tone.

"Callie, it's my bedroom." I wiggle my arm, and she digs her nails into my palm. "Fuck. You know how I make my money, right?"

"Step away from the door. Give me one minute, and I'll be out of your hair. You can screw Stephie all night."

"I'd rather screw you." There. The truth is out there.

She pales. "That was a one-and-done, pal, sorry." She puts her free hand on my chest. "Now step back."

"I'm going into that room." I twist the knob again. She doesn't have the strength to keep me out.

The door opens, and she jumps into my arms, giving me no choice but to hold on to her ass. "Please. I'm begging."

"I appreciate the begging, but it's unnecessary."

She grunts and scoffs, then unwinds her legs from my waist. "Fine. Have it your way."

When I move to the side, my eyes zero in on the edge of the bed. There's no lube on the nightstand. No vibrator for me to get her off.

I squint to make sure I'm seeing things right.

A baby outfit is laid on the bed with little booties and sparkly pink and blue confetti. I read the wording on the baby outfit: *Guess what... you knocked up Mommy.*

My breath stalls, and my gaze shoots to her. "Is this your idea of a joke? Fuck, what day is it?"

I mentally try to figure it out, but I know that April 1st has come and gone.

Shit. No way.

"This was you, right?" I point at the outfit. "Leighton didn't get confused and leave it for Hayes?"

Her eyes narrow, and her expression clearly says *you're an idiot, jackass.* "Yes, it's me. I get that you sleep with a lot of women, but I've only slept with you, so congratulations, you're gonna be a daddy."

A dad?

Me?

Fuck, no one wants that. My dad proved you're not born knowing how to be a father when your kid pops out of the womb.

"Reaper!" Stephie singsongs, knocking on the door and trying to turn the knob. "I can't get in."

Callie's shoulders slump, and she shrugs. "I thought it was cute."

I step farther into the room.

"Should I let her in?" Callie asks.

"Fuck no." I stare at the variety of pregnancy tests. Some pink lines, some plus signs. She's definitely pregnant. I read the baby shirt again to make sure I'm not losing it. "You're pregnant with my baby?"

She laughs. "That's why it's all on *your* bed."

I circle back around.

Stephie pounds on the door again, harder this time.

"You go handle that. Want me to take all that with me?"

I point at her. "You're staying right here. Give me one minute." I walk out of the bedroom, through the condo, and outside, shutting the door behind me.

"Oh, goodie, all ready?" Stephie asks, practically bouncing on the balls of her feet.

"Sorry, I have to help Callie with something. She's having a… dilemma, and she's… my best friend's sister, so I feel like I have to help her."

Her shoulders fall as well as the corners of her lips. "But I thought we were gonna…" She steps up to me and places her hand on my crotch.

Yeah, that thing is not going to perk up right now. He's grounded for the foreseeable future. I step back. "Maybe next time. I'll call you."

"Will you really?"

"You know what, Stephie, this probably isn't a good time. I'm midseason, and I need to focus on a few personal things as well as baseball. I'm sorry."

She stares at me for a moment. "It's her, right? You like her?"

Fuck yeah, but I'm not gonna tell Stephie that.

"She's Hayes's sister."

Stephie steps back. "Yeah, but I see you always looking at her, and at Saffire…"

Telling her I'm into someone else really is the easiest way to cut her loose. "Sorry, things were going on before you and I and—" It's not a lie exactly.

She smiles and shrugs. "Mind if I go talk to Easton?"

Well, she got over that fast.

I shake my head. "Not at all. Have at him."

Her smile grows wider. "Great." Rising on her tiptoes, she kisses my cheek. "Good luck with Callie."

I watch her bounce down the stairs, but I don't wait to see what happens with Easton. I don't care.

I walk into my condo, shut the door, and stare at Callie. "Start talking."

CHAPTER
NINE

Callie

"The T-shirt did the talking." I point toward the bedroom.

"So you were just going to leave it here and hope I knew it was you?" He goes to the fridge and grabs two beers, twisting the cap off of one and holding it out for me.

I raise my eyebrows.

"Fuck." He places it on the counter. "What do you want to drink?"

"Nothing."

"Shouldn't you have water or something? Are you hungry? I have peanut butter but no pickles." He turns his back to me and pulls a jar of peanut butter out of the cupboard.

"Listen." I go to the front door to grab my shoes. "I just wanted to let you know. I don't expect anything from you." I place my hand on my stomach, and his eyes zero in on the gesture. I retract my hand immediately. "This was a *you should know* obligatory telling. I'm not looking for a relationship or money or anything." I hurriedly slip into my shoes as he rounds the counter.

Damn, he looks good today. Of course he does. Low-hanging jeans, a black T-shirt, his tattoos sneaking out of his sleeves and above his neckline.

"Oh, I get it. You wanted to let me know, but I'm not good enough to talk it out with or have any part in the baby's life if you decide to keep him or her."

I glance up, and his eyebrows raise from what I suspect is a shocked expression on my face.

"Are you at least gonna tell me if you're keeping the baby? Do I deserve to know that much at least?"

I stand and grab my backpack, securing it on my back. "I…" I stutter because I assumed… shit, I'm the asshole now. "Well… I thought… You wouldn't want to? I mean I… do you?"

He puts the closed beer back in the fridge and dumps the other beer in the sink before tossing the bottle in the trash can. "You assumed I'd be a deadbeat dad. That I wouldn't want to know my own kid."

My stomach feels as though it slides down my leg and onto the floor. "That's not it." I glance away from him.

"I think you're lying."

I throw my hands in the air. He's cornered me, and it's apparent that I've clearly made assumptions about him. "Okay. Yes. I figured you might not even believe me and probably ask for a paternity test and then maybe you'd want to pay me a few bucks to go away. Which I wasn't going to take, for the record."

"Jesus, Callie." He runs his fingers through his hair and appears genuinely hurt. I'm surprised by how much it bothers me. "You're my best friend's sister, and you think I'd just desert you?"

I bite my lip as my shoulders sink. "I'm sorry, it was wrong of me to assume."

How could I be so stupid and judgmental to think he'd abandon the baby? His reputation as a womanizer doesn't mean he'd run from his own kid.

"I'm sorry. I think I got caught up in worrying how I'm to navigate this, and I wasn't giving a lot of real thought to how you would."

Foster sets his hands on his hips. "Are you keeping the baby? Have you made that decision yet?" His gaze falls to my stomach once more.

I follow his line of vision so we're both staring at my not-swollen belly. "I am."

He nods, steels himself with a deep breath. "Okay, well then, I'm in."

"Foster…"

"Goddamn it, Callie, don't. You might know what my dick feels like inside you, but you don't know *me*. You probably know what you've heard from gossip blogs and the reputation I've made for myself. Shit, I'm sure Decker told you to stay the fuck away from me, but that's my child in your stomach, and I'm not gonna have it grow up without me."

Although he didn't strike me, my cheeks heat as if he did. "You…"

He blows out a breath, goes to his bedroom, and I don't know if I should follow or just give him space. I couldn't have made this worse for both of us.

He comes back out with the onesie in his hand, staring at the small outfit. "I can't promise I'm going to be good at fatherhood. I'm going to fuck up, but I can make one promise to you that I'll never break." His eyes meet mine, and there's so much emotion swimming in those pools of blue, I can't see through to what he's really thinking. "They'll come first in my life. Always."

I suck in a sharp breath. "That's all you need to do."

He nods. "So, let's talk logistics. Have you been to the doctor?"

I shake my head, surprised he's thinking through the steps that have to be taken after he just tried to offer me peanut butter and pickles.

"You'll need prenatal vitamins."

"I know. I am the woman." My back goes up because who does he think he is to just tell me what I need?

"I'd like to go with you." His voice softens a little.

"Is this your first time getting a woman pregnant?" I ask, since he seems to know the routine so well.

"Yes, I'm not the manwhore you like to think I am. And just so you know, I would have known the baby shirt was from you. I haven't slept with anyone in Chicago but you."

I blink back my surprise.

"Shocking, I know." He crosses his arms, the onesie still dangling from his fingers.

"I feel like we should start over. I'm just…" I pause because Foster doesn't strike me as the kind of guy you want to pour your heart out to, but he is the father of my baby. "I'm not used to relying on people. I've just never been someone's first…" I let my words drift off, but he waits for me to finish. "I have hang-ups too, but it's no excuse."

He opens his mouth to speak, but I raise my hand. "I'm truly sorry for barging in here and leaving a bomb on your bed when I should've just asked to meet you for coffee. I should have talked it out with you. It was extremely selfish of me to assume you wouldn't want to be a part of this, and it was judgmental as well. I am sorry."

He doesn't say anything for a few seconds. My stomach sours. This is not how I wanted our co-parenting journey to start off.

"Have you eaten?" he asks.

I shake my head.

"Want to order takeout and talk it out?" I'm not sure of the look that crosses my face, but he chuckles. "You're used to being disappointed by people, and I'm used to being underestimated. How about we make a deal not to pick at the scabs other people have left behind?"

I don't know much about Foster's life, only bits and pieces, but if he feels the same about being underestimated as I do about being disappointed, I don't want to inflict that pain on him.

I nod. "Deal."

He pulls out his phone. "What are you craving?"

I shake my head, and he peeks up at me with a raised eyebrow. "Not peanut butter and pickles."

"But what?"

"Guacamole and chips. Pretty much all Mexican food."

He grabs some waters from the fridge and waves me into his living room. "Take your shoes off and stay a while."

I slip out of my shoes again, and my phone vibrates in my back pocket on my way over to the couch.

> Leighton: Okay, I've been a good girl and waited really patiently. When do I get my reward?

> I'm with him now. We're going to talk it out.

> How many flights of stairs did you have to walk up to reach him?

I giggle.

> Wouldn't you like to know?

> YES. YES, I would like to know. And you're gonna have to tell me who it is so I know if I have to tie Hayes down before you tell him.

> Keep your kinky sex games to yourself. I'll be over tomorrow.

TOMORROW?!? You're killin' me!!!!

"Work?"

I shake my head. My brother is a whole other ordeal, one I haven't wanted to focus on until after I told Foster he was going to be a dad.

Foster sits next to me on the couch and hands me a water after opening the top. "Food will be here in forty or so."

"Thanks."

We sit there awkwardly for a second, neither of us saying a word.

Finally I can't take it anymore. "Leighton knows about me being pregnant."

His head whips toward me, then toward the front door. I guess I know one thing Foster is afraid of. "Hayes?"

I shake my head. "And Leighton doesn't know you're the father. She knows it's either you, Easton, or Decker, but that's all."

He nods, seeming to take that in. "Thanks for telling me first."

"That's the one thing I did right in all this." I touch his arm. "Again, I'm really sorry."

He sips his water. "Don't sweat it, but…" He turns to face me. "I don't want us to be just co-parents. I want to be a part of our baby's life. And don't think I'm gonna have him or her at my place and have a woman over or something. I won't. We can make rules, and I'll abide by them. I want our child to have the kind of life I never did."

"A life you never did?" My head tilts.

"I'll just say this… I didn't have a role model, but I sure as hell learned how *not* to raise a kid."

I squeeze his arm, the fixer in me wanting to dig deeper, but Foster seems like a man with a lot of layers. Layers he's not going to shed to the person who underestimated him just minutes ago. He doesn't have to share anything with me, but maybe one day he'll feel comfortable enough to.

"The road might be bumpy, but as long as we keep this about the baby, we can make it work."

Foster brings his hand to the back of his neck and rubs there. "As long as your brother doesn't kill me. This isn't good for us or the team. I'm a jerk for sleeping with you in the first place."

"It's not your fault I'm so irresistible." I flutter my eyelashes jokingly, but his eyes don't stray from mine.

"I'm gonna be honest with you, I've never been that worked up before. I wasn't even thinking rationally. Maybe I didn't put on the condom right."

I sip my water and cross my legs. "Just what a woman wants to hear, that the man she slept with wishes he had been thinking rationally. And anyway, I don't think we... used one."

"It was more a compliment than anything, Callie. You made me see past all that." His forehead wrinkles. "We didn't use one? I always do."

"I'm on the pill, and I think I said..." I honestly can't remember the whole thing or how it all happened. Thanks, alcohol. I do remember his breath in my ear and the feel of his big hands on me though.

He made me forget myself too. I've never slept with one of Hayes's friends, and I never planned to. I never wanted to affect any of his friendships.

"We do have the fact he's engaged to my best friend on our side." I shrug.

"That's different though. You don't have a ring on your finger, and we're not in a relationship. It changes things." His voice is strained.

He's not wrong, but I'm fully prepared to give my brother shit if he decides to go after Foster. I'm a grown woman, and I can make my own decisions.

"Callie?" Foster's voice pulls me out of my thoughts. "Can I be there when you tell him?"

Whoever said Foster wasn't a stand-up guy was wrong. Oh, wait—that was me.

"Sure. If you want to."

He puts his hand in mine. His calluses are rough, but I love the way they feel along my soft palm. "I want to be there every step of the way. I'm not going to abandon you. I promise."

I squeeze his hand, feeling like real shit again considering how I thought this would go. "Thank you, Foster. I—"

"No. We start over now. Forget all that shit from earlier. I learned a long time ago that actions change people's perception, not words. So I know I'm promising you a bunch of things, and I mean every one of them, but I'll show you how serious I am."

Tears prick my eyes, but I suck them back.

This is not what I thought I was going to get out of Foster when I told him we were going to have a baby. It's a welcome surprise, but at the same time, I've heard a lot of promises from others who said they would be there for me, and when it came down to it, they weren't. I think I'll keep that wall erected a little longer.

CHAPTER
TEN

Foster

"You've been quiet. Something going on?" Hayes asks after we order our coffees.

We were hanging out today, and somehow, we were instructed to go get coffees for Leighton and Callie and drop them off at some bridal place where Leighton is trying on wedding gowns.

"Nah. Anyway, I thought it was bad luck for you to see the dress?" I'm trying to stop us from having to go to the bridal shop for two reasons. One, I don't ever want to be in a bridal store, and two, Callie is there. And although we've figured out our shit, the one thing we haven't figured out is how and when to tell Hayes. I have no idea if she's told Leighton I'm the baby's father, and if she did, Leighton clearly didn't tell Hayes since he's been more than fine with me all day.

Which only makes me feel like an even bigger asshole.

"I'm not going in. You are," Hayes says.

"No, I'm not." I lean against the wall and lower my hat, although my neck tats give me away.

The two of us together is like a flashing neon sign. So far no one has approached us though. I will say, I'm not sure if Chicago fans don't give a shit about their professional athletes, but I haven't had many people approach me in public since I came here.

"Yes, you are, because you don't want your best friend to start off his marriage with bad juju."

I scowl at him. "Juju? Who the fuck are you, man?"

He chuckles as the woman brings our drinks to the counter. Two to-go trays with eight cups.

"Who are all these for?"

Hayes chuckles again. I will say he's a happy fucker since Leighton and the kids came into his life. Makes me wonder if when this kid comes, I will be too.

"It's Kyleigh Landry's store," he says.

"Who?"

He picks up one tray, and I pick up the other, the two of us weaving through the mid-morning rush inside the coffee shop.

"Rowan Landry's wife. The center for the Falcons."

My head falls back in recognition.

As we approach the door, a gentleman holds the door open for us. "We're rooting for you boys."

"Thank you, sir," Hayes says. "We're trying our best."

I nod, and his gaze flashes to my neck, presumably to my tattoos, but he doesn't comment. "Good luck tomorrow. Toronto is gonna be tough."

Hayes is polite as always. I nod again since my stomach is in knots because my pitching hasn't exactly been stellar. I'm not getting the velocity I had last year, and it's hard not to wonder if I'm in some downward spiral toward retirement. There's no way I'm gonna be one of those guys who draws each drop of blood before calling it quits. I will go out on top as much as I possibly can.

The baby changes things a little. I'll have a little life to support and make sure he or she wants for nothing.

We walk down the sidewalk, and Hayes says nothing about me not conversing with the fan. He knows that's not me.

"Now that you have a family, is this where you see yourself wanting to stay?" I ask him.

I'm on a two-year contract with Chicago, and if I don't get my velocity up, I'm going to be traded before the end of that contract. I can't really talk to Callie about it at this point, but I refuse to live in a separate city from my kid. I know better than anyone the divide it causes. Makes for not knowing them, just like with my mom. Long-distance parenting ends up being a voice on the other end of the phone that eventually you don't want to hear.

He glances over with an expression as if to say, *what's going on in that head of yours.* "It would be hard to relocate the kids. I mean, Lake might murder me in my sleep. Then there's Leighton's job. I guess I'd have to talk to Leighton about it, but if it happens, we'll have to make a tough decision. Maybe it'll be time for me to hang up my glove."

I stop on the sidewalk. "You'd just quit baseball? For her?"

He laughs and shakes his head. "Sure, she trumps it all. I've had a long career, not always fulfilling, and it would suck retiring never having received a Gold Glove, but that's not up to me."

My mind wanders again to wondering what I want my life to look like. Now that Callie is pregnant with my baby, it changes things. I'm sure she feels as though I did a one-eighty when I told her I want to be part of the kid's life. It doesn't fit with my reputation, but I always promised myself if I ever had a kid, they would come before me. I guess that's what happens when you learn at an early age that parents don't necessarily have to stick around.

"Shit, I had no idea you were that invested," I say.

His forehead wrinkles. "Reap, I asked her to marry me."

I nod and walk. "Yeah, I know, but you only have so many years to play, and you fought so hard last year to get back on top." I shrug, knowing I'm not helping myself in the department of winning him over when he inevitably finds out I knocked up his sister.

"I can't wait until you're in my position so I can call you out on all the crazy shit that goes through that head of yours." He slides around me so he's close to the brick building. "Here. This is it."

It's definitely a bridal store. Mannequins dressed in white gowns are in the display window, and flower petals lay scattered along the bottom.

"I really have to go in?" I sound like a sullen child.

Hayes laughs, holding out his tray of drinks. "Afraid so."

I take the other tray and sigh, walking through the door that has Bridal by Kyleigh etched on the glass. A bell rings to alert everyone I've arrived. Awesome.

The heads of all the women seated on the couches in front of a huge mirror turn in my direction, and that's when I see Callie standing in the center of them, dressed in a fucking wedding dress. My arms lose strength for a second, and the trays tip out of my grip, but I recover before they fall to the floor.

"Oh jeez, look at him. He's gonna break out in hives." A brunette standing off to the side rushes over, laughing.

My eyes are locked on Callie, and hers are on mine through the mirror. Why the hell is she in a wedding dress? I don't like the image that comes to mind of another man around my kid. Or around her. And that second part is the problem—because a fast, brutal flash of *mine to protect* sears straight through me.

"We were just trying to convince Leighton how pretty a ball gown style with pockets is," the brunette I don't know says.

As if hearing the woman, Callie pulls her hands out of the pockets. She looks like a princess, though I'm definitely not her white knight. Regardless, I want to stomp over there and throw her over my shoulder.

Shit, where did that just come from? I shake my head.

"I'm Kyleigh, by the way. Rowan Landry's wife."

I've met Rowan and a few of the other guys from the Falcons a few times, but I've never met their wives. All I really know is they all have families and live on the same street. That's some close shit for teammates.

"Foster Davis."

She laughs and takes one of the trays from me. "I know."

I follow her to the table at the side of the group. She calls off orders and women raise their hands, all eyes on me.

"This is an absolute no." Leighton comes out of the hallway in a dress with a huge bow on her right hip. She sees all the women staring at me and ducks around a corner.

"He's outside," I tell her.

"Oh good." She comes back out, walking toward me. "You can come closer. Marriage isn't contagious." Kyleigh sets the last drink on the table near Leighton. "Thank you for this. I know Hayes probably sprang it on you."

I tuck my hands in the pockets of my jeans. "No problem." My gaze keeps straying to Callie, who is oddly quiet.

Leighton smiles at me and turns to the center stage area. "Oh, Callie, it is beautiful, but I think it suits you more than me. It's gorgeous." Leighton glances at me over her shoulder. "Don't you think so, Foster?"

Her smile says she knows, and if she knows, then I have to think Hayes is next.

Callie said we'd tell him together, but what if he finds out before we have a chance? The two of us decided we'd wait until we go to the doctor because why cause all that turmoil before the doctor confirms everything is okay? Still, something about Hayes not knowing feels like a knife is lodged in my throat.

"Yeah," I croak.

The entire room giggles.

"Oh, let the poor guy go. He looks like he could throw up," Kyleigh says.

Just then Hayes and Callie's mom comes out of the back-room, and her eyes light up when she sees me. My smile widens because I love Mrs. Carlisle.

"Foster!" She rushes over with her arms open, and I try to loosen my muscles and not seem so stiff as she throws her arms around me and buries her head in my chest. "Oh, you're a lifesaver. Hopefully the caffeine helps take the edge off."

"We're fine, Mom," Callie says with a note of exasperation.

Jennifer Carlisle is like a mom from television. She's patient, loving, and treats you as if you're the best person who was ever born. Even me.

Mrs. Carlisle rolls her eyes. "You know my Callie, she likes to get her way."

Callie inhales deeply, and she steps down from the pedestal. I finally feel as though I can breathe again. I hope she goes in the back and takes off that beautiful fucking dress. But she doesn't turn toward the back. She walks right over to me.

The dress swooshes as she walks, and the closer she gets, the more my throat closes up. "I was just showing Leighton the dress she's missing out on."

"I think *you're* missing out on the dress. Buy it for the future." Leighton sips her coffee, staring at Callie and me. "You never know when you might want to run off to Vegas and marry someone." She shrugs, looking at me from the corner of her eye.

"She'll probably sneak off and come back with a wedding ring on her finger and a baby in her belly." Mrs. Carlisle puts her arm around her daughter's waist and tugs her to her side. "She's impulsive, and we love her for it." She smacks a kiss on Callie's cheek.

Callie's eyes drill into mine again. Now my heart feels as though it's fighting a rip current—kicking for air, desperate to make it back to shore.

"I should go." I back step toward the door.

"Is Hayes out there?" Mrs. Carlisle asks.

I nod. "Yeah, he's adamant about not seeing Leighton."

She laughs. "Tell him I'll see him at Peeper's in a little bit? And you come too."

"Ah… I have some things to do." I am not going to be in the same room as Callie and everyone else until Hayes knows what's going on.

"Not anymore. Nothing is more important than spending time with me, your second mother."

Sadly, she is the closest thing I've had to a mother since I was eleven.

"Mom, let him be. He's a busy guy." Callie doesn't say it vindictively, and she's not throwing laser eyes my way, but still some part of me wants her to be just as uncomfortable as I am.

"I'll stop by for a little bit," I say.

"Oh good." Mrs. Carlisle brings her hands together in front of her.

"Thanks, Foster!" Kyleigh raises her cup. "And tell Hayes thank you too."

"Yeah… um, good to meet you."

We all stand there awkwardly, and my eyes soak in Callie one more time before I clear my throat and circle around, getting the hell out of the store.

"You survived!" Hayes pockets his phone and pushes off the brick wall. "I thought they swallowed you up in there."

Almost.

"Fuck no."

Now I just need to erase the image of Callie in a wedding dress from my head. She's gonna be the mother of my child, so of course some twisted part of me thinks there could be more here. But a relationship would only complicate our co-parenting dynamic, so I need to put her in a box that doesn't involve sex.

Easier said than done.

CHAPTER
ELEVEN

Callie

I've tried ten times to get out of going to Peeper's, but my mom was insistent—even when Leighton tried to come to my rescue by telling her I have a lot going on with the podcast.

So reluctantly, I walk into Peeper's Alley, dreading the fact I have to be around Foster without anyone knowing a piece of him is growing in my stomach.

I haven't been able to get his pale face out of my mind when he saw me in a wedding dress. It was probably his worst nightmare. He looked pale then green, as though he wanted to search for the nearest trash can so he could go vomit. I wanted to tell him he doesn't have to worry—I don't expect a proposal just because I'm carrying his baby. I thought that went without saying, but maybe I need to confirm to him that it's not the nineteen fifties.

"I know it's Foster," Leighton whispers as my mom

swarms Ruby with an unwelcome hug and we trail behind. "You're not hiding it very well."

"You have no idea."

I haven't told Leighton yet even though I said I would. Mostly because I don't want to put her in a worse situation with my brother. I kind of wish I would've just hung on to the news for a while, so she wasn't always pestering me about who the father is.

And she's a nurse and observant as fuck, so of course she noticed Foster ready to keel over in fear and anxiety when he saw me standing up there in a wedding dress.

"Exactly! Because you aren't telling me."

I steel myself and put on a brave face as we're about to go through the door into the private room. I have to ready myself to brave an hour or two of uncomfortableness as I pretend I'm not pregnant with my brother's best friend's baby, and also try to act as normal as I can with my best friend who knows what's going on. But before we go in, the door to Peeper's opens, and Hayes walks in with Foster and the three kids. Foster's talking to Lincoln about something, Monroe is in Hayes's arms, and Lake looks as though she'd rather be lying on a bed of nails than be in the bar.

"Oh, they aren't here yet." Leighton ditches the plan to head into the backroom and meets Hayes in the middle of the bar.

Monroe wraps her arm around Leighton without letting go of Hayes, and the three of them stand there in a little hug for a moment. I have no idea what Hayes whispers to Leighton, but her face flushes.

My mom calls Lake over to her side. There goes my buffer.

Foster and Lincoln walk toward us, and Lincoln puts a hand up for me to give him a high five. Foster says nothing, passing me and going into the backroom. I guess that's how this needs to go so no one suspects anything. I'd be a liar if I said it didn't hurt though.

Eventually I make my way into the room, and the rest of our group joins us. Somehow, I still end up next to Foster. He leans back with his arms crossed and his eyes on the television. I didn't realize he'd be so into watching contestants try to win a competition by climbing slippery steps but whatever. It's easier if we ignore one another.

Ruby comes in with chocolate milk for Lincoln and Shirley Temples for Monroe and Lake, their usual requests. She's really come around to having the kids here.

She slaps Foster on the shoulder. "What's with you?"

Hayes's eyes stray from the screen over to Ruby. "I asked the same thing."

Great. They're sensing something's off.

"I'm fine. Just didn't get a lot of sleep last night," Foster says.

"Keep your bedroom antics out of the kids' ears, please," Hayes says.

I want to stick my finger in my throat. It's terribly unfair that he has no idea Foster was up all night pondering being a dad and how it will affect the rest of his life.

Foster scowls at my brother. "Get your mind out of the gutter. I just couldn't sleep."

"What do you want?" Ruby comes over to me.

Of course the show goes to a commercial, so everyone is looking at me now.

"Um..." I'd usually have a glass of wine or at least a seltzer, but that's not happening. "I'll just have a... Sprite?"

Ruby's eyes narrow at me. "You're not drinking?"

Thanks, Mom.

I shrug, trying to play it off. "The coffee earlier made my stomach a little queasy."

Foster turns toward me, and his gaze dips to my stomach. I nudge my foot against his under the table. His eyes snap back up, and he turns to look at the television.

"Oh, I hope you didn't get mine," Leighton says. "You know how I take so much sugar."

Leighton for the win.

"Sugar? You don't take sugar."

Shut up, Hayes.

Leighton rolls her eyes. "I do when we get it out."

Just pile on the guilt that she's now trying to convince her loving fiancé that she takes her coffee differently at a café than at home.

"Since when?" Hayes, of course, doesn't let it go because no one knows Leighton like he does.

"Since I sipped someone's at work by accident and liked it."

Hayes's eyebrows shoot up. "Someone who?"

"She does know people you don't, Hayes." I try to get her out of the mess I created, but he narrows his eyes at her.

"Is this someone male?" he asks.

"Oh, how is Ilias? Did he ever get to Colombia for that bike trip he wanted to go on?" My mom came in for the save when she didn't even know it was needed.

Thank you, Mom.

"And you?" Ruby asks Foster, ignoring our back and forth.

He strips his attention from the screen and looks at Ruby. "I'll just have a… water."

"Water?" Easton says, walking into the room with Decker right behind him. "Since when do you drink water?"

"Since I want to." Foster returns his attention to the TV.

Easton and Decker both say hello to the kids and give my mom a hug.

"Where's Dave?" Decker asks.

Mom pats him on the cheek. "Golfing."

"We should've gone golfing," Easton says, sitting down. "Ruby, can I have a beer?"

Decker raises his hand. "Make that two. Thanks, Ruby."

She leaves and thank God the entire drink fiasco is over.

As they talk about the slippery stairs on the show and how one girl is almost to the top, a rush of nausea hits me. I've had a few queasy moments, but no real morning sickness.

Great, I manifested it with my lie. Karma is here to teach me a lesson.

I get up and walk toward the door.

"Where are you going?" Hayes asks, and everyone turns to look at me.

A sharp comeback is on my tongue, but my gaze snags on Monroe. "Bathroom," I mutter.

"Are you okay? You look pale," Mom asks, half rising off her chair.

"I have to go too," Foster mumbles and comes alongside me. "I've got her, Jennifer."

What is he doing? He's drawing more attention to us. I'm practically ready for Hayes to ask what the hell is going on, but Monroe asks him if they can make guacamole tomorrow for National Guacamole Day.

Thank you, Monroe.

I step out of the room, and Foster shuts the door behind me. Ruby eyes me from the bar, and I feel like I did the first time I smoked pot and was so paranoid I convinced myself the police were watching me through the windows.

I smile and walk toward the bathroom hallway, stopping outside of the men's.

"You need to snap out of it," I whisper, "and order a damn beer."

His head draws back. "Sorry if I'm not even done processing the fact that I'm going to be a father," he whispers back. "And then I go into that bridal store and find you wearing a wedding dress."

I tilt my head. "Your worst nightmare, right? Well, don't worry about it, big guy. I'm not expecting you to go down on bended knee just because your dick shoots magic sperm."

He looks as though he wants to say something, but I continue on. "If you don't start acting like your grumpy, pissed-off self, they're going to figure out that something is going on."

"Me getting you pregnant is the last thing they'll think happened." He frowns.

I rear back. "Excuse me? Why? Am I not good enough for you to sleep with?"

"Fuck, Callie, no. I just meant because as Hayes's best friend, I should've kept my hands in my pockets and my tongue in my damn mouth. And I definitely should've kept my dick in my pants."

He was a good kisser. Rushed, but good.

He sighs and takes off his ball cap, setting it back on his head right away. "I feel guilty as shit. Does Leighton know it's me?"

"She suspects, but I haven't told her."

His lips press together. "She acts like she knows. Maybe we shouldn't wait to tell your brother. We should just go in there and tell him."

I give him a *what the fuck* look. "Um... no. My mom is in that room. I get it. I do. I hate keeping this from him. It's all I can think of when we're with him. And poor Leighton. But we agreed to wait until we saw the doctor."

He sucks in a breath then nods. "Right. What if... the tests are wrong?"

I haven't told Foster that if he read the box of the pregnancy test, he'd see that it's unlikely they could all be faulty, but I also understand seeing a doctor and getting the news from a professional before we scream it from the rooftops and explode our world. I honestly have no idea how my brother is going to take this news.

"Regardless, you're going in there and ordering a beer." I thumb in the direction of the backroom.

"I can't."

"Why? I'm sorry, are you the one who is currently growing a human being in your body?"

He shrugs. "I'm not, but you are."

"What does that mean?"

Foster looks at me as though he'd rather spit razor blades than confess whatever he's thinking.

"Foster, what am I missing?"

He hems and haws, repositioning his hat once more. "I can't really do anything to help you through this, so I just thought, if you can't drink, I don't drink."

When I laugh, a flash of hurt hits his eyes, making me feel like a jerk.

I rest my hand on his forearm. It's so muscular. I wonder what it would feel like if his fingers were diving in and out of me.

What the hell was that?

I blink and shake my head. "I'm sorry. That's incredibly sweet of you, but unnecessary."

His eyebrows draw down. "I'm doing it."

There's a finality to his tone. I want to fight him on it, tell him he doesn't owe me anything, but I'm not sure I can change his mind.

"Fine, but you'll have to go back to making sarcastic insults to people."

A cocky smirk crosses his face, and my libido starts up like a racecar engine. "You telling me you want me to be a dick?" He leans forward a little, caging me against the wall.

I wish I could break the small amount of distance between us and kiss him. "I'm telling you to be yourself."

"You looked beautiful by the way." His voice is a low whisper. "In the dress."

My cheeks heat. Although his tough and rough act gets me hot, his compliments are like a simmer slowly heating up my insides—and my libido.

"Thank you. But I mean it, I'm not looking for any

dramatic acts of solidarity here. We're going to co-parent our little one, but that's all."

He nods, but his eyes don't stray from mine.

Shouldn't the fact that there's a baby inside me make the desire between us disappear instead of putting gasoline on a raging bonfire? We have much more important things to be worried about.

"Callie?"

I love the way my name sounds on his lips.

"Foster?"

"What are you guys doing?" Hayes's voice has us both turning to see him standing at the end of the short hallway.

I bend forward and cough, pretending I'm clearing my throat.

"She got dizzy, so I was trying to help support her." Foster's lie glides off his tongue faster than one of his pitches, so fast it's a tad scary.

"Dizzy?" Hayes breaks the distance, a concerned look on his face. "From all the sugar in your drink?" There's disbelief and questioning in his tone, despite his concern.

I'm not sure if we're fooling him as easily as we think we are.

I stand straight and cover my mouth. "I'm just going to go to the bathroom to splash some water on my face."

"I'll send in Mom or Leighton," he says.

I leave Foster to answer any more questions my brother might have. There's no way my brother bought that act, and if we're not more careful, he's going to find out before we can actually tell him.

CHAPTER
TWELVE

Foster

I haven't been in the right headspace since Callie surprised me with the news that I'm going to be a dad. It's hard to be around Hayes and rely on him when I'm keeping this huge secret from him. Omission is lying no matter how you try to excuse it.

Callie's doctor's appointment is tomorrow. Thank God. We had to cancel once because I wouldn't be back from New York in time. Fitting a doctor's appointment into my schedule isn't the easiest thing. But there should be no problem tomorrow. We're off right before we have a longer stretch of away games, going from Texas right to Atlanta. At least after that we're playing at home for a ten-day stretch with one day off.

Hayes is working with McCarthy since he's our starter today while I bullshit with the other pitchers after our warm-ups. I keep looking up at the stands to see who might arrive.

"Who are you looking for?" Hayes comes up next to me,

and I turn to see McCarthy talking to Coach Cal before the game starts.

"Just looking."

He rests his back against the one-way glass and eyes me. "You expecting someone again?" His cocky smirk says he still hasn't figured out that my dick only perks up at the mention of his baby sister. "Stephie done?"

I sigh, not seeing Callie but seeing Leighton—which means maybe Callie isn't coming. It felt presumptuous to ask her if she was. It's not really my business, and I shouldn't care if she is, but this odd feeling of protectiveness won't leave the pit of my stomach.

"She was a bit…"

"Much?" Hayes chuckles.

I shrug. "She was nice and all and said she was only in it for the sex, but I wasn't feeling it."

He rocks his head back. "Huh. Maybe pretty soon you might want more than sex from a woman." He raises his eyebrows.

Am I jealous of what Hayes has? Yes and no. The family that he's growing is something to admire. Something I've wondered if I'd be any good at. And maybe fatherhood will be good for me, but I'm positive I'd suck at being a husband.

"Maybe when hell freezes over."

He chuckles and turns, scanning the stands. "She made it."

My head swivels in the direction of where Callie always sits with Leighton, but there's no Callie—only Leighton. I realize Hayes hasn't been stalking the stands like me.

"Leighton was worried because of her schedule. I'm telling you, it takes more than a fucking village to align our schedules. My parents picked the kids up, but they're bringing Leighton's mom too." His smile is admirable—if I wanted something like he has. "I'll be thanking her tonight for making this work."

I turn away, telling myself it doesn't matter whether Callie comes or not.

"It's weird, you know? I played all those games without Leighton in the stands, but now that I have her, I want her at everything. We're going to try to get some babysitters so she can come to some away games. Too bad your sorry ass can't find someone to travel with." He laughs. "Maybe Callie will come with her as long as she's not busy with her podcast. Which…" He snaps his fingers. "Did you hear?"

My stomach drops. The only thing I've talked to Callie about is my spawn in her stomach. "What?"

"Brightwave is eyeing Callie's podcast for their network. Have you ever listened to it?"

I can't remember the last time Hayes was this chatty—especially before a game. I feel like an asshole having to ask him the name of it. When he does find out she's pregnant with my baby, he'll be asking, *You stuck your dick in my sister behind my back and didn't even know the name of her podcast?* Not a good show on my part.

"Her agent told her that for them to even consider her, she needs to get five big names on as guests, which isn't easy. I volunteered, of course, but she turned me down. Said they want names the majority of the public will recognize." His eyes light up. "You could do it."

Since all I really know about her podcast is that she walks around Chicago and talks to strangers who pour their hearts out to her, I'm not really the kind of person she wants.

"Sure, I'll tell the world about my shitty upbringing, my overly demanding dad, and how I don't really talk to my twin brother or my mother. Everyone will want to listen to that shit show."

"They actually would." Hayes gives me a lopsided grin.

I frown. "Well, it's not happening."

Neither of us says anything, and thankfully Coach Cal

tells Hayes and McCarthy it's time. We all fist bump, and Hayes winks, saying he'll see me out there. For the first time in a long time, I kind of hope I don't have to pitch tonight.

"Feel free to pitch a no-hitter, McCarthy."

The rookie pitcher looks as though he's about to throw up, but he gives me a smile that doesn't come close to genuine.

"You're gonna be fine. You've got me." Hayes talks him down as they head out to the field. He's good at that, so I'm not surprised he's such a good dad and partner.

I, on the other hand, do not share similar qualities.

"Does Hayes know how hot his sister is?"

My head whips toward Taz on the bench, and my fists clench at my sides.

"Her ass is…"

"Don't fucking talk about her like that. Hayes will kick your ass if you try anything with her."

My ass too, but that's beside the point. Right now, I'm holding in all my anger, so I don't pin Taz to the wall and knee him in the nuts for even thinking of Callie in that way. I can't very well go caveman on him and expect Hayes not to notice.

I don't even know why this dick is bringing up Callie.

It's the eighth inning, and the call comes from the dugout. All eyes look at me. Damn it. I was really hoping I'd get tonight off, go to the doctor appointment tomorrow, and then after we tell Hayes and I've taken my well-deserved beating, I can work with him behind the plate again.

The lights in the stadium turn down, "Crazy Train" by Ozzy Osbourne plays, and my intro pops up on the Jumbotron. I love the song, and I love the fact that my nickname is Reaper, but sometimes I wonder—had Decker and I swapped places all those years ago, would it be him who's seen as the darker brother? Maybe I just came out of the womb a grumpy egomaniac with a short fuse.

I jog onto the field and stop to have the umpire check me and my glove. He lets me go, and I meet the team manager, Ripley, and the guys on the mound.

I purposely don't look at the stands. I didn't see Callie arrive until the seventh inning stretch, but I'm trying to be at least halfway decent to Hayes, even if he doesn't know what's going on.

Ripley places the ball in my palm, and the infield steps back. Hayes jogs back to home plate, and I watch him, my eyes veering up.

Sure enough, Callie is sharing a pretzel with Lake. The two of them are laughing and talking. I love that she's taken on the aunt role to those kids just as Hayes took on fatherhood. The Carlisle family is one I don't deserve to be part of, that's for sure.

I throw my warm-up pitches to Hayes, and he's dodging a little.

"You good, Reap?" Easton asks. "You do see Carlisle's glove, right?"

My teammates laugh from behind me, and I tuck my glove between my arm and body, shaking out my hand. Fuck, I really need to get myself under control.

Hayes jogs back up to the mound, waving for the infield to take their positions.

He puts the ball in my glove. "I'm going to catch whatever you throw, so don't worry. All we need are two strikes, and we're in the ninth. You're the only one in that bullpen who can do it."

"I bet you say that to all your pitchers."

He laughs and doesn't argue. We've always had a special bond, but I haven't met a pitcher who doesn't love having Hayes behind the plate.

"Your slider looked good earlier, but they'll expect it, so let's throw them off and do a curve."

I nod.

"And we'll strike him out on the slider."

I nod again.

"Jesus, breathe. You look like McCarthy out here." He goes back to squat behind the plate, and I'm thankful he's not here psychoanalyzing me anymore.

My first pitch is so off Hayes has to get up to catch it. This isn't a great sign. But Hayes steadily gets back into position and calls the same pitch. A curve on the inside.

I wind up and throw the ball. It doesn't get as inside as I'd like, but Little does swing and miss.

I throw two more strikes. One more out and we're out of this inning.

The ball got in the dirt, so Hayes tosses it to the ball boy and asks the umpire for a new one. And damn if my eyes don't drift up to see Callie again while I'm waiting for a new ball.

If I thought my blood was hot from Taz's comment earlier, it's boiling now. Lake is with Mrs. Carlisle, and the two guys behind Callie are leaning forward talking to her. One can't keep his eyes off her tits while she laughs.

Fucking hell.

It was a bad idea to look over there.

Hayes tosses me the ball, and I almost miss catching it, but the top of my glove snags it before it sails toward Easton behind me.

Hayes gives me the slider sign, and I wind up, my usual throwing motion not feeling nearly as fluid as I'd like. The minute the ball leaves my fingers, I know. I don't need to hear the crack of the bat, the groan of the Chicago fans, or the roar of the visiting fans as the ball sails well over me, all the way over Ian's head, and into the bleachers.

"Fuck." My entire body gets tense.

Hayes calls time, and I try to wave him off, but he comes to the mound anyway.

"Hey, we're good," he says.

"No, we're not." My jaw is clenched so tight it hurts.

"Look at me." He stands there until I do.

I want to tell him everything. *I'm an asshole. I fucked your sister, and she's pregnant with my baby. I really hope you don't hate me, and I know I did a bad thing. I'll just stand here, and you can kick my ass.*

"It's one run. We'll get it back in the top of the ninth. Let's wash it and concentrate on the next runner. What are you feeling tonight?"

Soon all of the infield joins us. I want to throw a fit like usual and tell them to fuck off, but Jagger's words ring through my head. But really, it's knowing that I have a kid coming and that endorsement deals are even more important now that has me checking myself.

"You good, man?" Hayes asks.

"Best day ever," I respond dryly.

"It was only one slider," Easton says.

"It didn't slide." I cut him a pissed-off look.

My gaze veers up again, and I see the guy showing her something on his phone.

"Back the fuck up, clown," I murmur.

"What did you say?" Decker asks.

"Nothing. Just go back to your positions. I'm fine."

Hayes calls them back, and I inhale a deep breath.

"You too. Go. I'll get us out of this."

"What are you keeping from me?" Hayes asks point-blank.

I look at Callie, and this time he follows my vision and turns back. He doesn't say anything, but there's no one else I would be staring at, so I wait for him to call me out. I shouldn't be surprised that this is how it will all come to light—Hayes having to call me out because I'm a chickenshit. He's always been a more stand-up guy than me.

"You're gonna do the slider again, and we'll go from there."

He doesn't wait for my answer and goes back to squat behind the plate. And I think I'm so thankful he didn't ask me —or beat the shit out of me on the mound in front of millions of people—that I actually strike the guy out.

Decker saves me with a homerun in the ninth that puts us back up a run, and the Colts win. Thank fucking God.

CHAPTER
THIRTEEN

Callie

Foster demanded that he come pick me up rather than meeting at the doctor's office, so when there's a knock on the door, I grab my purse. I swing the door open, and there he stands in the hallway of my apartment, but his head is turned, staring to his right.

"Hey." I peek my head out the door to see what's caught his interest.

Jerry is staring back at Foster as he inserts a key into the lock of my neighbor's door.

Jerry is probably a little intimidated that Foster Davis is at my doorstep.

Foster turns to face me, and his blue eyes leave me speechless as they often do. "The door downstairs wasn't locked." He steps inside my apartment, leaving me no choice but to back up and allow him to invade my personal space.

"Come in, I guess…" I'm not sure why we're both not on the *other* side of the door.

"Callie!" Jerry calls, pulling me away from thinking that I should've cleaned up my apartment this morning.

I turn toward the open door to find Jerry standing in my doorway.

Here we go. He's probably going to fawn over Foster and ask me about tickets again. Not anything I'm in the mood for right now.

"Are you headed out?" Jerry glances over my shoulder.

"Yeah. Just for an hour or two."

Jerry glances at Foster again, whose chest is now pressed to my back, staring down Jerry over my shoulder. What the hell is his bodyguard behavior about?

"Oh good. I can look at that bathroom fan issue while you're out."

"Oh, Jerry, that's not me. I think you're confusing me with someone else in the building again."

He pulls out his phone and scrolls on the screen for a moment. Then he glances back at Foster, who I'm pretty sure is going to knock me down because he's even closer to me now. He's acting like a guard dog ready to attack.

"Oh, I thought for sure it was you."

"You're the landlord?" Foster's voice is gruff with a bite to it.

What am I missing here?

"That's me, Jerry. Foster Davis, right?" Jerry steps into the apartment, his hand extended. Foster winds around me, putting me behind him, but at least finds some manners and shakes his hand. "I'm a big fan of yours."

"Thanks." Foster doesn't sound any more friendly than earlier.

Jerry's lips thin, and his body stiffens. I glance to where their hands are joined, noticing that Jerry's knuckles are white.

I push Foster's side. "Anyway, we need to get going.

Hope you figure out which person needs their bathroom fan fixed."

Foster steps toward the door, giving Jerry no choice but to blindly back up into the hallway. Finally, we're all outside the apartment, and I lock my door, then say goodbye to Jerry.

"It was great meeting you, Foster, or do I call you Reaper?"

Oh, Jerry, quit while you're ahead.

"Foster's fine," he grumbles.

Foster waits at the top of the stairs for me to go down first, and he places his hand on the small of my back as if we're a couple. "I got us a car."

He takes one more glance over his shoulder before we exit the building. He stops and turns around. Jerry is at the top of the stairs, watching us.

"Maybe forget the bathroom fan and fix this door," Foster says. "I shouldn't have been able to just walk in. The residents' safety is your responsibility."

Jerry's face turns red, looking struck. "I'll get on it."

I peek my head around Foster's arm. "Thank you, Jerry." I tug at Foster's sleeve. "We're going to get going now. Bye."

I drag Foster out of the vestibule, and when we get onto the sidewalk, I release him. "What's with the bodyguard act?"

"I don't like him. He was coming out of that apartment next to you. He didn't say anything to me. The door to the outside was unlocked." He stares at the building as if he's a building inspector and is about to slap a red sticker on it that says CONDEMNED. "I thought your podcast was doing well?"

I stop beside the car he led me to before climbing in. "Are you judging where I live?"

"I just think you can afford somewhere that makes safety a higher priority."

I place my hand on his chest and laugh. "Let's remember our roles here, Foster. You're the baby daddy, not my keeper."

I climb into the car and get situated as he slides in beside me. Thank God there's more than enough space, and we're on separate sides of the SUV. The driver pulls into the traffic with the address already in his GPS.

"You're wrong. You're the mother of my child, so your safety *is* my concern. I don't like Jerry, and I don't like the apartment."

I laugh bitterly. "Well then, let me just move out." I glare at him, hoping he catches my sarcasm, but he's still brooding, holding my gaze in a stare down. "Jerry is harmless. He keeps forgetting which tenant needs help, and I'm sure after your mafia boss performance, he'll get right on the door."

"I guess we'll see when we get back."

"*I'll* see because I can get myself home after the appointment."

"I didn't say you couldn't, but I'll be taking you home after."

I swivel in my seat to face him and cross my arms. "It's funny, you know. The gossip blogs all say you're not a gentle-man, so I'm not sure why I'm getting such special treatment, but I can assure you I'm a big girl who can take care of herself."

I'm not sure how to describe the feeling swimming around inside me from him being so protective. Shock isn't even the word I'd use to describe how I felt when he was all in on the pregnancy, and now this whole act as if he's going to put me in a bubble until I deliver his baby.

Foster doesn't talk the rest of the trip, as if what he says goes. He's in for a rude awakening. We arrive at the doctor's building, and he tells the driver he'll text him when we're done.

"I can walk home." I don't wait for him to answer, heading toward the building.

"Is this doctor any good?" he asks, reaching for the door

handle before I can get it, which means his chest is once again pressed to my back.

"No, I picked her because her reviews are subpar. Figured I wanted to give her a chance to redeem herself." I step into the medical building. "This is the doctor the Falcon wives go to. I used to go to my doctor closer to my mom and dad, but I figured I needed someone in the city."

"If the Falcons trust her with their wives, then I suppose we can trust her."

I stare at him blankly as we wait for the elevator. He's standing so close to me, as if he's afraid I'm going to disappear.

I sniff his cologne. I don't know why. Maybe because it smells so damn good.

Shaking it off, I turn to face him. "Okay, you're scaring me. What's with this?" I motion with my hand down his body.

He glances down. "What?"

"You being so protective of me. Where I live? Hiring me a car? Judging the doctor I picked?"

Foster shoves his hands into the pockets of his black jacket, and his gaze falls to my stomach. I think I get it now. He can't control any of this, but he can make sure I'm safe and, as a result of that, so is his child. I feel a little enamored by it if I'm honest.

I sigh. "Let me put you at ease—I'm as invested in this little one as you. I'm going to protect it too."

The elevator doors open, and I step in without waiting for him to respond. I press the button for the fifteenth floor. He leans his back against the elevator wall and watches the numbers rise as we ride up in silence.

I have no idea what's going on in his head or how we're going to navigate this as we move forward. After we confirm that this pregnancy is healthy and happening, we're supposed to tell Hayes.

Which will make my life easier, but it's also hard to

process this new normal that will be my life. Raising a child with Foster Davis, the bad boy of baseball, the man who I'm pretty sure has never had a steady girlfriend. The hothead, the one who can't control his temper on the mound. This man is a part of my life forever now. It all seems surreal.

The elevator dings, and the doors slide open. We head down the hallway, following signs to the doctor's office. When we step inside the office, everyone's attention turns in our direction. Most of the women have swollen bellies, and there're only a scattering of men accompanying the women.

I ignore them all and head over to the receptionist.

"Good morning," she says.

"Hi. Callie Carlisle. I have an appointment with Dr. Amato."

She glances at Foster, who's acting as if we're velcroed together, and tilts her head, but then smiles.

How did I not think about Foster being recognized?

"Okay, thank you for doing the pre-check-in, and I show you have a forty-five-dollar co-pay." She holds out the payment processor.

I open my purse, but Foster pulls out his credit card and taps it on the keypad. I balk at him, but he doesn't grant me even a glance, tucking his card back in his wallet as if it's normal for him to be paying for things for me.

We really need to talk about this whole "I'm his to protect" thing he's got going on right now.

"Great. Here's your receipt, and have a seat. The nurse will call you back in a little bit."

Foster hands me the piece of paper.

"It's yours," I say softly.

"Use it for your flex spending." He pushes it between us again, leaving me no choice but to take it unless I want to make a scene.

"But..." I hold it limply as he walks away from me and

sits in one of the two chairs in the corner, behind a large potted plant.

I'm baffled that Foster Davis knows about flex spending like some middle-aged dad who budgets and tracks his spending.

I sit next to him, crossing my legs. He leans back, manspreading. I don't look, but I can feel a lot of eyes on us. It's either because he's Foster Davis, or it's his neck tattoos and the fact that he's hot. Probably both.

The only thing we have going for us is the fact that the Colts haven't had any stellar years lately where people recognize the players more, but Foster has a distinct look.

"Where do you want to go to lunch?" he asks, picking up a magazine and flipping through it, but he tosses it back on the table without reading any of it.

"What is going on right now?" I whisper, leaning in close.

He turns to face me, and we're so close, I draw back. It feels way too intimate.

"You need to eat, and I'm hungry. Plus…" He scans the room, probably judging who is listening to us, who is slyly trying to take a picture. This could be bad if anyone here leaks that Foster Davis was in an OBGYN office with a woman. "We need to get to know one another better."

"We need to get to know one another better?" I repeat what he said, hoping it makes more sense when I hear it from my own lips.

He chuckles. It always throws me when he laughs because it happens so rarely. He's so grumpy and brooding and matter-of-fact that it's weird when he's enjoying himself. "Sorry, you're stuck with me."

A weird sensation ignites in my stomach, and I realize I may have grossly underestimated Foster. What if he's just succumbed to being the person everyone believes he is?

Then again, how many times has a man fooled me before? How many times did I swear an asshole wasn't an asshole only to get burned in the end? There's no way I can try to figure out Foster *and* protect our baby. If their mom is heartbroken from thinking she saw something different than what everyone sees in their dad, that's not protecting them.

It's safer if we just stick to co-parenting.

"Callie?" a nurse calls.

"Here!" I bolt up out of my seat.

The sooner I'm in that room, the sooner I stop imagining that there's a different man under the tattoos and hard exterior. Because imagining is exactly how I'll end up hurt.

CHAPTER
FOURTEEN

Foster

When the nurse calls Callie back, I'm thankful to be away from the prying eyes. I purposely picked the two chairs in a corner with a plant in front of us so no one could get a clear picture. Who am I kidding though? They'll manage it if they want one.

All the patients' eyes were on us, as if they were trying to figure out our dynamic. It's not that hard to figure out. I'm with a woman in an OBGYN office. Two plus two equals four. Or plus one in this case.

The nurse doesn't do anything more than give me a polite smile and quick glance before asking Callie to follow her. Which is nice to see. Callie should have all the attention. She's the one taking one for the team between the two of us.

We're shown to an exam room, and the nurse leaves, telling us the doctor will be in soon.

I'm minding my own business, sitting in the chair the

nurse told me to, when Callie flips around on the table toward me. "You doing okay?"

Her smirk says she thinks this whole experience is funny. Probably because she believes all the rumors that to be in an OBGYN office with a woman I spent one night with would be a nightmare scenario for a guy like me. And maybe it would be… but it's her. Somehow, she seems to make all the difference in the world.

There's some truth to the rumors that fly around about me. I haven't been fucking celibate, but I'm not entirely who she thinks I am either.

"You think I'm gonna run or pass out?"

Her legs swing back and forth. She's cute as hell, and isn't that the number one problem with this entire situation? "It's a nightmare, right?"

I tilt my head and cross my arms. "Haven't we already been over this?"

"You wanting to be part of the baby's life and you still thinking this is the last possible thing you would have wanted are two very different things. Neither of us planned on this happening."

"True." I'm not going to lie and say I dreamed of this scenario. "But here we are."

"I can handle this, you know? You're midseason."

My first reaction is to go on the defense because it feels as though she's pushing me away. That old wound opens up, telling me I'm not good enough. That Callie would rather have gotten pregnant by anyone but me. But part of me suspects that Callie's hyper-independence has nothing at all to do with me.

So I inhale a deep breath before I say something I'll regret and decide to voice my suspicions. "Callie, who hurt you?"

Her usual teasing smile slips. I lean forward, ready to tell her to forget my question and declare my intentions again, even if they fall on deaf ears. Anything to see that smile again. But a knock sounds on the door, and a woman with a white coat walks in.

Maybe the interruption is the best thing that could happen because this isn't really the best time for us to have this conversation.

"Oh..." The doctor's attention snags on me. "Hello. Usually my staff tells me when we have clients who have more discreet needs." She steps over to Callie and holds out her hand. "Hi, Callie, I'm Doctor Amato."

"Hi." Callie shakes her hand. "So you recognize Foster." She puts her hand out as though she's declaring me as the prize.

I mentally scoff. I'm no one's prize.

Dr. Amato laughs. "You kind of stick out." She holds her hand out for me, and I shake it. "In a good way."

Her smile is kind, and I want to trust her to do what's right for Callie and our child, I do. But trust isn't the easiest thing for me.

She walks over to the computer. "Okay, so let me gather some information, then I'll have you change into a gown, and we'll take a look on the ultrasound." She looks really excited, but I guess that's why she picked this profession, right? "Let's start with the date of your last period."

Callie tells her, and I mentally try to figure out the math, although we only slept together once, so I guess the date of conception is obvious.

"So you're about six weeks then." Dr. Amato types on the computer. "And you're the father?" She pointedly looks at me.

I refrain from making some smart-ass comment. "I am."

"But we're not involved." Callie waves a finger between us. "I mean, it was just one night."

Dr. Amato smiles at her and nods. I wait for her judgmental look—like *of course you had sex with her and got her pregnant*—but it doesn't come. "Okay, and you're all right with him being here during the visits?"

What kind of question is that? Don't I have some rights here?

"Yes. We're doing this together."

Thank God, seems Callie finally got the memo.

"That's great. So, let's talk family history."

My gut twists. My family is the absolute last topic I ever want to talk about.

Callie gives the doctor her family history. Of course it's all picture perfect and could be wrapped up in a suburban home with four bedrooms, perfect parents, a brother who adores her, and a big fucking bow tied around the white picket fence.

Dr. Amato turns toward me, and I'm ready to excuse myself just to get out here. I feel as if the collar of my coat is strangling me.

Callie doesn't know a lot about my family or me, and divulging all the sordid details in front of the doctor seems wrong since all my fucked-up family problems will inevitably affect our child, no matter how much I try to keep them away from it. God knows I've tried to escape them to no avail.

"I'm a twin," I admit, figuring this is something the world already knows.

Dr. Amato's eyes light up. "Oh…" She types, then looks at Callie.

"I didn't even consider…" Callie cradles her nonexistent belly. "Could there be two babies?"

Dr. Amato laughs. "It's not as common as you think. If you were a twin, the chances would be a little higher. You can breathe now."

Callie's shoulders lose the tension, and mine do too, because I don't want that for my child. Being a twin isn't the dream most people think it is.

"Identical or fraternal?" Dr. Amato asks.

"Fraternal."

"Yeah, they're so different." Callie chuckles. "Not only in looks…"

Dr. Amato's eyes widen, and her mouth falls open. "Decker Davis is your twin. Sorry, I knew that. My husband is a die-hard Colts fan, and he'd be embarrassed that I even had to ask."

I shake my head. "It's fine. Really."

"Well still… so fraternal twin. Do you know if your mom went through fertility treatments or conceived you and your brother naturally?"

I never asked, and since my relationship with my mom is nonexistent, it's not like I can ask her. "I'm not sure."

"Well, it's really just for the probability. It's not that important. Anything health wise or family history I need to know about?"

She and Callie are looking at me. My neck beads with sweat, and at this point, I wish I would've done what Callie expected from me and bolted from this appointment. Why was I so adamant about coming here?

What do they want to know? My dad is a deadbeat dickhead, but other than high blood pressure—which could be from his temper and anger issues—he's in good health. My mom I have no fucking clue about, except she's still alive because she sends me a birthday card every year that I don't open.

"They're alive." I do my best to keep my voice even.

Callie's smile drops. I'm sure she's disappointed and appalled by my lack of family. I really hope she doesn't try to get me to patch things up with my mom. If so, I'll just have to get used to her disappointment.

"Okay." Dr. Amato slides away from the computer.

Thank fuck that's over with.

"I'll let you get changed and be back in a few minutes.

Then we'll do the exam and hopefully get your first picture of your baby." Dr. Amato smiles at me, pats Callie's knee, and leaves the room.

I stand to follow the doctor out.

"Where are you going?" Callie asks.

"I figured you'd want privacy."

Plus I need to take a second to catch my breath before all my insecurity about becoming a father suffocates me. I had a shit role model, so I'll be learning on the fly. Despite my best intentions, what if I end up making the same drastic mistakes my father did?

"Just turn around." She hops down from the exam table, and I hear the crinkling of the paper as I turn my back to her.

I'm still very attracted to Callie, so the fact she's getting naked right behind me is all I can think about. It takes all my self-control not to look over my shoulder.

More paper crinkles, then she says, "You can turn around."

I circle around as she places her clothes on the chair next to me. And although she's tucked her underwear under her pants and shirt, a satin piece of purple fabric peeks out, which I'm pretty sure is her panties.

Fuck me. My dick twitches. This is the worst possible time for me to be picturing Callie standing in front of me wearing just those panties.

The doctor knocks, and Callie tells her she's ready.

Dr. Amato smiles and glances at me, her grin growing wider. She goes over to the sink to wash her hands. "Okay, let's take a look."

She gets the stirrups out, and without instructions, Callie seems to know what to do. She slides down the table, and the sheet covers her lower half as Dr. Amato slides her chair between Callie's legs.

It's nearly impossible not to envision what's under that thin piece of paper covering Callie's lower half. I want to pull it away. Instead, I stuff my hands in the pockets of my jacket, clenching them and trying to appear as though my mouth isn't watering from thinking about touching Callie, tasting her.

"Because it's so early in the pregnancy, we're going to have to do a vaginal ultrasound." Dr. Amato puts on a new set of gloves, gets the machine ready, and puts a condom-looking thing over a dick-looking thing, and it disappears under the sheet.

My eyes widen as Callie shimmies a bit on the table. I feel as if someone put me in a torture chamber.

I'm not sure if I make a noise or what, but Callie glances over, smiling. "It's not as enjoyable as it might look."

I blow out a breath. "I am a bit self-conscious right now."

Both women laugh.

"It's just the tip," Callie says and turns her attention to the screen.

Not helping.

I stand to get a better view. I have no idea what we're about to look at, but Dr. Amato grins at me and nods. What she's seeing must be good then? The baby is good?

"So, this is the little one." She points at the screen. "And this little flicker? That's your baby's heartbeat."

My eyes transfix on the flicker. It's blinking so fast. It's nothing more than a speck, but that flicker means life.

A rush of emotion swells from my breastbone up my throat. My hands slide out of my jacket, and Callie reaches up, grabbing one hand for a moment, but she quickly tries to pull away. I clench her hand harder until her soft palm loosens.

"Everything's good?" I ask, my vision blurring for a moment.

Dr. Amato looks at both of us. "Perfect."

Callie and I lock gazes, and all the shit coming our way

disappears. We made that little one together, and it's going to depend on us.

So I make the same promise I already did to myself, but this time I make it for him or her. *I will protect you and love you forever. You'll never have to deal with the kind of shit I did. Ever. And in protecting you, I'm going to protect your mom, so you'll always have her in your life.*

CHAPTER
FIFTEEN

Foster

I'm still whirling from the doctor's office by the time Callie and I ride the elevator back down to street level in silence and climb into the car.

"That was terrifying as fuck," I admit when the driver pulls into traffic.

"Hello, it's my body. Did you see those diagrams on the wall?" She stares down at her stomach as if an alien's about to pop out of it.

"I purposely tried not to."

"What do you care? It's my vagina that's going to be all torn open."

The driver slyly looks through the rearview mirror, but I give him a scathing expression, and his eyes go back to the road.

"Thanks for the visual."

"You did this to me." She points at me.

"If memory serves—" The driver glances at us again, and

I decide we're going to stop talking until we're alone. He probably knows enough. Although I'm sure in his profession and with what he charges, he must be discreet, since this car service is specifically for clientele with a public profile. It's better if we table this conversation for now. "Let's go eat."

"I'm not really hungry."

Her mood has diminished since we saw the baby. I think reality has set in that we're going to be parents.

"You have to eat." I look at her stomach, and she covers it with her hands. "For, you know."

She rolls her eyes and sighs, turning toward the window. "Just spare me the overprotective bullshit self you've morphed into since I broke the news to you."

"Do you think I want to be like this?"

It's as though something has taken control of my body. And I'm still trying to figure out if it's the baby, the guilt that it's Hayes's baby sister, or just this thing in my stomach that won't stop craving Callie.

"Well, you're not trying very hard to stop. So far—"

I give a small nod in the direction of the driver, and she sighs but stops talking. Surely, she knows we have to be discreet. Then again, one thing that turned me on about Callie was her I-don't-give-a-shit attitude. I wouldn't care if someone knew she was pregnant, and the baby was mine. Hayes just needs to find out first.

We pull up to her apartment a few minutes later, and I tell the driver that we're done with his services, opening the door and waiting for Callie to slide out of my side before shutting the door.

"Thanks for the ride. I'll see you next month at the next doctor appointment." Callie pats my chest and walks past me toward her front door.

"I'm walking you up." I follow her.

She pulls on the street-facing door and walks into the

vestibule to the next door. She pulls on that door, but it doesn't budge.

Thank you, Jerry.

"Great." She opens her purse and digs inside. "Now I have to get my keys, but look, your wish was Jerry's command. So relax, big guy, your kid is all safe and secure." She nods at the door, pulling out her keys. "You can go now."

"I'll see you in." I know it's pissing her off that I'm being an overprotective asshole, but I can't squash this part of me that needs to know she's okay.

I've had women tell me they were pregnant before, but those all were attempts at extortion. The first time it happened was when I'd just arrived at college. I remember thinking it would destroy my entire life and everything I had worked hard for. Maybe it's different this time because I know Callie isn't lying, I'm late in my career, and although I never thought I was going to have a family, this might be my only chance.

"You're driving me crazy, Foster."

"Be careful, last time you said that to me..." I let my words trail off because she knows exactly what happened last time.

"Ugh!" She opens the door, walks through, and doesn't hold it open for me, continuing to climb the stairs.

"Should you be walking up these stairs every day?"

Callie stops midflight and turns around. "I'm pregnant. I'm not an eighty-five-year-old heart patient." She swivels back around and stomps up the stairs.

"It was just a question."

"A stupid one in case you were wondering."

She gets to her door, and I put my hand over hers as she's about to insert the key into the lock. "Listen. I'm sorry. I don't know why I'm feeling this way. These things are just coming out of my mouth. I've never been like this."

"You mean with your other one-night stands who end up

pregnant, you weren't trying to lock the woman in a padded room and force-feed her?"

I lean my shoulder against the wall and blow out a breath. "Hayes is really important to me. Our friendship is…" I try to excuse my behavior with one of my many theories.

"Ah." Her head rocks back. "It's about me being Hayes's baby sister. Well, don't worry, I'm a big girl and can take care of this little bundle."

It's not just because she's Hayes's sister, but it seemed like the better explanation than trying to tell her all the shit going on in my head.

"Go home, Foster." She puts the key in the lock. "I'll see you around."

Callie twists the key and swings open the door. She freezes in the doorway, and her jaw slowly drops. Seeing her stunned reaction, I push off the wall and peer over her shoulder into the apartment.

"Callie…" I try to keep my voice level. "I'm gonna need your help so I don't end up on the evening news in hand-cuffs." My voice is calm, but rage boils in my veins, hotter than hellfire.

She puts her hands on either side of the doorframe as if she could stop me from barging in. "Jerry?" She uses a calm voice as if he's a child. "Why are you in my apartment?"

"And wearing her fucking bra and panties?" I shout over Callie's shoulder.

Callie sighs and presses back against me.

His eyes are wide as he glances around like a wild animal that's been cornered. "Oh… I… I was fixing your shower and my clothes got wet…"

"Bullshit." I step closer so I can get my hands on him, but Callie continues to stand in the threshold, blocking the way, which keeps the beast in me at bay.

Just barely.

"I think we both know that isn't true, so how about you

get dressed and leave the apartment?" Again, with the placating tone.

Jerry walks to her bedroom, head hanging low. I don't want to know how many times he's done this.

Callie finally walks in and points toward the kitchen. "You're going to stand over there, behind the counter, and you can't come out."

"I'm not your dog."

"Don't act like a guard dog then." She pins me with a stare.

My fists itch to meet Jerry's face, but I do what she says because Jagger's words repeat in my head—don't do shit that's going to get you bad press. And I'm pretty sure beating Jerry to a bloody pulp will get me bad press. Even if they knew what he did, there would always be people saying, "I knew Foster was trouble. All those tattoos and bad energy. Of course I'm not surprised he beat up that innocent man."

Besides, the last thing I want is for my kid to find out I've been arrested when they get older.

Callie looks away from me in the direction her landlord went. "And, Jerry, you can go ahead and keep that panty and bra set."

"Did he have to put on *that* set?" I grumble.

She side-eyes me.

It was the set she was wearing the night we were together. Black, lacy, and see-through with flowers. Shit, I almost tucked her panties in my pocket that night like some prize to prove she'd actually slept with me. At the time, I thought it was the competition with Easton over who could have her, but I knew the minute my lips pressed against hers I'd been lying to myself.

Jerry comes out, his head angled down.

Callie crosses her arms. "I'll be changing my locks, and you won't have a key."

He nods. "I did fix that outside door." He peeks at me, and

I clench my teeth, wanting to growl at the fucker. "I'm sorry, Callie. I just…"

She opens the apartment door, waiting for him to walk out. "Goodbye, Jerry." Once he's past the doorway, she slams it shut and flicks the lock. She does a full-body shudder and makes a gagging sound. "How many times do you think he's done this?"

"May I come out now?" I round the counter and sit on a breakfast stool, crossing my arms. "I guarantee it wasn't his first time."

"Which means all of my panties and bras." She passes me, pulls out a garbage bag from under the sink, and heads down the hall.

I follow her, watching from the doorway.

Callie opens her drawer and shoves all her bras and panties into the bag.

"What about the ones you're wearing?" I raise my eyebrows. "Go ahead, I don't mind if you strip."

Why am I deflecting with humor? *Because you're an asshole, remember?*

She gives me a *not now* look, and I break across the room and sit on the edge of her bed.

"Sorry, that was stupid," I murmur.

I'm not surprised to see her bedroom is girly with floral wallpaper and lots of pillows on her bed. All the colors match but somehow contrast at the same time. There are pictures of her and Leighton in various frames, and my gaze snags on one of her and Hayes when he was drafted, then one of her entire family the same day.

I'm not sure I even took a picture the day I was drafted. If I did, it wasn't with my entire family.

"Believe me, I'm going to take a shower as soon as you leave, and I'll be going commando until I can get to the store." She cinches the bag after cleaning out the entire drawer. "Oh wait." She opens a bottom drawer and tosses lingerie onto the bed.

A babydoll number lands on my thigh, and I pick it up, envisioning Callie wearing it as she saunters over and falls to her knees in front of me.

Fuck my life right now. This is not the time to be thinking about that.

"I have no idea how I'll continue to see him around the building. I feel like I need to tell the neighbors. What if he's done it to them too?" She opens the bag and tosses the items from the bed in the bag.

I want to buy her an entire assortment of lingerie and fill that drawer up as long as she promises it's only for my viewing pleasure.

"You're not staying here." I get up from the bed, needing to stop thinking sexual things about a woman I'll never have and never deserve.

"Why not? I have a lease."

"That you can break now that you found your landlord in your apartment, wearing your intimates."

"Intimates?" She chuckles. "Foster Davis calls my panties and bras intimates?"

"Come stay with me." It's out of my mouth before I really think about it, but I cannot allow her to stay here.

She laughs and takes the bag into the family room, dropping it by the front door. "I think I'll just drop them off to Jerry. I'd hate for it all to go to waste."

"Callie?" I draw her back to the conversation, ignoring her attempt at levity.

She looks over her shoulder and goes into the kitchen, looking exhausted with me. "I'm not moving in with you."

"Why?"

She leans against the counter and stares me down. "Is that even a real question?"

"It is actually. Give me one reason why."

I may have been rash in suggesting it, but the more I think about it, the more I like the idea of knowing more about the woman who will be raising my child than just how she sounds when she comes.

"You're taking this protective bodyguard thing too far." She opens her fridge and takes out a water.

"Listen to me." I slide onto a barstool. "We have to learn to be around one another. We're going to be co-parents, and you can't possibly stay here now. He essentially broke into your apartment and wore your lingerie. Who knows what else he's capable of?"

"I'll get the locks changed."

"Take Jerry out of the equation. I want to get to know you better before the baby comes."

She goes to her purse on the counter to grab something and it falls over, the ultrasound picture slipping onto the counter. She stops and stares at it, and I feel as if there's a sliver of an opening to get her to agree.

"It's a ridiculous idea."

I lean back in the seat, staring at the picture. "What if I told you I'd help you get your five big names for the podcast?"

Her head flies up.

I've got her interest now.

CHAPTER
SIXTEEN

Callie

"How do you know about that?"

Hayes.

"It doesn't matter, but I do know you need five big names to interview for your podcast, and I can get them for you." His smug smirk says he knows he's piqued my interest.

The whole Jerry thing has me majorly creeped out, but I can look for a new place. Maybe stay with Hayes and Leighton for a little while, although I'd hate to disturb their and the kids' lives.

"You're bribing me?" I cross my arms.

I've already talked to Jarrah about my client list and the fact that, other than my brother—maybe Easton or Decker, who she thought would be too much of the same thing—I have no one. I don't know any celebrities, and I'm not popular enough to get the kind of people they want.

"I would have preferred you to just agree to it, but apparently I'm a desperate man and will resort to bribery."

Many women in my position would be jumping for joy. I'm certain most people don't know this side of him even exists. Sure, I was physically attracted to Foster and that obviously led to me sleeping with him, but had I known he was like this, I would've been crushing on him hard. If it's not all an act.

"The bad boy of baseball? The man who has never had a serious relationship wants his pregnant one-night stand to move in with him? Explain."

I gulp down some of my water because my mouth is dry from the thought of sharing space with this man, but at the same time, he's offering what I need to make this podcast thrive so I can raise this little one inside me.

"I know you don't know much about my past, and I'm not getting into it all today, but you know that Decker and I were raised separately since we were eleven years old. Even before that, there was never a real sense of family in my life. It's important to me that I give my kid a different kind of life. A life where their parents get along and are at least friends. I obviously never intended for you to get pregnant, and I never thought I'd find myself in this position, but I always told myself that if I did, I'd never make my kid choose. I'd always make my kid feel like they were a part of a family unit, no matter the circumstance. So, I want to spend this time getting to know you, become maybe friends."

"Friends?" I hope he can't hear the disappointment in my tone.

Not that I think being friends isn't a great idea, but I have this stupid attraction to Foster I haven't been able to shake. When he picked up my lingerie earlier, I almost said *let me model it for you*, which would have been the worst idea ever.

"Yeah." He runs his finger across my counter. "I'd like to tell our baby that I love Mommy. I might not be *in* love with her, and she might be with someone else, but I do love her."

My heart squeezes. I think I'm one of the rare few who

gets to see this side of Foster Davis. People would never believe he can be so sentimental. Now I'm more curious than ever as to what happened between him and Decker and what their childhoods were like.

"And it doesn't have anything to do with you being able to dictate what I eat, if I've eaten enough, or if I'm getting enough sleep?"

He chuckles, and those blue eyes that are the same color as Lake Michigan on a sunny summer day sear into mine. He looks so sincere. "I shouldn't start our friendship with a lie, so yes, I do like the idea of knowing you're doing okay. I feel like I should be the one to get you your cravings and get you a blanket or draw you a bath. I mean, like you said, you're doing all the hard work here."

A laugh bubbles out of me. "You're killing me. Who are you right now?"

He shrugs. "Your baby's daddy."

"But?"

"Callie, I don't want to bribe you to move in with me, but I can't stomach you living here with that creep of a landlord. I meant what I said. We're in each other's lives forever now, and it's really important to me that we get along. Form some sort of connection." His gaze falls to the ultrasound picture. "For this little one."

"We could have weekly chats instead. A bullet-point list of what we should share."

He slides off the stool and walks into the kitchen, leaning on the counter opposite me, and crosses his arms. "I just threw a huge truth between us. I'm showing you a side of myself I share with no one, not even your brother. I'm doing it for our baby, so I'd like you to consider it. Move in with me, and I'll get you five big names."

I'm still trying to wrap my head around how different he is from what I expected. "Will you be one of them?"

I know the answer before he even opens his mouth, but I

have to try because if I could get this Foster Davis on *If I'm Honest*, it would get a lot of attention.

He shakes his head. "Sorry, that's a deal I can't make. You and the baby"—he nods at my stomach—"are the only two who will see this side of me. But I promise I'll get you people better than me. After all, your success only helps my child."

My shoulders fall, and our eyes meet, neither of us looking away. He's waiting patiently for my answer. A part of me says this is a very bad idea. I'd be depending on someone again, and it will most likely end in heartbreak, but he's offering a lot. The five guests plus getting to know a side of him that I'd only get behind his closed condo door. And don't I owe it to my little one to at least try?

"Okay, but I'm putting down some rules."

His eyes widen, and I kind of like the fact that I've surprised him.

"Lay it out for me." He widens his legs and stares at me intently.

I inhale to keep my libido at bay. "No women at the apartment."

"No men either."

"No sexual partners at all?"

"Deal." He nods.

"You can't be asking me how much I've eaten or if I slept well. No papa bear vibes."

He chuckles. "Sure, I will not care about your well-being."

"Good."

His eyebrows shoot up. "Anything else?"

"You have to be clothed at all times."

He smirks at me. "So I can't sleep in the nude?"

A full zap of electricity ignites through me when I think about him being steps away from me and completely naked under a thin sheet.

"Behind your bedroom door, but not in communal places."

"Fine. And just so you know, you can feel free to be naked in communal places. I have zero problem with it."

I roll my eyes, but then I point at him, hating that I have to make this rule but needing to. "No flirting."

"Ah…" He bites the inside of his lip. "I'm not sure I can do that one."

"Flirt with your girls on the road."

His gaze flows down my body, and a little voice reminds me that I'm playing with fire. "There won't be any girls on the road until we decide on a different arrangement at some point down the road."

I pick up my water and down more of it to coat my desert of a throat. "That's unnecessary."

"Are you going to be sleeping with someone?" His jaw clenches, and his eyebrows are now straight slashes over intense eyes.

I really wish I hadn't noticed that. It brings to the forefront this attraction that still lingers between us. I think we're both doing our best to ignore it, and I really hope that moving in together doesn't make it a powder keg ready to explode, ruining everything we're trying to accomplish for our baby.

"No," I say.

"Why?"

Of course he'd ask. "It would feel weird to have another man in my body so close to the baby when he's not their father."

"Is that an invitation?" He smiles and laughs. "I'm kidding."

I decide to breeze right by that particular landmine. "No other men while I'm pregnant but expect some sex toys to be delivered to your place."

"As long as you buy me some." He grins again.

"I'll make sure to stock up your supplies of lube and tissues."

"Keep your moaning at a minimum in case I think you need me to come in and rescue you."

My body flushes hot. I need to send this conversation in another direction. "Anyway. Do you have any rules of your own?"

He pushes off the counter and steps toward me. "Only one." I wait for him to speak, but he hems and haws for a moment. "When I have a bad game, don't try to cheer me up. I'll be in a shit mood, but by morning, I'll be okay."

I nod, remembering how Hayes used to be like that. Lately he walks out of the stadium completely fine when they lose. Well, not jumping for joy, but he doesn't let it ruin his night anymore. Maybe it's the Leighton effect.

"Deal."

"Sorry, one more."

"Okay." I nod.

"Stay the hell away from Decker."

My eyes widen, but he doesn't add anything else. "I can't just ignore your brother."

"I don't want to find you in his condo. You can be polite but not best friends with him."

Friendly Foster has disappeared, and I see how serious and important this is to him.

"He's the baby's uncle." I run my hands over my flat stomach.

"Please, Callie." The strain in his voice makes it feel as though something's squeezing my chest.

I reluctantly nod, hoping one day I'll understand how two brothers, twins at that, can hold such disdain for each other. "Okay, but if he wants to help me carry groceries up three flights of stairs, I'm going to say thank you. But you'll never find me in his condo. Is that a deal?"

Foster nods and claps his hands. "Let's pack your bags." He pushes off the counter and walks down the hallway into my bedroom.

I follow and mumble, patting my stomach, "Daddy is a very complicated man, but he's ours."

When I get to the bedroom, he's already dug my suitcase out of the closet.

"I don't have to go tonight."

"Yes, you do, and we'll shop for more…" He looks toward the empty drawers. "Stuff for you too."

I laugh and fall on the bed. "Foster Davis, can you not say bras and panties?"

"I'm being polite here, Callie. Maybe you should go shopping with Leighton after all."

I prop my head in my palm. "You don't want to pick them out for me?"

His eyebrows raise. "You're breaking one of your rules already."

"Ugh. Sorry." This is going to be a lot harder than I thought.

I get up off the bed and pack a few of my things. I hope this isn't the colossal mistake that my gut is telling me it is. I have to keep thinking about the five guests and that I get to try to figure out exactly who Foster Davis is.

"So, do you want to play rock, paper, scissors for it?"

He sits on the edge of the bed. "For what?"

"Who tells my brother I'm your new roomie."

I laugh as his shoulders fall. I guess he forgot about that part.

CHAPTER
SEVENTEEN

Foster

My palms are sweaty as I walk onto our bus.

We're on the road for the next ten days, and Callie will be completely moved in by the time I get back. We hired a moving company, and she told me numerous times that she has it handled, and I'm to stay out of it. That I have more important things to worry about.

Callie's not wrong, but still, I don't love the idea of her having to be in proximity to that Jerry guy without me there.

Now that I'm in the front of the bus and see Hayes laughing with Decker and Easton at the back, my throat closes up. I have to tell him that his sister is moving in with me.

Callie and I did play rock, paper, scissors, and I lost, but I would've done it anyway. I initiated this little bribery to get her to move in with me. Another thing I do not fully understand. Why do I need her to live with me? If it was only about safety, I could have found her a better space with a doorman and a security guard, but I've chosen to share my space with her. And it's true that I want to get to know her better for the sake of us being co-parents, but we don't have to live together to do that.

"Reap, you're never gonna believe this story." Hayes waves me to the back of the bus, sliding over to the window seat.

I nod to a few of the other players as I make my way down the aisle. The DICs who think they're hot shit and make me wish I still batted just to play their little game with Hayes, Decker, and Easton on who can tag the most bases every month. It's the infield versus the outfield, and it just so happens that their names are Drew, Ian, and Camden—hence the DICs. But it fits. At least it fits Drew.

Last month, Hayes made them go over to his house when the infield lost, and he cooked instead of paying the tab at the fancy restaurant they usually go to.

I slide into the seat next to Hayes and see Decker's smile fall as if I'm a killjoy to his little party.

Good, you're my killjoy too, brother.

As usual, whenever Decker and I are together, we're like the elephant in the room. I hate it, but not much can change now. We're way too far gone.

The bus pulls away from the curb, headed to the airport, and Hayes tells me the story. "Easton and Decker went to the Trojans game last night and someone embarrassed themselves in front of the new general manager." Hayes laughs again, and Decker smacks Easton on the back.

Easton shrugs him off. "It was nothing."

"He hit on her like she was a diamond girl." Hayes laughs harder and leans forward, his feet coming off the floor. There must be more I'm missing.

"You didn't recognize her?" I ask, unsure if I would have

had she not entertained adding me to their roster last year before the Colts made a better offer while she was still debating because of my reputation. "She's the enemy."

"Yeah, it's bad enough we have to share a city with the Trojans," Hayes says.

"They're just baseball players like us," Decker chimes in with his "let's all be friends" bullshit.

It's one reason I never wanted to come here. I hate the fact there are two professional teams in Chicago, but I don't hate the rivalry. Especially during the Crosstown Classic.

Easton scowls at me and leans his head on the headrest of his seat, staring out the window. "It wasn't that bad last night."

A laugh barrels out of Decker. "Yeah, it was. That swagger did not win you brownie points. I hope you never want to be traded to the Trojans."

"Like I would." Easton scowls, but I've never seen his face so red, so whatever did happen must've been bad. Then his attention shifts to me, and there's a gleam in his eye like he's about to push me in front of the bus we're currently on. "But we have more important news to share this morning. Why don't you tell us what you did last night, Reap?" Easton's eyebrows lift in my direction.

Fuck. Callie and I left the condo this morning to grab breakfast, and I saw Easton and Decker climbing into an Uber. I'd hoped they hadn't seen us, but I guess I was wrong.

"Did you have a woman stay at your place last night?" Hayes asks, his grin so wide he assumes I have a funny story to share.

"Yeah, he did," Easton says.

I cut him a look to tell him to mind his own fucking business, but who am I kidding? He wants the heat off of him.

"Is there a Miss Chicago?" Hayes asks, his eyebrows waggling.

I crack my neck a few times to think about how to approach this. Callie isn't like the women I keep on reserve in each city, so she's definitely not Miss Chicago.

"Oh shit." Easton elbows Decker.

My brother only gives me a disapproving look as though he's my fucking father—although our dad wouldn't have given one shit about me fucking my best friend's little sister.

"This is going to be so much better than my story," Hayes says.

"No, it's not," Decker says.

"Do I know her?" Hayes interrupts.

"Actually, you do." Easton has a shit-eating grin.

There was a time when I was younger that I would've jumped over and pinned him to the side of the bus.

Hayes looks confused, and I know I just need to force out the words. I never want him to think he's the butt of the joke.

"Just listen to me first," I say.

Hayes glances at Decker, so I swivel my body so my back is facing them.

"No fair," Easton complains.

"It was Callie." I put up my hand to stop Hayes's reaction, but the fact that his smile falls immediately tells me how he feels about the idea of the two of us together. "We found her landlord in her apartment dressed in her bra and panties. She couldn't stay there, so I offered her my spare room."

"You what?" Decker interrupts, and I flip him off over my shoulder.

Hayes's eyes narrow. "You were at her place?"

Shit, we never talked about why we would say I was with her. I should've had answers ready for all this, but I know the right one isn't telling him that we were at the doctor's office to make sure everything is okay with the baby I impregnated his sister with. At least not here. Not now.

"I ran into her." And now I'm stacking lies on top of lies.

"And walked her back to her place. When she opened her door, her landlord—"

"That fucking Jerry guy, right? I told her he was weird." Hayes doesn't harp on any of the other details, and I breathe a little easier. "So, you offered her your place?"

I nod. "I didn't want her staying there. She said she'd change the locks and stuff, but still—"

He shakes his head. "Yeah, man, for sure. Thanks. She can stay with Leighton and me if she wants. I'm sure they'll talk about it while we're away. But thanks, it means a lot that you would look out for her like that."

Guilt hits me hard and swift like a baseball bat to the face. He's thanking me for being a decent guy, and I've been anything but.

"You're shitting me, right?" Decker says. "He's on board with his sister living with him?"

He must be talking to Easton, but I don't give a shit what his noble-ass opinion is.

At the same time, it feels weird to accept his gratitude because there's more he needs to know, but Callie and I decided last night to give it a little more time. After next month's appointment, we'll tell him. Dr. Amato said that's when the probability of a miscarriage will decrease drastically. Six more weeks before we blow up our world.

"I don't think Callie will want to move in with us though. Our lives don't really fit with a single woman who still likes to go out. I'll help her find a new place though."

"No rush." I straighten in my chair, thankful that part is over.

Hayes leans back against the seat and closes his eyes. I'm surprised he's not pulling out his phone to fill Leighton in on the news. Leighton has to assume I'm the dad, especially when she finds out Callie is living with me, so this next month needs to pass quickly so we can tell Hayes and not have this entire thing explode in our faces.

I pull out my phone to text Callie.

> Told him, and he's surprisingly cool with it.

Hmm… Leighton must have rocked his world last night.

> He actually thanked me for taking you in.

You didn't tell him that you bribed me?

> I like to keep some things to myself.

More than some.

> We'll play a game of truth or dare when I get back.

No. I'm going to introduce you to one for one.

> What's one for one? It sounds like torture.

Ask Hayes if you want to know. Good luck and see you in ten days.

She includes the blowing kiss emoji, and for some reason, that one little image makes me want to forget all our rules.

Decker leans across the aisle. "We have a good thing going here, don't fuck it up."

I turn to face my twin. "Stay the fuck out of my life."

"You're the one who came to Chicago."

"It's not an invitation to interfere. She's just living with me because her landlord is a sleazy bastard."

Decker straightens and grabs his headphones. "You're not as good a liar as you think." He puts them on, and I'm happy he's out of my head and my decisions.

Hayes smiles at me while he puts on his headphones, and I rock my head back, closing my eyes.

Callie and I have this totally under control. And when we're rocking the co-parent thing, they'll all see that we made the right decision.

If only I hadn't been up half the night, stopping myself from knocking on her door and asking for a little friends-with-benefits action. It'll get easier with time, right?

CHAPTER
EIGHTEEN

Callie

I say goodbye to the movers, walking them down the stairs, and make sure the security gate is shut behind them. It's odd to know I'm here all by myself for the next ten days. Maybe I'll go down and see Ruby at Peeper's.

Going back up to the condo, I can still smell Foster when I walk back in, making me smile. When he left this morning, I figured out the reason he always has this minty smell—it's his aftershave. Why is it so weird to think that a man like Foster Davis shaves and puts on aftershave? I should probably stop putting him in the box everyone else does. He clearly has some hang-ups.

My phone dings with a text, so I grab it off the kitchen counter.

Hayes: I heard you're living with Foster. You okay?

I smile at my brother and how much our relationship has changed over the years.

Yeah, it's temporary.

You're always welcome at our place.

I knew I would be, and I have to call Leighton to tell her the news—although Hayes might have already, I don't know. They have this little family they've created, and I'm not going to be the first crack in their perfect life. Plus, as weird as it is, I see Foster's point. We need to figure out our relationship since we're going to raise a child together.

I type my message as I make my way to my new bedroom.

I know, but he's not even here. It's like I'm living by myself.

True. I'm exhausted from the travel already. Let me know if you want me to go kick that landlord's ass. I always told you there was something off about him.

He did, I'll give him that. I just thought Jerry was a lonely and forgetful guy, not someone who broke into my apartment to wear my underwear.

It's fine. I'm good. Just getting settled.

Okay, you let us know if you need anything. Love you.

Love you. Good luck on the road.

Talk to Leighton about a date when you can both join us out here.

And what am I going to do while the two of you fuck like bunnies?

You can spend time with Decker. ;)

If he only knew I'd recently made an agreement to never be alone with the man.

I want to inquire if he knows what's up with the whole Foster and Decker thing, but I can't seem too invested. Hayes will wonder why I care so much.

Bye...

I toss my phone onto my bed, staring at all the boxes I have to unpack. Just wanting to tear off the Band-Aid, I dial Leighton, unsure if it's even her day off.

But she picks up right away. "It's about time. I feel like I've lost my best friend." From the background music, I'd say she's doing dishes.

"Me? You're the one in a love bubble. I'm just surviving."

She sighs, and I hear the music turn off. I keep her on speaker and explore the apartment rather than sitting in my room.

It's surprisingly neat.

"So... baby is good?"

"Yeah, everything looks good. I'm about six weeks along."

She screeches then coos. "I can't wait to hold him or her. So the father is okay with it?" She leaves her question hanging.

"I have to tell you something, and it's not who the father is. I promise I'll tell you soon, but I want to get to three months before I say anything to Hayes and the world at large. I don't know, maybe I'm stalling, but I feel superstitious about it."

"Ugh... Callie... it's killing me. You have no idea how thankful I am that he's gone for ten days so I don't have to look at him every day and think I'm keeping something from the man I love."

I cringe. "I'm sorry."

And I really mean it. I wish the circumstances were different. I doubt Hayes will want to kick Foster's ass, but he will be upset with us to a degree.

"I know, and I want to give you the space you need to figure this out. And since I'm the one who fell in love with your brother, I'm partly to blame. So, I'm going to stop giving you a guilt trip."

I really have the best friend anyone could ask for. "Okay, well… are you ready for the big news? Do you already know? Did Hayes message you?"

"No! Now he's keeping secrets from me?" She sounds offended. "What is it?"

"Well… I'm in Foster's condo right now."

"Are you trying to slyly tell me who the baby daddy is without outright telling me?"

I laugh and sink into the couch. "No. It's a weird situation because Foster happened to be with me when I went home and found Jerry in my bra and panties."

A sound rings over the line, and I think it might be her gagging. "Say that again?"

"You heard me. And he happened to be wearing my favorite set—the first date one, you know."

She sighs. "Not the black mesh one with the flowers?"

I nod although she can't see me. "Yup."

"I'm so sorry. How are you doing? You must feel so violated."

I'm not sure I've had time to process my feelings about what went down with Jerry. I do feel violated, and it only heightens my trust issues and my lack of confidence at being able to determine someone's character—men especially. I reported the incident to the building owner, but I have no idea what happened since I'm no longer there.

When I finally took a shower after all that, I swear I took off a layer of skin.

"Honestly, I've been more processing the fact that I've moved in with Foster Davis. I mean…" I let my sentence fade.

Leighton is a smart girl. She knows I wouldn't hang out with Foster on my own, so telling her I moved in with him pretty much confirms he's the father of my baby. I mean, I wouldn't be moving in with him if Decker or Easton were the dad. But I don't want to officially confirm it. It would just be one more detail she has to keep from my brother.

"Were you at a doctor's appointment with Foster?" Then she quickly says, "No. Don't answer that. I can't know."

"Anyway, he was kind of adamant about me moving in with him. And now I'm in his condo while he's gone for their back-to-back road series, and I'm not sure what to do."

"Want me to come over? I can help you unpack."

I'd love for her to, but this feels like something I need to do on my own. "How about we meet down at Peeper's later?"

For some reason, I want to have some time alone to reflect on everything that's going on in my life—how I got here, where it's headed.

"Sure. I'll call my mom and Aunt Iris to watch the kids."

"Great."

"Hey, Cal?" she says, and I know she probably hears it in my voice. "You got this. Like, you know that, right? You're going to be a kick-ass mom, and if Hayes gets upset, he'll get over it. And maybe…"

"Don't say it." I bring my legs up and hug them to my chest.

"I am going to say it because once upon a time, I needed someone to tell me when I was about to get in my own way. So humor me, okay?"

I don't say anything.

"I know your hang-ups, and the reasons you have them

are beyond valid, but you get to choose this. You're in control, and if Fos… er… whoever the dad is doesn't step up or somehow isn't a good person, you can pivot. I'll help you move out and everything, but I just want you to give yourself a chance at this."

"At what?" Tears fill my eyes.

She really does know me.

All the times I've felt second best in my life. The "rebound girl" was what my friends referred to me as in college. Just date Callie, then you'll meet the one for you. She's like a cleansing bath. Hang around her because she's so fun, have sex with her, and then you're ready to meet your one and only. They all meant it as a joke, but at some point, it didn't feel that way. Probably because that was exactly what kept happening. So I learned to laugh it off as though I didn't care, even though it burrowed under my skin, and I carried it with me everywhere.

"I don't need to spell it out for you, but I am wondering if Foster isn't who we think he is. I mean, he moved you in, right?" Leighton says.

If she only knew how adamant he was about it. How protective he seems to be. I can't lie, the desire still courses between us every time we're in the same room, but I refuse to allow it to ruin any kind of good co-parenting relationship we might have.

"We made a deal."

"A deal? Was it something sexual?"

I balk. "No. Jesus, Leighton. He's going to get me my five big-time guests in exchange for me living here."

She doesn't say anything for a moment.

I grow paranoid when she remains silent. "What?"

"Nothing. I'm just… I mean, I knew he couldn't be that bad if Hayes liked him so much, but why is he wanting you so close?"

"Jeez, remind me to call you more often."

She laughs. "I just mean… Hayes was telling me about… it doesn't matter—"

"Don't you dare. What were you going to say, Leighton?"

She sighs. "He kind of has a woman in each of the cities they visit. Like, he doesn't sleep around, it's just one woman in each city. So it surprises me that he wants you living with him. I think it says more about him. Things you might discover while you live there."

"Which would be?"

"That Foster Davis might be the bad boy of baseball, but he's far from a bad boy in real life. That there's a very different version of him not a lot of people get to discover."

"It doesn't mean he's going to show it to me."

I don't know why I'm arguing. Foster already has shown me some of those parts of himself. Maybe because I'm afraid for it to be true.

"I think he already is, but you're going to have to open your door a little wider and give him the opportunity to walk through."

"When did you get so philosophical?"

She laughs. "I'm just trying to get you out of your own way. Callie, you deserve all the happiness in the world, and so does that little one growing in your belly."

My hand falls to my stomach, and I really take in her words. "Thanks."

"That's what best friends are for. You did the same for me, but I must say I think I was kinder about it."

A laugh bubbles out of me. "Probably, but you and Hayes are so stubborn."

"And you're not? I think it's a Carlisle family trait to defy all reasoning and advice."

I chuckle, then sober quickly. "It's scary." My voice is practically a whisper.

"Yeah, it is, but the reward could be pretty great."

I'm sexually attracted to Foster, sure. But I barely know

him, and the thought of us taking a chance, and it not working out… plus, I have no idea where his head is even at.

"Okay, missy. I'll see you tonight."

We say our goodbyes, and I hang up, then look around the condo.

Open myself up to being hurt again? Might as well hold a loaded gun right to my heart.

CHAPTER
NINETEEN

Foster

I'm beat. All I want to do is drop my bags at the door, walk to my bedroom, and collapse on my bed. I never sleep well at hotels, and a ten-day stint in them has made me feel like an insomniac.

I type in the code for the main gate, and we all make our way into the building. Decker and Easton peel off on their floors, none of us bothering with a goodbye because we're exhausted and we lost earlier today, so we're in shit moods.

I push open the door, and the first thing I notice is a soft glow and the scent of… vanilla?

Stepping into my condo, I look around and notice a lot of changes since I left ten days ago. I lean back to make sure I'm on my floor. It would be just like Decker to have this girly feel to his condo.

Yep, definitely my place.

Callie steps out of the spare room, which I need to think of as her room now. "Oh, you're back."

Is she even wearing shorts under that giant sweatshirt? Two seconds in the door and I'm already faced with temptation.

But it's a Chicago Grizzlies sweatshirt, and the caveman who only comes out when I'm around her wants to tear it off of her and throw my Colts sweatshirt over her head. Fuck, I need to get this beast under control.

She must notice me staring at her shirt because she looks down. "Oh, I found this in the back of the closet. I wonder how long it was there for."

"I heard the condo was Miles Cavanagh's place before Tweetie's. Back when they called this place The Den."

She nods, appearing to have no intention of taking off the damn thing.

Fuck Miles Cavanagh.

"Sorry about the game, but you won the Texas series. That's good, huh?" She flits over to the fridge and pulls out a water. "Want one?"

I drop my bag by my bedroom door and walk to the kitchen, seeing that sadly, she is wearing shorts. They're just short as fuck, showing off her long, lean legs.

"Sure, thanks."

She smiles, straightens, and hands me a water. I peer into the fridge before the door shuts and see that it's filled with food.

She must notice me looking because she grabs the door and holds it open as though she's a *The Price is Right* model. "Look. Real food."

There's fruit and milk and eggs, and it looks like no fridge I've ever had in my life. At least not one I remember, but those years before I lived with only my dad are fuzzy at best.

"Good," I mumble, twisting off the bottle cap and downing half the bottle.

She pulls out a pouch of microwavable popcorn, puts it in the microwave, and leans against the counter. "Shit, I'm sorry. I'm not supposed to engage with you, right?" She cringes.

"I decompressed on the plane and bus. It's fine."

"Do you want to talk about it then?"

I shake my head. "I sucked and lost the game for us. Not much else to say."

She opens a cabinet and pulls down a bowl. Does she already know where everything is in my place?

Of course she does, asshole. You gave her full access, and you've been gone for ten days.

"I don't think it helped that the DICs didn't get one hit the entire game. They're definitely in a slump lately. All three of them."

"You watched the games?" I fiddle with the back of the breakfast stool, contemplating if I should sit or not. Is this what people do? Am I being presumptuous that she wants to talk to me if I sit down? Maybe she just wants to make her popcorn and go back to her room.

"Yeah, my brother plays for the team." She chuckles.

"Of course." I was a fool to think otherwise.

"I'm kind of invested in all of you. And in my opinion, Blue messed up two of those calls. Greer was out before he ever got that hit."

I'm not sure the last time I talked game to anyone outside of coaches and teammates. She's not trying to placate me with things like "it's just a game" and "the shitty comments don't matter." I like it a little too much.

"That's what pissed me off so much." I immediately regretted showing my emotions on the mound. Although I didn't yell at Blue like I normally would, I saw the replay. Hayes calling time right away and coming to visit me on the mound. Me giving the ump a death glare and mouthing off, just not directly to him.

"I saw, but you had good reason. You guys lost because

Blue called that one pitch a ball when it was right on the outside corner."

I slide up on the stool, and she takes the popcorn out of the microwave and puts it in a bowl. Then she places it between us.

"Did you eat on the plane?"

"We did, but who can say no to popcorn?" I grab a fistful, and she gets up on the counter, legs crossed. "Your brother got me addicted back in Seattle."

She laughs. "It's kind of a Carlisle obsession, honestly. I feel like it was a nightly snack in our house growing up. So now every time I want to get cozy and watch television, I make a bowl."

I turn to look at the family room area and see that the television is paused. There's a blanket thrown on the back of the couch. "Oh, you were going to watch something? Sorry, didn't mean to interrupt." I slide off the stool. "I can give you some privacy."

She chuckles. "Stop. I don't need privacy."

I've never felt like such a fool. I palm the back of my neck. "Oh."

She chuckles again. "It's weird, right?"

"It's been a long time since I've lived with a woman."

She slides off the counter, and I'm surprised by the disappointment I feel. I would've enjoyed a little more time with her.

"You lived with a woman?" Her shock takes me a minute to figure out—she assumes it was a romantic partner.

"I didn't mean it that way. It's just that I moved in with my dad when I was eleven. He wasn't big on comfort items."

She picks up the bowl. "I see. Well, now that you have a woman's touch back in your life, you might not ever want to go back." She smiles. "Want to join me and watch some reality television where we can worry about other people's drama instead of our own?"

I don't want to interfere, and I'm not sure where the line should be drawn. Sure, she's here because I want to know her better, but how much should our lives intertwine?

"Um…"

She places the bowl on the table and walks back over to stand in front of me. It's really unfair how hot she is. I mean, your best friend's little sister should not be this fucking attractive.

She says, "Go get changed into comfy clothes and come watch. I'll explain who everyone is to you."

"I don't know."

"What are you going to do in there?" She motions toward my bedroom. "Brood over the loss? Think how things should've gone differently? Let me take your mind off it."

I know a way she could get my mind off it.

She puts her hands on her hips and tilts her head, waiting for my answer.

I nod. "Give me five."

She smiles, appeased, and turns to walk away. "Oh, are you okay with the candle? You're not sensitive to scents, are you?"

"It's girly, but…" I look around the place, and it definitely has a different feel to it than it did ten days ago. "It smells nice."

She looks so happy that I want to admit that coming home tonight was, for lack of a better word, nice. Yeah, coming home to someone was really fucking nice.

Instead, I turn around and go into my bedroom, shutting the door. It's the one space she hasn't touched, and I can't help but notice how cold and bleak it feels.

My chest tightens.

Maybe living together was the worst idea I've ever had because she's already getting under my skin—in a good way. And nothing good can come of that.

CHAPTER
TWENTY

Callie

It feels surreal—walking next to a man in the grocery store as he pushes our cart is some serious domestic shit I never thought I'd be doing, let alone with Foster Davis.

"I figured you were a takeout kind of guy?" I eye the fruit as we walk through the produce section.

A few people have glanced our way. Foster is a little different than Hayes. While my brother almost always wears his ball cap out, Foster doesn't seem to care as much. Maybe because of his reputation, people don't approach him as much or don't feel as comfortable as they do with Hayes.

"I'll have you know that I can prepare a few meals." He winks at me, and my stomach flips.

"Oh, I have to see this." I stop and put a bag of red grapes in the cart.

"I'll admit following a recipe annoys the shit out of me, but after a while, I kind of wing it with the measurements, and it still turns out pretty good." He grabs a bunch of bananas. "Potassium is good for fetal growth."

I purse my lips to stop from smiling. "Maybe you just want to do the shopping. Then you can make a list of everything I should eat."

He chuckles, which is such a rare occurrence. I watch him for a second longer than I should. "Don't tempt me."

I lean in close, put my head on his shoulder and singsong, "Just so you know, I won't follow it. I'm not like your usual girls."

He pulls away and meets my gaze. "That's why I like you." I'm not sure the look I give him—one of surprise, probably—but he blinks a few times, seeming a bit flustered. "I mean… that's why I like spending time with you… shit, you know what I mean."

"Careful there, Reap, those sound like compliments." I pat his chest and walk behind the cart to grab some kiwis.

Mostly, I step away because I need a little space. Him doing research on what I need to eat is endearing. Yes, maybe it's a little controlling, but mostly endearing. It's not as if he's tying me down and force-feeding me. Great, now I'm thinking of being in bed with my wrists pinned to his headboard.

A woman comes along next to me, grabbing a plastic bag. "You're cute together," she whispers. She's probably in her seventies, perfectly curled gray hair with a tint of red.

"Oh, we're just…" I glance at Foster. He's picking out a bag of nuts from the bins, and I have no doubt they're whichever ones are good for pregnant women. "Friends."

She takes the kiwi I was about to grab and touches my arm with her free hand. "Sweetheart, he doesn't look at you like a friend."

The urge to tell her our story washes over me. To unleash it to someone else so they can help me figure it out. The fact that I'm carrying his baby. How he's my brother's best friend.

How he's now my roommate. How confused I am about what I want, what *he* wants—why he's being so thoughtful and helpful when most people would say he's the last man I can trust, especially with my heart. But Foster looks around, still finding me at the kiwis, and wheels over the cart.

I can't take my eyes off him as he approaches with that stern, thin-lipped look he wears all the damn time except when we're alone.

"It's always the ones who look rough who have the kindest hearts, I think. You should see my husband." She chuckles. "They might not show it to everyone, but the ones who see it are pretty damn lucky, if you ask me. Heart of gold, those rough ones." She pats my hand and looks at Foster before turning to her cart and putting the kiwis inside.

"Making friends?" Foster asks after she's wheeled her cart to the other side of the produce section. "She warning you about hanging out with a guy covered in tattoos?"

I laugh, feeling a little awkward. I could tell him what she said, but I don't want any reason for him to pull away and not let me see the real him. If I tell Foster someone else saw that there's more to him, he might do exactly that, so I keep quiet.

"She was just telling me how to spot a good kiwi from a bad one." I place the bag into the cart and walk alongside him. "Let's get back to the subject at hand—you making me dinner."

He stops at the meat section and grabs five packages of steak.

My eyes widen. "Are you throwing a party?" He gives me a wicked smile, and I shake my head. "Let me guess."

"Zinc, iron, B12..."

"Do you have a book somewhere?" I didn't see one around the condo, but he's clearly been reading up on what I should be eating during the pregnancy.

"Internet. I have a lot of time on the road."

"And you don't want to be a normal guy and just watch porn?"

He shrugs. "Not doing it for me anymore."

He doesn't elaborate, and I'm afraid to ask because deep down I know what I want the answer to be—that he feels this intensity between us and could only ever be satisfied by me.

The other night when he was on the road playing Milwaukee, I tried my vibrator, imagining it was him hovering over me. My tongue sliding over his neck tattoos, the growl he'd let out as he came. He looks like a growler. He didn't when we were together before, but I feel like he would be if he was on top, and we had more time than we did.

"Bread aisle!" I say a little too loudly.

Foster chuckles. "You look a little flushed there." He tips his head closer to mine. "You thinking about something dirty?"

God yes, and I'd be cutting this grocery trip short if we had the kind of relationship where I could have him whenever I wanted.

"No." I shake my head and walk ahead of him toward the bread aisle.

He puts a loaf of wheat bread in the cart and then puts a box of sugary cereal in the cart.

"Okay, so I have to eat steak and bananas, and you get what's practically a bowl of sugar?"

He drops another box of cereal into the cart. "It's my vice. No apologies."

"Foster Davis, heartthrob, bad boy, eats the same cereal as a six-year-old."

"And proud of it." He flashes me a smile, showing his full mouth of perfect white teeth—all except for one on the right side that's a little unaligned but somehow adds to his hotness. As though he's imperfectly perfect.

"If you get that, then I'm buying cookies, and you can't complain."

He holds up his hands from the cart. "You can have whatever you want. I told you your cravings are mine to fulfill."

"I think I'm too early to have any cravings. There hasn't been anything I've wanted so badly I had to have it."

Liar.

Well, one thing. But we're not gonna go there.

I turn the corner and almost run right into a little kid. I stop and draw back. He looks up at me, looks scared, and runs off screaming for his mommy.

"Well, that doesn't bode well for my future." I frown.

"Our kid is gonna love you."

I stop, and he strolls right past me. Two words from his statement hit me with a force I wasn't ready for—*our* and *love*. I hurry to catch up while Foster continues shopping as though that sentence wasn't earth-shattering.

"Oh, stop being so surprised. You're a likable person. I told you that already."

"Just what every girl wants to be called. Likable."

"If I told you what I really think of you, you'd probably knee me in the nuts, and this whole experiment of living together would end in disaster."

I want so badly to ask what he thinks of me. Does he lie in bed and think about how I'm only a room away too? Does he think about the things we could be doing to each other? When he sees I'm home, does his stomach feel as though it's full of helium and might float away like mine does?

They're all bad signs, but signs that aren't stopping me from continuing what we're doing.

When we reach the dairy section, I get distracted in front of the ice cream. So many choices, and I can't decide which one.

Foster comes over and makes a hmm sound. "Finally a craving?"

I shake my head. "Maybe it's a myth, like the five-month one."

"Five-month myth?" His forehead wrinkles.

"Oh, so you know every single vitamin I need, but not what most women experience around five months?"

"I haven't gone further than how far along you are. But now I'm curious." He pulls out his phone, but I place my hand over it.

I lean in close to him. "It's that a pregnant woman's sex drive gets more intense. Supposedly. But I'm gonna be honest, my nipples are so sensitive I'm not sure I could handle anyone's hands on them right now."

Foster groans then glances around. "Fuck, Callie, are you trying to get me arrested?"

"Arrested?" I frown.

"Having a hard-on in public. Jesus. I really hope I have a lot of away games during your fifth month. No offense."

I laugh because he looks so scared. "Seriously, I can handle it."

"You hope. But I guess if I have to take one for the team, you can jump into my bed."

I shake my head, then notice that he's added my yogurt to the cart. I give him a stern look.

He shrugs. "I saw you only had one left this morning."

My hand covers my heart. "Foster, you woo me."

"You'd be the first to be wooed."

My cheeks heat, and I open the freezer, grab the pistachio ice cream, and add it to the cart.

We finish our shopping while I'm trying to wrap my head around Foster and this flirting that seems to come so naturally for us, as well as how much I really like him and how I know he'll be a good dad.

I see the scared kid again, but this time his brother is chasing him. The mom is whisper-screaming, following them with her cart, but one of them bumps me. All I see is the display of pies on a table that I'm about to fall into before two hands grab my waist.

I fall back and Foster catches me. We're in a pose as if he just dipped me. For a moment, I lose myself in his eyes. God, he's gorgeous.

"I got you." His breath is warm and minty, and I want to wrap my hand around the back of his neck and pull him down to meet my lips.

"Thanks." My voice is more breathless than it should be.

"Of course. I'd hate for you to fall stomach first."

I stiffen.

Right. Of course. The baby.

I straighten up then pull away. The mom apologizes profusely then scolds her boys, who look a little scared of her now.

Foster goes about putting the items on the conveyor belt while I'm still reeling. I need to prepare myself for the fact that this attraction might be one-sided.

What was I thinking?

That I'd be Foster Davis's game-changer? What on earth would ever make me think that? Definitely not my past pick of partners.

Get your head out of the clouds, Callie.

"Oh yeah, forgot to tell you. I got you your first guest," he says absentmindedly as he loads items onto the conveyor belt.

"You did?" There I go floating up to the sky again. "You work fast."

"Keep that to yourself, okay?" He winks.

I laugh, and as we check out, head back to the apartment, and put the groceries away, it almost feels as though we're a couple.

Earth to Callie.

Houston, we have a problem.

CHAPTER
TWENTY-ONE

Callie

"So he just moved you in here?" Lex looks around the condo like a detective on a missing person's case.

"After we found Jerry dressed in my underwear, yeah."

She freezes and glances at where I'm getting ready for our guest today at the breakfast bar. "How many times did I tell you about Slummy?"

We're setting up the equipment for the guest Foster scored me, which I'm still in complete disbelief over. I haven't even told Lex about it yet because I want to see her expression in person.

"I know, but how was I to know that he liked my lingerie?" I shudder from the visual again.

"And now you get to live with the Reaper." She shoots me a wide smile and peeks into his bedroom. "Are you cleaning this place? Is it, like, a swap or something? He lets you live here, and you make his bed?"

"What? No!"

"So there must be a cleaning lady then." She slides up on the breakfast stool and takes the microphone from me to get it situated, since there's a reason she's the tech person and not me.

"Not that he's said or that I've seen. I think he's just a tidy person."

"Don't let that get out. You'll ruin his reputation." She laughs, unpacking her bag with the various microphones and cameras and cords she usually carries around with her.

"He can't be neat?"

She looks at me with interest as if she's trying to figure out why I sound defensive. I feel caught in a corner, unsure how to find my way out of this without her figuring out that Foster is different than what people expect.

She raises her hand. "Okay, I'm not going to address the fact you sound like a defensive girlfriend right now. I'm just saying an anal, tidy, and organized bad boy is an oxymoron. Am I wrong?"

I feel my lips tip up into a grin. I thought the same thing when I moved in. He picks up his mail every day he's home, and it rarely ever sits on the counter. He sorts through it as soon as he walks in, throws away the junk mail, and puts the rest somewhere in his room. He never goes to bed with dirty dishes in the sink. Even a cup gets put in the dishwasher when he's finished with it.

"I guess not everyone is who you think they are." I shrug. "I'm grabbing my jacket, and then we'll leave."

I hurry to my room, hoping she can't see it written on my face. Foster Davis is softening the part of my heart I prefer to keep frozen.

"I'll let you think you're fooling me. Now tell me the guest."

I stop in my doorway, sliding my arms into my jacket. "Ready?"

I'm so excited. I haven't even told Leighton yet just in case

Foster didn't come through. I wasn't ready for the pity or questions.

Lex rolls her eyes. "Stop with the antics."

"Maren Hale." My eyes widen, and my smile grows.

"Wow. Foster got you Maren Hale?"

Maren was a hugely popular influencer who was once engaged to a professional baseball player before her current husband. She documented their entire wedding planning, and it appeared as if the entire country was following along. So when he jilted her at the altar, it was big news.

She moved away from the influencer thing, but now she's back, but her star has risen even higher because everyone admired the way she handled the humiliation of what happened.

I nod and rush across the room. "That he did."

"Did he fuck her once upon a time before she married Eli Hale?"

I freeze as I grab my purse. I hadn't really considered it actually. From what I know, Eli Hale and Foster have never played on the same team. Eli never played for Seattle, and I would know since Hayes played there too. Would Foster really set up an interview where I'd have to chat with a woman he's slept with?

"I'm not sure."

"Sorry for putting the pin in your happily-ever-after balloon. I should've thought about it before saying it out loud." Lex grabs the equipment. I can tell from the look on her face that she legitimately feels bad.

"What are you talking about?"

"You and him playing house. You can't tell me that your imagination hasn't run away from you." She opens the door.

I would unload a lot of what Lex is saying, but I don't really want to dig into myself that much at this point. "We don't want to be late. Let's go."

"You're the boss."

I'm thankful Lex allows me the reprieve, and we walk out of the condo, heading down the stairs.

"I asked her to meet me at Peeper's." I push open the security gate.

"Do you want her to run away before you've even spoken to her? Ruby isn't exactly the welcome wagon."

I turn to face Lex after we're through the gate, seeing a new *Dugout* sign posted with a white piece of paper and *Reaper* written on the front of it.

Lex lifts the piece of paper and reads it. "'Reaper, I'm desperate for your slider to hit me deep and hard.'" She pretends to gag but puts the note back on the sign.

I resist the urge to rip off the note and tear it in two, or worse reply back that he's taken. He's definitely not taken.

"Yeah, I don't miss those."

We both turn to see Maren Hale standing outside of the bar.

She's as fresh-faced and beautiful in person as she is on social media. Her dark blonde hair is messy but somehow still appears styled. Her gold nose ring and her no-makeup rule somehow make her look younger than she is. She's wearing jeans, a T-shirt, and walking shoes.

Maren pushes off the door. "Callie, right?"

"Yes. I'm sorry—were you waiting long?" I break the distance, and Lex leaves the sign, following me.

"No, but that lady in there isn't very friendly." She laughs. "I told her that I knew Foster, and she told me that he's got more important things to worry about than getting laid." She shakes her head. "I tried to say I was a friend, but she wasn't having it. Thought I was here to screw him even after I showed her my wedding ring and a picture of Breelyn."

"She thinks everyone wants the guys," Lex chimes in next to me. "It's her thing."

I glance at Lex and back at Maren. "It's more of a protective thing with her, but I should've warned you. This is Lex, she'll be handling the camera. Are you still comfortable with walking and talking?"

Maren glances around the area. "Definitely." She lifts her foot. "Wore my comfy shoes."

Lex gets her hooked up with a microphone, and before we're about to start the walk, Maren says to me, "You must be important to Foster."

I don't want to kill the vibe by telling her the deal we've struck, but she continues on, and I'm wondering who is interviewing who here.

"No offense, but I told him no three times—more because I don't have the time with Breelyn now—but then he went into your whole story and said I'd be an idiot for not getting on your podcast now because it'll be the next big thing soon." She laughs and touches my shoulder. "You know how he can be. So I said yes, and here I am."

"Well, he's certainly been a big help and a good friend. Thank you again for agreeing to do this."

She gives me a knowing smile. "It's rare to find someone who has a kind thing to say about Foster." She takes me in, and I wonder if she sees all the feelings stirring inside me. "Anyway, I see you're ready." She touches my arm again. "Let's get started. I'm an open book—nothing is off the table."

We walk down Sheffield toward Waveland. Lex walks in front of us, changing angles. I'm glad that Maren seems okay being out in public, since it's the basis of my show. Thankfully, it's a workday, and the Colts have been away and don't play home until tomorrow.

"Start wherever you want." I prefer not to lead into our conversation with questions that will direct where the conversation goes. I want my guests to start where they think they need to because it's usually the exact right spot whether they know it or not.

Maren slips her hands into her jean pockets. "For a long

time, I thought my ex blindsided me by jilting me at the altar."

She goes into the embarrassment and shame she felt when things didn't work out with her ex. How she felt pressured to make it seem on socials as though they had the most magical love story, and having it exposed in such a public way was devastating. The mean comments from complete strangers who acted as if they knew them and the situation but really had no idea. How she got completely off social media— deleted all of her accounts and wanted to crawl into a hole.

"I was furious because I'd never asked for much from him," she continues.

We pass a couple arguing softly about which street they're supposed to get to.

"When he didn't show up," Maren says, "I didn't see it coming. I thought I'd been the perfect fiancée, planning it all myself, making sure everything was perfect and documenting it every step of the way. Sure, he never seemed thrilled with the videos and stuff, but I figured that was a guy thing. He didn't understand me chronicling our wedding planning."

My throat tightens because I can't imagine being dressed in your wedding gown and having all your guests there, only for the groom not to show up. It has to be the biggest embarrassment someone can go through. And to think she found a way to trust another man with her heart.

"I kept replaying it," she adds, "wondering what I could've done better. And that maybe I should have been… less." She glances at me, her gaze gentle. "But here's the thing no one tells you, and the one thing that took me a long time to understand. Oftentimes, the people who leave were hoping you wouldn't realize you deserved more."

Her words sink in slow and deep.

We stop at the corner, waiting for the light to change. Cars rush past, music thumping from one of them.

"When I met Eli," Maren goes on, her voice holding a

more loving note, "it scared me. Because he was so different, and so was I. I was becoming someone I was still getting used to." She laughs. "I turned him down at least ten times."

We turn the corner and glance at one another. She holds my eyes for a moment.

"He showed up," she says simply. "Every time. Not just with big bouquets and fancy restaurants. In quiet ways. He asked what I needed to feel secure in our relationship. He waited and took a step back when I said I wasn't ready to move forward. Most of all, he never made me feel like loving me was work."

The light turns green.

"And that's when I realized," she adds as we step off the curb, "the guy who wins you won't treat loving you like a job. He'll treat it like a privilege."

I swallow hard. It's clear why her fans love her so much.

We talk about her life with Eli and how having their daughter, Breelyn, is a difficult transition, but she loves being a mom—she just wishes she had more sleep. She's raw and honest and everything I hope for when I begin one of these conversations.

"I'm really glad I said yes," Maren says as we get closer to returning to the condo building.

My heart stutters. "Really?"

She smiles. "I'm picky with my interviews."

"I'm honored," I say, meaning it. "Your story… is beautiful."

Maren slows, glancing at me. "Foster told me if I came on, I had to be honest. That you don't tolerate any bullshit."

I laugh because that sounds exactly like Foster. "He would say something like that, wouldn't he?"

She nods. "He said you listen. That you want human connections that listeners can relate to."

My throat tightens, and we stop at the curb.

"You know," she says quietly, "the people who give others

room to be honest usually don't always give themselves the same grace."

I swallow. I'm starting to wonder if Maren should be doing this and not me.

We cross the street, and my gaze snags on Foster leaning against the brick wall of the building, head buried in his phone.

Maren follows my gaze and smiles. "He asked me because he believes in what you're building with this podcast."

As I'm about to respond, Foster glances up and smiles. It just about kills me. Maybe because so few people get it.

"Shit, are you Maren Hale? Wife of the Gold Glove winner Eli Hale?" he jokes.

Maren walks right into Foster's arms, and they hug tightly. "That's Eli Hale, husband of the amazing Maren Hale, you're talking about."

They both laugh, and although I have no reason to feel it, my chest stings with jealousy.

CHAPTER
TWENTY-TWO

Foster

I glance over Maren's shoulder as she squeezes me, catching Callie shuffling her feet and staring anywhere but in our direction.

No one would think I'm a hugger, and they'd be right. I'm not a hugger, but I've grown used to people like Maren who are, so I didn't think much of it when she walked toward me. From the day Eli introduced me to Maren, I've witnessed her hug almost everyone she encounters.

I step back and shove my hands in my pockets. "How'd it go?"

She looks over her shoulder at Callie, who is finally joining us, then back at me, putting her hand on my arm. "She's great. Don't fuck this up."

"She's Hayes Carlisle's little sister."

Maren rolls her eyes, but her smirk says she's not buying my act. I'm sure Callie didn't tell her that she's carrying my baby, and I know it's bad to hope that maybe Callie told her something about me that made Maren think there's something between us. It's stupid, since we have no future. At least not the romantic kind. I'm not telling anyone until I tell Hayes. Eli's great, I've known him since the farm league, and he'll be one of the first people I call after the news is out.

"You're back." Callie gives me an unsteady smile.

It feels too good to see her again after our last away stint. My gaze soaks her in as if she's a mirage in the desert.

"About fifteen minutes ago."

Maren's head volleys between us, and I can admit, we look really awkward. Like we slept together last night and haven't seen each other since. But Callie and I aren't used to interacting with each other in front of other people like we do behind the condo door.

"I'm Lex." The brunette with the camera slides out from next to Callie, hand extended. "Her right-hand gal."

"Oh sorry. Foster, this is Lex. She films for me and helps me with all the tech stuff." Callie motions between us.

"Where were you the other night?" I ask with humor.

Callie narrows her eyes at me because she called me while I was on the road because the internet went down. I tried to walk her through unplugging, replugging, what light should turn on, etc. In all truth, I was surprised, with Callie's age, how hard it was for her to figure it out. But at least our first time having to work on something together went smoothly, and no one lost their temper. It gave me hope for our future.

"Oh, she tried me first." Lex laughs.

Disappointment sinks in fast. I should be happy I wasn't her first option. I usually hate it when people rely on me.

"Oh, look at you. It's okay, big guy." Lex leans in closer. "You know how Miss Hyper-Independent is about relying on people."

"Lex!" Callie glares at her, but Lex shrugs.

I want to pull Lex aside and ask her how to get Callie to rely on me.

"It's not a big deal." I purposely look at Callie when I say it.

She just turns to Maren and starts her own side conversation.

"She gets a little ornery when she can't watch her reality television," Lex says.

I nod, unsure how to respond since reality television is becoming my own vice thanks to her. "Hopefully it was a one-time thing."

She laughs and looks at Callie, who is now deep in conversation with Maren. Lex seems nice, and I could get along with her, but I really want in on the other conversation.

"It won't be." Lex gives a look as if to say that Callie's tech issues are a constant thing. "She'd be lost without me." A buzzing sound comes from her pocket, and she pulls out her phone, sees who is calling, and shoves it back in. I like her more now. "But I'd probably be in a ditch somewhere without her, so we're even, you know."

I nod.

"Are you not going to ask why?" Her dark eyes take me in.

"Um…"

"Oh, someone did a number on you, didn't they? But asking me about my trauma doesn't mean I'm going to ask you about yours. Just so you know, not asking follow-up questions makes you come off like you don't give a shit." She leans in closer. "And if you act like that with her, you don't stand a chance. Just some helpful advice."

I draw back from her for a moment and try to find the right words but can't. I settle on, "Thanks for the advice."

Really what I want to say is *tell me more, Lex, like how to win Callie over.*

She nods as though she understands my unspoken words. Good. Now let's move on.

"I'm a recovering addict. Coke. After I got clean, I couldn't find a job. One day I see our girl over here at a coffee shop, trying to figure out her microphone. She's swearing and drawing a lot of attention, so I swooped in to help her. We've been together ever since."

The words *our* and *girl* together sound too good.

"She just let you take over?"

She laughs again. "Yup. Can you believe it? Did you see that pig fly by?"

I kind of like the way she talks about Callie as if we know her equally well, even though it appears Lex knows her a lot better than I do.

"Well, that was good of you to step in and help a stranger out of the goodness of your heart like that."

"I might be a lesbian, and Callie's hot, but I didn't do it because I wanted to get in her pants."

"What hope do I have then?"

"That depends, Foster Davis. Do *you* want to get into her pants?"

Yes. I do, Lex. I really want in Callie's pants.

I balk, though I have no idea why. She's bold, but I'm used to locker rooms and dugouts and the shit guys say to one another in those environments. Maybe it's Lex being so blatant when Callie is right next to us, or more likely, I just don't know how to handle my feelings for Callie. I'm attracted to her yes, but I also like her as a person, which makes sense. She's pretty much Hayes without a dick.

Jesus. Where the fuck did that thought come from?

Lex squeezes my shoulder. "My advice: keep showing up."

"Showing up where?" Callie interrupts, and I turn my head toward her.

She's clearly interested in our conversation. Maren is no longer beside her. I find her talking to a woman with a stroller farther down on the sidewalk. I assume it must be her nanny.

"On the mound, silly. I was giving Foster some unsolicited advice."

Callie shoots me an apologetic look.

I'm a little scared at how well Lex saw through me. Does one fuck-up see through another?

"Here she is," Maren says, holding Breelyn.

Callie turns and coos with excitement. "Oh, she's adorable."

"Want to hold her?" Maren holds her daughter out to Callie.

"Sure." She takes Breelyn and cradles her on her hip, smiling at her.

Fuck, I love the thought of Callie holding our own child. That visual is a life I never thought I'd want. Hell, one I never thought I'd get.

"Hi, sweet thing." Callie bounces Breelyn a little on her hip, walking around and looking like a complete natural.

"What about you, Foster?" Maren sets her gaze on me. She turns to Callie. "He always declines."

"Last time I saw her, she couldn't even hold her head up. I'm not going to be responsible for it falling off."

The women all laugh. Breelyn whines a little, and Maren runs her hand down her daughter's fuzzy blonde hair. "You're okay. Callie's good people."

"I think she wants her mom." Callie leans toward Maren.

Maren takes the baby back, but before she settles her in her arms, she holds Breelyn out to me. "You sure, Foster?"

I raise both hands. "I'm good."

They all laugh again, and Maren tucks her daughter in her arms.

My gaze falls to Callie. She's staring at Breelyn, but the hint of sadness in her eyes cuts me open for some reason.

"Well, I gotta go. Nice to meet you, Maren." Lex raises her hand in a friendly wave.

"You too, Lex. I hope I'll like all the angles." Maren smiles, and I'm clearly missing an earlier conversation.

"Only your best sides." Lex puts her hand on Callie's arm. "I'll see you tomorrow? For editing?"

"Oh, actually…" Callie glances at me. "I forgot I have something, so I'll call you. And then the next day they have their game. Um… the day after that, okay?"

"I'll forgive you if you get me a ticket to the game?" Lex looks at me.

"I can get you a set. I'll leave them at will-call."

Lex's mouth falls open, and she glances at Callie. "Look how easy that was. She's been holding out on me."

"Well, in her defense—Hayes has an army to get tickets for while I have…" I trail off. How pathetic is it that I have to say no one.

"Thanks." Lex seems to recognize that I need an out. I swear, she's my new best friend. "Now I have to figure out who I want to impress with really good Colts tickets." She eyes me, and I nod to confirm that they'll be good tickets. "I don't believe a word they say about you anymore." She laughs and walks down the sidewalk.

"I have to go too." Maren glances over her shoulder at her nanny standing down the sidewalk.

Callie thanks her again for doing the show. "I'll be in touch."

Maren and Callie say their goodbyes, then Maren comes over to me, giving me a one-armed hug.

"I promise she's not contagious." Maren laughs, and Callie is late to join in. "But no blaming me when you get some woman pregnant."

She laughs again, and Callie looks as if she wants to choke but manages a polite laugh.

"Tell your husband to fix the hole in his glove."

Maren scowls at me. "He told me to tell you to lift some weights, your velocity sucks."

I shake my head, and we smile at one another.

"Let's do dinner when we play each other." She walks backward, and Callie waves, turning to face me so her back is to Maren. Maren points at Callie and mouths, "Bring her."

I shake my head, and once she, the baby, and the nanny have crossed the street, I join Callie at the security gate. "So it went well?"

She throws herself into my arms, leaving me no choice but to catch her. "Thank you so much, Foster. That was an amazing interview and exactly what I needed." Her voice is slightly muffled since she's speaking into my neck, but my arms instantly wrap around her.

I've become addicted to the scent of her perfume. When a woman wearing it walked by the other day, I whipped around, hoping like hell it was Callie. Sadly, it wasn't.

No one has ever shown so much gratitude for anything I've done for them. It's usually their hand out and a quick "thanks, man, I owe you." But Callie… it's in her tone, in her tight hug. And it makes me want to open my fucking checkbook and give her whatever she wants.

None of this is a good sign.

CHAPTER
TWENTY-THREE

Callie

I turn on the lamp in the living room after rolling around in bed half the night.

Holding Breelyn was a massive mistake.

When Maren offered, I wanted to say no, but what kind of person am I if I tell the woman who might just change the projection of my career, *I don't want to hold your baby*? She'd be offended.

So I took Breelyn, and it felt uncomfortable and awkward. And after I gave her back when she got fussy, it left me with mixed feelings I'm having a hard time processing.

Finally, deciding that sleep isn't coming anytime soon, I got out of bed in search of a snack. I quietly make my way to the kitchen and open the fridge, looking for anything that might hit the spot, but I didn't make it to the grocery store in Foster's absence since I was preparing for Maren's podcast.

I tap my lips. I could order out, tiptoe out of here, and head downstairs to get it from the outside gate. But all that's open are the twenty-four-hour fast-food places, and I'm trying to eat better than that. Making popcorn would wake Foster.

I take a water and head to the couch because it's the comfiest couch in existence. Seriously, I'm going to have to try to swindle a deal with Foster when I move out and maybe use our kid as bribery to be able to take it with me. Or sneak it onto the moving truck.

Foster's door creaks open, and I freeze midway to Comfyville.

"You're up?" His voice is all rough and sexy, and for a moment, I get lost in a visual of him waking me with that voice telling me things he wants to do to me.

I swivel around to face him, and I'm pretty sure I need to pick my jaw up off the floor. If I thought his voice was making my traitorous body think unthinkable things, his body adds another heap of sexual desire on the pile. He's wearing only a pair of boxer briefs. Very tight black boxer briefs that don't hide his tattoos or his muscles or the inches of beautiful skin. God help me.

This is how you end up on the heartbreak train, girl.

My gaze finally reaches his again after trailing over the perfection of his body. His eyebrows are raised, snapping my thoughts back to reality and the fact that we are supposed to be friends, co-parents in the making, and nothing more.

"Go get on some pants and a shirt. You're breaking rules." I think my voice came out pretty even.

But maybe not, because he chuckles and surprisingly does go back into his room, emerging a few seconds later with a pair of sweatpants on but no shirt or socks. "Better?"

"Where's your shirt?"

He ignores me and walks into the kitchen, grabbing himself a water. "This is no different than me wearing a swimsuit. It actually covers more."

I blow out a breath. "I don't see a pool anywhere around here, so clothes would be appreciated."

"Tell me why you're up first."

I lean along the back of his couch, facing him in the kitchen, still unable to take my eyes off him. He really is such a beautiful man.

"I couldn't sleep. I was going to eat something, but turns out we're living like college students. Or at least I was while you were away."

He opens his pantry, then the fridge. "Sit." And then he takes out a box of pasta, and milk and cheese from the fridge.

"Oh, don't… I mean, I can make popcorn now that you're up." I join him in the kitchen, sliding around him to grab a pouch of microwave popcorn, but just as I have it in my grasp, two hands grip my waist and turn me back toward the living room, leaving me no choice but to walk that way.

"Popcorn isn't enough. I'll make you a meal. You barely ate your dinner."

"I ate."

He doesn't bother fighting with me. Instead, he pulls a pot out and fills it with water. "Just say thank you and sit on a stool and keep me company."

I slide up on the stool and watch him take a grater out to shred the cheese. "You should really cook with a shirt on."

He peeks up at me, giving me a look that says *really*, then concentrates back on the task at hand. "You do know you're breaking the rules too, right?"

I glance down at myself. "I'm wearing a T-shirt and shorts."

"The shorts are short."

"That's sort of the definition of shorts."

"And your shirt rises when you lift your arms." He doesn't look at me when he says this.

"Observant."

He stops shredding the cheese and glances at me again. "Hard not to be."

My libido flares to life like a struck match. I know this is a very, very bad thing, but I also can't help but love that he notices me like I do him.

"Okay, I'll give you a reprieve on the clothes thing since you're making me food. Can I sit on the counter though?"

He chuckles and pats the spot next to the stovetop.

I slip off the stool and round the breakfast bar, hopping up on the counter as he puts the pasta in the water. "So, whatcha making me?"

"Don't get too excited. It's just something I learned on the fly when I was younger." He puts butter in a pan with minced garlic and a few other seasonings. The buttery-garlic smell curls around us, and my mouth waters.

"Where did you learn this?" I ask.

"I made it up myself."

I see we're not going to get far in our conversation unless I push. This is the perfect moment for us to discover more about one another. "Hey, did Hayes tell you about our one-for-one game?"

He peeks up at me from the corner of his eye. "I don't generally ask questions that are designed to torture me."

I push at his leg with my foot, and he doesn't budge, continuing to stir the butter in the pan. "You're the one who said we should be friends and get to know one another."

He groans. "Fine… what is one for one?"

We're about as closed off to our true feelings as two people can get, so I'm not sure if this is a good idea or not, but here we go…

CHAPTER
TWENTY-FOUR

Callie

I straighten and clap my hands, although I probably won't be as excited when I'm the one having to divulge something—like why I could barely eat any dinner. I'm not even sure if he noticed how quiet I've been since holding Breelyn.

"Okay, one for one is where I ask you a question, and then you ask me one, and you *have* to tell the truth."

He drops the spoon next to the pan and pulls some flour out of the cabinet. "Isn't that just called having a conversation?"

I move my head right and left. "No. It's different."

"If you say so." He measures nothing, putting a few spoonfuls in the pan. "Since it's your game, I get to go first?"

"Since you're new to the game, sure. I won't make you lose at rock, paper, scissors—again…"

He shoots me an amused smile, and my stomach flips.

"Ask me whatever you want to know." I shift to get more comfortable on the counter.

He stirs and stirs, both of our eyes on the mixture he's conjuring in the pan.

"If you can't think of anything, I'm happy to—"

Foster eyes me. "I'm sure you'd like that."

"Immensely. I already have my question."

He chuckles. "Sorry to disappoint you." He puts in the milk, stirs, and moves over to the pasta, using a different spoon to stir the noodles, then stays there so my knee is touching his hip.

I'm trying to process being so close to him. It's really nice, but it also feels as if I'm leaning over a ledge, and one wrong move and I'll fall.

"Why are you up right now—other than the fact that you're hungry?"

"You don't beat around the bush, huh? I'll have to warn Hayes if he ever plays with you."

"You don't have to—"

I put my hand over his mouth. "Yes, I do. That's the whole point of the game. So be prepared, Foster Davis, because I'm hitting you just as hard."

He nibbles on my palm like what I imagine a rabbit feels like, and I retract my hand. He laughs, and for a second, his armor slips, and he's all warmth and soft edges. It happens more often now, but it still knocks me sideways.

"Holding Breelyn… I'm worried…" I pause, hoping he'll fill in the blanks, but he doesn't, so I continue. "I like to think I'm good with kids. Monroe, Lincoln, and Lake… but they're older. They can tell me what they need, and I can do something about it. But a baby? Babies don't give you instructions. What if I don't have that motherly instinct? What if I'm not a good mom when it counts—like in the beginning? Maybe I'll crush the toddler years, but the infant part? It scares me. Holding Breelyn felt like I had an eighteenth-century vase in my arms, and one wrong move and…"

My hands go to my stomach, and I stare down at them. There's no turning back now.

"Not to diminish what you're feeling, but I do think it's natural to feel that way. Especially for people who have never really been around babies." He picks up the spoon and steps away, and I hate how quickly I miss the heat of him beside me. "But Callie, the baby is going to be yours—"

"Ours."

A smile tugs at his mouth. "Ours, so you'll automatically feel more comfortable, and you're not a quitter. Being comfortable will come in time. I honestly think you'll be fine."

He tosses the parmesan cheese into the pan, stirring before grabbing the hot pads and picking up the pot of boiling water and noodles.

I watch the muscles in his back tense and shift as he dumps the pasta into the colander and turns on the water. "The trick is to cool the pasta immediately."

I can't stop admiring him when he can't see me. It's as if my eyes have a mind of their own. His dark blond hair is mussed from sleep, all rumpled and unfurled. Tattoos spill over his skin as though he's covered his scars in ink. The shape of him is all sharp edges and strength. His classic V torso, the narrow waist disappearing into his sweatpants, the waistband of his boxer briefs taunting me just above them. He's taller than any man I've dated, broader too, built like he could pick me up with one hand, and it would be nothing.

Foster turns before I can look away, and I don't have time to hide the way I'm looking at him. He freezes with the colander suspended midair, his gaze colliding with mine. The desire between us narrows into something sharp and tight.

He clears his throat, jaw flexing, as though he's fighting the pull between us as much as I am. I drop my gaze, drag a breath into my lungs, and grip the edge of the counter until my fingers ache.

I don't remember the last time I wanted a man as badly as I do him.

"This whole not sleeping with people thing getting to you?" He pours the noodles into the pan. For someone who hates talking about himself, he sure is eager to address the elephant in the room.

"I'm perfectly fine. Believe me, you'll break that rule before me. Just like the clothing rule."

He laughs and shakes his head. "I won't." He sounds so sure.

I figure we need a distraction because this line of conversation is not a road we need to venture down. "Time for my question. What are you most afraid of?"

"In regard to the baby?" He coats the pasta with the cheese mixture. His noodle dish is one of those you'd crave during a snowstorm, tucked under blankets and binge-watching a series.

"Yes." I chuckle.

He shrugs. "Just wanted to make sure I'm not giving more information than necessary."

I roll my eyes. "I'm sure this is killing you."

He pulls down a bowl and scoops some of the noodles and sauce into it, then sprinkles some parmesan on top. "Well… I'm scared… of becoming my father."

I resist the urge to jump off the counter and hug him because I know any show of sympathy would stop him from telling me whatever he's about to.

"His fatherly instincts never kicked in, and if mine don't either, I'm stuck with one example of fatherhood and…" He never looks up as he walks over.

I hold out my hands, ready for the bowl, but he stops in front of my knees and taps the drawer handle with two fingers. When I open my legs, he slides the drawer out, jaw tight like it was a second ago, grabs a fork, and shuts it again. Before I can close my legs, he steps between them.

He never hands me the bowl. Instead, he twirls the noodles, sauce dripping, and holds the fork out to me.

Our eyes catch, but this time, they don't let go. "And being like my father isn't an option for me."

I open my mouth, and he feeds me the noodles. As my lips close around the fork and he slides it out, I want to ditch the bowl and drag him in by the waistband. But the flavor hits—rich, garlicky, stupidly good—and I make a sound I can't swallow fast enough.

He sets the bowl beside my hip as if nothing happened and goes back to his water, the picture of calm confidence. It's as though he doesn't realize he's thrown gasoline on the match that was already lit.

"Oh my god, this is so good. How?" I mumble around my food, needing the intimacy in the room to dissipate quickly.

He busies himself getting a bowl for himself, not answering me right away. I almost fill the space with another compliment, but then his gaze meets mine.

"Turns out, even teenagers get sick of fast food when it's every damn day, so I started looking up recipes and winging it. I first made it with those little parmesan packets from the pizza places. I lived with my dad, and he worked a lot. If he wasn't working, he was with me at baseball. Eventually I took the money I'd blow on drive-thrus and went to the grocery store instead. So… there you go. Your first fun Foster fact."

"Well, thank you. I have a feeling our little one is going to grow up begging you to make this dish for them."

A hint of a smile lifts his lips, and he hops up on the counter opposite me. "I hope so."

"I know so."

"Same goes with you. We're gonna make this work, Callie."

My first instinct is to make a joke. To deflect and keep everything light. But the way he sounds so sure and confident… it's odd, but I believe him.

Regardless, it's still scary as hell.

CHAPTER
TWENTY-FIVE

Foster

I'm never going to get used to being in this doctor's office.

As Callie checks in, I look around the waiting room, seeing the spots by the plant where we sat last month are taken. So I search the room for anywhere else that might be more protected from all the other waiting patients.

Nothing.

The receptionist tells Callie the amount of the co-pay, and I hand her my credit card. As expected, Callie huffs. I'm not sure why she thinks I'm not going to pay. Would she prefer me to be like, *That's a you problem*?

I leave the area to go claim a seat and let Callie finish up with the receptionist.

Last night's one-for-one game in the kitchen left me feeling vulnerable. I lay in bed most of the night rethinking whether I should've told her anything. Wondering if I should keep the past where it belongs, in the past, as I always have.

But I was the one who put this whole living together thing into action. And maybe she needs to know my demons so she can protect our kid from having any.

"They said the doctor is in labor." She cringes and takes a seat beside me.

"The doctor was pregnant?" I frown.

Callie laughs. "No, she's delivering someone's baby, so she's running late."

The guy a few seats down on my right nods at me. Recognition. Fuck. I didn't even wear my baseball cap because I swear people are less likely to recognize me without it, since they usually see me wearing a baseball cap. But it's left me with nothing I can tip down to conceal my face a bit.

We're as far away from other people as we can be, but we're out in the open, so I pick up a magazine and hold it in front of me.

This extra time in the waiting room is just more time for someone to put a face to my name and snap a picture.

Callie glances over with an expression that says, *What the fuck are you doing?* But then she goes back to putting her receipt in her purse. She pulls out her phone and faces away from me, leaning one arm on the opposite armrest.

"Hey," I whisper.

She peeks at me from the corner of her eye, then leans over.

Fuck, now her scent is in my orbit again, and I have to control the urge to drag her onto my lap and kiss her.

"We need to tell Hayes." I know we already agreed to after this appointment, but for some reason, the fear that he'll find out from someone other than us washes over me.

She pats my arm. "We said after this appointment. We'll be at the end of the first trimester. I was thinking we could tell him after tomorrow's game."

I'm in the rotation tomorrow, and I was already thinking

that it wouldn't be a good idea to go over to Hayes's house tonight and tell him. Jagger said some bigwigs from the sports drink company who are looking at me for an endorsement will be there tomorrow, and I really need to have everything on my side. Meaning as selfish as it is, I need my best friend Hayes behind the plate, not hates-my-guts Hayes.

I nod in agreement.

She glances at the magazine and chuckles.

I give her a questioning look, wondering what's so funny.

She points at the magazine article and raises her eyebrows. "Trying to figure out what category you're in?"

I read the headline of the article the magazine is open to.

The Pleasure Gap Isn't in Your Head

I continue reading because I don't want to show my face anyway.

In over 566 straight-couple sexual encounters polled, men orgasmed in about 90%, while women only orgasmed in about 54% of encounters. That's basically a coin flip.

Heads or tails if you have an orgasm? That can't be right. And men are only at ninety percent? I've had an orgasm every single time I've had sex.

"Hey, Callie," I whisper and nudge her with my elbow.

Her head is buried in her phone, and she gives me a quick look, but I'm clearly annoying her from the way her lips thin. I nod for her to come closer.

"You're pretty needy this visit." But she gets closer, so I move the magazine so it's in front of both of us.

"Read this."

She scans the article and shrugs. "And?"

"That can't be right. Just over fifty percent? That has to be wrong."

Her eyebrows crinkle and a smile teases her lips. "Sounds right to me."

I scowl at her. "No fucking way."

Her face grows serious, and she nods. "Depends how much time we have, how much foreplay there is, and honestly whether I feel like putting the effort in to get there. Whether toys are involved. There are lots of factors for us women. Do I have a lot going on in my life at that moment, and I'm all up in my head…" She studies me then draws back, realization dawning. "Oh. Your ego a little bruised? You thought you rocked every woman's world, did you?"

I scoff. "Well, everyone I've been with has come." I can't help the way I puff my chest out a little.

She arches an eyebrow. "You sure about that?"

I rack my brain. Yeah, I'm sure. They scream, they tense, their pussy clenches around my dick before all that pressure releases. "Yeah."

A look crosses her face. One that suggests I'm very wrong. "You did, right?"

She bites her lip as if she's trying to remember.

How can she not remember? I mean, it's a little fuzzy because we'd been drinking, but the ending I remember pretty damn well.

"Yeah, sure." She shrugs.

"Not very convincing."

Her shoulders deflate, and she scans the room. "I don't think this is the place to talk about it."

The magazine drops from my hands and falls to my lap, and I turn to her. "You've got to be kidding me."

Her gaze shifts to look around the room again, and I scramble to pick up the magazine, opening it and placing it in front of us.

"This isn't hiding anything. If anything, we're being more obvious."

"I don't give a shit," I bite out. "Did you really not finish?"

"Callie?" the nurse calls.

"Here!" She springs out of the seat, and I follow her, bringing the magazine with me.

The fucking guy nods at me again, and I nod back, hoping to appease him so he doesn't try to get a picture and put something on the internet about me being in an OBGYN office.

I'm going to have Callie alone for a few minutes before the doctor comes in. I need answers.

CHAPTER
TWENTY-SIX

Foster

The nurse glances at the magazine in my hand. "Dr. Amato is almost done, but we're going to get you guys into a room, so you're all set when she gets here."

"Perfect." Callie hands me her purse as she steps on the scale in the hallway.

My mind is swimming. I'd really like to get Callie alone right now. Actually, I want to seduce her just so I can prove to her that I *can* give a woman an orgasm. She's the anomaly, not the norm when it comes to women having orgasms with me. Or maybe she's confusing me with someone else. She had an orgasm. I'm positive.

The nurse brings us into an exam room, and she and Callie talk about how nice the weather is outside and how nothing beats spring in Chicago, except for maybe Christmas. I grunt along with the conversation, and Callie keeps shooting me looks like *get your shit together*.

Finally, the nurse leaves us with one of those damn paper sheet things for Callie to put on.

"Time to turn around." Callie hops off the table.

I do as she says. "You're joking, right? Trying to get into my head or some shit?"

She huffs. "Are we still on the article thing?"

I start to turn around but then remember she's partially naked. "Yes, we're still on the whole 'you didn't orgasm when we fucked' thing."

"That sounds crude. You know, because we have the baby coming."

I roll my eyes even though she can't see me. "Callie, we had sex in a nightclub bathroom. We fucked."

"I'm just saying, I don't want our kid to know that."

"I'm not going to tell…" I shake my head. "Did you really not?" I sound like a desperate man with the begging note in my voice.

"Oh, you sound upset. You can turn around now."

I do, and all the thoughts leave my head at seeing that damn paper sheet over her lap—and instead of having placed her clothes on the chair next to me, she holds them out for me.

"Put these on the chair for me, please?"

I take them and place them on the chair. "Tell me."

Her body wiggles around as if she's turning to jelly. "I don't want to get into it. It doesn't matter."

"Yes, it does," I bite out.

"It's not a big deal. You're not the only man I didn't finish with. There have been plenty… I mean, not plenty of guys. That's an exagger—"

"I don't care how many people you've slept with, Callie. What I do care about is that I gave you a fucking orgasm."

Her head rears back. "Fine. No." She's so matter-of-fact. As if it's not a big deal.

"Fuck." I pull at the back of my neck with my hand, cringing.

It's like I used her to get off. Is that what she thought this entire time? I got off, and she didn't, and if that doesn't mean I'm a selfish bastard, I don't know what does. It makes me no better than my dad…

"In all fairness, we were rushed."

Most times I've had sex with a woman, it's been rushed. I'm not the kind of guy who takes his time… oh shit. I grab the magazine to keep reading, and sure enough, there's another statistic that stabs me right in the fucking dick.

81% of women orgasm when they masturbate.

There it is in black and white for all the men who don't make their women come. They don't need us.

"You're really freaking out about this, Foster. But I mean, you were in it for yourself. That's fine."

There goes the selfish bastard bell ringing again.

I say her name in a calm tone that I don't feel in any fiber of my body right now. "It is not *fine* that I didn't give you an orgasm."

Is this what she's grown used to? Disappointment by man after man? Is this why she puts those walls up around herself? It's gone so far that during sex, she doesn't even expect to have an orgasm?

She rolls her eyes. "You're being very alpha male right now, like I'm ruining your reputation or something. I'll tell you what. It's our little secret. I'm not gonna tell anyone, but…"

I inhale a deep breath. "What?"

"It's just… I'm probably not the only one." She shrugs.

My mouth falls open as the air is sucked from my lungs. It feels as if someone just punched me in the nuts. "So, you think there's like a *Foster Davis sucks at sex* thread somewhere, and all the women I've slept with comment about how shitty of a partner I am?"

She laughs. "Someone sure thinks a lot of himself." She shifts, and the wrinkling of the sheet echoes through the empty room. "There isn't a thread somewhere. I mean, I never went looking for one."

I stand in front of her, so she has no option but to look me in the eye. "So it was shit. Like you were waiting for it to be over?"

She shakes her head, and damn that smile for being so cute when I'm fuming at myself and can't really appreciate it. "Okay, calm down." Her smile fades as though she can read my mind. "We were really hot, right? Like, we went from arguing to me being pressed against the wall. And it was really, really hot. But then when we got to the bathroom…"

I lower my head and pinch the bridge of my nose, exhaling.

"You're a good kisser," she says as though she's trying to let me down easy. "And I'm sure with more time… You were rushed."

I squeeze my eyes shut. "You have no idea how much I want to lie you down on this bed and make you come right now."

"Well, that's not gonna happen."

"I owe you an orgasm."

She laughs, and it's so loud there's no way the people outside the room don't hear it. "No, you don't."

I lean into her, placing my hands on either side of her hips, the thin sheet crinkling beneath my palms. "Callie, you just shattered me."

"I'm sorry." She looks genuinely upset. Her hands come to my cheeks. "It's not that big of a deal."

"Please stop saying that."

Her head tilts, and we stare at one another. "Are you asking me for a chance to prove yourself? We're platonic, just friends. No complications, remember?"

I shake my head. "I can't find it in myself to care right now."

"You will after you have an orgasm."

"After *you* have an orgasm."

She laughs. "Okay, you need to go sit down. We'll talk about this after the doctor comes in."

There she goes erecting that wall again. After last night, we both know we're hanging on by a frayed thread already.

"One night. No strings. One repeat."

Her eyes widen, and she inhales. But she doesn't say no. "Foster…" Even her tone doesn't suggest no.

"You say the word."

"All so you can prove yourself?"

"Yes."

I can't even lie. It's not just about proving I can make her come. I want to show her that not every man is a selfish bastard who's going to disappoint her. That she's worth the time and attention.

"I—"

A knock sounds, and the door opens. "So sorry, guys," Dr. Amato steps in then comes to a stop. "Oh, do you want me to—"

"No, we're just talking." Callie lightly pushes against my chest.

I straighten and go take a seat. She'll probably never take me up on my offer, and I'm not even sure why I give a shit, but the thought of her always thinking I'm mediocre at sex just doesn't sit right.

I've made a lot worse mistakes in my life than sleeping with Callie Carlisle one more time.

CHAPTER
TWENTY-SEVEN

Callie

I lie in bed, my hand on my stomach, feeling relieved since the declaration from Dr. Amato that this pregnancy is moving forward. Not that I thought there were any issues, but late one night while Foster was away, I read a little too deep into some Reddit groups that suggested not to get your hopes up yet—a lot happens before that twelfth week.

Now that I feel more at ease with the pregnancy, Foster's obsession about me not having an orgasm and offering a do-over to prove himself is at the forefront of my mind.

It's ludicrous. I mean, we're doing something admirable here. We're being responsible adults for our unborn child. We cannot sleep together, but the truth is... I really wouldn't mind saying fuck being an adult and being a little reckless instead.

I've been so thankful for the kind of pregnancy I'm having so far. The little nausea I felt has subsided, and ever since Foster made me dinner, I've wondered what it would be like to be on my knees in front of him, my hands hooked on either side of his hips, drawing those gray sweatpants down as I watched his eyes turn feral. For me. To take a man like him to the brink of losing control would be like having a gold star pinned to my chest.

My grave would read, Callie Carlisle—daughter, sister, mother—the woman who made Foster Davis crack his quartz countertop when she went down on him.

Ugh.

I roll over and try to get comfortable again, but all I can think about is Foster taking his time with me, doubling down and making sure I have more than one orgasm. It's hard not to imagine what he could do with those large hands and long fingers. What it might feel like if he—

An alarm blares in the condo, and I bolt up, looking around as if someone is in my room.

Is someone trying to break into the condo building?

I throw off the covers and tiptoe across the floor so I don't alert anyone I'm in here. I'm not trying to be a jerk, but go pick the six-foot-three tattooed baseball player. I'm busy growing a human here.

My door creaks opens and a dim light floods in. I scramble to find anything to hit the person with, but I've got nothing, so I grab a pillow and cover my stomach.

Foster peeks his head in. "Stay in your room and lock the door." He slams my bedroom door shut.

"Wait!" I call and follow.

Foster is shirtless with a pair of athletic pants on, slipping into his slides by the door. "Do you ever listen?"

I ignore his ornery behavior. "What's going on?"

"It's the downstairs alarm. Someone must've tried to get in past the gate."

I rush to my bedroom, grab my sweatshirt from the chair, and go out to the main area, feeling safer in the condo now that I know the possibility of them being in here is slim.

"I told you stay in your room."

"I feel safer with you than being here by myself." I slide into my shoes by the door, hopping in place to get the backs on. I usually wear Foster's slides when I go get the mail and stuff.

He stops and stares, his delicious abs on display. I wait for him to argue with me so I can argue back. I am not staying here by myself.

"Fine. But you're not going past the security gate."

I salute him. "Yes, sir."

He grunts and opens his door, looking right and left before he signals for me to follow as if we're a pair of Navy SEALs on a mission.

The alarm is even louder outside the condo.

Easton and Decker are already at the bottom of the stairs, and Easton is pressing in a code, but the alarm isn't shutting off. I toss my hoodie over my head and cover my ears as we walk down the stairs to join them.

"Fuck, do you not remember it?" Decker asks loudly enough that he can be heard over the screeching alarm.

"Why would I remember the code to the alarm?" Easton presses some numbers again, but it doesn't turn off.

"Because it's gone off twice in the past month." Decker glares at Foster.

I turn to Foster with a questioning look because I haven't heard it go off. And why would Foster be to blame anyway?

Decker finally presses in the correct code and the blaring stops.

Easton's phone rings, and he walks off to the side. "Hey, Coop—yeah, Decker got it to turn off, but I'm not sure if there's a malfunction or what…" He listens, nods in understanding at whatever is being said.

"When did it go off before?" I ask Foster.

His eyes are on Easton, but he answers. "During the day.

You were gone both times. Ruby told us about it, and she called Cooper."

Decker's gaze drops to my sweatshirt, then flicks to Foster.

"Don't ask," Foster grumbles.

"What?" My head volleys back and forth between them.

"You live with a Colts player," Foster says matter-of-factly.

"Your neighbors are Colts players," Decker adds.

"Your brother is a Colt," Easton says. I guess he's done talking on the phone. "But Cooper will be happy when he sees you."

"Cooper's coming?" Decker asks.

"Yeah, security company called him, and cops are coming this time, so Cooper has to sign the paperwork."

"Cooper who?" I glance between them all, and their attention snaps to my sweatshirt at the same time. My confusion spikes.

"Cooper Rice. Grizzlies quarterback," Foster clarifies.

"Ohhh… I vaguely remember Hayes saying something about him owning the building."

Decker rolls his eyes.

I sit on the cement stairs and pull the sweatshirt over my legs. "It's comfortable, okay? And someone left it behind, I guess. I still love you guys the mostest though." I bat my eyelashes.

They all take turns glancing at one another then shake their heads.

"So who's going to go outside the gate and see if someone really is trying to break in?" I raise my eyebrows.

They all stare at me as if I've officially lost my last brain cell.

"None of us." Foster leans on the wall closest to me, crossing his ankles.

"Are you scared?" I ask.

"Fuck no." Easton scowls.

"Definitely not." Decker shakes his head.

Foster doesn't even bother to respond.

"Oh, I figured you'd all be fighting to be the one to find the guy trying to get in."

"Or girl," Foster says, and when I turn to him, he's looking at Decker. "I know you think these two are all innocent, Callie, but they—"

"We have a game tomorrow," Decker says. "And the women I see don't try to break in. That seems more your style."

Foster scoffs. "Yeah, I'm always the problem, right, Deck?"

"Okay, you two. We're a united front. I'll go out, and you guys better have my back." Easton walks toward the gate. He's only wearing basketball shorts, and I'm pretty sure no underwear. If it is a woman, she'll be drooling.

I jump off the stairs. "I'll be your wingwoman."

Someone pulls my sweatshirt hood and yanks me back. I land against a hard chest.

"No, you won't." Foster's voice is gruff and sexy as hell in my ear.

"Well, you guys aren't doing anything. You're kind of earning your reputation right now."

Easton turns around, crossing his arms. "What's that mean?"

I shrug. "Just that, you know... hockey and football players are rough and tough. Baseball players are... well... not."

Foster comes around in front of me, and all three of them stand side by side, staring me down. Easton's arms are crossed, Foster's hands are on his hips, and Decker's palming the back of his neck.

"I didn't mean to offend you guys. It was an offhand remark. I'm just saying, I think Miles Cavanagh would've been through that gate already."

Easton and Decker both turn to look at Foster.

"What?" His jaw flexes.

"This is your fault. She lives with you, and she's wearing his sweatshirt, and now she's saying he's tougher than us." Easton throws up his hands.

Foster blows out a breath and heads to the gate. Easton and Decker follow.

I smirk to myself. It really is too easy to bruise their egos and convince them to do something.

Foster pushes the gate open and walks right out, not even looking in either direction. "Just as I thought—no one. Except the fucking neighbors." He spins back around and the gate slams closed behind him. "And now a picture of me without a shirt on will be on the internet in about ten seconds."

"It was a nice thing you did. You made a lot of women happy just now." Somehow, I manage not to burst out into laughter.

His chest rises and falls, and I shrug with an expression to say sorry.

"Are you satisfied, Mrs. Cavanagh?"

Foster grunts in response to Easton's question.

"There already is a Mrs. Cavanagh, and I think she could kick my ass, so cool it."

The police show up shortly after, then Cooper Rice does as well. Holy hell, the man is drop-dead gorgeous. I can see why he gets all the endorsement deals even after retirement.

We all talk on this side of the gate, away from prying eyes, after everything has been settled with the cops.

"I'm going to go back to my wife who just got home from work. I'd like to discuss this further with you all though. I've never had this happen in all the years I've been renting this building out. So rack your brains for some names of people, and we'll meet up to chat about it." His gaze falls to my sweatshirt, and his head tilts. "And you are?"

"Oh, this is Callie Carlisle," Easton says. "Hayes Carlisle's little sister."

Cooper points at Foster. "I thought you took over his place?"

"I did." Foster doesn't offer any more information.

"It's just temporary. I'm staying here until, um…" I don't really know how to finish that sentence.

Cooper raises his hands. "None of my business. But I'm curious as to how you're wearing Miles's favorite sweatshirt."

I bite my lip. "Uh… I found it in the closet."

He blows out a breath. "He's bitched about that sweatshirt for years. We each got blamed for taking it."

"She should give it back, right, Coop?" Easton nods at Cooper like *say yes*.

"Ah, I don't think so. It's kind of funny that I can razz him about it."

"No, I definitely think his wife wouldn't like another woman wearing it." Decker gives Cooper a look.

"And you?" Cooper nods at Foster. "You want her to give it back?"

"I hate the thing, but it's not coming off right now."

"Excuse me." I look around at all four ballplayers. "You little egomaniacs. I don't belong to any of you." I shed the sweatshirt, leaving me in a T-shirt and boxer shorts that admittedly don't cover a lot.

"Jesus, Callie." Foster grabs the sweatshirt out of my hands and tosses it to Cooper. "There. We're going back up to bed." He grabs my hand and leads me up the stairs.

"This is pretty caveman of you, Reap." Easton's laugh follows his words.

"It's a turn-off, I'm sure," Decker shouts.

"My wife would kick all of your asses. You're a bunch of cocky assholes who haven't learned how to act around a woman," Cooper says as we move out of view.

When we reach our floor, Foster jams his finger on the keypad until his door opens.

Once we're ensconced inside, I whirl around. "You cannot act like I'm your property."

"Have you seen your shirt?" He motions to my chest area.

I look down and see it's white and yeah, okay… a bit see-through. Not my finest moment, but still, I can wear what I want. I cross my arms and jut out my hip, staring him down.

"I'm not apologizing." He slips off his slides.

"If you don't, you're gonna wake up to a cold bucket of water over your head."

He grabs his dick through his gray sweatpants. "Would you like it if I was down there with three other women, and you could see the outline of my dick?"

I'd probably have stood in front of him the entire time, blocking their view. But that's beside the point.

"Is that supposed to make me jealous?" I wave my finger between us. "We're not together."

He scowls at me. "Jesus, Callie, don't act like that."

"Like what? I'm not yours, and you aren't mine."

He stalks toward me, and I step back on instinct. My spine hits the wall. He plants his hands on either side of my head, boxing me in, and leans in so close that his warm breath skates over my lips.

"I'm about to sound like an asshole," he warns, as if that's anything new, "and I'm not going to apologize for it." His gaze is wild, and I wait with bated breath for whatever he's going to say next. "You're mine."

My pulse stutters. I tip my head, drowning in those baby blues, and his shoulders sag with a breath he's been holding back. He looks wrecked, not possessive, as if he hates how much he wants this, and I arch my back in offering because God, that second chance sounds so dangerously good right now.

Then his gaze drops to my stomach, and the heat in his face shifts to something else, something like panic. "At least until that baby comes."

I guess it's me getting the cold bucket of water.

CHAPTER
TWENTY-EIGHT

Foster

Too bad time machines don't exist, because I really wish I could go back to when I bribed Callie to live with me and take it the fuck back.

The lines between us are blurry at best, and we're crossing them every second we're together.

I asked her for a second chance to sleep with her so I can give her an orgasm. What the hell?

I've made her my pasta recipe, and my caveman mentality last night—telling her she's mine? Jesus. I'm sure my attempt to save myself by saying it was only because of the baby was transparent as fuck.

But Easton or Decker seeing the outline of her tits just wasn't an option. Not that I'm excusing my behavior. I already know she deserves a helluva lot better than me.

And now we need to be a united front after the game when we tell Hayes that I knocked up his sister. What has happened to me? I left Seattle to uncomplicate my life and now it's more of a dumpster fire than ever.

As I stand to get ready to leave the dugout after the game, my throat closes up because it's finally time to tell Hayes. Callie gave me a small nod after the last out when I came off the mound.

This is when shit gets real, and if I'm lucky, Hayes will be so pissed it'll burn every damn desire I have for his sister right out of me.

"You're really in your head." Drew comes alongside me. "You looked sick. Good thing I got us that run in the eighth. Let you breathe a little until you fucked up the ninth. That old arm hurting you?"

I whip around, fist his jersey, and slam him against the wall.

"Whoa, whoa, whoa!" a few teammates shout behind me.

Easton and Hayes intervene right away. Hayes puts his hands on our chests, and Easton drags Drew away.

"You just don't know when to shut the fuck up, do you?" Easton tells Drew. "And learn what being a good teammate actually is, asshole." He pushes Drew out of the dugout and toward the locker room.

I go to follow, but Hayes stops me. "Hey, man, what's going on? You've been moodier than usual today. I know you had a shit sleep with the alarm and everything, but is there something more?"

It wasn't the alarm keeping me up—it was the thought of his sister half naked in the next room.

"I'm fine. He just needs someone to beat the shit out of him, so he learns his lesson."

Razzing is normal. Ribbing is normal. Drew was taking aim at my motherfucking wounds, and I want him off the team.

"Really, man, I'm fine." I shrug off Hayes's hands.

He pins me with that look as if he can pry my thoughts out of me.

Not happening. I'm terrified of what he's going to do, so I keep dragging it out—waiting until the last possible moment until we get here. Like a punk.

"Okay. Okay." He retreats a step, both hands up.

I walk ahead of him. When we hit the locker room, I shoot Drew a look that says fuck off, and Hayes drops into the chair at the locker beside mine.

"I know I've been so busy with Leighton and the kids. But you know if you need to talk, I'm here. I'll find the time— even if you're doing pickup with me."

"I know." I yank off my jersey and unfasten my pants.

"Thanks again for having my sister. I'm sure that's not helping your mood. She hasn't found anything yet, huh?"

"No," I say a beat too quickly.

"I heard about Maren Hale. That's amazing. Who else do you have lined up?"

I sit on the seat, more mentally wrecked than physically tired. "I'm working on some people."

I have two other people already lined up, but I still need two more.

"I'm not sure who was more excited about Maren Hale— Leighton or Callie. You started big, man." He works the straps on his chest protector.

"Don't doubt my skills." I toss him a grin, trying to play it off, but it's forced and I'm sure he sees it. "I'm gonna go shower." I pat his shoulder and don't wait for an answer before heading to the showers.

"Don't forget we're going to Peeper's after," he calls.

I want to correct him that actually the plan entails that as soon as we get outside, we're going to let everyone else go in, then Callie and I will take Hayes and Leighton upstairs to our condo and tell them the news. Then I'm gonna pray he doesn't get blood on my new sofa that Callie's fallen in love with.

"Yeah, man. I remember." I lift my hand in a wave even though he probably can't see me.

I shower, get dressed, and stay away from Hayes because I'm so close to the moment, I'm about to crack. I want the secret out. I want it over with. I don't know how I've kept it in as long as I have, but every time he looks at me like *you okay?* I want to tell him. *I fucked your sister, and she's pregnant. Hey, we're tied together forever now, buddy. Lucky you.*

"Let's go, media room, guys," Wentzel points at Easton, Decker, Hayes, and me.

Just another fucking delay.

CHAPTER
TWENTY-NINE

Foster

Wentzel ushers us into the press room, and I step up on the platform and head to the far end of the table. Decker follows, which I'd normally be pissed about, but I'd rather have him next to me than Hayes at the moment.

Once we're all seated, Hayes takes charge as usual, pointing at one of the reporters.

"Foster, today didn't feel like a normal loss."

"Is there a question there?" I ask the reporter, and Decker hits his thigh against mine.

"Is something going on in the clubhouse?" the reporter asks and sits.

I lean forward on the table, hands linked. "Nothing happening in the clubhouse. I didn't execute. Fell behind in the count, missed spots. Those mistakes led to hits and a run. Sometimes two."

"Next." Hayes points at another reporter.

"Hayes, do you feel like the team's connecting right now?"

"Me?" He laughs. I hope to be him one day—not taking each and every loss so personally. "Yeah, I think we are." He glances down the line of us and back at the reporter. "It's not just one pitch. It's the stack of stuff that's been building. Breakdowns, loss of communication. We're connected. We're just not always communicating like it."

Another reporter stands, and I blow out a breath, wanting this to be the fuck over. "Foster, there were cameras on the dugout all night. You looked… angry from the start. Not locked in."

"I am angry. We were losing and ultimately lost. If that reads as 'something going on,' something's going on. We're not winning the games we should be winning."

"But don't confuse emotion with fracture. We all care, and sometimes that noise is loud," Decker says.

"We're not broken. We're frustrated," Hayes adds. "Next."

"Hayes, you went to the mound in the ninth, and it looked like an argument. Foster didn't even look at you when you walked away. You two are usually in sync."

Hayes straightens to answer without a glance to me, but I quickly interject. "I'll take this one. Hayes is doing his job. He's trying to slow the moment down. I'm trying to speed it up. That's the push-pull between a catcher and a closer. I'm sure it looked bad—"

"But we're best friends. And we've worked together a long time. He's the one out there doing most of the work. We have each other's backs."

Fucking hell, Carlisle. Don't say that shit right now.

The same reporter stands, and I wish he'd leave well enough alone. "Are you two okay?"

Hayes laughs. "Well, he'd rather chew glass than admit he needs a breather."

The room laughs, and it breaks the tension, but I shake my head.

Hayes points at another reporter, who says, "This is for Foster. At the end of the game, you pushed Drew Triggs against the dugout wall. Was it just teammates messing around, or was it serious?"

A camera clicks as my jaw tics.

I take a cleansing breath before I answer. "What, no one wants to talk to Decker or Easton?" A few laughs trickle through the gaggle of reports, but I only buy myself a few seconds. "Drew and I had words. I put my hands on him. That's not okay. Period. It doesn't matter what was said, it doesn't matter how heated it got—I was in the wrong."

Another reporter stands. "That's a first. You admitting you were wrong. Did you apologize to Triggs too?"

Who is this fool? Drew's dad?

I flash a smile that likely makes me look like an asshole. "Not yet. I thought he'd be in this room with me. But I guess I'm the lucky one."

Easton tugs the mic in front of him. "We all have egos, and sometimes we cross lines. It goes both ways. And I can assure you if Foster felt the need to put Drew in his place, there was a reason for it."

I stare down the line, and my shoulders lose the tension that's been locked there all day. Shit, I've never had a player besides Hayes stick up for me. Easton nods at me.

"We'll handle that ourselves." Hayes points at a reporter who hasn't asked a question yet. "Next."

"When something like that happens, people wonder if the clubhouse has a leadership problem. Who's leading this team right now? You, Hayes?"

"It has nothing to do with leadership. We're a new team, and we have some rookies. We're working out kinks. And as to who is the leader, our manager, Ripley, is our leader."

Decker leans into the mic. "We're all adults. We know

when to be accountable. How about we focus on the game instead of searching for issues that don't exist?"

A reporter stands without Hayes calling on them. "There have been reports about a competition and cliques within the team."

"I assure you we're not in high school." Decker shakes his head.

"Every clubhouse has groups. Guys who are closer than others. But we're a very close-knit group," Hayes says.

I'm not sure I agree, at least in Drew's case.

Another reporter stands and stares at me before voicing a question.

"I guess I'm the man of the hour, huh?" I do my best to keep the irritation out of my voice.

Another quiet laugh rings through the room.

"Foster, you're known to be a high-intensity guy. Do you worry you're the cancer on this team?"

My jaw clenches. "Well, thanks for going for the jugular there. Good thing I'm thick-skinned."

"I assure you, he's not," Hayes interrupts.

"Definitely not," Easton adds.

Decker says nothing because he probably believes I am the problem when Drew is the one who's infecting this team.

I hold up my hand toward my teammates. They don't need to fight my battles. "If my intensity becomes a problem, then it's not intensity—it's immaturity. I'm not interested in being that guy. Not here. Not anymore."

"Last question," Hayes says.

The same woman who called out Hayes last year about Leighton stands up at the back, and my stomach drops. Her gaze falls to me, then Hayes, and back to me. The cunning smile says she's about to blow my secret wide open.

I rack my brain for what proof she might have. Who she could have heard it from. What picture got leaked. She always focuses more on players' personal lives than the game.

"So, Hayes, you and Foster are best friends."

Hayes looks down the line at me, nods, and flashes me an easy smile. "Yeah."

Bile rises up my throat. He trusts me and has no idea that I'm about to ruin our friendship.

"So then you must be pretty excited—or are you not, and that's why there was tension on the mound today?" She turns to me. "Is that why you seem so off, Foster? It's gotta be stressful, especially for someone with your reputation."

Hayes looks down the line at me again, frowning.

"Just spit out whatever bullshit you have," Easton says.

"Fuck, Kodiak," Decker mumbles.

"Hayes's sister, the podcaster Callie Carlisle from *If I'm Honest*?"

My fists lock under the table. Callie's about to be exposed, and it's all my fault. I can take the heat, but she shouldn't have to.

Hayes rocks his head back as though he understands what she's getting at. "Oh, yeah, she had some landlord problems, so she's staying with Foster temporarily. Someone catch a picture or something?"

"Temporarily?" The smile hasn't left her fucking face.

Easton and Decker glance at me, and my teeth grind together. I have no choice but to wait for her to pull the pin on the grenade.

"Yeah." Hayes looks so certain.

I wish I had some superhero power to freeze time for everyone but him and me. Anything to keep him from being blindsided in the middle of a press conference.

"Well that's interesting, because a picture was taken of your sister and Foster at an OBGYN office yesterday. Isn't she pregnant with your best friend's baby?"

Wentzel steps forward. "And we're done."

Boom.

CHAPTER
THIRTY

Callie

"Hey." Lake hands me her phone as we're waiting for the guys to finish up and come out of the clubhouse.

"What's up?" I take her phone, hoping this isn't some preteen drama and people are spreading lies about her.

I read the screen, and my stomach drops like a semi-truck off a cliff.

When you have the same OBGYN as Foster Davis's baby mama.

And there's a picture of us in the waiting room.

I scroll as my stomach does that slow, nauseating drop because my body knows before my brain catches up. I'm about to be skinned alive in public.

northside.nyla: She's not who I thought he'd be with. 🙂
🤍 *2,983 likes*

Of course I'm not. I'm not a swimsuit model with a ring light.

wavelandwatcher: same… I'm confused 😵
💜 *611 likes*

ivyandheat: y'all act like you know him personally 💀
💜 *1,204 likes*

They'll never know the Foster Davis I do.

dugoutdaydreams: He could do better. 😔
💜 *4,112 likes*

filthyfourteen: Like me. 🙈
💜 *3,401 likes*

southside_sanity: Get in line
💜 *2,887 likes*

Congrats on having zero self-respect and a keyboard.

bullpenbabe14: Cry… I wanted to have his baby. 😭 💔
💜 *5,620 likes*

Sorry my uterus is crushing your dream.

extra_innings_girl: leave her alone. She's cute. 🫶
💜 *8,944 likes*

Cute. That's… kind. In the way you call a stray cat cute
right before you give it away.

bullpenbabe14: "cute" is generous 🙄
💜 *1,908 likes*

*extra_innings_girl: I'm exhausted from women ripping other
women.*

 *6,102 likes*

Same. And yet here we are.

petalsandpages: Nothing says 'please don't leave me' like a due date.

6,770 likes

Right. Because I planned this. Because I woke up one morning and thought, *You know what would be fun? Being permanently tied to a man with a mountain of issues who doesn't believe in love.*

futuremrsdavis14: Bet it doesn't last the season.
7,038 likes

Cute name, but there will never be a Mrs. Davis unless they're married to Decker.

midwestmoxie: y'all WANT people miserable and it shows
3,944 likes

Bless you, Midwestmoxie.

hannahhits: She got her fairy tale *...and the bank account locked in for 18+ years.*
9,821 likes

There it is. The one I knew would come.

buttercream.bria: love is temporary, child support is forever
2,410 likes

This one touches a familiar nerve. I already know that romantic love is temporary where I'm concerned.

windycitywhispers: What's with her hair. 😳
🤍 *3,118 likes*

My hair? What's wrong with my hair?

privatebutpetty: bad extensions.
🤍 *1,204 likes*

They're not even—I stop myself. I don't owe this comment section an ounce of my attention, but I keep scrolling.

kendall.kays: Congratulations. 🙂
🤍 *1,102 likes*

kendall.kays: (no really… congrats)
🤍 *804 likes*

Sure. Congratulations on being publicly dissected.

madisonrae_: I hope he's happy, he's so angry all the time. ☹️
🤍 *4,650 likes*

You don't know him.

jordynkay_: y'all project so hard in these comments
🤍 *2,911 likes*

morgan_923: What will happen when they ask her if she feels safe at home? 😬
🤍 *5,480 likes*

My numb fingers gain life. If this was my account, I'd be giving Miss Morgan 923 a piece of my mind.

modestep: that's a wild accusation to toss out for likes.

💜 *6,203 likes*

Thank you, Modestep.

morgan_923: I said what I said 🐍
💜 *1,002 likes*

Because you're evil.

LUV_CoLts_2: He really will sleep with anything with a pulse. 💀
💜 *6,911 likes*

A caustic laugh tries to claw its way up my throat but dies halfway. Because they're not just calling *him* a slut. They're calling *me* disposable.

futuremrsdavis14: Must have been dark that night.
💜 *8,210 likes*

extra_innings_girl: yikes.
💜 *9,114 likes*

Yikes isn't the half of this thread. These women are so vicious, and they don't even know me.

WAGsearching: Love is temporary. Signing bonuses are forever 💰

💜 *10,338 likes*

I blink hard, but it doesn't stop the sting.

ivyandheat: y'all are obsessed with his money like it's yours
💜 *5,477 likes*

oliviaa_13: men like him don't settle—they rotate 😼

🤍 *7,601 likes*

southside_sanity: imagine rooting for cheating. embarrassing.
🤍 *6,890 likes*

Then the comments shift, and I hold my breath as I continue to read.

statcaststacy: WAITTTT… that's Callie CARLISLE?? As in… Hayes Carlisle's sister?? 😳⚾
🤍 *15,908 likes*

My heart slams against my ribs.

northside.nyla: OH. That's why she looks familiar. I've seen her in the family section pics 👀
🤍 *4,112 likes*

wavelandwatcher: no wonder Hayes and Foster were fighting today…
🤍 *2,701 likes*

ivyandheat: y'all turning this into a conspiracy board is insane 💀
🤍 *8,220 likes*

Finally. A sane person. Please multiply.

dugoutdetective: Clubhouse messy 😬
🤍 *9,044 likes*

extra_innings_girl: or… hear me out… adults date adults.
🤍 *12,670 likes*

bullpenbabe14: it's still weird. sorry.
🤍 *3,110 likes*

wagswatchdaily: I wish my brother was Hayes Carlisle.
🤍 *11,330 likes*

Sorry, the position is taken.

podcastgirlypop: Wait I LISTEN to her… she talks about her "older brother" sometimes. THAT'S HAYES??🎙️
🤍 *7,884 likes*

My skin prickles because now it's going to spill over to my work, my life.

micdropmedia: yes!! she's mentioned "my brother is a Colt" before!!
🤍 *5,009 likes*

BrewCrew_68513: I'm screaming. the lore just expanded.
🤍 *6,441 likes*

Lore. As if I'm fictional. As if this isn't my actual heart. My life.

bleacherbarbie: imagine being Hayes and having your best friend dating your sister
🤍 *18,210 likes*

dugoutdaydreams: he's sick about it, you can TELL
🤍 *4,112 likes*

Stop projecting.

statcaststacy: or he's fine and you're writing fanfic in comments
🤍 *9,770 likes*

Thank you, Stacy. Please be my voice.
My eyes sting anyway.

Then the verified checkmark appears, and the air leaves my lungs.

hayes.carlisle10 ✅ : *She's my sister. Back the F off.*
🩶 *28,941 likes*

> *Oh shit.*
> Because that means Hayes has seen this.
> Because he knows.
> Because we waited too long.
> Where is Foster, and does he know that Hayes knows?

bullpenbabe14: uh oh…. sorry Daddy!
🩶 *2,701 likes*

> Gross.

southside_sanity: Hayes Carlisle playing protective big brother…
I die
🩶 *9,222 likes*

"Give that to me." Leighton swipes the phone from my hand and shoves it at Lake. "She doesn't need to see it."

"Hayes commented." I stare at Leighton, who is now shoulder to shoulder with Lake.

Before I can form the next sentence, the clubhouse doors swing open, and my brother storms out.

"Hayes."

He walks past me without a glance.

Then Foster steps out, his eyes finding me immediately, and he gives one small shake of his head.

And just like that, the ground drops out from under me.

CHAPTER
THIRTY-ONE

Foster

Hayes doesn't answer the question, stepping off the pedestal and out of the press room.

I follow, but Easton and Decker decide to as well, and somehow, they're the human version of a revolving door. Decker's shoulder clips mine. Easton throws a look over his shoulder as though he's about to try to tell me not to go after Hayes.

Just try it.

Questions still ring out in the room.

"Wentzel said no more questions," Easton mutters as though he's doing damage control for all of us.

"The rest of you have a good night," Wentzel says, ushering everyone out with the same tone a kindergarten teacher uses the day before Christmas break.

Once we're in the hallway, I push past Decker and Easton and head straight for the locker room.

Thankfully, the place is empty. The rest of the team went

home, probably already laughing about something on the group chat that I'm definitely not reading tonight.

Hayes is at his locker, packing his bag.

"Hey," I say softly, hoping to keep this between us. "I wanted to tell you."

"Funny how that works," he says without looking at me. His voice is tight and flat and not one he's ever used with me. He glances over, eyes sharp. "You're with me all the time, so if you'd wanted to tell me you fucked my sister and got her pregnant, I'm pretty sure you could have found your moment." He shoves a sweatshirt into his bag and zips it up —hard.

"I'm not doing this here. I'll see you at Peeper's." He slides his bag over his shoulder and walks out.

"Hayes, come on." I move after him. "Let's talk about it."

He doesn't stop.

I run back to grab my own bag that I packed earlier because I wanted to get to Callie right after the game.

We had a plan. We were going to tell him. We were going to do it like adults.

Not in a press room as Hayes's face went blank.

I exit the clubhouse doors and find everyone there.

Leighton and the kids.

Hayes and Callie's parents.

And Callie.

She glances up, and my chest tightens from seeing no color in her face. Her mouth parts. Her eyes flick to Hayes, and she steps forward, then she freezes.

We pushed this too long.

It's all our fault.

Hayes walks right by her as if he doesn't see her. Leighton follows, Monroe on her hip, Lincoln bouncing beside her, Lake dragging along behind, continuing to look over her shoulder at Callie.

I start toward Callie as she moves in my direction. Then her parents step between us, blocking my path.

"What happened?" Mrs. Carlisle asks me, already panicking. "Why is Hayes so upset?"

Here are more people who won't be screaming for joy at the news.

How did I forget we haven't even told her parents? Two people I've always respected. Who've always been kind to me in a way that now makes me feel like a thief because what should be a joyous moment for them—their daughter is pregnant with her first child, and they're going to be grandparents—is only going to cause turmoil in their lives.

Why can't life come with a pause button for moments like this?

My gaze shoots to Callie, and she exhales hard.

"Mom… Dad…" She bites her bottom lip.

Immediately their faces change and fill with matching concern. Mrs. Carlisle's hand flies to Callie's arm. Mr. Carlisle's gaze swings to me.

I'm done with the secrets, the delays. The truth needs to be out there.

"Callie's pregnant with my baby." I swallow hard.

Callie gasps and narrows her eyes at me.

Maybe that was the wrong way to tell them. This is not the commercial version where everyone cries and hugs and some acoustic guitar plays in the background.

Mrs. Carlisle shakes her head, apparently refusing to believe it.

Mr. Carlisle stares at his wife, more worried about her reaction than the actual news, I think.

"Are you…" Mrs. Carlisle looks at me. "Together?"

Callie steps forward, her shoulder brushing mine, and the anxiety racing through my veins slows a bit. I press back to let her know I'm here with her. We're in this together.

"We're just having the baby." She raises her chin a bit.

Mr. Carlisle turns his attention on me.

Her mom blinks. "So…"

"It was a one-night stand, Mom." Callie takes over the talking, which is probably a good thing.

Mr. Carlisle continues to look only at me. This is uncomfortable. I should say something, but I'm not sure what.

"I take full responsibility," I say, not meeting his eyes.

"Oh my god, Dad, stop the whole protective father act. He didn't take advantage of me. I was a very willing participant."

"Callie," I whisper out of the side of my mouth.

"Sorry." She massages the bridge of her nose for a second. "I get that's not what you wanna hear, but it's the truth. We… well, you know."

"Yes, we understand what happened. We don't need a play-by-play," Mrs. Carlisle says, voice neutral. She's usually overly sweet. I've never seen this side of her, and I have no idea if she wants to throw her hands up and be done with us or what.

"I wasn't going to give you a play-by-play. I was just saying that… anyway. We were together once, and now we're having a baby. Figuring out the co-parent thing."

"A baby?" Mrs. Carlisle glances at Callie's stomach.

Callie nods and tears fill her eyes. "Yeah. I'm twelve weeks along."

Mrs. Carlisle's eyes widen. "Three months?"

Callie nods again.

Mr. Carlisle's gaze still hasn't left me, and my guess is he's counting my neck tattoos and wondering why his precious daughter would pick a guy like me. I can only imagine he's second-guessing all those times he was nice to me. I snuck behind his back and made a mess of this situation.

"Everything is good? Baby is healthy?" Mrs. Carlisle steps closer to Callie.

"Yes, we were at the doctor yesterday. Everything is good.

We were waiting to tell Hayes until I was out of the first trimester, and now… well, a picture got leaked, and he didn't find out from us." Callie glances at me.

I exhale a deep breath because I think we're both in agreement that we're idiots.

"Hmm." Mrs. Carlisle glances at me. "So the roommate situation?"

I want to look away, but I stand firm. "The landlord was a sleaze, but we already knew she was pregnant at that point."

Her eyes widen, but she nods, absorbing all the information.

"Mom, I'm sure you're disappointed, and I'm sorry. It just…"

Mrs. Carlisle laughs and turns to her husband. "What do you think, Dave?"

He finally takes his eyes off me. "I think I'm gonna be a grandpa… for the fourth time." His face lights up as he smacks me on the back. "Congratulations."

"Come again?" Callie asks, forehead creased.

Mrs. Carlisle tugs her in for a hug. "Congratulations, you two. This is great news."

"It is?" Callie looks at me over her mom's shoulder. "You're happy?"

Mrs. Carlisle pulls away, holding her daughter's upper arms. "Of course we're happy. A baby—what's to be upset about that?"

"But I'm… I mean…"

Mrs. Carlisle waves her hand. "You're thirty years old, Callie. I'm not sure about your dad, but I'm aware you've had sex before."

Mr. Carlisle smacks me on the back and puts his hand out in front of me. "We'll just agree to call it an immaculate conception, all right?" I nod, and he slaps me on the back again. "Welcome to the family, Foster."

"Oh, Dad," Callie is quick to interject, "we're not getting married or anything."

"She really does take me for an old fool." He shakes his head lovingly at his daughter. "Foster is going to be in our family because he's our grandchild's father whether you're with him or not."

"Which I think may be in the future..." Mrs. Carlisle adds, her gaze shifting between the two of us.

This cannot be happening. They're really happy that I'm going to be part of their family?

"And Hayes will be fine," Mr. Carlisle says. "I brought him up better than to be a baby about this. No pun intended."

Mr. and Mrs. Carlisle switch spots, and soon she's wrapping her arms around my waist and pulling me into a hug.

I wish I had their confidence.

Again, Callie and I look at one another over the shoulders of her parents.

"Congratulations, Foster," Mrs. Carlisle whispers in my ear. "This is fantastic news."

I want to keep asking *Is it?* but I hold her and nod, even though I'm still digesting their reaction.

"Would you like me to go with you to talk to Hayes?" Mrs. Carlisle releases me from the hug and steps back.

"I think I'd rather go by myself." I look to Callie to see if it's okay with her, but I feel like I did him wrong, and I'm the one who needs to face the consequences.

"You're not going just to protect me from this, right?"

I shake my head. "It's not that."

"We're going to let you guys talk. We'll take the kids, so they won't be there. Congratulations again, you two. And you know we won't object if you want us at an appointment or two." Mrs. Carlisle winks and looks at her daughter's stomach one last time before the two of them leave huddled together, whispering and apparently over the moon about their family's new addition.

Callie crosses her arms.

I lift my hands. "I'm just asking to talk to him first. To explain myself to him. To come clean."

She looks at me long and hard, then nods. "Okay." She steps into me and wraps her arms around my stomach.

I tug her into me, and she lays her cheek on my chest. I have no idea what the hug is for but having her in my arms feels too good to ruin it by asking.

When she pulls back, she looks up at me. "Thank you."

"For?"

"For being here, standing next to me during all this. It's nice knowing I'm not alone."

I place my hands on her cheeks, cradling them, making sure she's looking right at me. I swallow, but summon the confidence to tell her, to put myself out there like she just did. "I'm not going anywhere, Callie."

Her hands cover mine, and she nods. We stand there for a few moments, and my entire world tilts, as if the world has shifted, though I can't explain why.

CHAPTER
THIRTY-TWO

Foster

Callie and I walk into Peeper's, both of us filled with anxious energy. Ruby glances up and shakes her head with a disapproving mom expression.

"Good news travels fast," I mumble, squeezing Callie's hand.

When we left the field, I wrapped a hand around hers and haven't let go. No one is going to mess with her when I'm at her side.

Ruby stops us as we approach the door to the backroom and blocks our way.

"Hey, Rubes." Callie gives her a smile that doesn't reach her eyes.

Ruby gives her a full body scan, then fixes her gaze on Callie's stomach. It's wild how the second people know, her belly becomes the only thing they see.

She flicks her gaze up to meet mine. "I hear congratulations are in order, but you better fix this." She thumbs toward the backroom. "We already have a problem with you and Decker. I'm not gonna have any more animosity between your group of boys. I swear, you're like a bunch of teenage girls." She gives Callie's shoulder a quick squeeze then disappears behind the bar.

"I guess that's the best we can expect from Ruby." Callie smiles at me.

"A scolding instead of a hug. Seems about right."

Callie twists the doorknob. I close my eyes for half a second and take one last breath then follow her in.

Hayes is planted at one end of the table, arms crossed. Leighton's beside him, leaned back with her legs crossed, wine in hand, smirking at us as though she already knows how this is gonna go.

"So did you guys know about this too? Was I the only one in the dark?" Hayes asks Decker and Easton.

"Fuck no. I didn't know." Easton sips his beer, shaking his head adamantly.

"And you?" Hayes swings his gaze to Decker. "I understand brotherly loyalty, but I expected more from you."

"You think I'd keep this from you? I warned him not to make a mess of things."

"They didn't know." Callie draws in a breath and tilts her chin up as though she's erecting a shield against the barbs about to be thrown her way.

Hayes's gaze lifts, his eyes snagging on our linked fingers. "Ah, the happy couple has arrived."

I hate the bite in his tone.

Leighton smiles and sips her wine, placing it on the table and standing.

"Leighton, united front." Hayes's eyes follow his fiancée.

The last thing I want is to cause problems between them.

She waves him off and rolls her eyes, safely out of his line of sight. "Official congratulations. I'm excited to be an aunt." She hugs Callie, then shifts her attention to me. "Foster? You were a mystery man for a while, and I'm happy it's you."

My head rears back. "You are?"

"I'm not." Hayes raises his hand. "In case anyone was wondering."

"Oh, shh…" Leighton waves at him again and sets her gaze on me. "Of course. You two are going to make a gorgeous baby, and I can't wait to spoil him or her."

"Thanks." I shift awkwardly in place.

Callie smiles at Leighton, then glances at me, and her smile blooms as though she can't fight it. It shouldn't hit me like it does. But something warm twists under my ribs.

Hayes glares at Leighton, but she doesn't seem bothered, going back to her chair and sipping her wine.

"I'm not in agreement." Easton stands and grabs hold of Callie, swinging her around. "Our baby would've been cuter, but congratulations, I guess. I'm ready to be a stand-in uncle." He winks.

Something like a growl rises up my throat, and Easton laughs, slapping me in the chest. "Congrats, asshole—or should we say Daddy Asshole?" He places his hand between us.

There was so much competition between us around Callie last year, but he doesn't seem to care now.

I shake his hand.

It does feel nice to have the news out. To not be hiding anymore.

"I'm the actual uncle." Decker follows Easton, hugging Callie respectfully. "Don't worry, there are good genes on our side. Foster just didn't get a lot of them."

I huff, knowing the beef between us needs to be squashed. I don't want my kid asking one day why I don't talk to Uncle Decker.

"Congrats, Uncle Decker. At least my kid will have one great uncle." Callie eyes Hayes, and he looks away.

Easton raises his hand. "I'm an uncle too."

"You are." Callie laughs and lets her head rest on my shoulder. Relief softens her whole body, as though the secret being out has allowed her to breathe again.

Hayes clocks Callie's body language, and a disgusted expression crosses his face. Winning him over won't be easy. It's clear Callie and I share a familiarity and intimacy, and he'll take it to mean we've kept a deeper secret.

An awkward silence descends over the room, until I decide to break it.

"Hey, man, can we talk?" I ask, willing to take the chance that Hayes is gonna come at me. Hell, I'll take him jumping over the table and smashing my head into the pinball machine rather than this silence.

Leighton nudges him.

"Come on, Carlisle, don't be like that," Easton encourages.

Decker doesn't come to my defense, but I broke the rules, and he's Mr. Rule Follower now. Guess he forgets the days when he wasn't.

Hayes downs his beer. "Sit."

Chairs shift, and everyone gets up to leave us alone.

"Why don't we go outside?" I don't want to do this anywhere near Callie. Depending on what happens... what's said... I don't want her even more upset.

Again Hayes acts as if I've suggested the worst thing, but Leighton nudges him again, and he sighs, reluctantly standing like Lake does when Leighton asks her to watch Monroe. As though talking to me is the last thing he wants to do.

"You've got five minutes." He starts to make his way across the room.

Callie steps in front of him, placing her hand on his chest. He glances down at it and then meets her eyes.

"I just want it to be clear this was both of us, okay? We both did this," she says.

He says nothing, and Callie steps aside, allowing him to leave the room.

I look at her. "If I don't come back…"

"I'll call 9-1-1 and then start searching." Callie smiles wide as though she has all the confidence in the world that I can fix this. Then she hugs me. "Just in case. So I can tell the baby what Daddy smelled like."

"Funny." I wrap my arms around her, and when I look over her shoulder, Decker's eyebrows are raised. I flip him off.

"I thought so." She puts her hands on my cheeks. "Just one last look to memorize this face in case any permanent damage is done."

I shake my head, and she laughs.

"Glad you find this funny. I'm about to get my ass handed to me."

She pats my cheek. "You asked for it, remember?"

And I'd do it again and again.

"Don't forget, duck and weave." Easton pretends he's in the boxing ring.

"You've always had a weak right hook, go with the uppercut," Decker says.

"Fuck both of you."

"He's not going to get physical. He's happy way deep down. He just doesn't realize it yet." Leighton takes another sip of her wine.

I stare at Leighton a beat, and she smiles sweetly, but I'm not sure she's right.

She shrugs. "Just trying to give you some encouragement."

With a resigned sigh, I walk to the door, but Ruby almost runs into me, coming into the room with a tray of drinks. I wait at the door, and she places the tray on the table then looks at Callie.

"Take your pick… Sprite? Water? Tonic water? I have a

non-alcoholic beer behind the bar." She takes the drinks off the tray, placing each in front of where Callie stands.

"Oh, that's sweet, Ruby," Leighton says.

"It really is." Callie looks at her best friend and smiles.

Are those tears in Callie's eyes?

"It's practical. Don't think too much of it." Ruby picks up her tray and walks away, stopping at the door and staring at me. "Don't you have someone's ass to kiss?"

"Going."

I leave the room, then weave through the tables in the main part of the bar. The regulars at the bar are already grumbling about my pitching and saying maybe I need to "see someone." Last week I was a diamond in the rough. Some nights I'm sparkling, and other nights I'm face down in the mud. Real inspirational crowd.

Hayes is outside the bar, and since a lot of fans are lingering around, I head to the security gate next to Peeper's that leads to our condo entrances. "Mind?"

He follows, and we walk through the gate. The Dugout sign is still there, with more notes posted on it to grab our attention. We go halfway up the cement stairs and take a seat. Neither of us says anything for a moment.

Then, with my heart in my throat, I break the silence. "I'm sorry. I knew what I was doing. I knew she was your sister, and I did it anyway."

Hayes says nothing.

"I can promise you that I'm gonna do what's right."

He glances over. "You're going to marry her?"

Bile rises up my throat, but it's not as bitter as it usually is when someone talks about marriage. And it should be—because I can't be the partner Callie deserves.

The corners of Hayes's lips turn down. "Thought so."

"Would you even want that? Me marrying her just because she's pregnant? That's what you'd want for her in a marriage?"

He leans his back against the brick wall, stretching his legs out in front of him, facing me. "I'm not sure what I want for her, but..."

"It's not me." I save him from having to say what we're both thinking.

He tilts his head. "What?"

I sigh.

"Foster?" He arches an eyebrow.

"You haven't been very shy in telling everyone that Decker is the only Davis brother you'd ever want for her."

He stares at me as though he has to think back, then bursts out laughing. "And why do you think that is?"

"I know why."

"But she doesn't want Decker—or at least she didn't. I'm not going to sit here and give you some pep talk and boost your ego by telling you you're good enough for my sister. She makes that decision. But fuck, Foster, I find out in a press conference?"

"I know." I lean on the opposite wall so we're facing one another. "I just didn't want—"

"You were worried about our relationship on the field? Your career?"

"Fuck no!" I shout, and my chest squeezes painfully. "You're the best friend I have. The closest thing I have to family, and I didn't want to lose that. Shit, man, I took your trust and did the unthinkable. I couldn't keep my dick out of your sister's pants."

"I'm gonna need one thing if we continue this conversation. I need to not think about your dick and my sister's pants, okay?"

I nod. "I'm sorry. I was ashamed and pissed at myself, but Hayes, we're going to do this co-parenting thing, and we're going to rock it."

He nods, and if he wasn't her brother, I might admit all the other shit—how much my attraction to her is building, how awesome of a person I think she is, and that the more time we spend together, the more I want from her. But this isn't the time to declare that I'm confused about my relationship with her and where it's going. I don't even know if Callie would be interested in anything more than co-parenting.

Shit, am I really considering a relationship?

"I'm sure you will, but I really wish you would've told me. I look like a fool. As far as me wishing it was Decker, get that shit out of your head. You're just as good as him, and I'd feel the same way I do now if it were your brother."

"You're telling me that if we would've come to you right away, you would've been jumping for joy?"

He shrugs. "You'll never know now. But I'm engaged to Callie's best friend. Do I really have a leg to stand on if I went into protective big brother mode?"

"In my head, yes."

He sits up straighter. "It was the secrecy that pissed me off, not that it was you. You need to bet on yourself, man, stop thinking you're a shit person. I know you'll do right by my niece or nephew. And Callie, for that matter."

We sit in silence because I'm not so sure.

"I'm not wasting a night out on this bullshit. Let's go celebrate me being an uncle." He stands then holds his hand out for me and helps me up, dragging me into a hug once I'm standing. "But, Foster, you fuck her over, and there will be a problem." He pulls back and laughs, hitting my chest. "Let's go."

I'm relieved that's over with. Relieved I have such a great best friend who seems to have enough confidence in me to think I won't fuck this up.

I have to navigate this situation carefully so this doesn't go south. Which means putting Callie in a box marked *Untouchable* and keeping her there no matter how much I want her.

CHAPTER
THIRTY-THREE

Callie

"So… you and Reaper." Easton leans back in his chair and sips his beer, stretching out his legs. "I mean, we all knew something was going on when he went all caveman with the security gate thing, but a baby?"

Decker hasn't said much, and I like him even more for it.

"It's going to be great." Leighton shoots me a reassuring smile.

Usually I'd have some smart-ass comment to shoot back at Easton, but all I can think about is what's happening outside.

Why did I let Foster take the first hit? Hayes would be nicer to me than him.

Leighton's shoulder hits mine. "It's fine. They're going to be okay."

I sip the water Ruby brought me. It's so much easier now that I don't have to pretend to be drinking. My foot taps the floor, and I let out a breath.

"Hayes isn't the type to go all apeshit on someone." Easton does his best to reassure me.

My gaze falls to Decker, and he forces a smile that doesn't come close to meeting his eyes. If Foster and Decker can be estranged all these years—twin brothers who don't talk to one another—the same thing could happen between Foster and Hayes, and I can't be the reason why.

"Sorry, I can't." I push up and head for the door.

"She just can't help herself. I'm proud of you for lasting this long." Leighton laughs.

I'm glad she finds this whole thing funny, and I wish I had her faith that this won't ruin Hayes and Foster's relationship.

I weave through the tables in the bar. Some Colts fans are filtering in now, probably because all the other bars are filled. Then again, there are a few tables of women who look me up and down. It's obvious from their judgmental expressions— they know who I am.

I push open the door and glance around, but Foster and Hayes are nowhere in sight. Then I hear Hayes's laugh, and my head snaps toward the security gate. The two of them walk through it. Foster sees me first and halts, smiles, and nods.

My shoulders drop as all the tension that's been there since we first found out about the pregnancy dissipates.

Hayes sees me next and opens his arms. "We're good."

I had no idea how much I needed to hear that, but the two of us still have some things to sort out between us as brother and sister. I force myself to walk to Hayes, grab his hand, and tug him back through the security gate.

"We'll meet you in there," I tell Foster over my shoulder.

"Callie, he's cool. It's all okay." Foster is frowning.

I crack the security gate and peek my head out, pointing toward Peeper's. "He's my brother, and I want to clear some things up too."

Foster holds up his hands, turning and going into Peeper's.

Don't get upset that he's about to weave through those tables with all those single women who would love to be his next conquest.

Hayes is leaning against the brick wall when I turn around, and the gate clicks shut behind me. "Callie, we're good."

"Sit."

His eyebrows lift.

"Please."

He sits on the concrete step, and I sit next to him, both of us silent for a second.

I want to say my piece, have everything out in the open so that we can move on. "I was just as big a part of this as Foster."

He nods. "I know."

"And it's my life, you know."

"I get it."

"I'm sorry we didn't tell you, but we were coming to terms with it ourselves. And then I wanted to wait until I was out of the first trimester."

"I know. I'm sure it's scary."

"Yeah… but now." I shrug. "I think I'm coming to terms with it."

"I knew something was off when he had you move in with him. It's a very un-Foster-like thing to do." He turns his head and looks at me.

"I was just as surprised. He's been a little alpha male since I told him."

He laughs and bites his lip, as if he's unsure how much to tell me about his best friend. I want to drill him with questions, but I'd rather have Foster trust me enough to tell me himself. "That tracks."

"You think? I'm kind of blown away by it all."

He nods. "He didn't have the best childhood. He's never

told me much, but his dad is… I've met him a few times, and let's just say he's about as far from our dad as you can get."

I figured.

"And then you have the whole Decker thing. He's told me bits and pieces, but they're brothers… twins… how could it be that bad? Anyway, I think overall, he's lived a pretty lonely life."

My heart aches at the words. "He's surrounded by people… women."

"It's not the same. He didn't grow up with what we did, Cal."

The pain in Hayes's voice cracks my heart open.

"I gotta ask you something," he says. "And it's none of my business, but I have to know… do you want more than he's offering?"

I stare at my hands. Because what I want is dangerous. What I want is a man choosing me on purpose—not because I'm pregnant, not because I'm convenient, but because he wants… me.

"Because from where I stand, from what I see, there's more than co-parenting going on." I snap my head up, and he nods. "I didn't say anything to Foster. I'd never put pressure on him since you're my sister. It really is between you and him, but I just have to tell you…"

"What?" I swear my heart is lodged in my throat.

"I'm Team Callie every day of the week. But I'm also Team Foster. I want the best for both of you. And the fact that you're making me an uncle together makes me pretty fucking happy, but raising a baby is going to bring you guys closer. Hell, you're living with him. You're holding his hand, and the ease between you when you're together…" He shakes his head. "I'm not warning you against him. He's worth the work it's going to take, but it is going to be work, Callie. It's going to take time."

"Sure sounds like a warning."

He shakes his head. "It's not. I love the guy, and I think the two of you would be awesome together. I guess I'm just saying that I don't want to see either of you get hurt."

"We really are just co-parenting together. I'm living there because he wants us to be friends."

He quirks an eyebrow, and I'm pretty sure we both know there's more to it, even if I desperately wish what I said was true. It'd make it easier on my fragile heart.

"I'm serious. He wants to be part of his child's life and thinks we need to become friends in order to give our baby a good family life."

"He's not wrong."

"But?" Now I quirk an eyebrow.

"There's clearly tension between you." He's quick to raise his hand. "I do not want details, but you slept together once and conceived a baby. Who's to say that tension won't boil over again? I just want to say, don't go into it lightly. You both have to hold one another accountable."

"When did you get your psych degree?"

"Maybe because when I went after Leighton, I knew the score. She came with three kids who were in it with us. Their hearts, their feelings would be affected by the outcome of our relationship. And it worked for us. It's the best thing to ever happen in my life. I want the same for you. If that's with Foster, awesome, but I'm only asking you to give him time. I know you've been screwed over in the past and—"

"We're not anything," I remind him.

He huffs. "Right now, maybe. I don't see it staying that way. Just be patient."

"Are you warning me because you know I suck at patience?"

He chuckles. "Well, you do. And he does too."

"Okay." I pat his knee. "I hear you."

"What did you hear?"

"I heard that if it goes south—which it won't because

we're only going to be co-parents—that you're not necessarily going to take my side."

He shakes his head. "Of course that's what you got from it."

I jump up and stand in front of him. "Well, congratulations, Uncle Hayes."

He stands and holds out his arms. "Congratulations, Mommy. I hope your kid's first word isn't fuck."

I laugh as he wraps me in his arms. "It most likely will be. You're really good with it?"

"Yeah, I'm good, but you two need to stop keeping secrets. I do not want to be surprised at a press conference ever again."

"Noted."

We part and step out of the security gate, almost running right into a guy standing there. He quickly turns away, lowering his Colts hat, and walks down the sidewalk. I give Hayes a confused look.

"No one said all the fans were female." Hayes chuckles.

"I guess not." Still, something sour knots in my stomach as I watch the man blend into the crowd.

If he was a fan, wouldn't he have wanted to stick around and ask for a picture or something? At least see which Colts player was coming out of the building?

"Let's go back so Leighton can tell me she told me so." He holds the door open to Peeper's, motioning for me to go in.

We walk into the backroom, and it's as if nothing happened. Decker and Easton are arguing about darts. Leighton and Foster are chatting. But when Foster glances up and our eyes catch, I see his relief—and I know Hayes is right. We're on the cusp of something, and we need to be certain before things go any further.

Which is a lot harder when he's looking at me like that.

CHAPTER
THIRTY-FOUR

Callie

It's been two weeks since Hayes and the entire country found out about the pregnancy, and thankfully the Colts have been traveling more than at home. It's the best thing that can happen when you're pregnant, sexually frustrated, and lusting after your roommate.

Because if Foster was here, I'm pretty sure we would've already slept together, which is why, since he's due home tonight, I'm going to get off before I have to see him in the morning.

I drag my vibrator down my body under the covers, opening my thighs, heat already pooling low in my belly.

The soft buzz starts, and my imagination drifts away to Foster.

It's not even a full, clear picture—just flashes of memory. The way he looks at me with heavy eyes, his mouth set as though he's holding himself back from tackling me onto the bed, his hands fisted at his sides as though he doesn't trust himself not to touch me. The way he stands too close, as though he wants to touch me but is trying to respect the line we put in place.

My stomach flips.

I'm doing this for relief. I'm releasing a pressure valve before he returns home tonight. Otherwise, I'm pretty sure the minute he walks in, I'd follow him into his bedroom and strip naked.

My body shivers with pleasure as the vibrator hums between my legs.

I think about his voice when he says my name—low, rough, like how he'd use it if we were in bed together. I think about his hands, big and capable, and the way they'd feel on my skin.

I squeeze my eyes shut, but it only worsens my want for him.

Heat gathers, tight and insistent, and my breath stutters. I press my lips together to keep quiet even though I'm alone and no one can hear me. I lose myself in the hum, the rhythm, and the delirious slow build.

And then my thoughts shift, too dangerous and, more importantly, too honest.

What if I took him up on his offer? A second chance with him, but this time, what if we didn't rush, but he took his time to prove himself? What if he made me tell him that I was his and made me hate him for it and love him for it in the same breath?

My body tightens. My pulse thumps hard in my throat.

I'm close. My arousal's rising, right at the edge where everything goes sharp and bright and—

The vibrator sputters to a stop.

No. No, no, no.

I press the button again.

It buzzes, but weaker now, like a car starter trying to turn over and failing.

"Fuck no!" I jam my thumb on the button.

One more pathetic little vibration sputters out.

Then nothing.

"You have got to be kidding me."

I click the button again. Once. Twice. Three times. And still nothing.

I throw my head back onto the pillow and let out a strangled, frustrated groan. Of course. Of course this happens when I'm finally—finally—almost there. I drop the vibrator onto the sheets between my legs.

My chest rises and falls. My body is still wired and unsatisfied. I stare at the ceiling again.

And the worst part?

If it really was Foster, I wouldn't have to worry about batteries.

I hate how much my body betrays me, wanting him all the time.

I toss off the covers and grab the vibrator, on the hunt for batteries. I know I haven't bought any, but Foster seems like a pretty prepared guy, so I'm sure he has a stash somewhere or at least a flashlight I can take them out of.

The living room light is on since I kept it at a dim setting, so Foster doesn't come home to a dark house. I head to the kitchen drawer he seems to shove a lot of miscellaneous things in. I dig around, but all I find is plasticware from takeout, chopsticks, some soy sauce packets, pens, and a few pads of paper.

I shut the drawer and look around his space, heading over to the table by the door. There's one drawer, but all that's in it are some chargers, charging cords, and a set of keys. I pick them up and inspect them, unsure what they're for, then put them back in the drawer.

"You have to have batteries somewhere."

Then the remote comes to mind. I head to the living room,

unclicking the back of the remote, but it takes double As, and I need triple.

"Damn it."

He'd probably have his electric razor with him. He only uses the microwave for a clock, which takes those off the list. My eyes snag on his bedroom door.

"Hmm…"

It's my last option.

I slowly push open his door. Being in his space without him knowing feels intrusive, but he's never told me I can't come in here. Just like before, his bed is made and everything is neat and organized. I search his drawers, trying not to move anything out of place.

His drawer of boxer briefs is all black. Seriously, no color? He needs a little color in his life.

His shirts are stacked, neat and orderly. No surprise there.

"Do guys keep toys?" I go to his nightstand, praying he's got something. A cock ring maybe? Although after our orgasm conversation, I'm pretty sure he's not into marathon sex sessions where you use toys and explore.

I open the nightstand drawer, and my shoulders fall, all hope dying because there's nothing but a box of condoms, a pen, and a pad of paper. Nothing of any use to me. I slam the drawer shut.

I pick up my vibrator and realize if I'm going to get off, I'm gonna have to use my fingers, which is fine but inefficient and doesn't always work.

As I'm about to step out of his room, like déjà vu, the lock slides over on the condo door.

Jesus, not now.

I cross the foyer and move past the kitchen to reach my room, but the door opens before I can escape inside it.

"Callie?"

I whip around, and the vibrator slips out of my grasp,

dropping with a thud onto the floor. You might as well strip me bare for him to see.

His gaze drifts down to it and back to me.

Foster steps into the condo without a word, shutting the door and flicking the lock. He looks good. Really, really good. Black jeans, black T-shirt with tattoos sneaking up over the neckline and down his arms, no hat. I bite my lip, my unsatisfied pussy begging me to throw caution to the wind.

"What are you doing?" He walks over to his bedroom door, drops his bag, and breaks the distance, getting closer.

I bend down and swipe the vibrator up, putting it behind my back. "Nothing. I was just—"

"Let's not insult my intelligence."

Damn me for being a polite roommate and leaving the living room light on for him.

I finally give up the act. "Fine, if you must know, I was pleasuring myself and my vibrator died."

"Pleasuring yourself?" His eyebrows raise. "Mid orgasm?"

"I hadn't gotten there yet."

"And you're out here because you were going to hump the couch?"

I scoff then glare at him. "Excuse me?"

He shrugs. "It is your favorite thing in this condo. It's a logical theory."

"It is not. I was looking for batteries. What kind of man doesn't have batteries?"

He chuckles and walks over to the fridge, pulls a water out, and twists it open, his eyes never leaving mine. "One who doesn't rely on sex toys."

"That's sad."

"My fist does the job just fine."

"Must be nice. You men have it so easy."

I haven't left the doorframe of my bedroom because I'm terrified I'll do something I shouldn't, because we're in worst-case territory here. I'm highly aroused, and now he's standing in front of me looking all bad boy hot with lickable tattoos after he saved the game today, and the Colts won.

"I don't know, your clit has more than double the amount of nerve fibers as my dick."

A laugh bubbles out of me. "Doing some research, I see?"

It's hot that he is. That after our conversation, he actually cares about giving a woman an orgasm and is reading up on it.

"If you know anything about me, you should know I don't want to be mediocre at anything."

"No one said you were mediocre."

"I didn't give you an orgasm. That makes me less than mediocre actually." He takes his water and heads toward his room. "Don't forget that the offer still stands. And tonight it looks like you could use a little relief." He shoots me a wicked grin over his shoulder.

I glare at him. "Don't play games."

He turns around and puts his water on his dresser, before resting his hands on the top of the doorframe, his long body stretching. "I'm not playing games. I might not vibrate, but I have fingers, a tongue, and a cock that you can use and abuse."

I stare at him, trying to quiet the noise of my pussy screaming at me, wondering why we're not already across the room.

"We shouldn't." Even I can hear that I don't really mean it.

"It's just bodies, Callie. And I'm gonna be honest, I wouldn't mind celebrating my win tonight."

I bite my lip, desperately wanting to accept his offer.

I press the button on my vibrator, and it doesn't magically start. Which means it's not an option.

His heated gaze sweeps down my body, and my resistance shatters on the floor like glass.

"One time only." I toss the vibrator on my bed and cross the main room to his bedroom. "One and done."

Yeah right, Callie.

His arms drop off the doorframe, swiftly picking me up when I get close to the door. I wrap my arms around his neck, and our mouths collide, his tongue meeting mine, my hand fisting his hair.

Fuck, why on Earth did we wait this long?

He's instantly hard, and I'm already halfway there, so there's no way I won't come this time even if he doesn't go slow.

We're crossing into dangerous waters, but I don't give a shit. We can handle whatever comes next.

CHAPTER
THIRTY-FIVE

Callie

His lips don't leave mine, his tongue continuing its exploration of my mouth.

His hunger for me is the hottest thing I've ever experienced.

I make a sound I don't recognize and grab his T-shirt in both fists, dragging him closer as though I'm scared he'll change his mind if there's even an inch between us. He tastes like mint, and coupled with the scent of his aftershave, it's all I can do not to rub myself against him like a cat.

This is so much better than I dreamed. He really is a good kisser, better than I remember from that night.

"Tell me to stop," he says in a low voice against my lips. It's a desperate plea, as if I'd be putting him out of his misery.

I should, but I don't care to, so I grind along the bulge in his jeans.

"Don't you dare," I whisper, and then he's kissing me again.

My back hits the wall softly, his body slotting into mine. The pressure of his solid weight pushing against me hits every fiber of my being.

This is exactly why the team being gone has felt like a mercy. Because if he'd been here, if I'd had to live with him every day, watch him walk around the kitchen as if he doesn't know what he does to me, I would've snapped sooner.

Not that it matters now. We've moved so far past the line it can't even be seen in the distance anymore.

Foster kisses along my jaw, then down my neck, and I tilt my head back, fingers digging into his hair. He says my name as though he's barely hanging on.

Join the club.

My stomach flips. My heart trips. My whole body tightens, bracing because he's about to ruin me. I'm certain of it.

He carries me into his bedroom as though he's done it a hundred times. As though I belong in his bed and in his space. Maybe this moment was inevitable all along.

The bed dips under our weight, then he's over me, braced on his forearms, staring down as he searches my face. I know what he's going to ask before the words cross his lips.

"Are you sure?"

I swallow, and for a second, my brain tries to put up a fight. Tries to list all the reasons this is a bad idea. Tries to remind me of the consequences that will be apparent once we see this through.

But his thumb brushes my cheek, and my body melts under his.

"Yes." It's true. I'm sure I want him, and although what will happen after scares me, in this moment, there's nothing I want more than to be with him.

His mouth finds mine again, the kiss slower and deeper. His hand slides down my side, and my skin sparks under his touch. I'm already achy with want.

This is going to be so good. It's been building for months. The tension. The eye contact. The way we try to pretend we don't have one eye on the other when we're together.

This is the moment I've been thinking about for days, weeks, *months*.

Our clothes are tossed aside, and he stares hungrily at my breasts before taking one nipple into his mouth, dragging his teeth along the taut peak, then doing the same to the other. My breasts no longer ache, but they're more sensitive than normal, so I can't help the moan that escapes me.

Next, he drifts his hand down to my lower abdomen that's popped in the time he was away. I'm not showing in a super obvious way, but there's a swell to my belly that wasn't there before.

"You have a baby bump now." His voice is filled with awe. Cradling my tummy with both hands, he moves his head down and places a gentle kiss there.

Something about the gesture almost brings tears to my eyes, but I blink them back.

Foster moves back up my body, and his mouth meets mine again. I slide my hand down the front of him, palming his long, thick cock, wanting it deep inside me.

He groans, then he's reaching toward the nightstand, but I place my hand on his. "Have you been tested?"

His head rocks back, realization dawning. "Yeah. You?"

"At the doctor. So we don't need to use anything if you don't want to. I mean, I can't get pregnant again."

His gaze falls to my body. "Shit, you just put me in a tough situation."

"Why?"

He kisses right between my breasts. "Because this is Operation Give Callie an Orgasm, and if I'm in you bare, I worry I'm gonna come too fast. Like when I lost my virginity, and I can assure you I know I never gave her an orgasm."

I laugh, and his lips trail over my body, his thigh nudging my legs open, answering my question.

He situates himself between my legs and hovers his lips over my mouth. "But I think I'm gonna take my chances. Can we agree on a third round, just in case?"

"At this point, I might agree to a third even if you don't make me come."

"Jesus, I hope it doesn't come to that, but at the same time, I wouldn't be complaining."

His lips press to mine as the tip of his dick pushes past my opening, and he slides into me. His masculine grunt only makes me wetter. I'm not sure the last time I was with a guy who made me feel as wanted as I wanted him. Dare I say this moment with Foster feels different than any time before.

He's good with his dick—circles his hips, doesn't move too fast or too slow, keeps up a good, steady rhythm—and as my fingernails are digging into his shoulder blades, and I'm close, my brain decides to come back online.

Why didn't I come the first time? He's not bad. In fact, this is amazing. Maybe this is different than the first time?

"Fuck, you feel so good, Callie. You have no idea the number of times I've jerked off to you."

My body heats with his words, but my mind continues to spin, telling me to hurry up and get there.

Pressure blooms in my chest.

Not because I don't want him. Not because it doesn't feel good. It feels amazing. Having him on top of me, whispering sweet dirty things is exactly where I want to be.

But I can feel the finish line up ahead, and instead of letting my body move toward it, my mind drags me back.

You have to come.

If you don't, he'll know.

If you don't, he'll think it's him.

If you don't, it'll turn into A Thing.

My throat tightens.

If I don't finish, I'll become a problem instead of someone he desires.

Foster's mouth moves to my neck. His breath is hot against my skin. His hand moves as though he's learning me, wants to memorize me. He whispers hot dirty words, but they're drowned out by my own anxious thoughts.

I should be where he's at. Both of us floating toward an orgasm.

But the article comes to mind. The numbers and stupid statistics I wish he'd never told me. The idea that there's some invisible scoreboard, and I'm about to lose. Not just for me, but for him too.

Mark one for Callie being too much work, not worth the effort.

Foster's head lifts, and his eyes meet mine, searching. "You good?"

I sink into those blue eyes like pool water, slipping deeper under his spell. He pulls one of my legs up around his hip, and my mind turns off for a second, relishing in the feel of the push and pull of his length in and out of me.

"You feel so good." I mean every word. He feels more than good. But my head is refusing to let me lose myself in him, to just *feel* and let the pressure float away.

"Are you close?"

"Yes," I lie, not wanting to hurt him.

Foster kisses me again, and I kiss him back harder, trying to control my thoughts and beat them back into silence.

His hand ventures down between us, and his fingers land on my clit.

I press my eyes shut and try to focus on the sensation. On him. On the way his breath stutters when I run my hands down his back. On the strength there. The way his muscles flex and stretch when he moves. On the sound he makes every time his dick hits deep inside me.

But the pressure is still there, building not in my body, but in my mind.

Any second now.

Don't ruin this.

Foster's breathing turns rougher. His forehead dips to my shoulder for a second, and it's clear he's barely hanging on.

I feel the shift. The change in his rhythm. The way his body tenses. The sounds he's making are even more guttural.

And my body snaps into panic mode.

He's close, and I'm not.

My throat closes.

I could say it. I could say, *I need more time.* I could say, *I don't think this is working.* I could say, *do this instead.*

But the words are lodged in my throat, and my brain is screaming at me not to make it awkward. Don't make him feel bad. Don't make him slow down when he's right there. Who knows if you'll ever come anyway?

So I do the easiest thing. The thing I've done a million times. What's the difference now?

I make my breathing hitch on purpose. I dig my fingers into his shoulders. I make like I'm right there with him. I slip out a moan and tense my entire body and hope like hell that I sell it.

Foster freezes for half a second, eyes squeezing shut as he's hit with his own relief. He says my name as if it's a blessing and a curse.

And then his face presses into my neck as he falls apart.

I stare at the ceiling.

My heart is pounding, but from guilt and not from an amazing release.

How do we start this co-parenting thing with me lying to him?

Foster stays on top of me, taking care not to put all his weight on me. Still, he's heavy and warm, breathing hard against my skin. Then he lifts his head, eyes soft, a satisfied little smile tugging at his mouth.

"You good?" His question is quieter this time.

This is the moment to tell him.

I force my lips into something that resembles a smile. "Yeah."

He rolls to his side, pulling me with him as though he can't stand not touching me. His arm wraps around my waist, and he kisses my shoulder.

And this moment would be perfect.

If I wasn't racked with guilt.

The room is quiet except for our breathing as it slows. His fingers trace absent circles on my hip, and I stare at his tattoos while the confession sits like a boulder in my throat.

I tell myself to let it go. To keep and bury the secret.

He got what he needed.

He thinks I did too.

It's easier than watching him leave because I'm such a disappointment to him.

No harm, no foul.

Except there is harm. It's in the way my body still feels tight and not fully satisfied. It's in the way my chest aches because I'm lying to him.

It's in the way I can already feel resentment trying to take root, not toward him, but toward myself.

And I refuse to let that happen.

I take a deep breath, then I turn my head to look at him.

Foster's eyes are closed, his face relaxed, as though he finally released some of the weight he's been carrying around.

My stomach twists. "Foster."

His eyes snap open. "You didn't, did you?"

The way he's able to read my tone unnerves me.

I shake my head. I hate that my reflex is always to lie about it.

For a beat, he looks at me. My heart hammers. My entire

body braces for him to be offended. Embarrassed. Annoyed. For him to make a joke about how something's wrong with me. Worse, for him to retreat.

"I didn't want to." The words tumble out, and I squeeze my eyes shut. "Fake it, I mean. I just—you were right there, and I could tell you were close, and my brain just wouldn't turn off—"

He touches my cheek, stopping my spiral with one gentle gesture. "Hey, look at me."

I do, and I see none of what I assumed would be written on his face. If anything, I see only concern.

"You having an orgasm isn't for *me*. It's for *you*."

My laugh comes out broken. "But…"

His mouth tugs into a small smile, but it's not cocky. "My ego has taken a second hit. It's okay though. I'll survive."

I swallow. "You're not mad?"

"Mad?" His forehead wrinkles as though the idea doesn't make sense. Then his gaze dips. "I'd never be mad. I just feel like a shit partner." He pauses, then adds, "It upsets me that you felt you had to fake it."

"I'm sorry," I whisper. "I think I've grown used to it."

I'd be embarrassed to admit how many times I've been less than fulfilled by a partner and stayed.

He shakes his head once. "Don't apologize." Then he kisses me, soft and slow. When he pulls back, his forehead rests against mine. "Tell me what you need."

My chest lifts with a shaky breath. The truth is, I don't even know how to answer that. Not without feeling as if I'm asking for too much.

So I say the only thing I can say. "I need to get out of my head. And I'm not sure I ever can."

His thumb strokes my cheek. "We'll keep it simple. You feel. I listen."

"And I need it not to be a thing," I add. "Not like… a scoreboard."

His eyes soften. "There's no scoreboard."

I release a breath I didn't know I was holding.

He kisses my forehead. "I'm not opposed to doing it until you get there. Practice makes perfect."

My stomach flips from his wicked smile. I close my eyes, and for the first time tonight, the pressure eases.

Not because my body is satisfied, but because my heart is feeling something it probably shouldn't.

CHAPTER
THIRTY-SIX

Foster

I'm a fucking failure right now, but I'll never make it about me and make Callie feel guilty that she didn't come.

Callie is on my bed, naked, hair spread across the pillow, cheeks still pink with embarrassment from admitting the truth to me. I want to do right by her. I need to get her there, and it sounds like I need to get her to relax and trust me enough to let herself go.

So as she lies next to me, my finger traces a path up and down her spine. We're way closer than we need to be right now, than we should really be, but I'm only thinking about how I can make this right.

"I want you to tell me how I can make this happen for you."

I hate that she ever felt like she had to fake anything with me. I hate that she thought my ego mattered more than she does. Like I was my dad or something, who always said *you take what you want and you win.*

So I slow us down. Even though my body is already lit up and ready for round two.

I brush my knuckles along her cheek first, giving her time to decide if she still wants me this close. If she wants to give it another go. Her lashes flutter, and she turns her face into my hand and nods.

I lean in and kiss her softly. Then I tease the seam of her lips with my tongue before going deeper. Her hands find my shoulders, running up and over to my back.

I pull back just enough to look at her. "Instruct me. Give me a sex lesson. Callie's choice."

She tenses for half a second. I don't think it's fear, I think it's pressure. How many times has she swallowed down what she needed because it was easier than saying it?

I keep my hand on her face, so she knows I'm in no rush. "You can take your time. I'm not going anywhere."

Her throat bounces as she swallows. "Okay."

I kiss her again, slower, trying to let desire build inside her again. Her body relaxes into the mattress. I want her to know that I'm not trying to get anything from her. She has the space with me to find whatever she needs.

My mouth drifts along her jaw. Her neck. The spot under her ear that made her breathe in sharply before. I've never kissed a woman this much, but I'm addicted to her soft skin and subtle scent.

Her body stiffens, and I know she's thinking, worrying, but I continue on my quest.

"You're so beautiful," I say against her skin.

"Foster…" Her fingers weave through my hair as I pull her nipple into my mouth.

I'm not sure I'll ever get enough of that feeling.

"Tell me if or when you want to stop. Otherwise, no apologies, and I'm going to keep going."

She exhales, and her shoulders drop a fraction.

I move my body back up and press my forehead to hers. "Okay?"

"Okay."

I kiss her once, then pull back. "I'm not in a hurry."

The words come out rougher than I intend because there's a lot of truth there.

She studies my face as if she's searching for the catch. I hate every man who has come before me. Hell, I wasn't much better in that department until her, I suspect.

I move lower, kissing along her throat again, my hand sliding down her side. Her skin is hot under my palm.

"Tell me," I urge again, softer.

Callie's eyes squeeze shut, and for a second, I think she's going to back out. Then she takes a shaky breath and opens them again. "I need you to…"

I wait. I won't fill the silence for her.

Her cheeks flush deeper. "I need you to go down on me."

The words land between us and hang there.

My body reacts instantly. A sharp pull low in my gut. A flare of want mixed with panic. If I fuck this up, she'll never ask me or anyone else again.

I've rarely gone down on a woman, if I'm honest. To me, it's more intimate and personal than sex, but here and now, it feels right. It's not as though I haven't been obsessing over how she tastes or whether she's shaved or has a landing strip. That night at the club didn't let me really see her. Not how I wanted to. She's asking me for something that requires trust, and it makes me have even more respect for her.

"Okay." I pull her nipple into my mouth and use my tongue against it.

Her eyes widen a little. "Okay?" Her voice sounds breathy.

I nod, still watching her as I move to her other nipple. "Yes. That's what you want?"

A tiny swallow. A small brave nod. "Yes."

I reach up and run my thumb along her cheek. "Then that's what you get."

Her breath catches, and it hits me right in the chest. That vulnerability. The way she's taking what she wants and asking for it. It's admirable, but I expect nothing less from her.

I move up and kiss her again, slow and deep, then pull away just enough to speak. "You tell me if you want something different. You don't have to pretend with me. Not ever."

Her eyes shine, and that throws me. She blinks fast, as though she's trying to keep it together and not show any emotion. Tonight was supposed to be hot sex, and now we've ventured somewhere I never thought we'd be. Hell, somewhere I never thought I'd be with any woman.

"I won't pretend." Her voice is a whisper.

"Good." I kiss her forehead like a promise.

I shift lower, keeping my hands on her with the hopes they anchor her. I keep checking her face, watching for any sign she's not enjoying this, that her thoughts are running away from her. Callie's fingers slide into my hair, hesitant at first, then firmer, as though she's grounding herself.

I wedge my shoulders between her thighs, my arms wrapping around and pulling her pussy flush against my mouth. I breathe her in and tease the tip of my tongue along her clit.

"That's good." Her words come out like a breath, barely audible.

"Talk to me. Like this?" I swipe my tongue along her core —tasting her, yes, but also myself. While I hope for a time when I can taste only her on my tongue, tasting the two of us mixed together somehow makes my dick even harder.

Her grip tightens. "Slower."

I swallow, my chest aching with her honesty.

I focus on her, on what she's telling me, on the way her breathing changes when I adjust. I keep my pace unhurried. Most of all, I try to keep my mind on point and not get lost in her to make sure I stay on task. At least until she feels comfortable.

Callie's hand trembles in my hair, then steadies. Her other hand finds mine, threads our fingers together, and holds on.

That does something to me. Something heavy takes residence in my chest.

I glance up, and her eyes are on me, wide and glossy, as though she can't believe I'm still here with her.

"Foster." Her whisper sounds as though she's not sure she's allowed to say my name right now.

"I've got you."

Her breathing turns ragged. Her hips shift, and she makes a soft sound that goes straight through me. Then she clamps her eyes shut and shakes her head once.

"No, no, I can't—" She swallows hard. "It's worthless."

I stop immediately. I'd rather load the bases in the bottom of the ninth in game seven than watch her shut down.

"Hey," I say. "Look at me."

She pops her eyes open.

"You're perfect. There's no deadline here. I'll eat you out all night."

A smile teases her lips, but then her mouth trembles. "I hate that it's this hard."

"I don't," I say honestly. "I hate that anyone made you feel like it had to be easy or there was something wrong."

She releases a shaky breath. "Just... keep going."

"If I must." I wink, then grin at her.

She laughs, and I suck her clit into my mouth, twirling my tongue around the hard nub. She grips my hair, not pulling, just holding me as though she's grounding herself. I bring my hand between her legs and circle her entrance with the tip of my finger.

"Yes, oh god, that feels good." She lets out a sound that tells me we're getting somewhere. "Push it in."

I do as she asks.

"Keep your mouth on my clit. Just light pressure."

My tongue flicks lightly on her swollen bud.

"Add another finger."

I follow her instructions, and her ass wiggles against me, her back arching a bit off the bed. If I lose her right now, I swear to god I'm gonna cut off my own dick.

"Arch them. Up... deeper..." Her hands leave my head, and she grips the comforter at her side.

My dick gets harder and harder the closer she is to coming.

"Right there. Suck my clit."

I am but her humble servant, happy to fulfill her every request.

"It's coming... fuck, it feels so good. Your tongue... your fingers... God, Foster..."

Her hands dive into my hair, and she pulls my head into her pussy, grinding and using me for her pleasure.

It's the sexiest thing I've ever seen.

She finally breaks, and if this is a fake orgasm, she should get an Academy Award. The way her whole face changes, the way her fingers lock on, the way she says my name as if I'm her favorite thing in the world. I was a complete moron to think she came earlier tonight.

I stay with her through the waves, until the strands of my hair aren't pulled taut and she's relaxed on the bed, catching her breath.

When I come back up over her, Callie's eyes are half-lidded, lips parted, cheeks flushed. She's fucking sexy, beautiful, and something unlocks inside me knowing I played a part of what she's feeling right now.

I brush my thumb over her bottom lip. "You have no idea how fucking sexy that was."

Her laugh is small and shaky. "Well. Congrats. You did it."

I smile, and it feels different than the cocky one I'm used

to wearing. Softer. Like it should be on Decker and not me. "*We* did it."

"Thank you, Foster. For taking the time with me."

I stare at the wall over her head and try not to let my heart burst out of my ribs because wasn't that the entire point? For her to see she's worth someone's attention?

"I had to prove myself," I say, wishing I could just own up to how doing this for her made me feel, but we're not a couple. We're supposed to be co-parents. Who apparently have the occasional sex lesson.

She relaxes against me, and the panicked urge to remove myself from her washes over me for a second before I kiss the top of her head.

I have no idea how we go back to what it was like before this moment. I don't think we can.

CHAPTER
THIRTY-SEVEN

Foster

We're in the locker room changing for the game. I should be dead tired after last night. Not from what Callie and I did, but from lying awake afterward, rehashing it all in my head.

She eventually got up and left my bed with the excuse that she can't sleep in the same bed as other people, but I guarantee she's lost in her head like me.

It wasn't just sex last night. At least not any sex I've ever experienced. And the trust she gave me, telling me what she needed… but even after that, it left me with so many more questions than answers.

"Hey, Reap, I have a question," Easton calls from his locker.

All of our lockers are right next to each other. Hayes is at the end, then me, Decker, then Easton. Not sure who thought it was a good idea for me to be next to Decker, but we make it work.

"Don't ask," Decker tells him.

I'm guessing they've already been talking on the side about the specifics of how and when Callie got pregnant, so it's pretty easy to figure out what he's going to ask. I figured it was coming.

"I'm pretty sure I'm with Goldie on this one. Let's all remember she's my sister." Hayes clips on his chest guard.

"Come on. We're all wondering. Either they were seeing each other behind my back, or it happened under our noses." Easton fastens his chain around his neck.

I give Easton a look. "Let's get one thing straight. You were trying to date her, but you never did accomplish that."

It's true. Easton and I were having a friendly little competition about getting with Callie. I went along with it because I'm a competitive guy, but I had no intention of ever following through. Plus, I never thought Callie wanted either of us, much less me, until that night. It was just us boys busting each other's balls.

"Just tell us when it happened," Easton says. "And I want it noted that you weren't dating her either. It was a one-night mistake."

"A mistake?" Hayes glances at me.

I shake my head. It wasn't a mistake. I might've been naïve and thought that at first, but now... fuck, I can't even process what's happening with Callie. I've never in my life wanted to spend every free minute I have with a woman before.

"Stop stirring up trouble," Decker says, tying his cleats.

"It's what I'm good at, but I'm not this time. It's genuine curiosity." Easton stands up and faces us, hands on his hips.

I glance at Hayes, knowing two things. One, Easton isn't going to let this go. Two, Hayes doesn't want to hear about the time I fucked his little sister.

I open my mouth, but Easton quickly puts up his hand. "Wait. I want to guess."

"Seriously?" Decker and I share a look that, for the first time in forever, says we're on the same page.

Then we divert our gazes just as fast.

"Let's see… how far along is she?" Easton stares at the ceiling as though he's trying to do the math.

"I don't like this game." Hayes pulls his phone out of his locker and texts who I assume is Leighton.

I wouldn't mind being able to text Callie whenever I wanted. "She's fourteen weeks."

Decker's eyebrows shoot up like he's surprised I even know.

"It's my baby too, asshole."

He holds up his hands.

"See, Kodiak… bad fucking idea." Hayes gives Easton a death glare.

"Was it that day we went to Lincoln Park? For yours and Decker's birthday? Yes." Easton points. "That had to be it. You were a little extra grumpy since you're turning into an old man, and you were looking for some comfort."

"Careful there," Hayes warns. "Don't make it sound like he was using my sister."

"Hate to break it to you, Carlisle, but it was a one-night stand. They were using one another."

Hayes stares down Easton, but Easton is oblivious.

"Was it your birthday?" Easton asks again.

I don't answer, pulling out my phone and burying my head in it, not entertaining this line of conversation.

"Let it go, East," Decker says. "It's their business."

Thank you, brother. Although I'll never tell him that.

"Fine," Easton says, and I glance up, not believing he's actually going to let this go. "I guess it'll be left a mystery…" Then his eyes light up, and he points at me. "Saffire."

I groan.

Decker glances at me quickly as if he knows.

"Math not your strong suit, Kodiak? She would have

already been pregnant then." Hayes shakes his head. "She's fourteen weeks along. We went to Saffire right after the season started."

That tells me Hayes has been wondering too. And maybe I should tell him, but would he really want to know? He wasn't even with us that night.

"Not that night." Easton rolls his eyes. "One night when your pussy-whipped ass couldn't go out."

"We're not fifteen. You can call me pussy-whipped all you want. I have responsibilities. Are you just jealous because I'd rather be with Leighton than your sorry ass?" Hayes uses a crying tone.

"It was, wasn't it?" Easton crosses his arms and stares me down. "You were at each other's throats that night, I remember."

"Which would imply it didn't happen that night." Decker eyes me, and it's the same look we used to give one another when we got caught doing something wrong, and our mom was badgering us with questions. Like, you don't tell, and I won't either.

Did my brother see something that night?

"Fuck no—come on. Reaper is totally hot for someone who gives it back to him. I should've seen it. I was trying to be all flirty and sweet with Callie, but the real way to get into her pants is to try to tell her what to do." Easton grins as if he's the mastermind who's figured it all out.

"Warning, Kodiak. You're crossing a line." Hayes doesn't even bother looking up from his phone.

"Sorry, man. I went too far there. But it's true, that's what gets you both hot. The hate-fuck thing." Easton carries on when he should really shut up.

"Second warning. Watch what happens the next time." Hayes's voice holds a touch more irritation this time.

"Okay, backing off now. Me and Reap can talk later." He winks at me.

All I can think about after his proclamation is there was nothing hate-fuck about last night. Not even close.

But Easton has a point. Callie's feisty side turned me on, but last night it was her vulnerability that really did me in.

I stand and pocket my phone. "I'm going to the bullpen."

"Me too." Hayes joins me.

"Oh, come on. We're friends. Give me a hint," Easton calls behind us.

"Let it go, man," Decker says.

On the way to the bullpen, Hayes asks, "It was that night? The one I wasn't there?"

I side-eye him. It's odd not being able to talk freely with my best friend. I could use his advice after last night, and with any other woman, I would've already cornered him to talk about it. Then again, no other woman has made me want to talk about my feelings.

I glance at him. "Do you really want to know?"

"I don't want details. Just when. I'm still processing."

"Easton's right. We went to Saffire one night. We were arguing a lot, and somehow it shifted and…"

I'll keep the details of us making out until we hit the bathroom to myself. How I flicked the lock, bent her over the sink, and fucked her. And he doesn't need to know that she lowered her dress afterward and walked out without a word or a backward glance.

He nods. "Let Kodiak keep guessing. It bugs the shit out of him."

I chuckle. "I had no plans of telling anyone."

"And whatever you two are doing in that condo you can keep to yourself too."

I stop, and he continues walking. No way he knows about last night. He wouldn't want to know. Some things are meant to be between Callie and me, and for us to figure out.

I think I've figured out what I want. Too bad I can't have it.

CHAPTER
THIRTY-EIGHT

Callie

I get home after interviewing the second podcast guest Foster arranged for me—a sports psychologist who is also a bestselling author and well-known on the internet. I have no idea how Foster has a connection to him, but Dr. Vaughn really went into what made him go into sport psychology in the first place. I think any listeners who are struggling to figure out what they want to do with their lives will love it.

I decide to relax on the couch before walking over to Webber Stadium to watch the Colts game and type out a text to Foster.

> Hey, thanks again for the hookup. Dr. Vaughn was amazing!

Three dots appear immediately, and I'm guessing he's in the bullpen about now.

He had a lot of nice things to say about you
too. Too many actually.

Isn't that a good thing?

Not when I think he's about to ask me for
your number.

He's old enough to be my dad.

Some women are into that.

Well, apparently, I'm into grumpy pitchers with tattoos who make me feel as though it's okay to be me.

Me: Not this one.

I bite my thumb, waiting for his response.

I wouldn't have given out your phone number
anyway.

Good luck tonight.

We should veer off this line of conversation and get back on the co-parenting track. Last night, I made the lame excuse that I can't sleep with other people to get out of his bed. He didn't argue, so I'm guessing he thinks we got a little carried away last night too.

A few minutes go by, so I figure our conversation is over. I should get ready to go to the game. My parents can't come tonight, so I want to go early to help Leighton with the kids.

I have some time, want to play a game of
one for one?

My stomach drops. I figure saying something snappy is

better than agreeing since I'm terrified of what he might want to ask me after last night.

> Shouldn't you be warming up that arm of yours?

> Just thought it might be easier for us if we do it over text.

Ignoring my question, huh?

> I could screenshot your answers and share them.

You'd never do that.

He's right. I wouldn't. But I like that he knows that about me.

Mind if I go first?

> By all means, you seem to be running this convo.

Are orgasms always hard for you, or just with me?

Man, this guy goes right for it.

> Jeez, warm a woman up a little.

Does he really think I'm going to put myself out there? But I guess I did last night. And it's the rules of the game. Otherwise, what's the point of playing?

That's not an answer.

> Why do you want to know?

You can ask that when it's your turn. Answer
the question, Callie...

It's never something that's come easy, but I...

Jesus, just tell him.

...

UGH, you're flustering me here.

It's me. You know the guy who gave you an
orgasm last night. ;)

Want a medal?

Finish your thought.

It can be more difficult for some women, and
I think I'm one of them. But I've wondered if
maybe... it's more about the guys I pick. I
think...

Help, I'm bleeding from a recently inflicted
stab wound... I AM said guy, no?

You made up for it last night.

And I'll do it again—whenever you want.

Just so I have it right... you pick shit men
who only care about getting off and don't
care if you do?

Way to just lay it out there.

I guess so.

So you've had shit boyfriends. Tell me
about one.

Hey now, it's my turn to ask a question.

Sorry...

Why do you care? We're done with that aspect of our relationship now.

Call it an ego thing. I kind of want to pound my fists on my chest and say I did what none of your ex-douchebags could. But I guess it's not that hard a job. You just need someone to give a shit about you.

And as far as we're done in that regard... I don't feel very done.

Do you?

Do I what?

I know what he's asking, but I need to keep us away from that topic. Still, it's fun to flirt with Foster over text like this.

All right then. Question #2 – Did you enjoy yourself last night?

What kind of question is that? Of course I did. Did you?

Is that your question?

No... well... I guess so.

Immensely. So much so that I can't stop thinking about it.

My stomach feels like a dryer tumbling round and round. He's been thinking about last night all day, just like I have.

And what do you suggest we do about that?

Hey now, it's my chance to ask a question.
Didn't anyone teach you to take turns?

I've never been a good sharer.

Something we have in common.

Don't you have a game to play?

I'm a closer, so I've got a lot of time.

Then by all means, ask me your question.

Would you be willing to give me some
lessons?

I read his question, then read it again. It makes total sense now why he's choosing to do this over text instead of in person.

Lessons on what exactly?

Sex lessons.

I cough, and a small bit of saliva gets caught in my throat, and I cough harder, causing me to get up for some water.

Well your silence doesn't bode well for me.

I lean over the kitchen counter and hammer out another text.

You know how to use your tongue, you just
need to use it more often.

That's just it. Right now, I'm no better than
those shitheads you've dated in the past. I
want to change, and since we both agreed to
not sleep with anyone else until after the
baby comes, I figure why not…

> Complicate our situation even more?

Haha… we just need some rules.

> This is a very bad idea.

So was you moving in with me, but—and this is me putting myself out there—I like coming home to you.

My breath catches. My heart soars, but my mind grabs it, tugging it back down. I'm breathing heavily as I stare at the phone screen and read it over and over. *I like coming home to you.*

Just going to leave me out here all by myself, all vulnerable? I see how it is.

My thumbs hover on the phone, but I have no idea what to type.

> I like knowing you're a bedroom away.

Shit, no. I delete that.

> Thanks.

I have no idea what to say. If I tell him what I'm really thinking, it'll only lead to trouble.

lmao… you're welcome.

So what do you say, help a poor soul out?

> I'm going on record as saying this is a horrible idea.

You said that already.

Things can go badly.

Like me, heartbroken in a hospital room and looking down at a piece of him.

It's just sex. No emotions.

We both know that's a lie. Or maybe not. I thought there were a lot of emotions in that bedroom last night, but maybe that was just me.

I opt to keep things light.

You sure you won't fall in love with me?

I'll try but no promises. ;)

I have no idea what I'm going to teach you.

And that's the truth. All of his moves are great, spectacular really. He just needs to devote more time to warming things up at the beginning, I think.

Everything.

Again, horrible idea.

Just until the baby comes.

There's a date when things would have to end. And I *have* been hornier than ever lately. And the idea of sleeping with Foster again appeals of course. He's my catnip.

Does this mean I don't need to buy batteries?

Hell no, I'm expecting you to be my guide with sex toys too. Want to know something…

I don't know. Do I?

I've never used a sex toy on myself or on anyone else. See how bad I need you?

I shake my head, smiling.

Let's talk rules… No sleeping in the same bed.

Never.

No relationship stuff.

Hello, remember who you're talking to.

Anything else?

Again…

Horrible idea. I heard you the first three times. What do you say, Callie Carlisle, will you be my sex instructor?

Twist my arm why don't you.

Perfect. I expect lesson number two tomorrow.

Tomorrow? Why not tonight? If I ask, I come off too eager though.

Just in case things go south for me in the game tonight, I don't want to break a promise.

Yeah, whatever. That's cool.

That wasn't nearly as smooth as I wanted it to be.

I gotta go. I'm playing a game here. Stop
pestering me.

Good luck.

:)

I drop my phone and stare at it, wanting to scroll through and read our texts over.

Did I really agree to give Foster Davis sex lessons?

When you're crying in the hospital bed, you can point that finger right back at yourself.

But I can't sleep with anyone else, and he's right here. Willing and able. And asking. This time is different. It's not like when I was dating other men or in a relationship with them. I know the score going in. As long as I keep telling myself that, I'll be able to compartmentalize and be satisfied sexually.

CHAPTER
THIRTY-NINE

Callie

I'm late to the game because I end up taking a call from a friend of mine from college on my way out the door. It's already in the second inning by the time I reach my seat next to Leighton. Thankfully, she doesn't have the kids with her, so my best-friend conscience is clear.

"Hey, you." I sit next to her. "Where are the kiddos?"

"They're not feeling great, so my mom came over to watch them."

I cross my legs, raising my hand to the hot dog vendor before passing my money down the aisle.

"You couldn't have stopped before sitting down?"

I shrug. "I was in desperate need to get to you."

She hands me my hot dog as it gets passed down the row. "I should've messaged you. Sorry."

"Foster delayed me. Marathon text exchange."

"Can I just say I don't like this? I don't like not being able to tell you about Hayes, and I feel like I know nothing about what's going on with you two. You can tell me, you know. Hayes is kind of like, 'Don't tell me anything unless one of them is going to kill the other' now." She swivels her body toward mine, turning her attention away from the game.

After what I just agreed to, I kind of don't want to watch the game, but would rather talk to my best friend.

I glance around. There are a lot of ears here. "How much will Hayes freak out if you're not sitting in this seat when he looks over?"

"I come to every game. I have three kids home sick, and I'm still here. He can deal with it." She stands and takes my hand. "Let's go up top."

Leighton leads me up the stairs to the strip of pavement where we can lean against the wall and still see the game. People are walking by, but this is as much privacy as we're gonna get here.

"So… what's going on?"

"I slept with him again last night." Might as well just get it out there.

"Callie!" she scolds, then draws back and runs her hand down her body as though that's going to compose her. "Sorry. No judging. How was it?" She grins at me.

"Bad."

Her eyes widen. "Bad?"

"I got in my head about having an orgasm. At the doctor's office, he read this article and…" I tell her the gist of the story, and she shrugs and rolls her eyes as though she gets it.

"Of course, he's surprised. Most men think they're practically porn stars in bed."

I chuckle. "Yeah, well, he wanted to try again, and before he got home last night, I was using my vibrator because the tension between us is insane, Leighton. Like…"

She smiles as though she knows exactly what I'm talking about, and I really want to do the immature thing and say *ew* over it because she's thinking of Hayes, but I don't say anything. Eventually we have to figure out this topic. Maybe I just need to pretend she sleeps with someone other than my brother.

"So you know… and then the vibrator dies."

Her mouth drops open. "No!"

God, it feels so good to talk to her about this.

"Right? And not one battery to be found in his place. I searched everywhere. Then he came home. I'm all hot and bothered and begging the universe to let me come, and he brought up the second chance."

"And then?"

"I said okay." I shrug.

"Oh shit. Hold on." She stops a beer vendor and asks for one. "What do you want?"

I shake my head and bite into my hot dog. "My new vice. Junk food."

She laughs. "Okay, keep going." She sips her beer.

"It was like out of a movie. I'm walking across the room, and he picks me up. I wrap my legs around his waist, and our lips just smash together. We're talking no teasing of the lips, just open mouth, insert tongue. It was so hot…"

"Sounds like it."

"Then the more we got into it, the more I got lost in my head, and I just couldn't come."

"That's the worst." She sips her beer again, then Hayes's walk-up song, "Seven Nation Army" by The White Stripes plays through the stadium. "Shit, hold on a second." She turns to the field. "Let's go, Hayes!"

I plug my ear closest to her mouth. "Jesus, Leighton."

"Sorry. I'm a big talker, but I saw him glance at the empty seats. And he's in a little bit of a batting slump, so I want to be extra encouraging."

We wait for Hayes to step up to the plate. He does his usual setup. The first ball comes in as a strike, and he doesn't swing. The next two are balls.

"Come on, baby," Leighton whispers. "You got this."

He swings and misses.

"Shit, that was fast. Like, hell, what does the radar say?"

I stare at her in disbelief. "Who are you, and what have you done with my best friend?"

She waves at me. "I'm the fiancée of a professional baseball player. Obviously."

The next pitch comes in, and it's a ball on the outside. She blows out a breath. You'd think she was the one at the plate.

"Full count. Way to work him up, baby, but if it's over the plate, hit the shit out of it." She's whispering to herself, and I reluctantly find it cute.

I know she wants the best for him, and maybe because I've seen Hayes go through a lot of slumps over the years, I don't think it's that big of a thing.

The pitch comes in, and I swear Leighton holds her breath, but Hayes swings, connects, and the ball sails through the air.

She jumps up, her beer going with her and spurting out of the top, but she doesn't even care. "Way to go!"

Hayes hits a double down the line to the left.

Leighton's hand covers her heart. "Thank goodness. I don't know if I can handle another night of watching videos of his swing, trying to decipher what's wrong. I love the man, but…"

I laugh and smile at her.

She points at me. "One day, it's gonna be you."

"Yeah, doubtful. Anyway…" I tell her about Foster and how great he was. How amazing the orgasm was when he went down on me and how patient and understanding he was.

"Foster Davis?" She points toward the field although he's in the bullpen somewhere.

"The one and only."

"I knew he was a good one, just needed those edges filed down a little."

"But then he messaged me a little while ago, and he wants to…" I glance around to make sure no one is paying us any attention. "You can't tell anyone this."

She zips her lips with her fingers and throws the key away.

I balk. "Okay, you're hanging around my mom too much."

"Well, at least Hayes doesn't catch the key and put it in his pocket."

"Yet." I'm a little scared Leighton is going to turn into my mother. I love the woman, but… "Anyway, he wants me to give him sex lessons."

Her forehead wrinkles. "He needs them?"

"No. I swear it's a me problem, but he says he has no experience…"

She laughs.

I narrow my eyes. "Taking his time with a woman. Not like he hasn't slept with enough women."

"Gotcha. What happened to the whole 'we're just co-parents' thing?"

"I guess we're co-parents who sleep together?"

She doesn't smile. Actually, inhales a deep breath before she speaks. "Be careful, Callie."

My hot dog turns to lead in my stomach with her confirmation that this isn't the brightest idea.

"It's different this time. See, I know the score going in. That this is just sex, and once the baby comes, we're both free to move on and do what we want. I'll move out, and we'll be good friends."

"Friends?" She gives me a *yeah right* look.

"Yes." I place my hand on her arm to reassure her.

Sure, I have my own qualms about this arrangement, but after the baby comes, let's be honest, my life won't be mine for a good long while. I won't be out dating or trying to meet guys I might have a future with. And I've learned that hope is what leads to heartbreak. I won't hope that Foster will change, so I'll be just fine.

"I'm not sure—"

"I'll be fine. I swear. I mean, Foster Davis isn't one to give false hope, so he won't be doing any sweet little boyfriend things. It's strictly about getting one another off. Enjoying ourselves until the responsibility for caring for this little one takes over." I rest my hand on my abdomen.

She's not saying anything, but I can read her expression. I don't really want to hear her doubts, so I change the subject.

"Did I tell you I'm in stretch waist pants now?" I run my hands down my abdomen, pulling my shirt tight so she can see the swell of my belly.

"Oh, Callie!" Her hand goes to my stomach. "You're showing."

"Barely, but yeah… every time I walk by a mirror, I stare at it. A human is in there. Isn't that crazy?"

She laughs and puts her arms around me. "I can't wait to meet them."

"I can wait for the delivery because now I'm thinking about how he or she has to come out. There's no turning back. Another reason to sleep with Foster—my vagina might never be the same after I deliver this baby."

She squeezes me. "You'll be fine. Many women have gone before you."

"Says the labor and delivery nurse."

We both laugh, and even though Leighton doesn't agree with my plan, I feel lighter having talked to her. It's been a while since the two of us have been able to connect. There's nothing like a little girl time to put a smile on your face.

We eventually go back down to our seats. Foster comes in the game in the ninth for the last two outs. He keeps looking up at the stands, and there's no way he's making sure I'm here. He never even asked if I was coming.

He ends up walking a runner, then giving up a double.

The outing isn't going well, and he's stopped glancing up here altogether. The next guy pops out to Decker. And then Foster strikes out the last batter, ending the game, the Colts winning by two.

"Good way to start the series against Colorado," I say.

Leighton talks to a few of the fans around us.

As we file onto the stairs to make our way up, a woman touches my arm. "Callie Carlisle?"

She's sweet-looking. Roughly my height, a little over average for a woman. A brunette with her hair cut short, but it's her eyes that tell me who she is.

"Hi, my name is Angela… Angela Davis."

I have no choice but to stay next to her the whole time we climb the stairs.

"I'm Decker and Foster's—"

"Mom. He has your eyes."

She nods, and tears well in those eyes that match the blue of her son's. I know absolutely nothing about their situation other than Foster moved away with his dad when he was eleven.

"I just wanted to"—her gaze falls to my stomach—"say congratulations. I heard the news, and Decker confirmed it. I'm not sure—"

Leighton is waiting for me at the top of the stairs. I'm not sure if she sees something in my face or not, but she swoops in, putting her arm through mine. "We should get going." She smiles sweetly at Angela. "Sorry to steal her away."

It's a typical thing we do when people find out we're the family of one of the players and a fan of the team wants to chat for too long.

"Um… are you here visiting?" I've never seen Angela, but I didn't come to a lot of games last year since I was on my podcast tour.

"I'm thinking about moving here," she says. "So, you two go. I'm sure I'll see you around again."

I nod, and Leighton waves at her. "I'm sure we will. Have a great night." She tugs me, and my feet practically drag along the pavement. "You look pale. Are you feeling sick?"

"That was Foster's mom."

She stops and turns to look over her shoulder. "Well, that's probably not a good thing."

Suddenly, it hits me. The whole sex lessons thing isn't the problem. It's the fact that I've been inching closer to Foster for weeks… and his mom just reminded me there are parts of him I'll never get to touch.

CHAPTER
FORTY

Foster

I walk out of the stadium after the press interview, leaving everyone behind. I told Callie we'd have lesson number two tomorrow, but we won the game today, so I'm hoping I can convince her to have a lesson right now. I can already feel the crawling sensation working its way up my spine, and if I don't shove all my thoughts away, my temper will get the best of me, and I'll do something I regret.

"Foster," Decker calls from behind me, but I keep walking. I already know what he's going to ask me. "Come on, man. Just hear me out."

I stop right before I leave the clubhouse when really, I should keep walking. Nothing good is going to come from this conversation.

I turn around.

Decker doesn't even have his shirt on. "She heard the news."

I'm surprised he's getting right into it.

"Good for her." I turn around again to leave.

"She's the grandma."

I whip back around. "And you're going to welcome Dad as a grandpa to your kid someday? Have him over for birthdays and holidays? Hell, let him babysit?"

He winces.

Exactly. How the hell does he think this feels to me?

I was completely blindsided to get on that mound and look at the stands to search for Callie, only to see *her* eyes staring back at me.

"That's different, and you know it."

I pull my bag farther up on my shoulder because I need to get the hell out of here.

Decker steps closer. "She wants to talk. Coffee? A drink? She'll take whatever."

My teeth hurt from clenching my jaw so hard. "She had a lot of years to talk. She chose not to."

"You know Dad. He didn't make—"

"That's bullshit." I point at him. "And you know it. That's what's most fucked up to me—you know exactly what she did, but you continue to stick up for her. Asking me for a few minutes because what? She wants to look like some fawning grandma? Post some pictures on Facebook about her other son and his kid? Give me a fucking break."

He doesn't say anything in return. Because what can he say? Sorry Mommy chose me? That's only going to pour salt in wounds that will never heal.

For a moment, my brother's face looks tired… and sad. "I just… the baby changes things, no?"

I balk. "Why would the baby change anything? I should invite her to do the same thing to my kid that she did to me? Not on your life. She'll never have anything to do with my child. You can run back and tell her that."

"I get it. I understand. There's a lot of shit there, but there are things you need to hear."

I huff. I should walk away. I should leave before this turns even nastier. "Funny, brother, I thought you learned a long time ago that actions speak a helluva lot louder than words. I don't need your explanations. And I sure as shit don't need to hear hers."

A door down the hallway opens, and Penelope steps through it.

Perfect fucking timing to prove my point.

"Have a happy life, but she's never gonna be part of mine."

I give Penelope a look, and Decker turns to see who I'm looking at. I take my chance at escape and leave them. I have someone way more important to see.

I push through the door and see some family members sprinkled around the room. My eyes search out the only person I care about until I spot her. I don't even give a polite nod to anyone. I just walk up to Callie, link my hand with hers, and drag her away from Leighton.

"Well, okay then. Good game, Foster," Leighton calls behind us.

"My game sucked, and you know it, Leighton. Hayes will be out soon," I call back.

Callie comes with me, doesn't push back or try to fight me. Had I tried this alpha maneuver even a week ago, she would've literally dragged her feet and told me she's not going anywhere. Makes me think she's discovered something tonight, but I really hope she didn't. She'll want me to talk about it, and that's the last thing I want to do.

Once we're outside, I keep us in the shadows, walking toward our building.

"I thought we could go out to eat with Hayes and Leighton." She's practically speed walking to keep up with me.

"I'd really like that lesson tonight."

"You said tomorrow."

I tug her and press her back to a light pole, moving closer, sheltering her from the view of others. "I'd like to move it up, if it's okay with you?"

She places her hand on my chest. I love when she does that, but sometimes I wonder if it's her way of keeping people from getting too close. "Foster."

It's in the tone of her voice. Good ol' Ang got to her already.

My eyes narrow. "You talked to her?"

"She stopped me on the stairs." Her shoulders fall, and her eyes give her away. Those big brown eyes show all her emotion, and right now they're filled with pity—the one emotion I fucking hate more than any others.

"Tomorrow it is then." I leave her at the light pole and walk toward the condo myself.

"No, come on." She catches up to me. "Don't be like that. Let's talk. It's clearly bothering you."

"There's nothing to say."

"Talk to me, Foster. I'm a really good listener."

I stop and stare at her.

A group of guys walk by. "Hey, Reap, great strikeout at the end."

"Way to end the game," another says, and I wait for them to walk away.

I meet her gaze. "That's not our relationship, Callie."

She flinches but quickly masks the hurt in her eyes. "Neither was you trying to give me an orgasm. But you had no problem crossing that line last night."

"Yeah, because my ego was hurt." The lie tastes bitter on my tongue.

"That's not true?" The fact that it sounds like a question tells me I'm far from proving to her that some men do care.

"Just go have dinner with Leighton and Hayes. I'm going home." I turn and walk toward the condo.

"Well, I'm not hungry." She walks alongside me.

I grunt like the caveman I'm channeling right now. "You need to eat for—"

"Oh, save it." She walks faster to get in front of me.

I let her go, watching her the entire time as she walks to the building and turns the corner. I slow my steps because I need to cool down and not take it out on her, so some space between us will be good—if only for the walk back to the condo.

As I round the corner, there's a group of people outside Peeper's, which I should've expected. We won, and they've all congregated here, knowing that we hang out here. I'm willing to ignore them, but my gaze snags on Callie talking to two guys. All the anger I've been feeling since I stepped on the mound roars back through my veins.

I walk by and take her hand to pull her away from these douchebags wearing Colorado shirts.

"Hey, man," one guy says.

Callie twists her hand out of mine, and we stare each other down.

"Seriously, what's your deal?" The guy continues to come at me, stepping between Callie and me. "Are you okay? Do you need away from this guy?"

I huff out a laugh, and his friend turns to me.

"Shit." He nods to me. "It's Foster Davis."

The guy looks over his shoulder and then up since I tower over the little shit.

I cross my arms. "Hey."

"Don't let him intimidate you," Callie says, then looks me in the eye. "They were just asking for directions."

"I don't care."

"Guess what? I'm not your property."

"I'll be your property," a woman walking by says.

I shake my head. "Fine. Stay out here. I'm going home."

I flip around and walk over to the gate, staring at the cardboard sign before I type in the security code. The scribble on one of the notes looks really familiar. I tear it off, read it, and crumple it, tossing it on the ground.

Awesome. Things have gone from shitty to worse. Love that for me.

Then I press the code and open the gate with one look at Callie. Her arms are crossed, and her eyebrows raised. I exhale, and our eyes remain on one another as if we're waiting for the other to apologize first.

Who am I kidding? There's no chance I'm leaving her out here alone.

"Fine. I'm sorry. Will you come with me?" God, I do not sound like the Foster Davis everyone thinks I am.

"Say it again?" she asks, cupping her ear as she walks toward me. "I don't think I heard you."

"Fucking hell, I said I was sorry."

"Better." She smiles.

I shut the gate after her, then I cage her against the wall, placing my hands over her head. "I'm sorry for acting like a Neanderthal, but I really don't want to talk about it."

She frowns. "I wish you would."

"I'd rather you be my distraction." I bend and kiss her neck.

"Hmm… I don't know." Her tone suggests she might be on board.

I keep placing kisses up her neck to her ear. "I need you, Callie."

Her fingers tiptoe their way up my chest and around my neck, pulling me down so our lips meet. "You have me, but you have a lesson to learn first."

"Lead the way, Miss Carlisle."

I pick her up, her ass in my hands, and walk up the four flights of stairs to our condo.

I hope she's going to go along with me and not ask any more questions because I can't go there. I'm not even close to ready to share how fucked up my past really is. If I do, I'll most likely lose her.

CHAPTER
FORTY-ONE

Callie

I feel like I'm giving in again. And I haven't done that with Foster, but he clearly doesn't want to talk about what's bothering him. Do I let the issue go and play this part of being an outsider to his life, or do I push him? And if I push, am I okay with him retreating?

He carries me up the stairs and presses my back to the side of the wall as he punches in the security code. It gives me enough pause to know what I have to do. But I'll wait until we're settled in the condo.

He releases me, and my feet hit the floor. Then he drops his bag by his bedroom door. "Where do you want me?"

I take his hand and lead him into the living room.

"You sure you want to dirty up the couch?" He laughs, and I slide us between the couch and the coffee table, signaling for him to sit first.

When he does, I straddle him, placing my legs on either side of his hips.

His hands fall to my ass. "I like this." He's all smiles now.

I place my hands on his cheeks and kiss him briefly. He tries to slip his tongue in, but I pull away.

"Foster." I stare into his eyes. "Do you remember when you asked me to move in here?"

He squeezes my ass. "Good call, right? Look where we are now."

I nod. "In a pretty great place. But do you remember the point of it?"

His smile dims, and his eyes bore into mine. "What are you doing, Callie?"

"I'm reminding you that I'm here so we can get to know one another. So we can be friends. It would be really easy for me to seduce you right now, but what would that get us?"

His head rocks back, and he blows out a breath. "I should've known you agreed too easily."

"I'm not asking for specifics, but I can't let you use my body to hide what you're feeling. Seeing your mom clearly got under your skin."

His hands fall off my hips.

I pick them up and put them back there.

He stares at me for a minute—waiting to see if I'll back down, I think, but I hold his gaze. "I don't want her in my life."

I nod. "Okay."

"And I have my reasons for it."

"Do you want to tell me about them?"

He shakes his head.

I sit back on his lap a little, placing all my weight on him, running my fingers over his T-shirt, feeling the hard muscles underneath. "They used to call me Rebound Callie."

I want him to know that this is a safe space between us, and maybe the only way to do that is to confess something about my own past.

"Meaning?"

I don't look in his eyes, concentrating instead on my finger tracing the lettering on his shirt. "Because it seemed like every time someone dated me and broke it off, they found their person right after me. At first, I laughed it off."

His fingers flex on my hips.

"But when it kept happening… it's not like they all got married after me, but I started to believe them anyway. That I was fun for a moment, but not someone to settle down with. I think maybe that's why I stopped asking guys to take a little more time with me or asked if we could slow it down. I just…" I shake my head. "I started to think I wasn't worth it, and if I made things difficult, they'd leave."

Foster's jaw flexes. "You're going to give me a list of names, right?"

I laugh and my forehead falls to his shoulder. "But last night, you didn't make me feel that way. You made me feel the opposite, that I was worth the effort, and I'm not sure you know how much that means to me. I have no idea where we're headed in the future. This entire co-parenting-with-benefits thing we've initiated is probably going to end in disaster, but no matter what, you helped me realize that it's okay to ask for more. I want to be a sounding board for you. If you'll trust me."

"Fuck, Callie. Now I have even more emotions swimming through me."

I run my hand over his cheek, loving the way the day's growth scrapes against my palm. "Tell me."

"First, I want to kick the ass of every guy who ever made you feel used." I give him a soft smile. "And second, if I go there, I don't want you looking at me like I'm damaged."

"Damaged? I would never."

He licks his lips, and I place my finger under his chin, so he looks me in the eyes.

"Trust me." I hold up my hand. "I know how hard it is, but we're growing this little one." I take his hands from my hips and bring them to my small belly. "We need to under-stand one another."

He stares at our hands over my belly. My small ones on top of his large ones.

"Did you know they're developing facial features and muscles right now?" His palm runs over the bump.

"They are?"

"If they're like their mom, they're probably eyeing me pretty hard right now."

"I think they're smiling at us."

I let him think about it while he strokes my small baby bump.

"Our parents divorced when we were nine." He doesn't bring his gaze up to meet mine. "At first, they did the split custody thing. But when we were eleven, they split us up. I went to live with my dad, and Decker stayed with our mom."

His focus remains on my belly, his long fingers gliding along the swell before he lifts my shirt a little so his palm meets warm skin.

"My dad moved us south because you can play longer seasons down there. The first Christmas after we moved, we all saw one another, but after that, it was one excuse after the other as to why we couldn't go home. My dad had me in camps, in extra lessons, and I wasn't allowed to miss anything. Mom never came to visit. She and Decker stayed in Philadelphia. They just raised us separately. She didn't have time for me, so why should I have time for her now?"

His fingers gently tap my belly, and he lifts his gaze to mine. "She said her and Decker were coming down to visit for this one birthday. I remember I was so excited. She was finally going to see me play, and I'd been doing really well that season. And then she just didn't show up. Then I see Decker share pictures of the season's hot new bat she bought him and a cake, celebrating at some restaurant with her."

My heart breaks when I think about him going through that at that age.

"I don't want anything to do with her. I don't want our child to get to know her. And why would I? So she can send them a birthday card once a year? That's not a relationship. Her showing up here now, right after the news broke, I don't need that. She can wait until Decker has a kid to play grandma."

His anger is valid, and my chest squeezes painfully for him.

"I understand now, and I'd never push you to have a relationship with her. I'm not a believer that just because you're blood, you're family. But would you ever consider talking to her?" He opens his mouth to say something, but I barrel ahead. "Not for her, but for you. To tell her how what she did has affected you. It might be healing for you."

He huffs and runs one hand over my head, pushing some hair behind my ear. "This is the reason I didn't want to tell you. You come from this perfect family, and you only know love. Don't take this the wrong way, but I don't think you can relate."

I'm starting to understand his edge. He likes to keep people out.

"Can I ask you a question?" I ask.

"Well, you did just skin me alive. I guess one more question isn't going to kill me." He laughs, but it doesn't come close to landing.

"Why do you think you're not good enough?"

His cheeks fill with air, and he blows it out. "Shit, digging right into the wound now, huh?"

I lean forward and hug him. He wraps his arms around my middle and tugs me closer to him. "I'm sorry."

"Don't be. I think you can be my new therapist."

So he's had one in the past?

"I wasn't good enough for her to fight for me, or keep me,

or raise me—she abandoned me but stuck by my brother. It's a pretty big gaping wound. I try to bandage it with a I-couldn't-give-a-shit persona, but just like you with Rebound Callie, it's still there under all the layers of scar tissue."

I squeeze him tighter. "I'm sorry, Foster. That she did that to you. That she made you feel that way."

He runs his hands up and down my back. "Thank you."

I pull back, and there's something like relief in his eyes.

"If you hadn't pushed, I never would've told you. Somehow it actually feels good for you to know," he says.

"Look at us adulting."

"You're a good influence on me. And I'm sorry... for pulling you away from the clubhouse, those guys... acting like you're mine. There's no excuse, but I saw red, and I just wanted to get out of there, but I wanted you with me."

I smile. He has no idea how much he's killing me. "I'll always be here for you. But next time, maybe just say, 'Hey, Callie, let's get out of here. Alone.'"

He nods. "I will." We stare at one another for a beat until he breaks the silence. "How about we order in and watch the finale of that show you love?"

"No sex lesson?"

He shakes his head. "Tomorrow—morning—but tomorrow."

I laugh and lean forward a bit to get my phone out of my back pocket so I can order takeout.

"You're the bravest person I know," he says before kissing my neck. "You just charge headfirst into unknown territory."

My fingers sink into the hair at the back of his head as he sprinkles kisses along my neck.

This feels like something different than what we've done thus far. This intimacy and sharing our trauma and wounds are going to get me in trouble. But it's all in the name of love for our baby, right?

CHAPTER
FORTY-TWO

Callie

I 'm ungodly hot, and my eyes slowly drift open, looking around to get my bearings. A heavy arm is swung around my waist, and a hard body is pressed against my back. Oh… Foster.

We must have fallen asleep after eating and watching the final episode of *Southern Charm*.

I shift, but his hand presses gently on my stomach, nudging me to stay where I am.

This is bad. Like, really bad.

He nuzzles into the crook of my neck. "That was the best sleep I've had in a long time."

"We should probably go to our beds," I say, slightly panicked by this intimacy and the way I love being this close to him.

What would it be like if this were my life?

"Nah, I'm good where I am. You're like my real-life teddy bear."

"Um… not a compliment." I roll onto my back so at least I'm not feeling his morning wood pressed to my ass.

A low chuckle leaves him. "Sorry, it happens."

But even with me moving, he only scoots closer, his hand tucking under my ribcage and pulling me closer to him. His mouth finds my neck, and I tip my head to the side without even thinking about it, giving him better access.

A low sound leaves him, as though he's relieved I'm offering more skin. Foster slides his hand along my waist, his palm warm through my shirt, and holds me close, but does nothing else.

My body is like fifty live wires, and I'm aware of every single place we're touching.

His kisses are slow, but after a few minutes, they're delivered with more intent.

"Tell me what my lesson is," he whispers.

"Have you ever just made out with a woman before?"

"You'd be my first," he murmurs against my neck, and my back arches.

My eyes slip open, and he lifts his head, his gaze on me. Making out might quickly end up with us having sex.

"How about you learn about erogenous zones?"

He's found my neck and just under my ear, and I'm already half panting. I'm not sure what shape I'll be in after I show him the rest.

"I'm an eager student." He props himself up on his elbow. "Point to one."

"First, I'll let you choose. Front or backside first?"

He hums, and I swear I grow wet just from that noise. "Backside."

I roll onto my stomach. The couch is squishy enough that it's not pushing up or digging into my tummy. It remains the best couch ever.

"You're going to undress me as you explore my body."

"Sounds amazing." His large hand cups my hip. "Point me in the right direction."

I tap the back of my neck, sliding my hair to one side.

"Hey, that's my job." He tugs away my hand. "Don't make me tie you up."

"Oh, we'll get there."

His deep chuckle rings out behind me. "I hope so."

His fingers slide into my hair, so it falls off one shoulder, and although I know he's going to do it, when he presses a soft kiss to the back of my neck, shivers race up my spine. The kiss lingers. He's taking his time, kissing only an inch over.

"This good?" His voice is low and rough as he continues placing feather-light kisses, each one warmer and softer than the last.

My breath catches, and my eyes drift closed. "Perfect. Move to the sides now and use your hands to skim your fingers or knuckles along my skin."

He slides his hands under the hem of my shirt, his fingertips gliding up my ribcage, and I squirm under his touch.

"You like that." It's not a question but more a confirmation of my body's reaction.

"I do." I let him keep kissing me there because I love having the back of my neck kissed. "Now you're going to slide my shirt up and kiss down my spine. Don't forget your hands need to be doing something too. And no groping me. Try to think of how it might feel to me, not you."

"Hey, no judging something before I even do it."

I giggle, but then he shifts so that he's partially draped over me, keeping his weight from crushing me. His hands slide under the hem, bringing my shirt up as he runs his nose along my spine.

Holy shit—he's a fast learner.

I lift my torso so he can push my shirt up, and then with his help, I slide my arms out, and he tosses it on the floor.

"I feel like it's too early to remove a piece of clothing," he says.

"Are you complaining?"

"Hell no. But when do I get to unhook the bra?"

He chuckles as though he's not serious, then his lips fall to the top of my neck, and he trails them down my spine. I moan, my breath stuttering the farther down he goes, and when he's right above my pant waistband, I want to say fuck it, just have sex with me—but that's not the point of this exercise.

Instead of asking about continuing his path down, he shifts and runs kisses up the side of my body, his hands sliding ahead of his lips, grazing my side boob.

"You can unhook my bra, but you're going to do it and leave my bra on for a few minutes." God, this whole thing now feels like a lesson in patience for myself.

Foster's hands slide up either side of my torso, and he unhooks my bra with more ease than I'd like. I'm smart enough to know that he probably mastered that move at a young age.

"Now I'm going to roll over, and you're not going to remove my bra, got it?"

"You don't have to sound so mean."

I laugh and roll over, but as soon as I see the heat in his eyes, my laughter dies. It's clear I'm not the only one who is turned on right now.

"Did you know that blue is my favorite color?" His eyes fix on my nipples poking through the see-through blue material of my bra.

"Mine too." I stare into his blue eyes.

He sits on my legs, not putting his entire weight on me, and his calloused palms run up and down my ribcage. His hands are so large that his fingers are splaying all the way to my sides. His thumbs tease the bottoms of my breasts, and I suck in a sharp breath.

Foster's gaze bounces around from my face to my breasts to where his hands are splayed over my skin. "You have no idea how beautiful you are."

"I don't mind you telling me."

He smirks and lifts the edge of my bra, testing his touch on the underside of my breast.

"Did I tell you that you could go there?"

"Sorry. It felt natural. Should I not go on instinct?"

I slide the strap off one arm, then the other but keep the bra covering me. "Your instincts are good. Surprisingly."

I giggle, and he pinches my nipple through the fabric.

My giggle morphs into a moan. "Kiss my stomach and travel upward."

I tilt my head, and he bites his bottom lip, sliding down and settling himself on his stomach, kissing my small belly first. The space between my thighs is humming, begging for some attention.

"Now come up as slowly as you can. You're going to leave my bra on. You can use your lips, your tongue, your fingertips, but that's it."

His tongue slips out, and he trails it over my belly button and up to my breasts. He takes the strap of my bra between his teeth and pulls it off my body so that I'm completely exposed. Continuing up the valley of my breasts, up my throat and over my chin until his lips are hovering above mine.

"I don't think I told you to remove my bra."

"Again… instincts. And I really wanted to have my face between your tits. Sorry, not sorry."

Before I can respond, he presses his lips to mine, the kiss like a caress until he slides his tongue through my parted lips. Even then, he doesn't fight for dominance, doesn't try to control it. He lets our kiss ebb and flow naturally.

My hands run through his hair. One thing I absolutely

love about kissing him is weaving my hands through his thick head of hair.

Foster lifts his mouth and trails down to my collarbone. "Where to next, professor?"

"You're going to feel me through my pants. No going under the waistband yet, and you're going to keep kissing me the entire time. Remember, the slower the better, the gentler the better. You have to warm up the engine before we can kick it into high gear."

"Got it."

We continue to kiss, our mouths melding together as his right hand travels down my body until he reaches my hip. He runs his palm all the way down my outer leg, sliding to the inside and back up at a painfully slow, delicious pace.

Thank God I'm wearing yoga pants.

He runs his thumb along my clit, and I close my eyes, the sensation after all this foreplay nearly making me come.

I pull my mouth from his. "Okay, you can go under now."

"You said not yet."

"I lied."

"Either I'm a fast learner, or you're an excellent teacher."

"The latter. Please, Foster… now you need to read that if you don't get me off in the next ten seconds, you might lose your chance." I've never been this hot and desperate in my life. "Just slide your hand down and use your thumb on my clit, but use very little pressure at first."

His fingers tiptoe up until he reaches my waistband, then he slips his hand underneath, but not under my panties.

"I need your fingers on me." There's a begging note to my voice now.

"We'll get there." He bends over and sucks on my nipple.

My back arches off the couch. "Foster…"

He moans and pulls my nipple between his teeth. He touches me over the fabric of my panties, and I want to scream and tell him to give me what I want. That we're long past the teasing stage. But fuck, it feels so good.

He brings his other hand up, running his thumb along my bottom lip, and I nibble the pad of his thumb.

"You're so hot. I thought about nothing but fucking you all day yesterday."

"Keep talking. That's perfect."

He pushes the tip of his thumb into my mouth and applies more pressure on my clit. "This good?"

A moan is my answer, then I suck on his thumb.

"My instincts are telling me to suck your tits. What do you say?"

I nod, more noises falling out of me. He bends and sucks, dragging my breast into his mouth. Oh shit, it feels so good.

"I'm thinking I should use my fingers now. Slide them into this wet, needy pussy. Sound good?" He slides my panties aside.

"God yes. One first, not all three."

His mouth moves up to mine, and I grab the back of his neck, bringing his mouth down to mine. There's no softness, and he pushes one finger in while still massaging my clit.

He groans, a deep, desperate sound. "You're soaked."

I pull him back down to kiss him more because I'm almost there. I'm so close. "Another."

Foster pushes a second finger inside me, using his knowledge from when he went down on me to angle them perfectly.

I lock my hand on his wrist, taking no chance that he'll stop. And I come explosively fast—my entire body tenses, my pussy clenching, my torso jolting. All I see is black and stars until it washes over and out of me.

I open my eyes to find him staring at me.

He slips his hand out of my pants, and I'm about to tell him to lick me off his fingers, but he does it anyway. I've never been more ready for round two so fast.

CHAPTER
FORTY-THREE

Foster

"So you're coming in too?" Callie's head tilts as we approach the hotel.

It's my day off, and I figure why not go with Callie to this podcast appointment? This is the third one I've arranged for her, and I wouldn't mind seeing how it all comes together.

I had her text Lex the address to meet us here, but I've been keeping who the guest is, or guests as it were, a surprise.

"Yeah," I say.

"You're not just walking with me here?"

One thing I've learned about Callie is that she asks a lot of questions when she doesn't know what's going on.

"Yes. Now don't make me ruin the surprise."

The doorman for the hotel holds the door open for us, and I wave her in first.

We head to the venue area. I follow the signs to go where I was instructed. There's security outside the room, but I give them my name, and they check their list.

Lex comes up next to Callie. "Hey, this is weird. What are we doing here?"

"Hey, Lex." I nod to her. "She's with us too."

The guy nods and tells us to follow a woman who he waves over. She leads us into the event space that has been set up for the show.

"Holy shit, you got us into *Iron Ink*?" Lex's voice is loud but impressed. "I love this show."

We're kept offstage, and I watch Frankie Owens walk around the set, checking out the tattoos the contestants did, pointing out what's good and what needs improvement. She's a little cutthroat compared to her husband, Jax. He usually offers friendly tips and is always more complimentary than judgmental.

Jax notices me standing behind the cameras and gives me a little nod.

"Do you know him?" Callie asks in a low voice, so we don't get in trouble.

"He's your guest. And so is his wife."

Her mouth falls open. This is why I wanted to be here with her. Because I knew she'd be impressed, and part of me wanted to see her reaction.

I grin at her. "I don't let just anyone ink me."

"Yeah, but… they're, like, famous. I heard their daughter, Jolie, is better than both of them."

As if summoned by Callie's declaration, Jolie steps onto the set. She doesn't have a single tattoo, but she's definitely the artist most celebrities gravitate toward these days.

The show ends, and Jax puts his arm around his wife's shoulders and turns her toward me.

Frankie's eyes light up. "Foster Davis!"

"Oh my god, I was not prepared for this," Lex whispers, grabbing Callie's arm. "She's so hot."

"Frankie Owens. Still making artists second-guess their calling, I see," I say.

She laughs and hugs me with a pat on the back. "Do you want shitty tattoos on your skin? You should be thanking me." She eyes Callie, then Lex. "Which one is Callie?"

Callie raises her hand. "Me. I'm sorry to interrupt—"

"We're done for the day, but we'll be back at it tomorrow. Jolie has a private client right now, so you only have Jax and me."

"You're icons." Lex's eyes are wide, and she appears a little star struck.

Frankie laughs. "Well, thank you, but it wasn't always like this for us." She turns around and waves Jax over.

He joins our little group, giving me a handshake and a once-over. "What are we doing today?"

"Ah, not until the season is over."

"Callie?" Jax looks right at her as if he's done his research and knows exactly who she is.

They shake hands, and Lex can barely control herself when I introduce her.

"I have an idea. I'm starving, and I've yet to have Chicago deep-dish pizza since we've been in town. Would you mind walking, having lunch, and then we can walk it off and finish the interview? I don't want to change whatever plan you had." Frankie directs her question at Callie.

"I'll take whatever you'll give me. Honestly, I'm just so grateful you agreed to this." Callie's brown eyes sparkle. It's likely not a great sign how much I love being the one who put it there.

Frankie laughs, and Jax joins in, putting his arm around his wife. "Please, we're just normal people. Our friends from Clifton Heights would tell you we're not anything big. One of our friends married a prince, so… we're small potatoes."

This is why I thought they'd be perfect. They tattoo some of the biggest celebrities in the world, but they're also self-made. Plus, they didn't have it easy in their younger days.

Lex gets them set up with microphones, and Callie

decides she'll interview Frankie on the way to the restaurant and Jax on the way back.

Jax and I hang back on the walk to the restaurant, letting the girls do their thing.

"So… a baby?" Jax says.

I nod. "A baby."

"Crazy. You knew her before?"

"I'm friends with her brother. Hayes Carlisle."

"Oh yeah, you brought him by once."

Probably.

"Feels like a real grown-up move. And here I thought you were calling for another tattoo."

"Maybe after the season. I'm trying to help her get some celebrities on her show. Her podcast is gonna be huge soon, so you should be thanking me for getting you in so early."

He chuckles and shakes his head. "I never thought I'd see the day."

I frown. "What day is that?"

"The day Foster Davis was smitten."

My defenses immediately go up. "It's not like that. We're just going to co-parent."

He nods and doesn't say anything.

"What? It's true." I scowl at him.

Jax shrugs. "Okay, if you say so. But you went to a lot of trouble to get Frankie to agree. How many times did you call her?"

"Well, if you could be the man of the house and make the damn decision yourself, I wouldn't have to go through your wife." I chuckle.

Jax nods toward Callie's back. "Just wait. You'll see."

I don't bother asking what he means by that.

We reach the restaurant, and Lex spends most of our meal asking Frankie and Jax questions about their journey becoming famous.

The way Jax and Frankie still look at one another after all

these years is amazing to me. They tell her about how they met, how Jolie isn't Jax's biologically, but he adopted her when she was young. That they have another son who wants to chart his own path. How both of them had many struggles when they were younger, and how they hope their stories help people through Callie's podcast.

At some point, Callie goes to the bathroom, and I excuse myself to get a few minutes alone with her.

When she comes out, I'm standing against the opposite wall.

"Oh." She startles for a beat, then relaxes when she realizes it's me and smiles. "Thanks again, Foster. They're great. Like, couple goals, right?"

"They've been together a long time. Went through a lot of shit to be together."

She nods, and our eyes lock.

I want to open my arms and welcome her into them. Seeing Jax and Frankie always touching each other has made my hands ache to touch Callie. Just a hand on her thigh. Or my arm around her shoulders. My fingers running along the length of her neck. Hell, I'd take the outsides of our thighs pressed together.

Callie's head tilts. "What's with you?"

"I just wanted to make sure you were happy with your number three."

"So happy. I feel like me living with you isn't payback enough."

"I'll take a kiss." It's out of my mouth before I can think it through.

"A kiss? Do you need a lesson on how to kiss a woman in a dark bathroom hallway?"

"Yes. I'm terrible at it." She steps closer, and once she's close enough, I swing my arm around her waist and tug her into me. "You know you're really starting to show. Sixteen weeks now."

"Thanks for the reminder. I hadn't noticed my swelling belly."

"It's sexy as hell. Makes me want to tell everyone it's my baby in there."

"News flash—everyone pretty much knows already. The trolls on the internet for sure."

My eyebrows draw down. "Don't listen to them."

"Easier said… anyway, I thought I was teaching you how to kiss."

"Oh yes. Please show me." I grin at her.

"First, your hands are in a good position, but I need to slide mine around you, so our bodies are flush together." She shifts so there isn't an inch of space between us. "Then you need to say something sweet or hot…"

"Like… I've wanted to kiss you all day?"

She shrugs. "A little generic, but it might work because you're Foster Davis."

"I told you I'm not mediocre."

"Then try again."

I think for a moment. "I've been holding back all day, and I'm done with it. I can't take it any longer. I need to taste you."

Her head rocks side to side. "Pretty good."

"You're satisfied then?"

"I should say something sassy back, but honestly, we're on borrowed time, and you're lucky you're so hot."

I nudge her closer somehow and capture her mouth with mine. Our kiss starts off innocent, but as I knew it would, it grows desperate because I can't get enough of her. Alarms blare in my head, but I don't give a shit. I don't want to come up for air.

"Oh."

We strip our mouths off one another.

Frankie is standing at the entrance of the hallway. "Jax owes me." She grins and goes into the bathroom.

Callie's forehead lands on my shoulder. "I look really unprofessional right now."

Jax rounds the corner and comes to a stop when he sees us. "Oh, you're here too. Frankie lost a contact—we'll be right there." He disappears into the same bathroom Frankie went in and locks the door.

"I think you're safe."

We both laugh and head back to the table, but I link my fingers through Callie's, and she doesn't stop me. It makes me too fucking happy, even if it is just temporary.

CHAPTER
FORTY-FOUR

Foster

I'm getting ready to leave for my game when there's a knock on my bedroom door.

"Come in." My back is turned toward the door as I face my bag on top of the dresser.

The door creaks open. "Leaving soon?"

"Yeah, in, like, five. What's up?" I toss a clean shirt in my bag. Since it's a home game, I don't need much. Just a change of clothes. We're supposed to go to dinner with everyone afterward.

"I was hoping you were still here." She hugs me from behind, her hands reaching around my waist, fingers going right for the button on my jeans.

"What are you doing?" I watch her fingers manipulate my button and zipper flawlessly.

"Turn around." Her voice is a whisper.

I turn to face her, and my dick goes from soft to rock hard in record time.

Shit.

"Callie." I almost choke on her name.

I only get a glimpse of her standing there in a blue lingerie set. The sexiest thing about it might be the swell of her belly over her panties.

She falls to her knees and looks up at me. "You've been such a good student, I think you deserve a reward."

Her fingers hook into the waistband of my pants, and she drags them down my legs.

"Is this, like, my gold star?" I run my hand through her hair, pushing it out of her face because I don't want to miss one moment of this.

"Keep doing such good work, and you can expect a lot more gold stars." She rubs her palm over my boxer briefs, her eyes never leaving mine. "Do you want to sit or stand?"

I run my hand over her face, my thumb running across her bottom lip. "Hate to tell you, but you can do whatever, and I won't be complaining. My body is a pretty simple machine."

She chuckles, nibbling on the pad of my thumb. She does that a lot, and every time, my dick twitches.

"Standing it is." She pulls down the waistband of my boxer briefs, resting it under my balls.

Her gaze on my dick undoes me. It's like she's salivating for a taste of it, stirring something feral inside me.

She wraps her hand around my length, and my body goes tight, every muscle constricting. I swallow hard and reach for anything to grab onto.

Callie glances up, and the look on her face punches the air out of my chest. Her desire to do this, to please me, is so clear. She's clueless about how hot she looks on her knees in front of me, my dick inches from her mouth.

"Callie," I breathe, but it comes out strangled.

She adjusts her hands, using light pressure on her stroke, and my head tips back. A groan slips out of me. My skin prickles, my heart rate picking up.

She moves with patience that feels on the edge of cruel because she's going painstakingly slow. But I have no complaints—she can delay my gratification all she wants.

I look down again, the urge to watch her too hard to fight, but I regret it instantly. Her tongue is out, and I squeeze my eyes shut as soon as she licks up my shaft.

Holy hell.

"Look at me."

I do as she says and her eyes don't stray from me, watching me like I do her when we're together—studying what makes her tick, what brings her pleasure. Even though she could do just about anything, and I'd be good, she wants to be sure I'm enjoying it. She wants to learn how to please me. Nothing is sexier than that.

I slide my fingers into her hair, gathering it gently and holding it in my fist. My other hand lands on the edge of my dresser, and I grip it so hard my knuckles ache.

She moans around my dick, and it unravels me. My breathing turns rough when she encases my entire tip in her mouth, and her lips stretch around my length.

All too quickly, her hot mouth is gone, but she continues to work me with her hand.

"Tell me if you need me to do something different." Her voice is quiet, as though she's offering me control while having no idea that her taking charge is hot as fuck.

"I don't."

Her big brown eyes flash with satisfaction, and she continues, remaining unhurried, and my mind goes blank. My only awareness is of *her*—her hand, her mouth, her saliva, her sounds.

Damn. The sounds coming out of her make it seem as though she's enjoying herself as much as I am. But I can guarantee that isn't the case.

The pressure in my balls builds too fast. I tense, trying to slow it, to make it last, because I don't want this moment to end.

"Callie," I warn breathlessly.

She glances up at me, continuing to stroke my base, to pop her mouth up and down on me. I swear she's smiling with her eyes.

She takes more of me in, and my hand tightens in her hair, desperation clawing up my spine. My hips jerk forward a fraction, and my hand grips the dresser corner until the wood creaks.

"Fuck."

The room grows fuzzy, my pulse skyrockets, and sweat beads down my spine. My knuckles are white. I'm barely able to stand, watching her work me as if she's done it for years.

I push myself to look anywhere but at her, but the need to watch her takes hold, too strong for me to fight. And as I glance down and see her doe eyes looking up at me, something hits me in the chest.

This isn't just sex.

I've been a fool to think this is some transactional swap between us. Because I'm already thinking about picking her up after this, laying her down on my bed, and eating her out. Making sure she gets hers. And that's not me. She's found something inside me I didn't think existed.

The thought snaps something in me.

I'm gone.

My head drops back, my chest heaves, and every nerve in my body lights up like a switchboard.

"I'm gonna come," I warn her, but she doesn't move, continuing to work me over. "Shit... Callie... fuck... God." I'm a mumbling mess until my balls draw up, and I jolt forward, catching myself on the corner of the dresser for the millionth time.

My release barrels up my shaft, and she doesn't move,

swallowing me down. After she's done, she licks my dick while her hooded eyes stare up at me.

When the orgasm fog clears, I'm still in the same position with one hand on the dresser and one in her hair.

Callie slowly rises, hands sliding up my thighs, then my waist, and she presses her cheek to my stomach for half a second, trailing kisses the rest of the way.

I'm completely wrecked for this woman. There's no denying it anymore.

I place my hand on the back of her neck and taste myself on her tongue. She ends our kiss too fast for my liking.

"You okay?"

I'm pretty sure she's asking about the orgasm, but I can't help but relate it to her presence in my life. I laugh breathlessly. "No."

Her eyes soften. "Good." Then she smacks my ass. "Now you have a game to play."

She steps back, but I grab her hand, pulling her into me, kissing her one last time.

"You'll be in the stands?" I ask, already knowing she will be, but for some reason, today it seems more important.

"I'll be there waiting for 'Crazy Train' to blare out of the speakers."

I rest my forehead on hers, unable to stop my smile, because I'm starting to want things that are really dangerous, but I can't seem to stop myself from taking them—even if they're only temporary.

The buzzer rings in my condo.

"I think you're being summoned," she says.

I draw back from her and soak in the sight of her in blue lacy lingerie. "You're going to wear that again tonight, right? So I can take it off of you?"

"Do you need a lesson on how to undress a woman?"

"Yeah, I always fumble my way through it."

She laughs. "Well, I hate to break it to you, but these

panties are really wet right now. I should probably change them."

My dick perks up. "Shit, Callie, I'm hard again."

She laughs again and turns toward the door, stopping in the doorway. "Good luck, Reaper." She winks, and I bite my lip while watching her leave.

Jax was wrong. I'm not smitten—I'm obsessed.

Callie

I'm already outside Webber Field when my phone vibrates in my purse.

Running late but I'm coming…in case you
see Hayes.

I'll let him know if he comes to the fence line.

Thanks. I messaged him but he's probably
warming up the pitchers.

No problem. Take your time.

I stop at the vendor and get a pretzel with cheese and a water before going to my seat. Usually, Leighton is already here when I arrive. My parents are on vacation, promising to be back for my twenty-week appointment and then staying in town until I deliver. I let them know they don't need to do that, but I was told not to argue.

Staring at the four empty seats around me, I quickly grow bored. Isn't that always my problem? I don't love being alone.

Then I realize the manager's daughter is sitting in front of me with her daughter, who looks to be about seven years old. Being Hayes's sister and now the baby momma of Foster's kid, I should probably introduce myself. Plus, they're all alone as well.

I tap her on the shoulder. She looks over her shoulder and smiles instantly. She's dressed casually, but wealthy casual. Her clothes are higher-end, and her designer purse is a glaring "I have money" sign.

"Hi. I'm Callie Carlisle. Hayes's sister."

Her little girl looks up from her coloring book at me.

"Hi." She stands to face me and holds out her hand. "Penelope Ripley, and this is Hazel." She puts her hand on her daughter's shoulder. "Say hello."

"Hi." Hazel waves and goes back to her drawing. She has golden-blonde hair like her mom's, long and straight, and a matching complexion with porcelain skin and peachy cheeks.

"This is our first time sitting here," Penelope says. "We're usually up in a suite, but Hazel said she wanted to be with the fans."

I smile. "It's a little rowdier down here."

She laughs. "I only really don't like it because the fans sometimes say bad things about my dad, and I've been known to go alpha daughter, unable to bite my tongue." She tilts her head toward Hazel. "I'm trying to be a good role model."

"I hear you. One time I almost got physical with a woman who was saying stuff about Hayes. But now I let Leighton fight those battles. She's his fiancée and should be here shortly."

Her head rocks back. "I know Leighton already. We've met. Another reason why Hazel wanted to sit down here. They have children, right?"

I nod. "She'll love Monroe. She likes to color too." I aim it more at Hazel, but she looks at her mom.

"We just moved here. It hasn't been easy," Penelope says. "I always thought friendships just kind of happened when you're young and that it was when you were older that they got harder." She looks onto the field, and I assume she's looking for her dad.

"So sorry I'm late!" Leighton rushes down the stairs with three bags hanging off her arms.

"No Lake?" I ask, seeing only Monroe and Lincoln in tow.

"She's too cool for the game today." She rolls her eyes and plops down next to me. "Oh, Penelope! Coming down with the common folk?" Leighton laughs and gets back up and hugs her.

"Thought we'd lower our standards and see what it's all about down here." Her smile says she's joking, and Leighton laughs.

"I'm kidding. Monroe, you remember Hazel." Leighton drops her bags and pulls out Monroe's coloring stuff.

The two little girls say hello, then look away from each other.

Penelope and Leighton share a look that says *what do we do to get them to talk to each other?*

"Want to get a closer look?" I ask the girls. "Sometimes the players come to the netting."

I stand and take Monroe's hand, leading us down the aisle, then we wait at the next row down for Hazel. Penelope encourages her, and Hazel eventually weaves past the other people who are already here and joins us.

As I predicted, Easton and Decker come over on their way to the dugout.

"Making friends, Monroe?" Easton winks at her.

She shrugs. Usually Monroe is talking a mile a minute. I have no idea why she's so quiet today. I thought she'd be talking Hazel's ear off by now.

"You guys know Hazel," I say, placing my hand on her head.

Decker raises his fist to knock knuckles, but Hazel doesn't do anything.

Lincoln joins us and tries to be helpful. "Like this." He holds out his fist and Decker hits his knuckles.

Decker keeps his hand out for Hazel, and she eventually bumps her fist against his. "There you go."

"So tell us, who's your favorite player?" Easton asks Hazel.

"Why is everything a competition with you?" I shake my head at him.

"Well, you broke my heart and decided to have Foster's baby. Now I'm looking for validation anywhere I can get it."

I tilt my head and run my hand over my stomach, which is growing by the day. "Cute."

He winks. "I think so… sorry your guy is in the bullpen, and I heard it's your fault he was late this morning."

"No, it wasn't." My face heats.

"Something about putting too much soap in the dishwasher? I swear if it leaks down into my place, there's gonna be hell to pay."

My tension eases, and I'm glad to know that Foster isn't a kiss-and-tell kind of guy. "Relax, it's all fixed."

The guys talk to Hazel, Lincoln, and Monroe about whether they're excited about the game. I notice Hazel is very quiet, and Lincoln is the one leading the pack. By the time we say goodbye and go back to our seats, Penelope is up in our row. Leighton tells Monroe and Hazel to sit in front of us.

"Thanks. Maybe she'll talk more if she's sitting with her," Penelope says. "I was telling Callie the move has been hard, but…"

Leighton and I nod.

"Big life changes are difficult." Leighton pats Penelope's

leg. "I lost my cousin last year and became the guardian of these two, plus their older sister. It's an adjustment."

Penelope's eyes widen.

Leighton says, "They're doing great. It wasn't the easiest path, but we're figuring it out. And so will you. Sometimes it just takes longer than we'd like."

"Aunt Callie, can I have a piece of pretzel?" Lincoln asks me, and I turn my attention to him, allowing Leighton and Penelope to talk.

Just then Hayes comes out of the bullpen with McCarthy, and they're walking toward the dugout. He waves to Leighton, and she blows him a kiss.

"It's rather sickening, these two," I say to Penelope after Hayes disappears.

"It's cute." Penelope smiles at Leighton.

"You know who's cuter?" Leighton interjects, and I groan. "Did you know that Foster and Callie are having a baby?"

Penelope smiles at me, but it's one of those apologetic smiles for knowing something she shouldn't. But it's not her fault that social media hasn't yet let go of Foster Davis having a baby with his catcher's sister. "I heard."

"As did everyone," I say with an eye roll.

"And they're so cute," Leighton goes on. "Especially since Foster is..."

A look crosses Penelope's face, almost like fear, but she masks it with a smile that doesn't reach her eyes.

I can't help the gut feeling that I'm missing something here, but I have no idea what it could be. I mean, Ripley did coach in Seattle while Foster was there, but Penelope was married then.

Sourness hits my stomach, and I tell myself not to think too hard about whatever this gut reaction is. It's just fear scratching at that scab.

"...so into it. I mean, you'd think he wouldn't be so on

board with this pregnancy, but he's all protective…" Leighton continues, but I don't hear much of what she says because my mind spirals somewhere it has no place going.

"I'll be right back." I hand my pretzel to Lincoln.

"Wow, thanks, Aunt Callie."

I walk up the steps and into the bathroom, pulling my phone out of my pocket. There's a message from Foster that I must have missed.

> Step away from Easton.

I smile to myself, all those fears disappearing.

> He was talking to the kids.

> Sure he was. FYI, I told them something happened to our dishwasher and that's why I was late meeting them downstairs. In case he brings it up.

> He did, and I played along. After having a heart attack that you told them I was on my knees in front of you in blue lingerie.

> Just so you know, if I pitch like shit, it's your fault because I'm gonna be seeing every batter as you in that sexy lace. I want to tear it off with my teeth next time you're wearing it.

> Is this sexting?

> Probably not the best time, but you started it.

> One for one?

> You first.

> I loved making you fall apart.

I loved you making me fall apart.

I hug the pone to my body, knowing we're playing with a Costco size box of matches, but I can't seem to care.

CHAPTER
FORTY-SIX

Foster

When the stadium goes black and the sound system plays "Crazy Train" by Ozzy Osbourne, adrenaline pumps through my veins. I'm more excited to go out there than I've been in months.

I want to see her right there behind home plate. I want to see her smile and hear her cheering for me.

As I cross the field, my eyes search her out as Art checks my glove and hands, but I'm not close enough. Hayes, Easton, Decker, and the rest of the infield wait for me on the mound. Ripley holds the game ball in his hand, and I blindly hold out my palm. He places it there.

Hayes says something to me that I don't really hear because I'm searching the crowd, and when my eyes find her, as cheesy as it sounds, calmness flows through my body. Now all I care about is ending this game and going to dinner with our friends with her next to me.

I'm not thinking about strikes or balls. My slider or my fastball.

I'm thinking about us returning to the condo tonight.

Until I see who she's talking to.

All that elation gets smothered with a hundred-pound weight because sitting right next to her is Penelope Ripley.

My hand clenches around the ball.

I'm fucked.

CHAPTER
FORTY-SEVEN

Foster

I have no idea how I manage to do it, but I pitch better than I have all season. So much so that there's a text from my agent waiting for me when I get in the locker room.

> Jagger Kale: Finally… this is good. We have a lot of eyes on you right now. Keep it up and something will come through.

Hayes slaps me on the back. "Great job tonight." He sits on the bench to undress.

"Thanks."

I would be ecstatic if not for the fact that a woman from my past was talking to the woman carrying my baby, and she didn't even know it. Now I have to have a very difficult conversation with Callie with the hopes that it doesn't change our dynamic.

I should've seen this coming, but I don't give Penelope any thought if I'm honest.

I head to the showers, the water washing over me not calming me one bit. The fear that I'll lose everything we're building and Callie will walk away from me is eating me up inside.

Hello, childhood trauma, great to see you again.

And just like with the pregnancy news and Hayes, I want to tell Callie as soon as possible. I can't stomach this torture.

I leave the shower and get dressed, stopping right before I walk out. "Hey, I need to talk to Callie about something. We'll meet you at Peeper's, okay?"

Hayes nods, a few lines forming on his forehead. "Everything okay?"

I could tell Hayes, and he might tell me I'm overreacting. That Callie will handle this fine. Surely, she knows I wasn't celibate before her, but I'm not sure Hayes is aware of how hurt Callie still is from her past relationships. How hard she fights to trust people, men especially. And I've worked really hard to get her to trust me. Hell, I even told her about my mom, which is something I've never done—with anyone.

"Yeah." I play it off as best as I can. "It won't take long."

I hope.

"Cool, see you there."

As I walk out of the clubhouse, everyone nods and tells me good game. It's been a long time since my pitching felt so flawless and effortless. Like I could depend on my arm again.

Some of the families are waiting around, and Callie is with Leighton, having a conversation, as Lincoln and Monroe run around with Penelope's daughter, Hazel. Standing next to Leighton, Penelope glances up from her phone, and our eyes catch for a moment. She offers me a small smile, but I shut it down immediately.

"Hey, you!" Callie hits my chest with the back of her hand. "What a game. Congrats!"

She's all smiles. What I really want to do is swoop her into my arms and kiss the shit out of her, but there are a lot of eyes here, and she's not really mine.

"Foster, they said your fastball hit 103!" Lincoln's mouth is open, and his eyes are wide.

I ruffle his hair. "It was a good day on the mound."

He smiles up at me. "Are you coming for pizza?"

"Can Hazel come?" Monroe asks Leighton.

I leave Leighton to answer Monroe and lean into Callie. "Can I talk to you before we head out to dinner?" This time I act nicely instead of taking her by her hand and dragging her away from her friend.

"Look who learned his manners." Leighton laughs.

Callie smiles. "Okay, sure." She slides her hand into mine. "Let's go check that dishwasher." She winks.

I feel as if I'm about to be sick. She probably thinks I want to celebrate my win, and I hate that I'm about to blindside her.

"We'll meet you there," I tell Leighton.

I really hope Penelope and Hazel will not be joining us for dinner.

We walk out of the stadium, and thankfully it's a weeknight, so not as many fans are hanging around the bars and restaurants. The sidewalk isn't that busy, and I want to spit the words out, but they clog my throat. I should wait until we reach the condo anyway, since I'm not sure how Callie will react.

"People were going crazy. Did you hear them all cheering and yelling for you?" she says.

God, she's oblivious, and I fucking hate it.

"A little, but I end up with tunnel vision when I'm in the zone like that."

She tugs on my hand. "Hey, be happy. You should be on a high."

"It's just my job." I'm struck for a moment because I've never once thought of baseball as *just my job*. It's always been my priority, my number one, my life. There is nothing bigger or better than who I am on the mound.

"And you deserve a raise after that performance."

I shake my head.

"Foster, you came in during the seventh with bases loaded and the leading run on third. No outs. You got out of the inning with three strikeouts." She's practically jumping at my side with excitement. Definitely way happier than me. "Then you came back in the eighth and not one player got to first base. And don't make me talk about the ninth. It was a stellar performance."

Thankfully, we reach the condo, and I don't even bother to look at the cardboard sign because I just want to get this over with.

"I'm gonna be honest, I expected a little more than this. I give you a blow job, and you pitch amazing, and you're still grumpy?" She stops outside the door of our condo while I enter the code into the keypad. "Why aren't you saying anything?"

We step inside, and I shut the door, flicking the lock, then rest my back against the door.

"I slept with Penelope." Getting it out doesn't feel as good as I thought.

Her smile and excitement are doused like a bucket of water on a flame. "Oh…" She turns and heads to her room, but stops in the doorway and circles back around. Facing me, her eyes meet mine, strong and steadfast. "When?"

Oh fuck. I'm an idiot.

"No, I mean… Jesus, I knew I'd fuck this up." I pinch the bridge of my nose. "Not recently. I'm sorry, I should have phrased that differently."

She shakes her head. "It's fine. It's not like we're anything, right? I mean, we're just co-parenting, but I did think we had agreed—"

"Callie, it was back in college." I push off the door. "I swear to you. It was so long ago."

She nods. "Oh, okay then."

I take her hands, and she lets me lead her to the couch. "Her dad was my coach in college, and it was a short-lived attempt at a relationship. I, of course, fucked it up and was a total dick to her. But I wanted you to know. I didn't want you in the dark when she obviously knows what happened. It felt unfair to you."

She's staring at her hands, but she nods. "I knew you slept with other people. I have no right to be mad, but…" She looks up, and there's not really hurt in her eyes but something else I can't figure out. "I thought you meant now and… well…" She shakes her head. "I mean, it's fine. I've slept with people. Not anyone you know, but clearly, we've both had partners. It's a little weird since I'll have to see her and stuff, but we aren't anything anyway, right?"

I take her hands and want to tell her we *are* something. Ask if she feels the same way I do because I've never felt anything like it before. But she doesn't need my bullshit while she's pregnant. And what if this doesn't last? What if right after I tell her, those feelings disappear? I've never been a person someone could rely on. Never been the kind of person someone wanted to stay for.

"I'm sorry." I grip her hands. "That you have to deal with this."

"She's really sweet."

I nod. "She's a nice person. At least she was. I've barely spoken to her since I came to Chicago. And I want you to know, and maybe you don't care, but she was just some girl in college. It was a really fucked-up time for me. We went to the same school, and Decker was in college the next town over, and… I thought my brother and I were getting our relationship back on track, but…"

She looks at me and waits.

So I tell her the whole story—Decker, Penelope, and me. How messy and shitty that part of my life was.

Callie seems to understand better after she hears the story. "So you weren't in love with her?"

I let out a somewhat caustic laugh. "Callie, I've never loved anyone."

That flicker in her eye burns out, and her usual shine dulls. My gut twists because she was probably hoping I'd say I had loved someone before.

"I'll love our baby though. I know that for certain."

She gives me a sad sort of smile. "I know." Then she kisses my cheek. "Thank you for telling me. Let's go see our friends now." She stands, putting my face level with her belly.

It's growing, the swell becoming more pronounced. I want to put my hands on it as I always do, but this doesn't seem like the right time.

"Just like that?" I ask.

She smiles and nods. "One for one?"

"Sure."

"When I thought you slept with her last week, I was going to move out, and this whole thing was going to end. I have feelings about what you just told me of course, but I can't be upset, Foster. I know there were women before me."

Sure, there were women, but Penelope is really the only relationship I ever gave a go. But I keep that to myself, so she doesn't think I'm too much of a screwup.

"And I really appreciate you wanting to make sure I wasn't blindsided." She briefly kisses me on the lips. "That's what's most important to me—you put my feelings ahead of your fear of telling me."

"I was terrified this was all going to end." I give her one last confession for the night.

"Well, no worries. Now let's go celebrate your performance. You deserve it." She takes my hands and urges me up off the couch.

Once I'm standing, I wrap my arms around her, holding her against me. "You're really a rock star."

She shakes her head and puts her hand on my chest. "You're the rock star. Now come on."

Then she slips out of my arms.

I want to tell her I want to stay here in the condo with her, that I want to be alone with her. But that's something that couples do, and we aren't one. It's just hard to remember sometimes.

CHAPTER
FORTY-EIGHT

Callie

A couple weeks later, my hand lands beside me on the shower wall, my fingers running along the steamy glass, needing something to anchor myself to. "Oh my god, Foster."

"You have no idea how bad I wanted you all night."

His head is buried in the crook of my neck, his cock deep inside me.

It was supposed to be a sex lesson, but as they all have lately, it morphed into just sex. It turns out Foster is a fast learner and a committed student, because he's playing my body as though he's known it for years.

"Remember the penetration talk?" I say, my voice breathless.

His hand slips between my legs, and two fingers land on my clit. My back arches up, but he keeps me in place with his hand under my ass. The water is warm and streaming over us, but my back is pressed to the glass of his shower.

"Yes, clitoral stimulation is a must." He groans when I clench around him.

"It's just unlikely that I would…" But at this point, I'm thinking we should see if I can come from penetration alone because holy shit, this angle or whatever it is—I'm about to fall to pieces under his spell.

"Doesn't seem like you're having a hard time…" He laughs into the curve of my neck, his tongue licking upward until he encases my earlobe in his mouth. He nibbles on it and his fingers dig into my ass, manipulating our angle so he can get even deeper.

"Foster, you feel so amazing."

"That's it. Keep praising me." I swear he practically growls. "I get off when you tell me I'm doing well."

"Want me to call you a good girl?"

He rears back. "Hell no."

"Well, if you have a praise kink." I grin at him.

"Just tell me that no one has ever fucked you this good." He uses his hips to give a particularly brutal thrust, and a moan slips out of me.

"Only you, only you're this good," I rush to get it out, praying he doesn't stop anytime soon.

"That's right. Only I can get you like this."

"You're being really alpha." My fingers curl along the fogged glass. "That's okay, you deserve it after all your hard work and the orgasms you've given me."

"I had a great teacher." He applies a little more pressure to my clit, and my body turns to Jell-O from the sensation of my orgasm drawing near.

He continues to fuck me and play with my clit, and I extend my foot to the shower shelf to use it as leverage and lock in our position.

"It's happening," I say. "I'm coming."

"Good girl."

I didn't think I had a praise kink, but holy fuck, that was really hot.

I come hard, and he smashes his mouth to mine, the kiss hungry and desperate until he stills, emptying himself inside me. We remain locked together, panting with him plastering me against the shower wall.

"You know what sucks?" I say.

"That a man needs time to recover before he can do it again?"

I chuckle, but there's a sort of sadness to it. "That I made you into a sex god for some other woman to enjoy." As the thought comes out of my mouth, I realize that that painful truth is too raw and real, and I wish I'd kept it to myself.

He rests his forehead on mine. "What sucks for me is that the only one I want to enjoy is you."

Oh heart, don't soar. Don't hope that this could be something more than what we agreed on.

We stay like that a bit, each digesting the other person's words, until Foster gives a quick swat to my ass. "I hate to be the bearer of bad news, but we need to get going."

"You started this." I slide my leg down and his dick slips out of me before he positions my feet on the floor, taking care to make sure I have my balance before he lets go. "Now I really do have to shower."

He turns the water on us, and we both shower, washing ourselves. I admire his body when he's turned toward the water, and I hope he's doing the same when I wash the soap off mine.

When we step out, he wraps a towel around my shoulders before grabbing one for himself. It feels very much like a relationship, and I wonder if the blurred line between us has now been erased completely.

Foster Davis and I have entwined our lives completely, and it's going to be a mess to try to unravel.

CHAPTER
FORTY-NINE

Callie

It's Foster's only day off for the next ten days, so after our escapade in the shower, we decide to use the opportunity to go out and shop for the baby and have lunch together.

The moment we step into the baby store, a woman greets us, beaming.

"Oh, we hoped you two would pick our store." She folds her hands in front of herself.

Foster places his hand on the small of my back, his fingers flexing then relaxing.

One of the things I've realized about him is that he hates social media and the insight it gives people into his life. I've also realized that he has better restraint than I do when it comes to reading the comments.

"Really?" I ask. Clearly, she knows who we are.

"Yes, and you can rest assured. We take care of all the Grizzly and Falcon families. Even a few of the Trojans, but we're a little far north for them." She steps closer.

Foster's hand does the whole flexing and unflexing thing again, as though he's going to attack if she comes any closer. I'd never tell him, but I've grown to love his protective nature even if it's only because I'm carrying his baby.

"We're just browsing today," I say.

She glances at my stomach. "How many weeks are you now?"

She phrases the question as if she's been following my pregnancy. Sure, I have a social media presence and have been chronicling the pregnancy a little, but I feel a little creeped out that she phrased it the way she did.

"Eighteen weeks," Foster answers for me.

"The bigger you get, the more uncomfortable the heat will be for you. I can give you the name of a maternity store that all the WAGs use."

Foster growls under his breath, but I'm proud of him. At least he's not just walking away from her.

"And are you going to find out the sex of the baby?" she asks.

Foster's fingers dig into my side. If I don't get him out of this situation, grumpy Foster is going to make an appearance.

"Um… we haven't decided." I wave my finger in the air. "We're going to look around, then maybe we can make a date to register." It must be what she's looking for, to make sure all of our friends and family come here to buy stuff.

"Yes, of course. Sorry, we're just so excited to see you." She smiles.

I'm not sure who *we* are, since there doesn't appear to be anyone else here, but I take Foster's hand and lead him to the opposite side of the store.

"So, this is going to be our life."

I don't recognize a lot of the items. The more we look around, the more panicked I become.

"What is this?" I pick up an item by a crib.

"You put that around your head." Sally, the saleswoman—

whose nametag I can read now—puts the contraption on her head. A pole shoots out from the headband with something dangling off of it.

My head tilts. "It's a wearable mobile?"

She nods, and it bounces.

"You gotta be shittin' me," Foster mumbles.

"This way when you're changing the baby's diaper, he or she has something to look at." She demonstrates over a changing table where a plastic baby lies.

"They can't just be happy looking at Mom or Dad?" Foster looks at the woman as though she's an idiot.

She takes it off and puts it back on display. "You don't want the baby to be bored."

"Boredom never killed anyone." To his credit, Foster's voice isn't the grumpiest I've ever heard it.

I smile at Sally. "Thanks for explaining it to us."

Foster picks up something else and gives me a questioning look.

"It's a nasal aspirator." Sally takes it from Foster. "See, you put this in the baby's nose and then you suck."

"I what?" Foster palms the back of his neck.

She smiles at him. "You suck, and the boogers come out."

He looks at me, and I think he might be starting to panic.

"It's one of our most popular sellers," Sally assures us.

I pick up a spatula-looking thing. "And this?"

"To spread the diaper cream so you don't get it on your hands." She again demonstrates on the doll as if we can't put two and two together.

"What haven't they invented?" Foster continues to pick up items and put them down, each one seeming to make him more baffled.

"Thanks, Sally. This is all a lot for first-time parents, but you've been more than helpful." I give her what I hope looks like a sincere smile.

"Of course, I'll leave you two to it, but just grab me if you need me." She looks at Foster, and her gaze feels a little covetous to me.

I'm about to growl and show my teeth.

What the hell was that?

Foster is oblivious, hitting a mobile with his finger. "Hey." He turns to me after Sally leaves us alone. "I don't want anything baseball."

I stop, but he continues checking things out, so I follow him. "What?"

"I don't want any baseball things for the crib or on the walls. Nothing baseball, okay?"

He tries to walk away, so I take his wrist and tug him back to me. "Why?"

He glances toward Sally. Thankfully, the phone rings, and she walks away to answer it. At this point, I don't even care that she's probably telling whoever is on the phone that we're here.

"Because I'm not going to shove anything down my kid's throat."

I frown. "But you love baseball, no?"

I don't have any specific plans on what I want for the baby's room, but I'm thrown that a major league pitcher doesn't want anything baseball in his child's room.

"I do love it, but I didn't always. And I don't want him or her to feel like they have to like something just because I do."

It sounds as though this really matters to Foster, and I figure this is a fight I have no say in, so I nod. "Okay, no baseball. But just so you know, lots of people are probably going to give us baseball-themed gifts."

He shrugs. "That's fine. But we won't buy any."

This isn't the place for me to push him to talk about it more, so I let it go. The last thing we need is Sally gossiping to her friends about us any more than she already will.

"What should we buy today? The stroller? Crib? I suppose we'll need two of everything, but I was thinking—do you think you should stay for a while after the baby is born? I'll be in the off season, so we can tackle it together." He wraps his arms around me and pulls me into him. "Plus, I might need more lessons."

I draw back and look up at him. "First of all, I think your lesson days are drawing to a close. And you do know that after this baby comes out, I can't have sex for at least six weeks, right?"

He looks down between us. "Really? I guess that makes sense. You're pushing a baby out."

I shudder. "Don't remind me."

I ignore the tug at the back of my mind that says that's all he really wants from me.

We both look around the store and at one another. "Lunch?" we say at the same time.

Are we ignoring our future, the inevitable? Yeah. We tend to ignore a lot of things that are coming our way. There will be a day I'll have no choice but to face it, but today isn't that day.

Foster

It's as though my mind can't filter my thoughts before they come out of my mouth when I'm around Callie.

Telling her that I don't want any baseball stuff is just waving another red flag in front of her. She didn't push me this time though. She let it go, but I need to be prepared that she'll ask me again.

We ate at a small Mexican restaurant that makes their own tortillas. I'll definitely be back. The place was phenomenal.

Now we're walking back to the condo, but she stops outside a white building that has big green letters saying *The Last Chapter Book Shop*.

"Want to do the very cliché thing of buying baby name books so we can each highlight our favorites and compare?" The way her entire face lights up, there's no chance I can say no.

"Only for you."

Her smile grows, and she preens before moving toward

the door. I reach around her, opening the door for her to walk in.

"It's adorable." She moves to a display table, perusing the books there.

I've never been much of a reader. It wasn't like my dad ever pushed me to be. Not even an inspirational athlete's story. Academics were always secondary to baseball. Hell, *everything* was secondary to baseball.

"Hi, welcome to The Last Chapter." An olive skinned woman with long dark hair and glasses greets us from where she's shelving some books.

"Hi." I follow Callie around as she says, "We're looking for baby name books." She runs her hands over her baby bump as though the woman wouldn't have noticed that she's pregnant.

"Oh, I'm sorry, this is a romance-only bookstore."

"Romance only?" Callie asks and glances at me. "I didn't realize there was even such a thing. Thanks, we'll look around."

"If you have any questions or want any suggestions, my name is Amanda." She turns to me. "Sports romance is over there." She points.

Callie turns toward the wall, where what looks like all the categories of romance are highlighted. She looks as though she's trying to decide where to start. "Thanks. This is so fun."

I decide to head to the sports section, figuring I'll buy myself some time until she's done.

"Don't go falling for some fictional man when you have me at home," I say to her.

She waves me off and ventures down the row.

The door to the store opens. I turn to look and am shocked to see Conor Nilsen with his wife, Eloise, walking through the door.

Shit, I thought Callie's stomach was growing. Eloise looks ready to pop.

"Eloise!" Amanda walks over, and the two of them hug as best as they're able to with her stomach.

Conor stares after his wife but catches me watching and laughs. "Shit, what are the chances?" He comes over and puts out his hand.

"Enjoying off season?" I ask as we shake hands.

"Getting some reading material since Eloise just got put on bedrest until the baby comes. This is her happy place, so here we are before we head back home." He pats me on the back and glances at the sports romance shelf I was looking at. "Didn't figure you for a romance reader."

"No. My…" I have no label for Callie. Baby momma makes me want to throw up. Friend isn't nearly accurate enough.

Conor must realize my hesitation because he laughs again. "Carlisle's sister, right?"

I nod, thankful for the out. "She's back there somewhere." I thumb in the direction Callie disappeared.

"Piece of advice? Don't get all jealous of her falling for some book boyfriend. If the book is good enough, you'll reap the benefits." He winks, and I huff out a laugh.

Conor and all the Falcons are cool. Sometimes at Peeper's, we all end up in the backroom together, and it's usually a lot of fun. From what Hayes told me, Hayes, Decker, and Easton came into the building after Conor, Tweetie, and Rowan moved out. All three of the hockey players bought houses on the same street as Henry Hensley, and the four of them are raising their families together as neighbors. I can't even imagine being that close with my teammates.

"I hope you're not thinking you'll find a baseball book up here." He points toward the wall.

I turn to inspect all the covers, realizing quickly that the majority of them have hockey players on them. One after the other—hockey, hockey, hockey. Puck this and puck that.

"What the hell?" I raise my hand. "Hey Amanda, can you come here for a second?"

Conor laughs and crosses his arms, settling in. Amanda walks over, and Eloise follows. Conor gives a brief introduction between his wife and me.

"You here by yourself or with someone?" Eloise looks around, and her eyes light up when she sees Callie walking around the end of the row. "Callie!"

Guess they've met before.

Then she's gone.

Amanda looks at Conor first. "Hey, Conor. Sorry, no book has been fan-fictioned off of you yet that I know of."

"I heard Piper Rayne might be writing one." He shrugs.

"I'll keep my eyes out." She shakes her head, and I get the feeling this is a conversation they've had before.

"Look for *Mr. Swoony*. I think the title fits me. Right, Lulu? Me as Mr. Swoony?" Conor calls to Eloise, and she smiles, but it's appeasing.

"Amanda, are you hiding the baseball books in the back or something?" I scour the covers, and hockey outnumbers baseball twenty to one. There are even more football books than baseball ones.

She cringes. "I'm sorry, hockey is really big in sports romance."

"Why?"

Conor's eyebrows rise. "Do you really have to ask? We have to chase a little black puck around with a stick while we're on skates and our opponents try to slam us into the boards. What's the most you guys get—a pinkie sprain or a calf pull?"

I tilt my head. "First of all, look at me. I look a helluva lot tougher than you."

"Why, because you have neck tattoos?"

I purposely position my head so I'm staring down at him. "I've got you by a few inches."

"I don't think this is a competition," Amanda says. "If they write 'em and they sell, I'll stock 'em."

"You can't blame her because the romance girlies don't want to read about your lame-ass baseball players," Conor says.

"Sure, they'd rather read about a bunch of goons throwing punches on the ice." I roll my eyes.

"What's going on over here?" Callie comes over with Eloise, and both have a stack of books in their hands.

Conor and I reach to take the books from them and are met with a scowl and a look that says *I am perfectly capable of holding a few books.*

Callie looks between the three of us. "Are you guys bothering poor Amanda?"

Eloise looks at Amanda, "Sorry if their egos get out of hand."

"Look at the wall and tell me what's wrong with this picture?" I say to Callie, motioning with my hand up and down the wall.

Callie slides between us and inspects it, picking up a hockey romance called *Faking it with #41.* "Oh, this looks—"

I swipe it out of her hands and put it back on the shelf.

Conor cracks up laughing.

"I can't read that one?" Callie arches an eyebrow.

"You should let her, then she can be thinking about a hockey player when—"

"Don't finish that sentence." I point at Conor.

He just laughs harder. "You are too easy to rile up."

"Leave him alone." Eloise shakes her head at her husband. "If it helps, his ego soared to new heights the first time I took him to a bookstore, and he realized that hockey heroes are a big thing in romance. I'm really the one to blame."

"I'm going home to email every romance author I can find online and ask them to write a baseball hero." I frown.

"Oh, here's one!" Callie picks a book up off the shelf. "*The Hotshot*. Can I buy this one?"

Conor's eyebrows rise, and I groan.

"Buy whatever you want," I grumble.

Callie reads the back of the book and puts it back. "Never mind, it sounds too much like Hayes and Leighton's story. I'm gonna stick to these Eloise recommended."

Both women accompany Amanda to the checkout while Conor and I hang back.

"Holding up okay? How far along are you guys?" he asks.

Is this what happens these days? People talk about pregnancy as a *we* thing?

"Eighteen weeks."

"Wait until after twenty, that's when the shit gets real. But it's great. When you feel the baby move… it's unreal."

His face is so bright with happiness that it makes me excited for what's coming. The only difference is that Eloise is his wife, and Callie isn't my… anything really. The baby coming brings a finality to what we have. It's very different from what Conor has.

I look at Callie laughing with Eloise and Amanda, picking up bookmarks and completely enthralled with this store we stumbled upon, and all I can think is that I don't ever want to let her go.

Sure, she'll always be the mother of my child, but that's not the same as what we have now. And though I can't tell her… I really like what we have.

CHAPTER
FIFTY-ONE

Foster

"I'm so excited to go home and read." Callie's been beaming since we left the bookstore.

"So happy we found that little gem of a place." Do I want to sit and watch Callie reading about men who are probably more emotionally intelligent than I am? Hell no.

"Oh, stop it. You look jealous." She knocks her shoulder into mine. "They're fictional."

I know she's right, but I'm a little salty over the fact there aren't enough baseball romance books. We're tough. So what if we don't fight like neanderthals on the ice? Have these writers ever heard of bench-clearing fights? A hundred-mile-an-hour fastball to the arm? Besides, baseball is a thinking man's game. It's definitely more appealing.

We stop at the corner, waiting for the light, and Callie glances at me. "You're brooding."

"Do you think hockey players or football players are more... manly than baseball players?"

She laughs, but when she notices I'm not, she cuts it short and tries to school her face. "It's just fiction, Foster."

"I don't care. I'm gonna tell the guys about it."

She laughs but contains herself once again. "Hey, I'd pick you over one of the hockey guys any day."

"They're all married." It's true. All the professional hockey players in our orbit are married with families, so her point is moot.

"Not the Chipmunks."

"Who?" My brows draw down.

"You know those rookies who come to Peeper's sometimes? They're young and cocky and play for the Falcons. All unattached."

My head rocks back, remembering them now. That trio needs to grow the fuck up. Always thinking the backroom is theirs when we're out of town.

"And your point?" I ask.

She pulls me over to a wall, getting us out of the foot traffic. "Now I'm getting jealous. You want a bunch of women fawning over fictional you?"

I shrug. "Yes."

"I'm not enough?" She huffs and walks away from me.

"Shit, Callie, you know what I mean."

"I don't know if I do. I think maybe I'll go to a Falcons game."

"It's their off season," I remind her.

"Then I'll ask Conor or someone to fix me up. I think one of the Chipmunks hit on me last year. Simon maybe? I can never keep them straight." She pretends to think about it.

"You're not going on a date with any of those squirrels."

Unless she wants me to get into a bar brawl.

"Then stop being so grumpy 'cause there aren't baseball romance heroes. You have me."

I grab her from behind and tuck my head into the crook of

her neck, kissing there. "Brooding officially over. Let's go home, and you can give me a lesson on using a vibrator."

She turns in my arms and pushes at my chest. "You got that lesson already but…" She swings her head back and forth. "You could use another lesson just to make sure you really nail it."

I grin at her. "You're too good to me."

I love when she gets all sassy, and I can't fight the smile on my face when she says, "I'm nice like that. Come on, I'll also give you a lesson on reading spicy sex scenes to your partner."

"As long as I don't have to pretend to be a hockey player." I let her tug me along.

"Oh, I'd never make you do that, but how do you feel about having Illyrian wings and referring to me as your High Lady?"

"A what-what?" I ask, falling in line with her.

We're two blocks from the condo when my phone vibrates in my pocket with a text. I pull it out, and my stomach drops.

Fuck. This isn't what I needed today.

I push my hand through my hair and look at Callie. "Hey, I'll meet you back at the condo. I forgot I have to run an errand."

Her forehead crinkles. "What do you have to do?"

"You go and get a head start on your books. I'll be, like, twenty minutes tops." I lean over to kiss her, but she puts her hand on my lips.

"Where are you going, Foster?"

The flash of fear in her eyes is quick and says that we still haven't reached that full trust stage, but then again, I'm keeping this from her, so how could we?

"I have to go to the bank. It's something…"

She waits, and I don't blame her for not giving me an out. I wouldn't either.

"For my dad."

She nods and hooks her arm through mine. "Let's go then."

"Callie…"

She smiles up at me. "Where you go, I go."

I groan, but as I lead us to the bank, hoping it's not too late for a wire transfer to go through, I feel a little less lonely with her on my arm.

CHAPTER
FIFTY-TWO

Callie

As I stand outside the bank and watch Foster shake hands over the banker's desk and smile at him, I contemplate what he could be doing. I want to grant him the privacy to go do whatever he has to with regards to his dad. But my suspicion is that he sends his dad money every month. Helps him float his income. I don't even know where his dad lives, but Foster looks friendly with the banker, as though this isn't the first time he's been here doing this. Then again, the guy could just be a Colts fan.

But the pit in my stomach widens—how much leash do I give Foster before I demand he tells me what secrets he's keeping?

And honestly, does it even matter? I'm already too invested.

Heartbreak is inevitable.

CHAPTER
FIFTY-THREE

Callie

It's been a week since Foster went to the bank. I've waited for him to talk to me about it and yet, nothing. It's really none of my business what he was doing at the bank, so I feel like it's not my place to ask, even though I wish he'd open up to me.

His inability to open up to me hasn't dampened my craving for the man though.

We have our twenty-week appointment next week, but he'll be gone this entire week, playing a back-to-back away series.

I can't get comfortable in my bed. I've fallen asleep with Foster on the couch, but we've never broken the rule to never sleep in bed with each other. Even if I think joining him in his bed right now would do the trick, I won't be the one to ask.

So I toss and turn, wishing my brain would turn off and let me sleep, but then the building alarm goes off again.

It hasn't happened again in a while, and I haven't heard

anything about it since the night I met Cooper. I have no idea if the three guys ever met with Cooper after that night.

I open my bedroom door, and Foster is by the condo door, already slipping into his slides. "This shit has to stop."

I step out of my bedroom and make it halfway across the condo before I think to turn back around and grab a sweatshirt. Although it's hot outside, I want to cover myself up given what happened last time.

"I've got you." As though he was prepared for this, Foster holds his Chicago Colts sweatshirt for me.

"Territorial much?" I snag it from his grasp.

"No more Grizzly shit."

"Or Falcons?"

"Nope." He shakes his head.

The alarm continues to blare.

Foster palms the back of his neck. "I gotta be on the bus early, so I hope this isn't gonna take all night."

As we leave the condo, the alarm stops, and when we reach the ground floor, we find Decker and Easton are already down there.

It's complete déjà vu, except for Easton's explanation as he jogs up the steps. "It was just some girl. She tried to use a crowbar to open the gate. Ruby saw her when she was closing up."

I'm thankful we don't have to wait for cops or Cooper at least.

"What can I say? I'm irresistible." Easton grins.

"Good. See you fuckers in the morning." Foster turns and holds the door open for me.

"Like the new merch, Callie." Easton's grin gets bigger.

Foster rolls his eyes, and we make our way back up to the condo, where he shuts the door and locks it. I take off the sweatshirt and hand it back to him.

He shakes his head. "Keep it."

We stand in the foyer area, gazes locked and neither of us heading to our bedrooms.

I don't feel like having sex, but I do want to be with him, even if it breaks all rules.

But when he doesn't say anything, I see no point in continuing to stand here. "So, good night." I wave like an idiot and head toward my room.

"I was thinking…"

I stop and circle back.

He says, "I mean, I'll be gone for a week and…"

"Yeah…" *I'll miss you like crazy. Will you miss me too?*

"Do you think… I mean…" He pushes both hands through his hair, then leaves his hands resting on the back of his head so his torso is stretched out. "I mean… I've never slept with a woman before. Like *just* slept. Do the lessons extend to that?"

My entire being lights up at the thought of sleeping with him for the entire night in his bed.

A small smile makes its way across my face. "I think I can help you out."

He holds his arm out, signaling that I should head to his room first, so I do, Foster following.

"The first thing you should do is pull down the covers for her."

He reaches past me and pulls the covers open. I slide in, scooting to the other side.

"Now you get in after her and pull the covers up over her."

He does, the mattress dipping when his weight settles on it.

"Now turn around so you're the big spoon, tugging her into your chest."

He nuzzles close to me, wrapping his arm around my torso, and nudges me back so our bodies are aligned. "Like this?"

I lose my voice for a moment. "Perfect."

We lie cocooned with one another, and if sleep wasn't coming for me before, it's definitely not coming now. The faint scent of him is on the pillows, and with his warm, strong body wrapped around me, I've never felt safer than this moment. His hand drifts to my stomach, running up and down over the swell of my belly.

"I never knew this would be so nice." His voice is soft in my ear.

"Me neither," I admit.

We lie there for a while, and I swear I feel his heartbeat against my back. I slide my feet up his legs and back down.

"Callie?" he whispers.

"Yeah?"

But he doesn't say anything for another minute or two.

"Sleep."

Utter disappointment hits me because I thought maybe he'd say something more heartfelt. Which is stupid because that's not us, that's not who we are. But sometimes… the way he looks at me, the way he touches me… it makes me think that maybe we are there or could be at least.

"Don't go trying to throw your leg over mine or anything." I try to use humor to cover my disappointment.

He chuckles. "Don't press your ass into my dick… actually, feel free to do that."

I chuckle then try to relax. My mind is still whirling that I'm in bed with him, in his arms, and eventually I hear his breathing even out.

Hours later, I awaken to a dark room, but a soft light comes through the edges of the curtains. I don't want to move to see what time it is.

I'm still on my side, tucked under the blanket, Foster behind me. His chest is pressed to my back, his arm around my waist, his hand resting flat on my stomach as though he's protecting the both of us. Did we really not move the entire night?

I should try to go back to sleep.

But that's impossible with the weight of him against me, the heat of his body turning my thoughts to wanting something I can't have.

His breathing is even. I'm the only one fretting about us being in bed and not having sex.

For a few minutes, I relish the quiet and safety of being in his arms. I don't want fear to leak into this moment—I just want to enjoy it for however long I get.

Foster stirs behind me, his fingers flexing over my belly. With his touch, my spine straightens, and my breath catches from that familiar twinge of excitement when we want one another.

Foster's mouth brushes the back of my neck, the exact place he knows I love. He moans, and I tilt my head to the side, giving him more skin to explore so he knows I'm in. His exhale is warm against my skin, and his arm tightens around my waist as he slides even closer. I didn't think there was more space to fill between us, but he found it.

"Tell me if you want me to stop." His voice is low and sleepy.

I shake my head. "Don't stop."

All it takes is my permission.

His mouth finds my neck again, and he kisses me slower this time. He kisses the same spot twice as his fingers run up and down my side, purposely teasing me.

It's the gentlest kind of ruin.

I press back into him before I can overthink it, and when my ass hits his dick, a guttural groan escapes him. Getting him to make noises that tell me how much he enjoys being with me is so addictive.

His lips graze my ear. "You feel so warm… so nice. I like waking up with you."

A sharp ache pierces my heart, and I almost laugh at how unfair this situation is. How much I want to change the game on him and hope he's on board.

Because this... this isn't lust or co-parents getting closer and becoming friends. We've fallen in love. And it was so easy to do that I'm still shocked. I tried to deny it as long as I could, but I've fallen in love with Foster Davis, and I'm pretty sure he's fallen in love with me.

It was the quiet kind of falling, so it sneaked up on me. One day he was a hot guy to have sex with, then he was my friend, and now I want him to be so much more.

I turn in his arms carefully, shifting until I'm facing him. In the dim light, his eyes still find mine.

His hand cups my cheek, thumb sliding once along my jaw as if he's committing it to memory. "I don't want to go."

"I don't want you to go."

It's only a week. We've gone through longer stints during our time together. This shouldn't be a big thing.

His forehead rests against mine for a beat, and it's so tender that my throat burns with my unsaid confession. Foster lowers his head, and his lips meet mine.

It's slow. No frenzy or panic. As though he's savoring me and putting all his emotions into our kiss. My hands rest on his shoulders, then his back, pulling him closer, desperate to hold on to this moment in case I never get it again.

He shifts over me, the mattress dipping, the blanket tangling around our legs. He hovers over me, careful to keep his weight off my belly and pausing to look over my face, staring into my eyes as if asking permission.

I nod, unable to find my voice but wanting him so much.

He slowly undresses us both, then kisses me again and again, each one less hurried than the last, as if he doesn't have to leave to meet the team soon.

His hand slides into mine, threading our fingers together,

and it pulls me out of my head and back into my body, back into him.

I want this.

I want him.

The only sounds in the room are our breathing, the soft shift of the sheets, the small noises from each of us.

Foster's mouth leaves mine only long enough for him to whisper, "God, Callie." He slides into me, slow and sure.

My heart stutters because this feels different. This is new. The slower pace. The unbroken eye contact. The trust between us.

"Foster…" I manage, my voice barely working.

His eyes hold mine, clear and honest. "You are… amazing. You're everything."

The fear, the loneliness, the part of me that always expects to be the only one who wants more breaks at his words, and my chest opens up to expose my heart, inviting him in.

"You are…"

He kisses me before I can finish my thought.

Then there's no more talking.

He touches me as if I'm precious. There's no pressure. No invisible finish line. No panic flaring through me. I'm completely lost in him.

Just him moving inside me, as though we're learning each other in a completely new way. His hands are linked with mine, holding them over my head, clenching and unclenching our fingers together.

My orgasm comes slowly, like a rolling wave before it crests and crashes. When I come, it's not hard or crushing, but a feeling of euphoria wrapping around me, and I know I'll never have this with anyone else.

He comes right after me, with a quiet moan and my name whispered in a tone holding so much awe and adoration. I stare at him, losing myself in his blue eyes. He unhooks our hands, and I cup his cheeks, overcome with emotion.

"I love you," I whisper.

Foster opens his mouth then shuts it. He blinks, and that dreamy expression he had a moment ago vanishes, replaced with fear I haven't seen in months.

"Ah…" He slips out of me and catapults off the bed as if I'm contagious. "I forgot I have to get to the clubhouse early for the bus to the airport. Shit, what time is it?" He checks his phone.

I sit up in bed. "Foster," I say, but he's scrambling around the room. "I know it's scary, but—"

"I'll call you from the road, but I gotta go." He throws on a pair of sweatpants and a T-shirt, shoving stuff into his bag.

"Foster…"

He leans over the bed and kisses me briefly on the cheek. "I'll call you."

Then he's out the door, and the condo grows quiet as I lie in his bed naked and embarrassed, tears welling in my eyes.

Which is stupid, because I knew how this would end all along. I only have myself to blame.

CHAPTER
FIFTY-FOUR

Foster

I go down to Decker's, having nowhere to go until the stadium is open.

He swings open the door, rubbing his eyes, wearing only his boxers.

"Spare me this early in the morning." I cover my eyes and walk into his condo.

It's my first time being in his space. Where's all the candles and soft lighting? This place is all masculine and dark colors. Nothing is overly neat or organized. There's some stuff lying around, and mail piled up on the table.

"Why are you here?" he asks, not shutting the door in my face like he should.

"Because you already think I'm an asshole." I go to his living room and sit on the couch since it's the same layout as my own condo.

"What did you do?"

"Don't worry about it. Go back to bed, and if anyone calls, you don't know where I am."

"Foster…" He stands over me on the couch. "Did you hurt her?"

"What do you think? Of course I fucking did." I lie down and turn over, putting the pillow under my head. "Your couch sucks ass."

I hear him breathing over me for at least a full minute before his bedroom door shuts.

Did I want to come to Decker? Hell no. But I meant what I said, he already thinks I'm an asshole, and it's the last place anyone will look for me.

As I lie on the couch, I pull my phone out of my pocket and press on Callie's name.

I desperately want to reach out to her and apologize and tell her I can't be what she needs. That for one brief moment when she said those words, I wished I was anyone but me. I wished I could be one of those guys who could just confess to her that I feel the same.

But I don't trust that feeling. Every time I've ever loved someone, every time anyone has ever said they love me— they've left. My mom, my brother, and even my dad, once I cut him off. And they're my blood. If your blood doesn't love you, what hope do I have with someone who's not?

It's better this way. Better for Callie.

She can find one of those men who are in tune with their feelings and can tell her how awesome and perfect she is without being paralyzed by the thought of losing her just because he loves her.

CHAPTER
FIFTY-FIVE

Callie

Thorere's a knock on Foster's condo door, and I swing it open.

Leighton holds up two grocery bags. "Ice cream, pizza, popcorn, chips, Twizzlers, and three bags of Hershey's bars."

She steps in and drops the bags, pulling me into a tight hug.

"Today we veg and cry. We'll figure everything out tomorrow."

The tears come because how was I so stupid to think that I could be a game-changer for Foster fucking Davis?

CHAPTER
FIFTY-SIX

Foster

Word travels fast because Hayes sat away from me on the bus and the plane. He hasn't said a word to me today.

When I corner him in the bullpen before the game, seeing Callie's eyes reflected back at me with the same pain I saw this morning tells me it's a stupid endeavor to try to explain my side.

"Not yet." He walks away but turns back around. "I'm not saying never, but I need some space."

He leaves with McCarthy, and I sit in the chair to watch the game, wondering where she is now.

I don't get called in until middle of the eighth, and of course the bases are loaded with one out. I reach the mound, and they're all waiting for me. I'm met with Decker's usual disapproving glare. Easton can't even look me in the eye. And Hayes is fuming for good reason.

Ripley hands me the ball.

"Hey, guys, let's just win the game." Easton steps in, trying to ease some of the tension, which I suspected he would. "Put the personal shit away and get out of this inning."

"Just throw a fucking strike." Hayes turns and walks back to the plate.

"Fuck, man, what happened?" Easton asks. So he doesn't know. "This is going to tear up the team."

"Kodiak," Decker says, in a tone that says shut up.

My jaw clenches. "Stay out of it."

I throw a warm-up pitch that's high, making Hayes get up to catch it.

"You have to fix this," Easton continues.

I whip around before throwing my next pitch and point my glove at him. "Stay the fuck out of it."

Coach Cal runs onto the field. "Guys, let's focus on the batter."

I turn back around.

"We don't know what happened. Why are you automatically blaming him?" Decker asks.

I'm shocked he'd even question whether I was at fault or not.

I throw another pitch, and it's inside.

All I can think about is Callie and wanting her and wishing I wasn't the fuck-up I am.

Somehow, I get out of the eighth, but we go three up and three down, leaving Pittsburgh up one run in the top of the ninth.

We've got two outs down when I walk a batter.

Hayes calls time, and I wave him off to go back to the plate, but he comes over anyway.

We step off the mound, and he covers his mouth with his glove. "Get your head out of your ass. I get that you're all lost in your feelings, but you caused it, so suck it up and actually throw a strike and get us out of this."

Hayes has never talked to me like this, and I thought he never would.

But what do I expect? I fucked over his little sister.

Blood is always thicker than water, and what does it say that my blood doesn't want me?

"Why don't you guys score some runs and make it a little easier for me?"

He shakes his head, and his eyes bleed anger. "It's always someone else, right? When are you going to actually get over this chip on your shoulder?"

"It's not a chip." My words are delivered through clenched teeth.

I should back down. I'm in the wrong here. I'm the one who needs to apologize. I took liberties I shouldn't have.

"You're right, it's a fucking boulder. So you had a shitty childhood. I'm sorry, but it doesn't give you license to fuck around with other people's feelings. You hurt her."

"You think I don't know that?" I shout.

Art comes up from behind the plate to interrupt and get us playing, but I want this over with. I want to have this out with Hayes for reasons I don't understand, but I want it over and done with.

"Go back." I point at Art to go back behind home plate, but he keeps coming. I step toward him, arm still extended. "Art, go the fuck back, we'll be done in a second."

"Foster," he says, shaking his head. "This is a warning."

Ripley steps out of the dugout, on the line ready to call time and cross, but I point to him to stay back too.

Decker jogs over, puts his hand on my chest, and I fling it off.

"Everyone, just go back to your positions, and I'll fucking throw the ball."

"Stop it," Hayes says, but why would I stop now?

After all, I'm Foster fucking Davis. I fuck up everything. This is what I do. This is who I am, right?

Art continues to approach me. He waves Ripley in, and he crosses the first base line, joining our party.

"You better calm down, Foster," Art tells me.

"Fuck off." I spit off to the side, into the grass.

"Out!" he yells, making the ejection signal.

I chuck the ball into centerfield. "Happy to."

"Davis!" Ripley shouts. "Get in the locker room. Now!"

Fuck all of them. I walk through the dugout and right into the locker room, throwing my glove as hard as I possibly can.

I pull my phone out of the safe in the locker. I sometimes carry it with me, but I didn't want to be tempted to contact Callie or read our text threads again.

There are two messages waiting for me.

> Jagger Kale: Way to lose the endorsement. They're not interested in you anymore.

The other one makes my heart stop for a second.

> Callie: I'll survive, don't flatten your career on my account.

She hs no business messaging me, showing once again that she's way too good for a fuck-up like me.

CHAPTER
FIFTY-SEVEN

Callie

At least if Foster was going to break my heart, he did it right before he's gone for a week.

"Cal!" Leighton calls, and I meet her in the foyer of Foster's place. "Hey." She drops the empty boxes in her hands and wraps her arms around me. "We're going to be okay. We're going to rock this single parenthood thing. And I don't want to hear it—you're staying in our guest room for the foreseeable future."

She hugs me so tightly, I almost believe her that the pain will fade.

"It's only until I find a place." I pick up the boxes and go into my bedroom.

"Hayes wants you to stay. Says he wants to be a hands-on uncle." She goes to my dresser and fills a box with my clothes.

I don't say anything.

"How was this morning?" she asks hesitantly.

I shrug. "I pretended that I like Foster too."

My taping with the fourth guest Foster secured for me was earlier today. I didn't tell Lex anything was going on, and I pretended to be as happy as I normally am as I chatted with the sports reporter who was involved in a scandal because she had a relationship with her boss. She talked about how cruel the internet is, which I understood perfectly. But also about how she found love, and she didn't want to apologize for that. It was a real feel-good story. Had I interviewed her before Foster ran out on me, I would've probably been even more delusional afterward that Foster and I could ride off into the sunset together.

"I think my fifth interview will have to be one of the guys. I don't want Foster's help anymore."

"That's right, we're not taking anything else from him." She points at me with an intense expression on her face.

"Okay, we can't hate the guy, he is this one's father." I rub my stomach as I've been doing constantly for the past two days, as if I'm consoling the baby too. "It's bad enough that he'll bomb his own career."

"Hayes said he's suspended."

When I heard the news earlier, my heart sank, followed immediately by me wishing I wasn't still so invested in him. I should say go to hell and be done with him, but part of me knows that the Foster Davis I saw is the real one and that he's just scared. But it doesn't make it hurt any less.

Then again, what does that say about me? Did I not show him how safe he is with me like he did for me?

"Two games, right?"

She sits on my bed. "Yeah."

I continue to pack my things. I can't believe how at home I've become here in just a few months.

"You know I want to burn him at the stake and all that for hurting you, but at the same time, I feel so bad for him. I mean… he's clearly scared," Leighton says.

I turn and glare at her.

She holds up her hands. "I said I want to burn him at the stake. But I think he really is a good guy. From what I gather, he didn't have a great childhood. At least not one where he felt he could be himself."

I sit on the bed with her, grabbing a pillow and hugging it. "He hasn't really told me much except that the issue with him and Decker started because their parents split them up. There's animosity there. But he's trying to live like it doesn't affect him, like it didn't shape him."

That's basically common knowledge in our group, and I won't say anything more than that. Certainly not what he told me about college. I may be irate with him, but I would never betray his trust.

"Don't take this the wrong way, but I don't think you understand what it's like not to be raised in a perfect family." I open my mouth to refute her statement, but she holds up her hands again. "I'm not suggesting that you haven't gone through things, and you don't have your own wounds. It's not even something that you should feel bad about. It's wonderful that you and Hayes can't empathize in that way. But when you're young and bad things happen… when you don't feel safe, you believe the lies. Both the ones you tell yourself, and the ones other people tell you. Kind of like Rebound Callie."

I stare at the pillow, my hands running along the edge.

"I think it was poor judgment on his part not to deal with it before getting into a relationship with you," she says.

"We weren't in a relationship." I look at her.

She pushes my leg with her hand. "Callie, you guys can tell yourselves whatever you want, but you were in a relationship. You were openly kissing and hugging and holding hands. You can only have sex with someone for so long before intimacy sneaks into the mix. I think that's what happened with you guys. You thought you could play it safe, but you fell in love. You wrapped your head around it and put yourself out there, and he ran. But for the record, I do think he loves you. I'm just not sure he'll ever come to terms with it. And that's why I feel sorry for him. He'll live a very lonely life if he can't get out of his own way."

Tears push at my eyes, but I suck them back. "Let's just get this packed up. I don't want to be here when they get back." I drop the pillow and get back to packing up my stuff.

"I think you should take the couch," she says, getting off the bed.

"When I leave here, I'm not taking anything that would remind me of him." I look down at my stomach. "I already have a piece of him forever. I kind of hope brown really is dominant so this baby comes out with my eyes."

She frowns, and her shoulders fall.

I shake my head at her. "Nope, no tears today. We're moving on."

We work to pack up the room, not saying much, but then Leighton says, "Hey, Cal, just do one thing for me?"

I look at her.

"Don't build that wall back up, okay? This is on Foster and has nothing to do with you. You're worth it, and it's his loss. It was really beautiful the way you loved him so freely."

Tears prick my eyes again, threatening to fall.

How can the biggest heartbreak I've ever felt not crush me? But then again, I have a little one who needs my love, so I'll pour all of mine into him or her.

CHAPTER
FIFTY-EIGHT

Foster

What a banner week. Two-game suspension, a blown endorsement, and now I'm back to face what I've done.

Decker and Easton peel off to head to their condos, and I continue up the stairs to my own. My finger hovers over my keypad because I have no idea what I'll find when I get inside.

I didn't message Callie while I was away because I didn't want to have the conversation over the phone. Hayes warmed up a bit as the days went on. At least he's being cordial now, but it's not like it was.

I punch in my code, and when I push the door open, the consequences of my actions hit me square in the face.

There's no candle scent.

No soft glow of a lamp.

No throw blanket over the couch.

Most of all, there's no Callie.

It's as if all the life has been drained from this place. It's an empty shell, a husk of what was.

I cross the room and push open her bedroom door to find it empty like before she moved in.

You really did it this time. Fucked up good.

Why did I think she'd even entertain staying here after how I acted?

The couch feels like a beacon of loneliness, so I lean against the wall and slide down onto my ass, my arms resting on my knees and my head falling forward so my chin hits my chest.

I'm so mad at myself. I want to destroy the condo. Lash out. Take a knife and shred the couch so it matches my shredded heart.

For the millionth time, I wish I could do it over. That when she looked up at me with so much love and vulnerability, I didn't crush her. I could have stayed, talked it out, but I ran—like a fucking coward. An undeserving coward.

I hear the electronic beep of the keypad at my door. Someone is punching in the code. I scramble to my feet and jog over to the door, but when it opens, it's Hayes and Leighton.

"Hey," Hayes says. From the pity in his eyes, I know he can see my disappointment that he's not his sister. "Yeah, she's not coming."

I nod. "She moved out?" I look at Leighton.

She nods. "She'll be with us at least until the baby comes."

I inhale a sharp breath and go back to the living room, but instead of sitting on the couch, I go back to the floor.

"There something wrong with the couch?" Hayes asks, about to sit on it.

"It's a thing with them." Leighton makes a gesture like he should sit.

"Like I shouldn't sit on it?" He turns to inspect the couch.

"Just sit." Leighton rolls her eyes.

"Listen…" Hayes starts off the conversation.

I brace myself for a lecture I really don't want. I already know I fucked up. I know I'm at fault. I know I'm the puppeteer of my own misery.

"I was really mad when I first heard what went down with you and Callie the other day. But I'm pissed at myself that you lost that endorsement because of our fight on the field. So I'm sorry for that, but I've calmed down now, and I have some things I need to say. You should know that when I first found out about you two, I told my sister I was Team Callie *and* Team Foster."

"Be Team Callie."

He huffs out a laugh and glances at Leighton. She nods for him to continue.

"I don't know if me telling you this will make a difference in what has already happened. Maybe you and Callie will just be co-parents for real," he says.

Knife in the chest.

"But I think it needs to be said, for the future I still want you to have because you're my best friend, and you're missing out on something pretty great. What you need to know is that you're enough, Foster." He glances at Leighton, who nods. "I feel like a therapist," he whines.

"You sound like one too," I grumble.

Hayes stands. "See? I told you guys don't talk like this to each other."

Leighton tugs him back down by the sleeve and slides closer to me. "What Hayes is trying to say is that you deserve love, Foster. You deserve Callie's love. And I can tell you, as someone who has been loved by Callie since I was a freshman in high school, she's worth the risk. She's loyal, and has your back, and always wants the best for you."

"I know all this," I say. "It's not her that's the problem."

They stare at each other for a beat. I'd like them to leave so I can wallow for the foreseeable future and then pick myself up and move on with my life as if these past four months never happened.

Even if that feels impossible right now.

"Do you love her?" Hayes asks. "And don't bullshit me. If you don't, that's fine, but do you?"

I've never told any woman I loved her. Hell, the last time I told anyone I loved them was when I was young and I told my mom. Look how that turned out.

Still, I can't deny the truth. I give Hayes a sharp nod.

"Thought so. Then you have to fight, man."

"What Hayes means—"

Hayes looks at his fiancée. "I said what I meant."

Leighton slides off the couch and onto the coffee table across from him. "Yes, and it was great." She taps his leg a little condescendingly.

Hayes shakes his head and leans back on the couch.

I bite my lip to stop a small smile from forming.

"You have to fight for yourself, Foster." Leighton meets my gaze and holds it. "You need to realize that you deserve this. You deserve to have Callie love you. This isn't about fighting for Callie. She already wants to be yours. But you have to work on you. Put Callie out of the equation. How do you see this going with your unborn child? How do you expect your child to feel deserving of love if all he sees is a father who doesn't?"

Fuck... she has a point.

"I'm gonna be honest, no one gets to love you more than you love yourself. You can't keep destroying the relationships in your life, because it will inevitably trickle down to that little one growing in Callie's belly. It's admirable that you want to be a different parent for your baby, but you need to do the work first. And yes, it will be unpleasant, and it will hurt, but once you're on the other side of it... well, I think you'll find that Callie and your child are worth it."

She sends a questioning glance at Hayes, and he gives her a small shake of his head, but she rolls her eyes.

A crease forms between my brows. "What?"

"It's up to you, of course. But if you wanted, you could take the first step today… your mom is downstairs at Decker's." She raises her hand before I have a chance to speak. "You don't have to forgive her. We have no idea what happened, so maybe you're right—maybe she doesn't deserve your forgiveness. But I think you deserve some healing. Maybe in order to do that, you need to hear her out. And if you still feel the same way, okay. But I think you need to handle that part of your past so you can move forward with your future."

Hayes stares at me.

"I'm not a psychologist or anything, so take my advice as a friend who really wants to see you happy… and maybe with her best friend." Leighton smiles sweetly, then pushes herself up off the coffee table. She puts her hand on my shoulder before walking over to the door. "I'll be outside."

Leighton opens the door to leave but then turns around. "If he says no, Hayes, ask him for the couch." She laughs and walks out.

"She's just joking," Hayes says.

"Take the couch for Callie," I tell him.

He doesn't say anything for a beat before he gets that look in his eye. The same one he gets on the field when we're on the cusp of winning a game.

"All right, now that she's gone, let me tell you what you're gonna do." He leans forward and rests his forearms on his knees. "You're gonna get off your ass. You're gonna go down to Decker's and hear your mom out. And then you're gonna do one big grand fucking gesture for Callie. You love her, and she's what you want. Sure, fight for yourself, but fight for the love the two of you have together. You never would've hooked up with my sister behind my back if there wasn't something there from the get-go. I knew that all along. So stop wallowing like a punkass and go do the work to win her back."

Hayes stands from the couch and takes a few steps before turning back around. "I'm telling you, it's a great life. Don't miss out on it."

He walks out, and the door shuts behind him.

I rock my head against the wall and close my eyes, steeling myself for what's to come.

CHAPTER
FIFTY-NINE

Foster

I'm not sure whether it's going to do me any good, but what I've been doing hasn't been working. What's the definition of insanity? Keep doing the same thing and expect a different result?

So I steel myself and knock on Decker's door.

He answers and manages to keep his expression neutral. Thank God. If he'd looked smug, I would've turned around and left.

My shoulders lock up the second I step inside and see my mom on his couch, sitting comfortably, as though she's at home here in his space. The sting of rejection hits because I'm not at all comfortable—not in his space or around either of them. It's just another reminder of their relationship that I don't share.

"Foster." My mom stands, an expectant and surprised look on her face.

"Angela."

She flinches when I use her given name. Good.

Decker clears his throat. "I'll be out doing errands." Then he's gone, shutting the door behind him.

My mom gestures to the couch. "Will you come and sit?"

I take the chair in the corner by the window instead. It's as far away as I can get and still be in the same room as her.

She nods as though she expected me to keep my distance. "Thank you for coming."

The urge to make it clear to her that I'm not here for her rises up. I'm here because Callie's pregnant, and I'm trying to figure out how to not screw up the one thing in my life that matters. But having this conversation devolve into an argument in the first two seconds won't get me any closer to my goal, so I bite back my retort.

I cross my arms. "Just tell me what you want to tell me."

She takes a breath, and I notice her hands are shaking as if she's trying to hold herself together. Did she forget that she's the one who gave me up?

"Your father and I got pregnant young." Her mouth tightens. "That's not an excuse. It's just the truth. It was hard—raising twins, our marriage, all of it. We weren't happy for a long time. Probably longer than we admitted."

I stare at the wall behind her head because I cannot look at her face.

"When you started getting attention for baseball and your dad wanted to move you south, I told myself I was making the right choice. For you." She swallows and takes a second to compose herself. "You had a real shot. Your dad wanted you in the elite programs, playing against better competition. You wanted it too. And I agreed to let him take you."

I run her words through my head for a beat. "You could've come too." My voice comes out sharp. "You could've brought Decker."

It wasn't as though he wasn't also playing baseball at the time. Sure, my talent developed a little earlier than his, but he would've benefited from the move too.

Her eyes shine with tears. "I could have."

"And you didn't."

She nods once. "I didn't."

I wait for the part where she blames my dad. Where she tells me she had no choice. Where she tries to make it seem like a noble sacrifice.

Instead, she looks me straight in the eye. "The truth is, I chose what was easier."

Her words hit me harder than I'd like. My chest squeezes painfully. "You're saying you left me with him because it was convenient."

"No." She shakes her head. "I'm saying I didn't fight hard enough. I told myself it was for you, but it was also because fighting your father felt impossible. There had already been years of it, and I was exhausted. I couldn't take any more of the arguments and the manipulation. So I gave in. I thought there would be time. I thought I could fix it later."

My jaw clenches. "And?"

"And I blinked." Her voice cracks, and tears run down her face. "And you were grown."

My throat tightens and fills with a painful lump that keeps me from responding.

She wipes her cheeks as if she's angry at herself for crying. "I called. I tried to visit. Your dad told me you had practices, games, travel, that distractions would mess you up, that you didn't feel like talking to me. It was always something." A shaky breath slips out of her. "I should've gotten in my car anyway. I should've shown up anyway."

I thought I was over this. I thought that nothing this woman could say would affect me anymore. That I was numb to her and what she did or didn't do in my childhood. It's obvious now that I've been carrying around a thousand-pound sack of issues where she's concerned.

I don't say anything because I don't trust myself to speak right now.

She reaches for a tissue on Decker's coffee table. Of course he has fucking tissues in his condo.

"I'm not crying for your pity." She blots her tears. "I'm crying because I lost you. And I did it while telling myself I was doing the right thing."

I sit back, stretching my arms over the armrests of the chair, my hands flexing on the leather.

"But I came here because you're about to have a baby. And I don't want you to make the same mistake that I did."

"I'm not you." My words lash out like a whip.

She flinches, but I don't take it back. It's the truth. It's the whole reason I'm here talking to her today. I'm not her, and I won't ever do what she did.

A sad smile tilts her lips. "You're not. And I don't want you to be."

She stands, but she doesn't move away. She just looks at me as though she's trying to memorize my face after years of not seeing it in person.

"I know I've made a mess of our relationship. I might never earn you back." Her voice drops. "But I'm still your mother, and I still want the best for you."

A bitter laugh threatens, but I swallow it down. "How do you know what's best for me?"

She frowns. "Because from the outside, you don't look happy."

I hate that she's right. That I'm that transparent to her.

She steps closer. "You can tell yourself you're fine. You can tell yourself you'll figure it out later. That's what I did. And later turned into months that turned into years." She lifts her chin as if she's forcing herself to stay strong. "All that hurt you have inside you—because of me, because of your father" —she presses a hand to her chest—"it poisons you. It leaks in and contaminates things you don't expect. How you act. How you think. How you give love. How you receive love."

My stomach turns over. Because I already know that. I've felt it every second since I walked out on Callie.

"I heard that you and Callie aren't together right now."

My body goes rigid as if she just lodged her finger in an open wound. She has no right to know what's going on in my life. Fuck Decker.

Her expression softens. "When I saw you with her—from afar—you looked… lighter. Like you'd set down some of that weight you carry around."

I stare at my hands.

"If you love her, go to her and tell her. Show her."

My mouth opens, ready to argue. Ready to say it's complicated. That she doesn't know the whole story, and she never will. Mostly, to point the finger at her.

She cuts me off before I can. "Don't go to win. Apologize without defending yourself." Her voice breaks. "Choose her even if you're scared she won't choose you back. Let her see all of you."

My chest burns as if I just walked into a smoke-filled building.

"I'm leaving town tonight. And I won't be moving to Chicago." She gives me a small, sad smile. "You deserve space. You deserve to become the father and partner you want to be without me in your face as a reminder of everything that went wrong."

I don't know what to do with that.

She moves toward the door, then stops with her hand on the knob.

"I don't know what your father told you over the years." Her voice shakes. "But I love you, Foster. I always have. I just didn't love you the way you deserved." More tears fall, and she wipes them off her face.

Then she leaves.

I sit in the chair, staring at the empty space where she was standing as though my brain is trying to decide if I should chase her or pretend none of this even happened.

Part of me wants to run after her.

The other part of me wants to say fuck it all and stay numb. Push away the way her words made me feel.

I finally stand and look out the window.

Decker is on the sidewalk with her. He pulls her into a hug as though it's normal. As though this is what families do. She nods, saying something. His hand stays on her back as if he doesn't want her to fall apart.

My head tips back toward the sky, tears burning in my eyes.

When does the pain stop?

I rub my chest.

I'm so tired of living like this. This isn't the world I want my child to grow up in. This isn't what I want Callie to feel when she looks at me.

The change has to start with me. Whether or not she takes me back is up to her, but I have to at least try. For her. For our child. But mostly, for myself.

CHAPTER
SIXTY

Callie

"Lex, I told you I have an appointment." I'm on speakerphone, still half-dressed and staring at my reflection. I'm going to need a lot of makeup to fix this. "We can do it tomorrow."

"Just meet me at my place," Lex pleads. "Your doctor is literally a mile away. You can walk with them there, our shoot will be done, and you'll still make your scan."

I groan. "You're acting like this is a hostage negotiation."

"It is," she says as if she's proud of it. "This guest has limited time."

"And you're still refusing to tell me who it is." I run my brush through my hair, figuring I have to start somewhere.

"They want it to be a surprise."

My stomach twists thanks to the real reason for my mood today. "I messaged Foster. He might be at the doctor."

"Why would you do that?" Lex's protective chihuahua side comes out whenever Foster's name is involved.

"Because he's the father," I say as if it's obvious. "And I want him there when we find out what we're having. I'm trying to be the grown-up here."

Which is hilarious, considering I'm the only one. He never really responded to my message with words. Just a thumbs-up.

A dumb, little yellow thumbs-up like he didn't just break me open and then act as if I asked him to pick up a container of milk on the way home.

Whatever.

Lex keeps talking, but I'm already annoyed and want to get off the phone.

"Fine. I'll be there in thirty. I have to put some makeup on, so I don't look like my heart was ripped out and stomped on. See you then."

I hang up.

By the time I make it downstairs, Hayes is on the couch. It's his day off, which means he's lounging. Leighton's at work. The kids are at school. The house is quiet in a way it never is when everyone's home.

He pops a piece of popcorn into his mouth. "Where you going?"

"To meet Lex to film a podcast segment," I say with a sigh. "Then my appointment. I find out today whether you're going to be an uncle to a niece or a nephew."

I do a small dance, trying to mask the fact I'm missing a very big piece today. A six-three pitcher to be precise.

Hayes smiles, but it comes off as pitying. "Can't wait."

I say goodbye, then get in my Uber, which drops me at Lex's building. She's already outside, bouncing on her toes.

"You're acting weird," I tell her as I get out of the car. "Where is this magical guest?"

"They're ready to go." She grins. "I already got them mic'd up."

"Well, I'd like to talk to them for a minute before we start recording." I follow her toward the sidewalk. "I need to know what I'm walking into. Tell them what to expect."

"You're late." She reaches for my shirt to clip on my mic.

I smack her hand. "Lex. Dinner first, remember?"

"Okay. Real talk. I know you've been in your head lately. I'm just trying to help. So just… don't bite me."

I fake a smile.

"Better." She literally presses her fingers into my cheeks to push my smile higher.

I groan.

She laughs. "I'll be right back."

"Okay." I stand alone on the sidewalk while traffic hums by and my brain does what it does best.

Spiral.

Because it's impossible not to think about Foster.

I hate myself for missing him.

He's acting as if he doesn't give a shit about me, so why should I care?

Why did I even text him about the appointment?

Because I want him at the scan. Because I want him there when they say boy or girl and my whole life shifts again. Because I'm mad and I still want him anyway, which is the most humiliating part of it all.

"All right," Lex says, popping back into view as though she's on a game show. "Here we go. Your fifth guest…"

I turn around.

And my entire body goes cold.

"What is this?" I whisper, because my throat is suddenly too tight to breathe.

Foster stands there. Hands in his pockets. Eyes on me. Looking contrite and hopeful.

My chest hurts instantly. Anger, relief, desire, fear. All the emotions drown me, overwhelm me.

"Lex," I say, voice sharp. "Nice joke."

Lex lifts the phone she's recording with and points at our

mics as though she's proud of herself. "This is why I mic'd you."

I take one step backward. Then another. Before turning and walking away.

Foster moves fast, catching up to me, his hand lightly cupping my elbow. "Callie." His voice is soft, maybe softer than I've ever heard it. "Will you just walk with me?"

Tears come quick and hot, which pisses me off. I swipe at my face as if I can erase their existence. "I'm not doing this. I have an appointment."

"I know." He nods. "That's why we're walking to it."

I can only stare at him. I've been starving to set my eyes on him all week, but now that he's in front of me, it feels too overwhelming and painful.

"I'm not asking for forgiveness." His voice goes rough. "I'm asking for you to listen. That's it. You deserve to know everything. Then you can do whatever you want with it."

The way he says deserve hits me in the soft spot I've been loathing lately.

I look at Lex. She's watching us as though she's holding her breath.

Traitor.

I look back at Foster and nod once. "To the doctor's office."

He nods too and exhales a long, deep breath. "Yeah. That's what we planned."

I shoot Lex a look that promises revenge. She just smiles as though I'm going to thank her later.

We start walking. I'm stiff at first, the ground feeling unsteady under my feet.

Foster doesn't touch me again. He just matches my pace.

"When I was eleven, my parents decided to split Decker and me up," he begins, and he tells the story he already told me, but it's more for the listeners than me.

"After we moved, things intensified. My dad was always

hard on me, but now that it was just the two of us, he was even more brutal. Baseball above all else. If I had a bad game, I'd hear about it for days. I was punished with lectures and cold shoulders, forced to practice until I'd corrected whatever he thought the problem was. If I had a great outing, he was all smiles. Would brag about my performance to anyone who would listen. About how his son was going to be a superstar someday. How he always knew I had it in me."

We stop at a corner and wait for the light.

"It taught me that love was conditional. And when my mother abandoned me and left me with my dad, I knew I hadn't met all the conditions."

I glance at him. Foster's jaw is tight, and he's looking forward.

"As I grew up, the competition got better, got stronger, and I got good at being the version of myself people could handle. The version that didn't need anything. The version that could take a hit and act like it didn't hurt."

His eyes flick to mine for half a second.

"But you changed that." He's so quiet that it feels as if I'm betraying him by recording this. "What I felt with you… Callie… it's not something I know how to explain."

My throat tightens again. I want to fold into him, but my brain revolts, reminding me of the pain he caused.

"And what I did…" He clears his throat. "Taking what you said to me… and then turning it around and making you feel like you imagined it all, like it didn't mean anything… that was cruel." He swallows.

"I'm sorry," he says, eyes glossy with unshed tears. "I'm trying to do better. Not just because of the baby. But because I'd kick someone's ass if they made you feel that way. And the fact that it was me who inflicted that pain on you makes me physically sick. I don't want our child to ever think my love is conditional. And I don't want you thinking you're only worth what you can give."

The light changes, and we cross.

"I'm tired of being this angry version of myself filled with repressed pain. It's time for me to tackle the monkey on my back. Starve it out rather than keep feeding it my pain and resentment. I don't want to be that person anymore."

He talks more about his childhood and some of the things that went down, the mic catching everything. As he speaks, I can hear the listeners in my head already. People taking sides. People judging. People turning our real life into content.

It's not something either of us needs.

We get another red light and have to wait to cross. Foster turns toward me this time, and something about the look in his eyes steals my breath. The sounds of the city fade away. I find myself scared of what he's going to tell me.

"I love you." His voice is filled with strength and certainty. "So much. And I took that love and I threw it away like it didn't matter. If you give me another chance, I'll never do that again. You have my word. You don't have to decide right now, you don't have to—"

I should make him sit in it.

I should make him say it again.

I should make him prove he won't take it back the second he gets scared.

But my heart has my body moving before my mind can catch up.

I throw my arms around his neck. "I love you. I love you too."

His arms go around me tightly, as if he's worried I might change my mind.

"You're making this too easy," he murmurs into my hair.

"No." I pull back enough to look at him. "I'm making it about us. I needed you to stop fighting what you feel. To stop being scared of it."

He stares down at me and cups my face.

Then I remember the mic.

I glance over my shoulder.

Lex is standing on the sidewalk wide-eyed, holding her phone as though she just captured podcast gold.

Then he says, "There's more."

My stomach tightens.

I pull out of Foster's hold and take off my mic, then his. I hand them back to Lex. "Thank you. It means a lot that you did this for me. Now please… go away."

Lex looks between us. "Well… you're welcome," she whispers without her usual snarkiness. Then she walks down the sidewalk, leaving us alone.

"You have to know it all before you accept me back in your life," he says.

A cold shiver shoots up my spine.

We pass the doctor's building and keep going, cutting into a small park with benches and a fountain. He leads me toward a bench tucked away from the sidewalk.

When we sit, he keeps my hand in his. "I had to leave Seattle last year."

I stare at him. He's made it clear he wanted out of Seattle without really explaining why, but saying he *had* to leave feels different. "Why?"

He looks at our joined hands. "Because my dad was betting on my games."

I go still. My skin goes cold. How could a father put his son's career in jeopardy like that?

"The bookies came to me with a bill." He looks around for anyone eavesdropping. "It was big. They said they'd leak my name if I didn't pay up. So I paid. And then I did everything I could to get traded and away from my father. Jagger put out the feelers, and Chicago wanted me, so I pushed for it."

My heart is pounding hard and fast.

"But then my dad got himself in hot water again, and probably knowing they can't get blood from a stone, they came straight to me to pay up. It wasn't like last time. Not as much. I tried to ignore it, ignore them, but they kept resurfacing and threatened to make it look like I was betting on games if I didn't settle my dad's debt again." His jaw clenches. "The security gate break-ins… I'm pretty sure that was them too. They left a note on the gate once. That's why I went to the bank that day. To wire the money and make it go away."

My breathing stutters.

"The only person who knows is Jagger. You should also know that I've been paying my dad too. Every month. Not because I want to. Because it keeps him away."

He finally lifts his gaze to mine, and there's a rawness there I've never seen before.

I feel sick at the thought of Foster paying the man who brought him so much pain. It must be like a constant reminder every month, a revisiting of all the trauma. No wonder he hasn't been able to move forward.

"I told him the checks would stop if he ever tried to contact me again." He squeezes his eyes shut for a moment. "If this gets out, I'm ruined. And now you're in my life, and there's a baby… but I can't… I can't keep secrets from you anymore. I'm done with that."

My throat tightens.

"It's behind me," he adds quickly. "It's paid in full now. But I needed you to know. Because I don't want there to be anything between us."

I stare at him, my mind still trying to catch up to everything he said. All the heartbreak he's endured.

Without thinking, I scoot closer on the bench and lean into him. His arm wraps around my shoulders, and he sighs as though he's waited to have me next to him again.

I close my eyes. "Okay." The one word isn't good enough, but I'm not sure what more to say. "Thank you for trusting me with it."

His hand gently tightens on my shoulder. "I'll always be

transparent with you, Callie. I don't want anything to poison what we have." He bends down and kisses me. "I love you."

I smile up at him and lay my palm on his cheek. "I don't think I'll ever get tired of hearing those words from you."

"Good, because now that I've said them, I'm not sure I can stop."

We laugh, and he kisses me again. We have so much to look forward to in our future.

CHAPTER
SIXTY-ONE

Foster

Having the weight off my shoulders now that Callie knows everything I've been trying to hide feels indescribable. I feel like a fucking idiot for avoiding this for so long.

Her hand is in mine as we walk into the doctor's office. No more worrying about someone taking our picture. No more pretending we're something we're not. Although I'm still wrapping my head around the fact I fell in love with someone, and they love me back, even after unpacking all my trauma for her to lay eyes on.

Callie checks in with the receptionist, then we go sit down.

This time not behind the plant.

Not shoved in a corner.

I pick a spot right in the middle of the damn room.

Callie smirks at me as I wait for her to sit first because we're on the same page.

"Want a magazine?" She picks one up off the table and holds it out to me.

"Yes, I do." I accept it, but I'd really rather talk to her. "Look where my reading got us the first time."

"I think it would've been inevitable even without the magazine article." She knocks her shoulder into mine. "I was hanging on by a very, very frayed thread."

"You?" I balk. "You were prancing around in those tiny pajama shorts and threadbare T-shirts."

"You were shirtless the majority of the time. You purposely broke the rules."

I shrug, and her eyes widen.

"You did it on purpose? Tried to get me to break the rule?"

I smile and wrap my arm around her, kissing her temple. "I just really wanted you."

She lays her head on my chest. "Me too."

"Callie," the nurse calls.

As we head toward the door, I catch a woman smiling at us.

Yeah, we're lucky as hell. If you want to report that to the internet, go ahead.

I hold Callie's purse while she gets weighed, then she sits on the table.

"You know, it's a little disappointing that the first time I'd be free to help you undress, you don't have to put on one of those paper gowns."

She shakes her head and lifts her shirt, palming her belly.

I stand and walk over, placing my hands over hers and kissing her stomach. Then I place a chaste kiss on her lips. "Do you think we should leave the sex of the baby a surprise?"

I've been going back and forth on whether we should find out or not.

"We could rock, paper, scissors for it?" A competitive gleam enters her big brown eyes.

"You do know the odds are in my favor to win eventually, right?" I take a seat.

She puts her fist in her palm. "Want to test your fate?"

"No. I want to know what we're having. It was just a thought." I shrug.

A knock lands on the door, and I stand when Dr. Amato comes in.

She stops and smiles. "You guys are my favorite couple. But don't tell the others, okay?" She washes her hands.

I slide to the side of the table to hold Callie's hand, and Callie looks up at me. "We're our favorite too."

Dr. Amato laughs and comes over with the stethoscope to listen to the baby. "It all sounds good."

She moves the ultrasound machine over and squirts some gel on Callie's stomach.

My heart races because this is such a pivotal moment for us. We finally figured our shit out. Well, I figured out my shit. Now we're about to find out if we'll be raising a girl or a boy.

The screen flicks on with an image that looks so different from the first time Dr. Amato did this.

I can actually see the shape of the baby. There's a head, a body, and are those feet?

"Shit," I murmur, emotions swelling in my chest.

Callie turns to me, squeezing my hand.

"There you are," she says to the screen. I realize she's probably been talking to the baby more than I have.

"It's so real."

Callie laughs. "That's because you're not lugging it around everywhere, but this does put a whole new perspective on it."

Dr. Amato points out the feet and the hands. The baby moves, and I have to swallow past the lump in my throat.

"They're being a little stubborn. Let me see if I can get a better view." Dr. Amato shifts the probe a bit on Callie's abdomen.

Callie and I share a knowing look. Our child was bound to be stubborn.

"There you are." The doctor points at the screen, and I tilt my head to see what she does. "Nothing between those legs."

"Nothing?" I panic, and Callie laughs.

"It's a girl." Callie turns to look up at me. "A baby girl."

"Yep. And she's very healthy, strong heartbeat, but there she goes moving around again. She's very active."

"Oh." Callie stares down at her belly. "I felt that." She smiles up at me. "It was like a little flutter."

"That will happen more and more." Dr. Amato pulls the wand back, cleaning it and Callie's belly, then washes her hands again. "Everything looks great. Keep up everything you've been doing, and I'll see you in a month."

She leaves, and the nurse comes in and gives us pictures to take with us. I fold one up and slide it into my wallet.

Callie gets ready, but before we leave the room, I stop her.

"You're happy?" I ask her.

"Of course. I didn't care."

"A girl."

Callie tilts her head as though she can hear it in my voice. How a daughter scares me. What will I do with a girl?

She laughs and puts her hand on my cheek. "You're going to be an amazing girl dad." I blow out a breath, and she raises her other hand, cradling both my cheeks. "I know it's scary, but we're in this together."

I nod. "I hope she has your fighting spirit. And I hope like hell she gets your ability to read a room, but most of all I hope she has your heart because it's so pure, Callie."

Tears glisten in her eyes.

"I hope the exact same. I hope she has her daddy's heart." She places her lips to mine.

"Let's go home." I tuck a strand of hair behind her ear.

"Sounds perfect."

CHAPTER
SIXTY-TWO

Callie

A month has passed, and I never would've thought we'd be where we are. Things with Foster are exactly how I always dreamed they'd be. He even decided to go to therapy again. Apparently, he'd been before for a short amount of time, but as he says, it didn't stick, so he's looking for a new therapist in Chicago.

"Now who's freaking out?" Leighton nudges me in the arm.

This has been a repeating pattern this year—Foster coming in with the bases loaded. We're two outs from getting out of the inning. "Crazy Train" plays, and our little girl kicks me as if she knows it's her daddy's song. I cradle my stomach and stand, watching him walk to the mound. He stops at the edge, and Blue checks him over, but right before he joins Hayes and the other guys, Foster's gaze lifts to meet mine.

The Jumbotron catches it. They've been doing that a lot

lately. The camera seems to always land on me when he's pitching.

He smiles and tilts his head at me. I don't blow him a kiss, and he doesn't do anything else because that's not us.

Ripley hands him the ball, and I see Foster grip it in his palm.

We're tied one and one so far in this three-game series against Milwaukee. We really need to win this one. It'll get the Colts one step closer to making the playoffs.

I sit, and my knee bounces as he throws his practice pitches to Hayes.

"He looks good," Leighton says.

"Really good," Penelope says on my other side. She's been sitting with us lately, and Hazel and Monroe have become fast friends.

I'm not wasting any energy worrying about what she had with Foster. It doesn't matter. And I know it doesn't compare.

"Go, Reaper!" Lincoln shouts, raising his gloved hand.

I bite my lower lip as Decker, Easton, and the rest of the infield head back to their positions. Hayes stands one more time, fixing his guards, before squatting behind home plate.

My nerves multiply as I realize it's the top of the lineup for Milwaukee. "Jace Castillo. Of course. He's probably gonna win the home run derby this year."

Leighton giggles and presses her hand to my bouncing knee. "Nothing Foster hasn't encountered before."

Foster gets one strike on his slider. Another on his inside curve. Jace takes a crack at the third pitch, but it dribbles to third. Decker fields it cleanly and throws it to Hayes at home. One out.

"Just one more," I say to myself.

Foster nods at Decker. Those two are really making great strides lately. Foster even went to dinner with his mom when she was in town last week. He was nervous beforehand and in his head about it when he got home, but he talked to me about how he was feeling. That's all I can ask for.

I'm hoping he'll make some kind of amends with her, if only for himself. But that's up to Foster. Just the fact that he was willing to be around her is a big step forward for him.

Warren Kincaid steps up to the plate next. He and Foster have beef over what I don't know, but at last night's game, Foster might have purposely hit him in the ninth after their pitcher, Whittaker, hit Decker the inning before.

So it's no surprise that Warren looks as though he wants to hit a line drive right at Foster's head.

Warren takes a swing on the first pitch and misses.

I catch Foster almost smiling, but he steps off the mound after Hayes throws it back.

The next two pitches Blue calls as balls.

"That was a strike!" I stand and shout.

Leighton tugs me back down to my seat. "Let's not make beef with Blue."

But everyone around us is on board with the fact that it was a strike.

Foster leans forward and gets the call from Hayes. They've been such an in-sync duo this past month, and I'm so thankful that what happened between us didn't sever those ties. Foster needs Hayes in his life as much as Hayes needs Foster.

The pitch comes in, and I have no idea why they would choose a fastball, but it comes in really fast.

"Holy shit, he hit one hundred and four." Lincoln points at the Jumbotron.

"Lincoln," Leighton scolds. "Language."

I lean a little closer to her. "Man, is ten the new sixteen?"

"Apparently." She gives Lincoln a look to say he's in trouble later.

"Finish him off," I call.

Leighton laughs. "My, how the tables have turned."

She's smug and deservingly so. I made fun of her many times for freaking out when Hayes was in the box.

Foster throws a curve. It's the one pitch that hasn't quite been doing what it used to for him, but this one tails right at the end. Warren swings, and I close my eyes until I hear the roar of the Chicago fans.

I spring my eyes open to see Foster walking toward the dugout.

Easton runs up behind him and pushes himself off Foster's shoulders, shouting, "Let's go!"

Hayes waits for him, and Foster fist bumps him, but right before he dips into the dugout, Foster's eyes find mine, and he smiles. A big, toothy smile that he's never once given me in public.

The camera catches it, and soon side-by-side pictures of us are on the Jumbotron with heart emojis and kisses sprinkled over the screen.

"You guys are the 'it' couple," Penelope says. "I'm glad to see him so happy."

"Me too."

We share a look, and I pat her hand, hoping she figures out that I know about her past with Foster, and I'm okay with it.

The Colts win, and everyone decides to go to Peeper's to celebrate.

We fill the backroom. Even Penelope and Hazel join us for the first time. We order pizza from down the street, and Ruby comes in with her tray of non-alcoholic drinks for me.

"You gonna pick one soon so I don't have to keep bringing a whole tray in here. My back is killing me," Ruby complains, but then without waiting for me to choose what I want she puts a glass of milk in front of me. "You should have this. It's good for the baby."

"Foster!" I shout across the room.

He's competing in a game of darts with Hayes, Easton, and Decker.

He sees the glass of milk and winks at me. "Milk has vitamin D, protein, calcium."

I shake my head, but I don't care. I love that he worries about the baby and me.

"He made me do it. Threatened me by saying he would invite those Chipmunks if I didn't give it to you." Ruby walks away and out of the room.

Later that night, when my feet are hurting and I'm tired, I see Foster pull his phone out of his pocket and check it. His smile falters for the first time since the game ended.

My stomach drops because whatever it is, it's about to rupture our happy little bubble.

He walks over to me, taking the chair next to me, and swings my legs over his lap. Then he hands me his phone and massages my calves.

Jagger Kale: Your guy just got arrested.
Buckle up, this might get bumpy.

CHAPTER
SIXTY-THREE

Foster

Callie tells the group she's tired and that we're going to head up to the condo. They all believe it, but I hate that my bullshit is keeping her from having a good time with our friends.

As soon as we're behind closed doors, she turns to me. "Okay, let's call Jagger."

I can see fatigue weighing on her as she sits on the couch and stretches out her legs.

Taking a seat beside her, I bring her legs over my lap again and massage her feet. "Go figure, right? Things were going way too well."

I concentrate on her feet, but she pokes me in the stomach with one when I don't look at her.

"Things are still great. You're innocent, and sure at first people will… well, we're getting ahead of ourselves. Let's just call Jagger and figure out a plan."

I sigh, meeting her gaze. "We leave in the morning for the Seattle game."

I don't want to tell Callie that maybe she should stay home. I left a lot of shit in Seattle. I thought it was all cleared up, but now I'm walking into a shitstorm and bringing her along with me.

"Call him." She pokes me with her foot again.

I pull my phone out and dial Jagger, putting him on speaker.

"Hey, sorry to ruin your night. I figured you were celebrating. You've been on fire on the mound lately. Keep it up and those endorsements will come. Well, depending how this all shakes out. How likely is it that your name will come up in this investigation?"

"Since I paid my dad's debt, and we share the same last name, I'm guessing pretty likely. Do you think he keeps records like that?"

Jagger blows out a breath.

Callie slides in next to me, resting her head on my shoulder. I wrap my arm around her and pull her as close as I can get her.

"It depends how big of an operation he's running, but since they nabbed him, and it is somewhat news, I'd say your name is somewhere. They're certainly going to be able to track it when they dig into his banking records."

I groan, and Callie takes the phone from me. "Hey, Jagger, this is Callie."

"Callie, can't wait to meet you."

"Do you think he should just go public and make a statement?"

Jagger chuckles but sobers quickly. "Sorry, it's just... of course you'd think that."

"People are going to talk."

"Foster hasn't even been named yet. I don't think we bring

shit up that they haven't figured out. If and when the cops want to talk to him, it may not leak to the public. They might interview him, be satisfied with what he says, and move on, no one the wiser. This could die down in a couple days. Or they might arrest him, and the case could get thrown out of court. Let's not be rash. Let's wait and see what happens over the next few days."

Callie and I look at each other, weighing what Jagger said in our minds. Eventually we nod in agreement.

"Okay, Jagger. Sounds like a plan." I kiss Callie on the temple.

"So, you're in Seattle this weekend. I'll be there too. We're gonna put on our happy faces and pretend like nothing is out of sorts. If it comes out, we'll address it at that time. Just keep your head down."

"Okay. I will."

"There's one more thing…" I can hear the hesitation in Jagger's voice, something I don't hear often.

There's a long pause as Callie looks at me quizzically.

"I'm hiring security." Jagger's statement lands like a bomb.

My chest tightens, and my hand flexes on Callie's shoulder.

"What? Why?" Callie straightens a bit. As best she can with her belly.

"Foster?" he says.

"She knows everything," I tell him.

"This bookie has people. People who are looking for who ratted him out. I don't think you're in danger or anything like that, but I don't want them bothering you guys. I know you're an 'in the stands behind home plate' girl, Callie, but this weekend, you'll be in a suite."

"But—"

I squeeze her shoulder and nod. I'd feel more at peace with her in a suite rather than out in public.

"Fine." She sounds like a sullen child, and my lips quirk up.

"We'll talk more this weekend. Since it's, like, a couples thing, I'll bring Quinn," Jagger says.

"Good, I have a question for her." Callie glances at the romance books in the corner on the table, one of which has Quinn's name on it.

"I always love it when my clients want to talk to my romance author wife," Jagger says dryly. "Sit tight, and if anything happens, I'll be in contact. Otherwise, see you tomorrow night. Security will be waiting for you at the hotel."

We say goodbye, and Callie tosses my phone on the other couch cushion, moving to straddle me. As I always do, I place my hands on her stomach. My number one priority is to keep them safe, and I can't help but think Seattle is the worst place for them.

"Do you think I can convince you to stay home?"

She shakes her head. "The whole reason we picked Seattle as the away series I tagged along for was because I knew it would be hard for you to be there. I want to be with you to remind you that it's us now, not just you."

She kisses me, but when she goes to pull away, I weave my hand through the hair at the back of her head, keeping her there.

I knew she'd still want to go, and Leighton is going for Hayes. Who knows when Callie will be able to travel again once the baby comes?

So I'll try to push aside my concern and lose myself in her, hoping like hell when we wake up, I'm not headline news.

CHAPTER
SIXTY-FOUR

Callie

Leighton and I have a fun girls' day once we arrive in Seattle. We do a little shopping with the bodyguards tailing behind. I'm sure most people looking at us are wondering if they've seen us before.

Nothing about the bookie and Foster has come out, thank goodness.

By the time we reach the suite at the Seattle ballpark, some people are already there.

A tall man in a sharp custom suit with perfectly gelled hair comes right over to us. "Leighton and Callie." He kisses Leighton's cheek, then puts his hand in front of me. "Jagger Kale."

"The man in charge of most of the guys on that field's career." I shake his hand.

His gaze shifts to my stomach briefly before they pop back up to meet my eyes. "That's me. And your man is taking up too much of my time lately." He chuckles and shifts his attention to Leighton. "Hayes's turn was last year." Then he waves us into the suite. "Come and meet my wife, Quinn."

He leads us farther in, and I can't stop eyeing all the food and drinks. The best thing about pregnancy is being able to eat what I want without feeling guilty about it.

Then I see that Angela Davis is here too, talking to who I suspect is Jagger's wife.

"Angela." I nod and give her a small smile.

She returns it and nods back.

I know she and Foster have a complicated relationship, but she is the grandmother of my baby, so I break the distance and hug her. "I didn't know you were coming."

"I try to always come to the Seattle games." Her confession strikes me as odd because she's from Philadelphia, from what I understand. "How is the pregnancy going?"

"It's good." We both look down at my stomach. Never have I ever taken so much time to stare at one part of my body as much as I have these past months. "She's moving a lot more these days."

Leighton says hello to Angela, then Jagger introduces us to his wife.

"This is Foster Davis's girlfriend, Callie Carlisle, and Hayes Carlisle's fiancée, Leighton."

"Oh yes, I've heard about you both." Quinn shakes our hands, giving us a big smile.

Jagger kisses her on the temple. "I'll be back."

"He's always got someone to schmooze." She stirs the straw in her drink. "How was the trip out here?"

We all make polite talk for a bit.

Yes, I'm six months.

Oh, it's a girl.

Quinn can definitely lead a conversation.

"Just so you know, Foster is going to ask you why there aren't more baseball hero stories in romance. Just a warning." I roll my eyes good-naturedly.

She laughs. "They're always so concerned about being a hero in a book. I guess it's those egos. But thanks for the heads-up."

We chat a little longer, then the game starts, so I take my seat between Angela and Leighton.

Everything is going great, we're winning, and for a moment, I think Foster won't even have to come in. But late in the ninth with only one out left to get, he's called in.

"It's weird to see it with no music and the lights on," I say.

The minute he steps out of the bullpen, boos ring through the stadium. A strangled sound comes out of Angela, and her body tenses.

Leighton puts her hand on my knee. "He left. You know how it goes."

True, but I still feel for Foster.

"You're fucking kidding me," Jagger whispers behind me, and I glance over my shoulder to see him walking out of the suite.

My eyes snag on the television screen in the suite, and all the breath whooshes out of my lungs. The headline flashing on the screen reads, *Foster Davis bets against himself with big Seattle bookie. More names to come.*

My head drops forward, and I excuse myself to go find Jagger. He's walking in as I'm walking out.

He gives my shoulder a reassuring squeeze. "I'm heading down to the locker room to meet Foster right after the game. Go back to the hotel and wait for us there."

"No, I want to see him."

Jagger blows out a breath. "Please don't be difficult. This is bad, Callie. Like, career-ending bad."

"Which is why I'm going to be by his side the entire time." I grab my purse off the counter. "I'm going with you."

"He did it, Cal. Struck them out, and we won! Take that, Seattle and your shitty fans." Leighton sounds really tough right now, even though she's the sweetest person I know.

I look over my shoulder and see her spot Jagger with me. Then Leighton and Angela look at the television and read the caption, their smiles fading.

We're going to get through this, and I'm going to prove to Foster that he has an entire army at his side.

Jagger agrees to take me to see Foster, and Leighton and Angela decide to come too. I'm hoping that Angela doesn't make it worse for Foster, but if anything, she can be there for Decker.

Jagger gets into the locker room because he's Jagger, and the rest of us are put in some room for the visiting team's guests.

"Did you know about this?" Leighton asks me once we're alone.

I nod. "He didn't do it."

"I know that." Leighton gives me a look as if she's insulted I'd dare to think otherwise.

"He's behind it, isn't he?" Angela asks.

"Who?" Leighton looks between the two of us.

I nod to Angela, and she shakes her head, walks away, then comes back with her phone. "Listen, Callie…" She pauses but then seems to convince herself of something and continues. "Has Foster shown you a picture of his dad?"

I shake my head.

She holds her phone out to me. "This is him. I have no doubt he's in this stadium somewhere. When we were in the suite, I felt okay, but now that this news has come out…and with you being pregnant… he's going to show his face."

I stare at the man who looks more like Decker than Foster. Dark hair and eyes, shorter than both of his sons.

"This is why I come to the Seattle games," Angela says.

"Why?" Leighton moves in to look at the picture. "You couldn't have known that this news would come out."

"No, but I knew he reached out to Decker for money and things. And I knew with both boys here… and if he knew you were here too, Callie, he'd try to work some angle to get something from the boys."

Emotion hits me when she says *the boys* because that's how she'll always see Decker and Foster. As her sons. She still wants to protect them both.

I take out my phone and see that the story is everywhere. I don't bother scrolling through the shitty comments from people who have no idea what they're talking about or the man they're pointing their fingers at.

"I just need to see Foster."

CHAPTER
SIXTY-FIVE

Foster

Walking off the field, I want to flip off the Seattle fans for booing me, but I'm better than that now. I have to be for Callie and our little girl.

As I'm about to duck my head and step down into the dugout, a woman leans over the railing, with the most venom in her eyes I've ever seen from a fan. And I've seen some bad looks.

"Your mother should be ashamed. Betting against yourself? I'm glad you're not with Seattle anymore."

I stop dead in my tracks.

Fuck.

It's out.

There's no way this lady just happens to be the one person who figured it out or has the inside track.

My gaze shifts to the suite Callie was in earlier. I don't see her, Leighton, or Jagger. Which means shit went down at some point in the ninth while I was pitching a great outing.

I jog down into the dugout and rush into the locker room, but Ripley stops me before I reach my locker. He touches my elbow and nods for me to follow, leading me to a nearby room.

No surprise, Jagger is waiting for me.

"I didn't do it," I say to Ripley.

He chuckles and sits in a chair. "I know that."

"Do you?" I arch an eyebrow, my heart beating a mile a minute.

He tilts his head. "Kid, I've known you for how many years? I know you'd never be part of something like this, but I know who would. I really wish you would've come to me."

I look at my lap. "No one else needed to be dragged into it."

A soft knock lands on the door, and Hayes peeks his head in.

"Come in." Ripley waves him in.

Easton and Decker file in behind him, and Hayes takes the seat next to me. Easton pats me on the shoulder before taking the seat next to Hayes, while Decker sits on my other side.

"Why are you guys in here?" I ask.

"Because this is bullshit, and we're on your side." Hayes clamps his hand on my shoulder.

"I'm assuming this was Dad's doing?" Decker asks.

I nod.

He inhales a deep breath, but I never hear him release it.

Jagger claps his hands together. "Okay, we're gonna get out of here and head to the hotel. I have the suite, so you can come up, and we'll figure out what statement we want to release." Jagger turns to Ripley. "I'll get in contact with the front office, keep them in the loop, make sure they're good with whatever we decide."

I cross my arms and stare at my lap. "People won't believe me."

"You're right, some won't." Jagger's always one to keep it real.

I already have a shit reputation with the fans and some players. Something like this will be easy for them to believe.

Ripley clasps his hands in front of him, leaning closer to me. "Some people will believe it, but those people don't know Foster Davis. Not the guy we know." He looks around the room. "This is your home base, and it's all that matters. You remember that."

I nod, anxiety welling up inside me because people will think I did something I didn't do and there's probably nothing I can do to make them think differently. It's a hard pill to swallow.

I was okay with people thinking I slept with too many women. I was okay with the rumors about me starting fights at bars. I did those things, but this... this accusation is the ultimate worst thing I could do.

It disrespects the game, the other players, my teammates and coaches. Hell, myself.

There's no way I want my daughter thinking her dad would do something as shitty as throw a game to win money on a bet.

I look straight at Jagger. "Tell me what to do."

He smiles and nods. "First thing we need to do is get you to Callie. If I don't, I'm gonna have one angry pregnant woman who wants my head on a stick."

I stand. "Where is she?"

"She's in another room with Leighton and your mom."

My head swivels toward Decker.

"She likes to come to the Seattle games." He shrugs.

Decker doesn't have to say it. It's because Dad is here.

"Go shower, and we'll meet you at the hotel," Ripley tells us. He comes over to me and puts his hand on my shoulder. "This will pass. I promise it will."

I was on my way to having it all, but I should've guessed that my dad's drama would throw one more stone. I just hope it's the last one.

CHAPTER
SIXTY-SIX

Foster

We all shower and change, and when I finally have Callie in my arms again, I feel as if I can overcome this. Maybe everyone might not believe me, but some people will. And Ripley is right—does it really matter as long as those people who truly know me believe in me?

"You okay?" She places her hands on my face, searching.

"I am now."

Her smile is soft and loving, and I thank whoever sent her to me because had I not had her, this moment would've sent me spiraling.

"Jagger said we're meeting him at the hotel?"

I nod. "Ripley said we don't have to take the bus, so Jagger got us some cars."

Callie, Decker, my mom, and I walk out of the room and down the hallways, but as soon as we're through the doors reserved for the players, I see *him*. Guess I shouldn't be surprised he's waiting for us.

Leaning on a light pole, my dad takes a drag of his cigarette and releases a puff of smoke.

Callie freezes, her hand going cold in mine.

How does she know who he is?

"Boys, great game." He pushes off the light pole and walks toward us.

Decker steps in front of our mom, but she slides out from around him.

"Go home, Jason." There's anger and years of exhaustion in her voice.

"Oh, you're a momma's boy now, are you, Foster? Saw her up in the suite with that woman you knocked up." He looks at Callie, and I slide her behind me. But much like my mom, she doesn't stay there. "Never thought I'd see the day you'd forgive her for abandoning you. For not wanting you and only wanting your brother."

"Enough with your lies." Decker's voice is filled with contempt.

Our dad's gaze flicks over to Decker. "Your mother wanted you all to herself. We knew Foster was the bad seed, and she was worried he'd sour you."

My chest squeezes, hearing all the same shit I did growing up.

My mom looks at me as if asking if he really told me those things. I don't engage. I just want to get Callie out of here.

My dad holds up his hands. "Hey, I abided by your rules. Never left Seattle. So I expect that those checks won't stop."

Callie steps forward until I gently pull her back. "He's not paying you anymore."

My dad laughs at her. "Because you're gonna get all his money, is that it, sweetheart? Think just because you can spread your legs, you're owed something?"

I release Callie's hand and move toward him, but she grips my shirt from behind, and I stop.

"Hate to break it to you, but whatever this is between you

two will be short-lived. My son here can't do relationships thanks to all his abandonment issues from her." He nods at my mom.

"You know what, Jason, I let you win long enough, but today it stops. You need to leave right now."

He looks at her as though she's nothing, less than nothing. "Or what, Ang?"

"I'm going to call the police." She pulls out her phone, but Decker places his hand on it.

We don't need the press here.

"Let's just go." I walk us out and see our cars waiting for us just outside the gate. Once we're in them, I can get my head on straight. We can figure out how we're going to deal with this.

"After everything I did for you," he says to my back, "all the time and money and attention I put into building you into the ballplayer you are today, this is how you act?"

I whip around, keeping Callie's hand in mine, and get into his face. "You did nothing for me. I was the one who did all the work. I was the one who threw the baseball. I was the one who stayed late at practices. I was the one with the special coaches. You were the one who took advantage. And now you come to me for what? You blew up my career. Thanks to you, everyone thinks I made some shady bets and threw games. That's not even mentioning the amount of money I've wasted on you, which was a helluva lot more than you ever spent on making me into the prodigy you wanted. Callie's right. There's no more money coming your way. I have a..." I stop myself. He doesn't deserve to hear from me if it's a grandson or granddaughter. "A child coming."

I turn and usher Callie into the waiting car.

"It's probably not even yours."

I release Callie's hand, step forward, and cock my fist back, but Decker beats me to it. He rears back and punches our dad right across the face.

He wobbles a little then falls to the ground.

Decker stands over him. "Go to hell and stay the fuck out of our lives."

"Deck, man, I didn't think you had it in you," Easton says.

My brother shakes out his hand. "Didn't want you to fuck up your pitching hand." He walks to one of the other cars and gets in.

I stand there for a second, feet planted, watching my dad stagger to get up.

A part of me wants to help him. Maybe he's right, and I wouldn't be where I am today without everything happening exactly as it did. But he only ever did more damage than good. He's only ever given me grief and made me feel shitty about myself.

A hand slips into mine, and it's not Callie's soft palm. I look to my left and see my mom squeezing my hand with eyes filled with sorrow and regret.

I choke back tears because I don't want this for my life.

She wants to make amends, and she's admitted to doing wrong. How can I continue to punish her?

Maybe we'll never have the relationship she and Decker share, but maybe we can have more than we do today. The only way to know for sure is to try.

CHAPTER
SIXTY-SEVEN

Foster Davis Denies Betting Allegations in Brief Press Conference: "I Never Placed a Wager"

Written By Bryce Cavanagh | The Breakout

CHICAGO — Chicago Colts closer Foster Davis addressed allegations of gambling-related impropriety Tuesday afternoon, firmly denying any involvement and placing responsibility on his father.

"I did not make any bets. I never placed a wager," Davis said, standing at the podium wearing a dark-navy Colts polo, jaw tight but voice controlled. "If there were bets, they were not mine. They were my dad's. I had no knowledge of it until it became an issue I couldn't ignore."

The press conference, held in a small media room beneath Webber Field, lasted under eight minutes and included no questions from the media. Davis's agent, Jagger Kale, stood along the wall, watching on. Colts' management and legal counsel were present but did not speak.

Davis, 33, has become one of the league's most reliable late-inning arms since arriving in Chicago last season. The allegations—circulating online over the weekend—suggest improper betting activity connected to games during his final months in Seattle. Davis did not name teams, dates, or individuals, only repeating that he was not the bettor and that he was "fully cooperating" with all investigative authorities.

Colts, MLBPA Announce Separate Reviews

In a statement released shortly after Davis exited the room, the Chicago Colts confirmed they will conduct an internal review "in coordination with the appropriate governing bodies." The Major League Players Association also stated it will be opening its own inquiry "to ensure due process and protect the rights of the player involved."

"As of this moment, Foster Davis has not been found to have violated any league rules," the Colts' statement read. "He is presumed innocent while the matter is reviewed."

A representative for the MLBPA echoed that language, emphasizing that speculation online has "outpaced verified facts."

What couldn't be ignored wasn't just what Davis said—it was how he said it.

This is a pitcher long known for his edge: the glare, the clipped answers, the sharp turn-and-walk exits from interviews. But Tuesday, Davis looked… steadier. Still unmistakably Foster Davis but grounded in a way that had reporters exchanging looks.

"He seems different," one national columnist murmured as Davis stepped away from the podium. "Like someone finally got through to him."

That "someone," depending on who you ask, was standing a few feet outside the frame.

Davis has been at the center of an entirely separate wave of attention in recent weeks after news broke that he is expecting a child this year with Callie Carlisle, sister of Colts catcher, Hayes Carlisle. Neither Davis nor Carlisle took questions about their relationship, but the pairing has become a favorite topic for fans and commentators alike, with clips of Carlisle in the stands going viral after recent games.

Then came the moment that will likely be replayed all over social media for weeks to come.

As Davis walked out of the media room, shoulders tight, he paused near the hallway entrance where Carlisle stood off to the side.

Davis didn't hesitate.

He pulled her into his arms and held on for a beat longer than necessary. It didn't seem performative, not for the cameras. Carlisle's hand weaved through his hair. His eyes shut briefly, as if her presence was the only thing that made the room stop spinning.

When he let go, Davis didn't look at the reporters. He didn't say a word to anyone.

He just took her hand and kept walking.

Love looks good on Foster Davis.

EPILOGUE

Decker

Losing sucks.

We had a great season, an excellent second half. We all thought we had it.

We fought hard each game for it to come down to the seventh game of the World Series.

As we walk off Webber Field, Toronto runs out, all of them cheering and celebrating, jumping around and congratulating one another.

It's a hard thing to watch when we came so close. But we should be proud we gave it our all.

We all file into the locker room where there is no champagne. The lockers aren't covered with plastic. There aren't any reporters waiting to interview us. They'll get around to us after they're finished interviewing the champions.

We all go to our lockers, and even Drew doesn't say a word.

We've been here before. Sure, not in a series like this, but in other big games that didn't go our way. You reevaluate every play, every at-bat. What could we have done differently? What caused the loss?

Ripley comes out, gives us an inspirational speech about how proud he is, that we have a great clubhouse, and we'll work hard in the offseason and come back stronger and better next season.

It's a good speech, but at this point in our careers, we know the drill. Some of us will be here next year. Some of us won't. Changes always happen in the offseason, and each season's team is never exactly the same.

We all get into the showers then get dressed. There's a contemplative mood in the locker room, not a celebratory one.

An intern rushes into the locker room, stopping short and frantically looking in all directions. "Foster!"

At the tone the intern uses, my brother bolts up from packing his bag. It's clear it's something big, most likely involving Callie.

Game seven wasn't the best timing with Callie being in the last week of her pregnancy. Of course Foster told her to stay at home, and of course she said over her dead body. They agreed on her sitting in a suite. See? They're learning to compromise.

"Is it Callie?" Foster grabs his bag and jogs out of the room.

Easton, Hayes, and I share a look, each of us grabbing our bags and following. Suddenly, the loss of the series doesn't sting so badly.

Foster's already at Callie's side, and someone brings a wheelchair, which is good. Otherwise Foster would probably carry her out of here.

"Someone call an ambulance," Foster says.

"No… no." Callie shakes her head. "We can make it to the hospital."

By some miracle, we all get out of the stadium and into

Ubers. Leighton and Hayes have to wait for an XL for their whole crew.

Everyone is here.

Hayes and Callie's parents.

My mom.

Leighton and the kids.

Easton's parents.

And the new addition to our group recently... Penelope and her daughter, Hazel.

We're all so busy picking cars and getting everyone to the hospital since we're all going to be there for Foster and Callie that I don't realize until I look at the seat behind me that I have Mom, Penelope, and Hazel in my car.

Well, this is awkward.

My mom makes conversation because she's like that. Foster and I didn't get her conversational skills.

Penelope answers her questions politely while I try not to hang on to every last detail she shares so I can know what her life is like these days.

Penelope is my *maybe someday*. Our paths have crossed, but we've never been able to stay. She also married the man she referred to as the love of her life, so there's that.

I'm in misery for the brief ride to the hospital, and after we get out of the Uber, we file into the hospital, looking like an overly close family that doesn't have any boundaries.

Not that far from the truth actually.

Somewhere in the midst of Callie and Foster disappearing, we all end up in a labor and delivery waiting room, vying for chairs.

We stay for fifteen hours, taking turns going in and seeing Callie as she sucks on ice chips and complains, deservingly so. We order food, we fall asleep, but all of us stay.

Finally, right before noon the next day, Foster comes out and gives us all the news. "Ellis Riley Davis has arrived."

He looks as if he played all seven World Series games in one night, but I never thought I'd see that smile on his face.

I'm proud of all the work he's done. He allowed himself to fall in love and managed not to blow it. I glance at Penelope playing with Hazel and Monroe. Foster is more courageous than I am.

We all take turns visiting with Callie and the new baby, and when my turn rolls around, I'm paired with Penelope.

Is the universe trying to tell me something?

Callie is in the hospital bed, and Foster's at her side, running his hand over the top of her head. Ellis is in the bassinet.

"She's beautiful." I'm probably more sensitive than my twin brother, but I'm not an overly emotional guy, so I'm surprised by the surge of emotion I feel when I look at my niece.

"We're hoping the blue eyes stick." Callie smiles at Foster.

Foster comes over, picks her up, and holds her out. I'm a little surprised by how comfortable he seems maneuvering with the baby. "Ellis, this is your uncle Decker. Don't go to him when you get in trouble, he's one of those rule followers. Easton's probably better for that kind of thing."

The two of us chuckle, and he hands her to me. I'm a little awkward with the pass over, but I manage.

My brother and I are mending our relationship, which has resulted in me making some decisions about the woman to my right and why I need to keep my distance. There's still so much between us that hasn't been discussed. Maybe it should be buried and left to rot, never to be dug up again. Leave it where it is, and we just all move on.

"She's going to be a rule follower too," Callie says.

"There's nothing wrong with being a little wild." Foster winks at Callie.

"A little bit maybe." She smiles at where Ellis rests in my arms.

Penelope peers over my shoulder, her perfume surrounding me. I swear it's the same one she used to wear.

"Here, did you want to hold her?" I hold her out to Penelope, and she takes Ellis with ease, of course, because she's a mother.

Penelope rocks her and sways as if it's all second nature. "Now I want another one. You forget what it's like."

"I'll call you to handle the 3 a.m. feedings, and you can tell me if you still want another one." Callie has so much love in her eyes as she watches Penelope with Ellis.

"Very true. But those days aren't long in the grand scheme of things. And now someone is off for the season, so you have an extra set of hands." She eyes Foster.

He goes to Callie's side as if he needs to reassure Callie about his feelings for her, which is ridiculous. Anyone can see that my brother is head over heels for the woman who just gave birth to his daughter.

Ellis fusses, and Penelope holds her out to Callie. "You have a lot of guests who still want to love on her, so I'll get going. Congratulations, you two." She bends and hugs Callie, then nods at Foster.

Yeah, dead and buried is definitely the way to go.

I say my goodbyes to the happy family, and as we walk down the hallway toward the waiting room, Penelope tugs on my sleeve.

"So, does everyone know what went down with all three of us back in college?"

The End

ALSO BY PIPER RAYNE

The Dugout

The Hotshot

The Wild Card

The Rulebreaker

The Troublemaker

The Nest

Mr. Heartbreaker

Mr. Broody

Mr. Swoony

Mr. Charming

The Nest Before Christmas

Hockey Hotties

Countdown to a Kiss

My Lucky #13

The Trouble with #9

Faking it with #41

Tropical Hat Trick (Novella)

Sneaking around with #34

Second Shot with #76

Offside with #55

Chicago Grizzlies

On the Defense

Something like Hate

Something like Lust

Something like Love

Kingsmen Football Stars

False Start

You Had Your Chance, Lee Burrows

You Can't Kiss the Nanny, Brady Banks

Over My Brother's Dead Body, Chase Andrews

Modern Love

Charmed by the Bartender

Hooked by the Boxer

Mad about the Banker

Single Dads Club

Real Deal

Dirty Talker

Sexy Beast

Hollywood Hearts

Mister Mom

Animal Attraction

Domestic Bliss

Bedroom Games

Cold as Ice

On Thin Ice

Break the Ice

Chicago Law

Smitten with the Best Man

Tempted by my Ex-Husband

Seduced by my Ex's Divorce Attorney

Blue Collar Brothers

Flirting with Fire

Crushing on the Cop

Engaged to the EMT

White Collar Brothers

Sexy Filthy Boss

Dirty Flirty Enemy

Wild Steamy Hook-up

The Rooftop Crew

My Bestie's Ex

A Royal Mistake

The Rival Roomies

Our Star-Crossed Kiss

The Do-Over

A Co-Workers Crush

Holiday Romances

Single and Ready to Jingle

Claus and Effect

Merry Kissmas

Yule Be Mine

The Baileys

Lessons from a One-Night Stand

Advice from a Jilted Bride

Birth of a Baby Daddy

Operation Bailey Wedding (Novella)

Falling for My Brother's Best Friend

Demise of a Self-Centered Playboy

Confessions of a Naughty Nanny

Operation Bailey Babies (Novella)

Secrets of the World's Worst Matchmaker

Winning my Best Friend's Girl

Rules for Dating Your Ex

Operation Bailey Birthday (Novella)

The Greene Family

My Twist of Fortune

My Beautiful Neighbor

My Almost Ex

My Vegas Groom

A Greene Family Summer Bash (Novella)

My Sister's Flirty Friend

My Unexpected Surprise

My Famous Frenemy

A Greene Family Vacation (Novella)

My Scorned Best Friend

My Fake Fiancé

My Brother's Forbidden Friend

A Greene Family Christmas (Novella)

Lake Starlight

The Problem with Second Chances

The Issue with Bad Boy Roommates

The Trouble with Runaway Brides

The Drawback of Single Dads

The Complication with the Best Man

Plain Daisy Ranch

One Last Summer

The One I Left Behind

The One I Stood Beside

The One I Didn't See Coming

Chasing Forever

Chasing Love

Chasing Home

Love in Apartment 3B

Hit or Miss

Three's A Crowd

Good on Paper

The Abbott Brothers

Rent a Husband

Buy a Boyfriend

Standalones

Don't Mind if "I Do"

COCKAMAMIE UNICORN RAMBLINGS

WHOA… this was our longest sports romance book to date!

What can we say, Foster and Callie really were the most stubborn couple we've ever written. They just wouldn't stop talking to us, and clearly Foster had a lot of shit he had to work through.

We're halfway done with this series, and we're already mourning the finish line. After all of our worries about writing a baseball series after The Nest, this group of characters has been so enjoyable to write. We've fallen head over heels for the found family in The Dugout crew.

Before we get into what changed from plotting to book, we wanted to address the biggest struggle we faced while writing this book. Time to get vulnerable… you know, like we always make our characters do? LOL

We released the cover of *The Hotshot* when we were about five days away from our deadline for *The Wild Card* and only halfway through writing the book. As with all our covers, we were so excited to finally show it off. We'd put so much into this new series and *The Hotshot* release, and finally getting to share Hayes and Leighton with all of you was indescribable.

And then someone posted over on our Threads accusing us of using AI for the cover.

We were stunned speechless.

Because we know our covers are not AI.

We immediately noticed that our designer wasn't tagged on the post (just a human error made by the person who put the post up, no biggie) and rectified it immediately, tagging the designer on the post. Please note, it's the same designer we used for *The Nest*.

We denied all claims, but even after that, some people still came after us. And some people came after us in what felt like a very personal way. Let us tell you—having a bunch of strangers who don't know you at all tell you what a piece of garbage you are on the internet is not a good time.

It paralyzed us.

Both of us completely lost the ability to concentrate on the book. Days were lost. Productivity dropped. We just sat in confusion, hurt, and we were honestly heartsick that something we were so proud of had turned into something else entirely.

We do not condone generative AI in our work. We never have. We had already had that conversation with our designer before she even started working on the cover. So to be accused of something we didn't do—something that goes against our values and our livelihood—is a hard thing to swallow and just try to move on from.

We aren't denying that AI is a real issue in this industry right now. Artists are being exploited. Their work is being scraped and repurposed without consent. So we understand why people are on high alert.

But understanding it didn't make the accusation that we were liars hurt any less.

Because we *do* pay artists. We *do* work with real designers. We *do* believe in protecting creative labor.

So when people implied that we were cutting corners or being dishonest with our readers, it felt like everything we'd built over the last ten years was suddenly being called into question.

We have always tried to build our writing career the right

way—with hard work, investing in our craft and our business, and integrity. And we won't even get into the hours we work, or the sacrifices our families have made for us to pursue our shared dream.

You trust us with your time, your money, your emotions, your late nights when you stay up too late to read "just one more chapter." We have never taken that lightly.

So to have that trust questioned over something we didn't do hit harder than we expected it to.

We almost didn't talk about this publicly.

We debated staying quiet and pushing through the deadline, pretending it hadn't affected us the way it did. But the truth is, it did affect us.

And pretending otherwise felt dishonest too.

So here is what we want you to know…

We did not use AI for the cover of *The Hotshot or any of our covers or character art.*

We believe in human-made art.

We believe in paying creatives fairly.

And we believe that Hayes and Leighton's story, and this whole new world we're building still deserves to be met with excitement and joy.

This shook us, but it also reminded us why we do this in the first place.

We do this because we love telling stories.

We do this because we love building worlds for you to immerse yourself in.

We do this because what you do after you're knocked down is what's most important.

This community means everything to us. Afterall, it gave both of us a chance at a second career that we love.

But we just can't sit in the corner and allow people to point their finger with no proof. It was insulting to our designer who did an amazing job on the cover. And it was insulting to us. We've worked our asses off to build this career and believe us—we wouldn't throw all of that hard work out the window to save a few bucks on a cover. We invest a lot in our work (good illustrators/designers and a full cast audio are *not* cheap).

Eventually, we had to put it aside and allow the naysayers to believe what they wanted and move on, because it became very clear to us that they weren't actually interested in the truth. But that moment will always taint this series for us, just a little bit. Which is a damn shame because we truly love these stories we've created.

And in moving on, you know what we decided to do? Use our experience as inspiration for our story and pour our feelings about it into there. So you saw Callie read the horrible comments about herself after her pregnancy is leaked and Foster being accused and judged for something he didn't do, you understand their feelings were our own.

We never thought we'd go through something like this, but here we are.

Okay… moving on… we've spent enough of our time and energy on that.

What changed from plotting to story?

Hmm… at this point we can't even remember.

- Hayes was going to find out about the pregnancy earlier in the story, but we wanted Foster and Callie to have time to get to know each other without that pressure.
- The bookie thing was never going to be there. It was only going to be the dad showing up.
- Penelope's storyline just popped up in The Hotshot and finally Decker and Foster's real problems came to light (just wait because we have written ourselves into a corner with that one. Let's see if we can get ourselves out of it).

- His mom wasn't going to be his sounding board to finally get back with Callie.

That's about all we can remember, but like we said, lots of distractions while we were writing this book.

As always, we have a lot of people to thank for getting this book into your hands…

Nina and the entire Valentine PR team. Thank you for taking our emergency call the day it all went down and for talking us through our feelings. We appreciate you SO much!

Cassie from Joy Editing for the line edits and who always graciously works with our chaotic schedules. This was a monster of a book we surprised you with and you still worked your magic meeting our return date!

Ellie from My Brother's Editor for line edits and proofreading. We threw this at you with hardly any time before we needed it back and of course you made it work for us. We love you!

Olivia Winston for giving our manuscript one final look over before we hit publish. And thank you for your kind words always after proofing.

Simone and Angela at Buerosued for our illustrated cover. Your work is amazing as always, and we're so happy to be working with you on another series. Callie and Foster couldn't be more adorable.

Amanda from Last Chapter Book Shop for allowing us to write her and her incredible romance only Chicago bookstore into this story. Adding another real slice of Chicago made the world feel more authentic, and we couldn't love it more.

All the bloggers and influencers who choose to read us when you have so many options out there. We're appreciative and honored to be on your list of must-reads and love reading all your reviews, edits, and more.

All the Piper Rayne Unicorns who support us all day, every day. We'd be lost without you answering our polls and telling us what you love and hate. We strive to listen to you and give you what you love about our books with a twist every time.

You, the reader, reading this now in real time, who has an abundance of books to choose from—thank you for picking up one of ours. Word of mouth is always the best form of advertising, and we appreciate you sharing your love for this series with the romance community!

It's no surprise whose book is next. Like we mentioned above, we'll be writing ourselves out of the corner, but honestly it makes our job a lot more fun. How boring would it be if we had everything plotted months ago? At least that's what we're telling ourselves. We do think Decker is going to rock you guys… we feel a little Henry and Jade vibe coming, maybe. No promises though.

See you soon!

xo,
Piper & Rayne

ABOUT PIPER & RAYNE

Piper Rayne is an Amazon Top 100 and *USA Today* Bestselling Author duo who believes in soft places to land, big laughs, and happily-ever-afters.

Piper runs on tea. Rayne runs on Diet Coke. But they both have one boy and one girl and are married to men who patiently listen to book talk they'll never quite understand.

Piper's the one who turns up the heat and humor—spinning tension, spark, and steam into moments that make you blush into your pillow and grin through the next chapter.

Rayne's the one who tugs on your heartstrings—mixing locker-room laughs, brotherhood banter, and the kind of heart-punch moments that hit when you least expect them.

Together, they create stories that feel like family—sometimes found, sometimes blood—but always the kind that stays with you long after the final word.

At the end of the day, Piper and Rayne write love stories that they hope feel real, funny, with just the right amount of steam… ones that make your heart race and your world a little warmer.

www.ingramcontent.com/pod-product-compliance
Lightning Source LLC
Chambersburg PA
CBHW051128130726
47988CB00005B/1750